M000033812

# ALT

a novel

ALEKSANDAR NEDELJKOVIC

*atmosphere press*

www.alt-novel.com

Published by Atmosphere Press
Cover design by Aleksandar Nedeljkovic



Atmospherepress.com

*For Luca*

## A lot can happen in a second.

You can decide if you're going to love someone for the rest of your life inside of a second.

It's enough time to recognize an idea that can lift up a civilization or start a war that will destroy countless lives.

It's about how long it takes the AI mind of Newseam Neural Network to construct a tailored news story to fit a headline like this one: The Systems That Aren't Busy Being Born Are Busy Dying.

A second is a measure of singularity closest to zero in which the past, present, and future are all contained as one, where what has been, what is now, and what might be, can still change one another.

# DAY_1

For nine months now, Theo has been struggling to resolve the strange conflict between elation and apprehension that gnawed at him ever since the Atlantic Commonwealth first approached him about working on "Sundance."

Having a chance to help redeem and continue his father's legacy by being a part of the team of scientists tasked with recreating his father's long-lost invention, feels nothing short of exhilarating. The thought that, after decades past, the world finally caught up with Augustus's vision of the future, filled Theo with a newfound vitality, sense of belonging, and hope that humanity might, after all, find a way to save itself from itself. Life has come full circle.

But along with the excitement of discovery and the thrilling pursuit of greater purpose, retracing his father's steps has awakened an old pain that he spent years learning to evade. It reopened a never-healed wound deep in his being, a painful reminder of the surgical indifference of fate, a memento of cruel injustice that people robbed of a loved one too soon, carry buried inside them, like a shattered stone whose jagged pieces can never be assembled back together.

"Dad..." Miles pops through the door, interrupting Theo's thoughts.

"Give me an hour," Theo says. "This thing is about to start."

"Okay. It's just..."

"I know. The quarterfinals. Don't worry buddy, we'll

make it work, one way or another. You'll get on."

Just then, an eyes-only message leaps up on the display, prompting Theo to shoo his son away. He waits for Miles to shut the door behind him then decrypts the viewing permission key and joins the meeting.

The video feed shows a who's who of the Atlantic Commonwealth Intelligence Service, seated around the oval table in the strategy room, engaged in subdued collegial banter. After a little while, the room quiets down and Guy Phillips, head of the Commonwealth's Department of Energy, walks in and takes the head of the table.

*"Thank you all for coming,"* Phillips starts. *"It's good to see everybody. I'm sure we can all agree that other than hitting Malachy's for happy hour on Friday nights, the coordination between the Department of Energy and the Intelligence Services hasn't always been ideal. Sure, everyone has their own shop to run, but when priorities change, expectations change.*

*These are precarious times. The world is in the throes of a grave urgency to alleviate the energy supply disruption caused by the devastation of the war in the Middle East. Oil production in the Arabian Peninsula and in the Gulf region has been practically obliterated with little chance of meaningful recovery. The damage inflicted on infrastructure is irreparable. Oil field fires are beyond the point of containment. The market considers these resources as gone, though before the war they represented more than sixty percent of remaining global oil reserves. The cost of a barrel has increased more than nine hundred percent over the last three years and is still trending up without significant restraints.*

*Simply put, the scarcity of oil is a tectonic blow to the elemental foundation of modern life. The geopolitical stakes could not be higher. There is a great reshuffling of alliances and resource flows as the search for sustainable alternatives to meet these new realities on the ground heats up. Things are moving very fast and I'm afraid the worst is still ahead of us.*

*Now, more than ever, we must not forget our values and our duty. We must be ready for whatever comes our way. An energy crisis of this magnitude presents a huge destabilizing threat to society as a whole. It's an existential civilizational challenge that we must address. We need all hands on deck, all working as one, if we're going to make it through this. We must find a way to engage with one another and to collaborate more closely and effectively. So, in that spirit, I'm here today to give you some insight into our work on a project that most of you are not familiar with."*

The display behind Phillips showing the current political map of North America fades to white and the word *"Sundance"* appears.

*"Energy independence has always been a paramount goal and one of our most important national interests. In that sense, Sundance is not a new endeavor. It's been an important component of an inevitable transition to a future of low- and no-carbon energy sources, ever since it was founded by the Gates administration, as a part of the Atlantic Commonwealth Strategic Energy Independence Act. As you know, the SEIA was one of the first pieces of legislation passed after the United States' dissolution, so I guess it's fair to say that Sundance is almost as old as the Commonwealth itself. It's a collaborative effort between the Department of Energy and the Department of Defense and it's under the direct supervision of the president.*

*Sundance was envisioned as a preemptive measure to counter the type of extreme scenario unfolding right now by mitigating our reliance on fossil fuels as a primary source of energy. It's a vital technological blueprint that holds tremendous promise to change the world for the better, a possible solution to the two biggest challenges our civilization is facing right now: the energy crisis and climate disruption.*

*So, without further ado, I have invited our chief engineer, Dr. Maya Savage, to join me here today, to lead you through some of the technical aspects, since she seems to be the only one who actually knows how this stuff works."*

Phillips yields the floor to Dr. Savage with a chuckle. As she steps up to the middle of the room, the words *"Harvesting the Sun"* pop up on the display.

*"Hello everyone. Secretary Phillips gave you a little background information, so I'll just jump to my area of expertise."*

Dr. Savage's presentation starts with a three-dimensional animation of Earth revolving around its axis under the sun's rays, ringed with onion skin-like atmospheric layers.

*"Sundance is an exosphere-based solar energy collection and delivery system. The exosphere is basically a vast transitional zone between Earth's atmosphere and interplanetary space. Its lower boundary is about four hundred miles above Earth's surface and it stretches out some one hundred twenty thousand miles, or about halfway to the Moon. There, in the geocorona area, our access to the sun's rays is uninterrupted by the filtering properties of the ozone layer, and the neutral hydrogen environment of the exosphere minimizes electrical turbulence experienced in the lower layers of the atmosphere. These are the perfect conditions for large-scale solar energy collection.*

*The ultimate goal of Sundance is to set up a network of solar collection farms across the exosphere, along with an efficient energy delivery process to Earth. We already have approximately five hundred photovoltaic cells up, launched during phase one, two, and three project trials. These trials proved to be quite successful, and we now have a full working model of our system. Presently, we are receiving about one hundred fifty megawatts of electricity from the solar panels already in place, and while this amount is negligible, it represents the potential viability of Sundance once the project is fully realized.*

*There are two critical components of Sundance—collec-*

*tion and delivery. The delivery part was never much of a problem; since the very beginning we knew that microwave transmission is the way to go. After initial testing, we settled at two hundred sixty gigahertz, extremely high-frequency microwave signals. Each solar panel is equipped with a microwave transmitter that's designed to safely transmit electrical current to substations on Earth. From there on, it's delivered to end users via the existing electrical grid. However, the collection part of the equation is far trickier due to the technological constraints of the photovoltaic solar cell as we know it.*

*The development of the photovoltaic method of generating electrical current from sunlight hit the proverbial wall early in the century as its limitations became all too evident. Simply put, the overall efficiency of today's photovoltaic solar cell is still as mediocre as it was decades ago. Add to that the steep production cost, hefty environmental footprint, and chronic shortage of critical production materials like tellurium, gallium, and germanium, and you'll quickly understand why we are still greatly dependent on the nineteenth-century practice of burning hydrocarbons, like coal, oil, and natural gas, all while destroying the conditions that make life on this planet possible.*

*A fresh approach to solar energy gathering is long overdue. We need a new technological template, completely different than the old photovoltaic model, that will enable us to develop a new, vastly more efficient generation of solar panels. Our team is currently working on a couple of prospective projects that one day might emerge as a solution.*

*The clear glass solar cell, which is sensitive to ultraviolet light, has been around for many years. We included about fifty of them in our phase two trial and so far, they're the best performers of all of the models sent up. Most of the ultraviolet light gets filtered by the ozone layer. Only about two percent of it hits Earth's surface. In the exosphere, these capture levels are much higher, up to ninety-nine percent. Our development teams are trying to adapt the existing clear glass cells to take full advantage of the abundance of ultraviolet light in the exosphere. The challenge is to make the new cell capable of absorbing these high levels of UV light and transforming a significant portion of it into electricity. We have a good starting point with these existing cells, but we haven't been able to fully verify the feasibility of this approach. Another possibility, and I say possibility here with reserved caution, is something known as artificial photosynthesis."*

Dr. Savage pauses for a moment, gauges the room, and then advances her presentation. A picture of a man in his early fifties appears.

*"The man in the picture is Augustus Smith, one of the pioneers of alternative energy technology from the early days of the twenty-first century. He is known primarily for his contributions to biomass energy generation through his revolutionary discovery of the Rapid Cellulose Solvent RCS enzyme, which unlocked the energy-generating potential of green algae, switchgrass, and other cellulose-rich plants. He became a subject of controversy after his death for his claim that he had discovered a way to capture the sun's energy through chlorophyll and resonance energy transfer, a process later known as artificial photosynthesis. This is a video of Mr. Smith addressing the board of a venture capital firm he was negotiating a financing deal with for his Chorus project."*

Theo's chest knots up as the still picture of his father comes to life.

*"The human race has wandered half-blind through this world for a long time,"* Augustus begins. *"We are often unable to see what's right in front of us, unable to comprehend the simplest laws and mechanisms of nature, let alone adhere to them. Sometimes, in our struggle to overcome our limits, we even go against these laws or try to bend them to fit our narrow interpretation of them. It's our responsibility as conscious beings to understand the world around us and to live within it*

*in a responsible and sustainable way. But instead, panicked, frightened, and lost in the absence of answers, we choose to maintain the short-sighted status quo, doubling down on our repeated mistakes, hoping that our Faustian bargain won't ever come back to haunt us—and if it does, that the price won't be too high to pay. We cause damage to the planet, other species, and ultimately ourselves, by living against the rules of nature. This can't go on forever. There will be a moment of no return, when the abyss starts gazing back at us, a moment when it will be too late to preserve life on Earth as we know it, no matter how hard we try. I hope we're not there yet.*

*The human condition is a struggle with natural forces from birth until death. Everything we have achieved so far as a species exists because we wrestled it from nothingness with our bare hands, our will, and our intellect. The hard way. But nature is still a great, dangerous mystery to us only because we often perceive it as an adversary, something outside ourselves, something to conquer and overcome. We will not be able to understand it fully and be one with it until we start obeying its laws. The truth is, we have already been given everything we'd ever need to sustain our precious opportunity to exist on this planet. We just have to attune ourselves with the divine harmony of nature and reap the benefits.*

*Every single day, the sun sends us a gift of limitless power, more than we'll ever need for any task imaginable. Our only challenge is to properly harness it. The best we have come up with so far is the photovoltaic cell which, although an admirable first step, is proving to be a false hope. It's expensive, inefficient, and unsustainable, a half-measure that falls short of truly solving the problem. There is another way to think about solar energy collection. And the answer is right under our noses. In fact, plants have already perfected this process millions of years ago."*

Augustus reaches out of frame with his right hand and brings a green rectangular panel the size of a big book into view.

*"This is Chorus, a new generation of solar panel that uses the same energy-generating mechanism found in plants, chlorophyll, and resonance energy transfer. Much like plant leaves, it's a self-regulating, regenerative, and lossless solar energy receptor and transformer. It's vastly superior to any other solar panel on the market today. All three prototypes that I have built are showing a similar conversion rate—between ninety-two and ninety-eight percent—meaning that the Chorus panel will convert over ninety percent of the sun's energy it's exposed to into electrical current. There's still work to be done, but I think that with its minuscule carbon footprint, zero emissions, low production cost, and the limitless energy source of the sun, I can safely say that we are on a good path to finding a permanent solution for our energy ails."*

Dr. Savage stops the video, then continues.

*"About a month after this video was taken, Augustus Smith died when his Brooklyn laboratory caught fire and burned to the ground. Although it was officially deemed accidental, the circumstances surrounding his death seem murky, to say the least. The document trail left behind does not offer much clarification. It does, however, show a glaring lack of investigation into the cause of the fire, which has never been determined. An independent chemical analysis commissioned by Augustus's widow found the presence of fire accelerants in the debris, but the results were ultimately dismissed as inconclusive.*

*The real twist came about two years later, when an unrelated investigation revealed that the venture capital firm with which Smith was negotiating financing just before his death turned out to be a key financial arm of the oil industry lobbying group. The firm was found guilty of predatory business practices with the goal of suppressing and eliminating the competition in the renewable energy sector.*

*The initial investigation snowballed into a full-fledged*

*scandal, and the venture capital firm ended up also being charged with criminal data infringement and theft, intellectual property fraud, six counts of industrial sabotage, and twelve counts of burglary and property destruction, all directed against small and mid-size enterprises in the alternative energy sector.*

*Four of the six identified industrial sabotage cases involved arson. All of these facts add up to the plausible conclusion that Augustus Smith might have been a victim of crimes perpetrated by the same group. The truth is, we might never know for certain what happened. But we do know that none of the three Chorus prototypes he said he had produced survived the lab fire. Most of the project documentation was destroyed as well, so we can't tell if Smith indeed had cracked the code of artificial photosynthesis—and if he did, how he did it.*

*Ever since, his chlorophyll and resonance energy transfer approach to solar energy collection has been a subject of great debate in the scientific community. Over time, it was mostly dismissed as a great romantic notion and a nonpossibility. He was even called an impostor, a sensationalist, and an alchemist by some. Others still believe that he was a genius who saw what no one else could and that with his passing we lost a chance to make a perfect, efficient, energy-generating device with a minimal environmental footprint. Even after all these years, Chorus solar panels continue to be the Holy Grail if you will, an elusive, perfect answer for our energy troubles. That is, of course, if you choose to believe that the concept of artificial photosynthesis is even possible. If not, you can easily dismiss this whole notion of a perfect energy source as one of those crazy stories from the past that only got bigger and crazier as time went by.*

*Right now, we're not in a position to ignore even a remote possibility that Smith's solar panel was real. A high-efficiency solar panel, like the one he claimed he invented, would be an ideal answer to the obstacles we're experiencing today with Sundance. Having a lossless, self-regulating collection panel that requires practically no maintenance is the only way that Sundance can achieve its full potential and deliver true energy independence. Mr. Phillips?"*

Having finished her presentation, Dr. Savage returned to her seat at the table and Guy Phillips resumed control.

*"Thank you, Maya. There you have it, ladies and gentlemen of the intelligence community. As you can see, we have our work cut out for us. If we had one of Smith's Chorus panels, we could reverse engineer it to uncover its secrets. If we had his records, we would be able to figure out what he did and how. But we don't. As Dr. Savage mentioned, most of Smith's documents perished in the fire, and the little that survived is not of much use. What's left behind is this mythical hypothesis that lacks validation and the only way to prove it or disprove it is to attempt to re-create this technological concept ourselves. So, we set out to do just that.*

*Over the last eighteen months, we've built a solid team at the department, dedicated exclusively to resurrecting Chorus. Expectedly, we found ourselves in uncharted waters, but we did not start from zero. A lot of good research has been done on artificial photosynthesis since Smith's time. Most of this research is theoretical, and sometimes inconsistent, self-contradicting, or incomplete, but it gave us a good point of departure.*

*In addition to our own resources, we also found ways to engage some of the most notable experts in the field, whose skills and commitment to the project gives us an edge. Some of these names might be familiar to you from the vetting processes your department conducted for us, or from the standing protective assignments that you've been tasked with when these individuals started working with us. I have invited one of our independent contractors, Theo Smith, to join us today from his home in Concord, California, and shed some light on the most recent simulation modeling predictions pertaining to the Chorus project."*

The video feed of Theo pops up on the ACIS strategy room display and he nods lightly into the camera, greeting everyone.

*"Mr. Smith is a preeminent computer scientist and we're lucky to have him. His work using quantum simulator applications is at the very core of our method of operations, the best tool we have in our effort to advance Sundance. Theo's devotion is unparalleled, and we're very grateful for his contribution. A scientist by blood, a humanist by nature, he is an inspiration for the entire team. And as the son of Augustus Smith, he also has a very deep emotional connection to this project..."*

------

Sentimental feelings aside, working on Sundance has been an exciting and professionally challenging experience for Theo, but the delayed compensation agreement he has with the Atlantic Commonwealth Energy Department in the form of share payment is not going to make him cash-rich anytime soon. Although his motivation from the beginning was altruistic and not monetary, he stands to make a good chunk if they manage to successfully replicate the Chorus panel. Adoption of this new technology would hopefully be instantaneous, and its application limitless. Even his tiny share of the enterprise would amount to a huge pile of money. In the meantime, he's going to have to make do with what he has, and keep fixing this rickety home solar power system until its last leg.

A sweat drop crawls down Theo's eyebrow, dissolving into a salty sting in his eye. He wipes his face with his sleeve and then steps over a row of solar panels, kneels down, and starts jiggling the DC switch cable.

"How about now?" he yells out.

"Come on!" Miles pleads at the flickering zeros on the voltmeter LED.

"Miles? Anything?"

"Nothing," Miles yells back, then walks out of the garage and, shading his eyes with the palm of his hand, looks up at Theo's silhouette on the roof. "Not a thing."

Mumbling something to himself about flux and alloys, Theo opens up the photovoltaic inverter box, plucks out the motherboard, and twiddles it around, examining the city of circuitry on its surface. He notices a black smudge under one of the chips, gives it a small pull with his nail, and the chip comes loose. He picks up the chip between his thumb and index finger and raises it up toward the white corona of the sun.

"What is it?" Miles asks from below.

"MPPT controller."

"Again?"

"Yup."

"Do we have a spare one?"

"Nope. No more."

"What are we gonna do? Do we have enough juice left in the batteries? Can we fire up the generator?"

"Let me see if I can work something out with Tischman first."

Theo straps on a helmet, mounts his bicycle, and with a few powerful uphill sways gets onto the country road above their house. Miles watches him zoom through the shadows of treetops and tall roadside bushes before disappearing altogether. A hawk scream breaks out from somewhere in the woods, piercing through dozy cricket chirps and the choppy hissing of garden sprinklers. Miles picks his pockets for a LinkUp bud, then remembers he didn't have it on him when Theo called him out to help and goes inside to look for it.

He finds the LinkUp right where he left it, impatiently blinking on the kitchen counter next to his Allcom. He sticks the squishy bead at the base of his temporal skull bone, behind his ear, prompting a small melody of chimes from CALO.

*"Hi, Miles."*

"Stax, give me new messages."

*"Sure. A new message from Elle: Are you studying for tomorrow's test? I can't make myself start. History's such a bore."*

"Reply: Not yet. Power out. Was dealing with that."

Miles goes upstairs to his room and starts digging through a clump of pillows and blankets on his bed.

*"Ugh. Solar crapped out again?"* A new message from Elle comes in. *"What about the game tonight?"*

"Dad's fixing it. Will be fine."

*"Ready to rule the world?"*

"Ack!"

*"Nervous?"*

"Like a leaf in a tornado, haha."

Miles catches a glimmer of crimson glass among the pillows, yanks the sheets off, and finds his immersion set lodged in between the mattress and the headrest.

*"Such a tough guy! I better get to it. Butt-chin Spaulding is getting hard to impress lately."*

"That's Professor Butt-chin to you, young lady!"

*"Haha... I'll be lurking tonight. Will hit you up afterward. Good luck!"*

"Thanks."

Miles grabs the immersion set from its hiding place, then goes back downstairs and slumps into the living room sofa, trying not to think about tonight's game.

He's in a good spot, he just has to let his strategy of jacking up scientific research and culture to the max play out. Maybe send a few more units down south, in case Kafka reneges on his alliance commitments and leaves Miles's Antarctica bases vulnerable to sneak attack. Chasm has been dying to reestablish his presence there ever since Miles took stewardship of the continent. He must defend the integrity of the Ross Ice Shelf at any cost! Miles's entire civilization depends on maintaining the current global temperature levels. If he lets Chasm back in Antarctica, he'll drill every little corner of it for oil and minerals, the ice shelves will splinter apart, and temperatures will most certainly rise beyond his civilization's level of tolerance. He'd be finished.

------

Angry at himself that he allowed their home solar system to fall into such a sorry state, Theo pedals his frustration forward, past Main Street, toward Tischman's place. This is the third time this month it crapped out. Patching it up is not going to cut it anymore. It's time for a real overhaul. MPPT controllers need to be bumped up to S-14 type, panels replaced, breaker box rewired, new inverter installed. It won't be cheap, but it's not like it's not doable. In hindsight, he should have known better than let his usual diligence be blunted and recondition it while he still had the convenience of having the main electrical grid to fall onto. The things we take for granted. Now that the grid has become an unreliable mess, it's almost certain that they'll end up being without power for days on end while the work is being done, and he can't afford to be without power.

Time has been at a premium as of late. Sundance has been consuming more and more of his work hours to the point that he had to forgo a high-paying job to build a localized climate forecasting system for a farming association out of Coachella Valley. That one job could have paid for half of the cost of the new system, but it was a solid month's commitment and he couldn't take a month off from Sundance. He wasn't worried though, there will be other offers coming. All he needs is a string of smaller jobs that he could squeeze in between Sundance sessions.

It wasn't uncommon for Theo to receive unsolicited job offers but, strangely enough, almost every single availability inquiry he received over the last month was from oil industry companies. They came from different places and from different entities; a tar sands operation in Saskatchewan, another one in Alberta, a couple of Dakotas frackers, and a wildcatting outfit in Texas. What struck him as odd was that they were all offering the same type of contract and that the job descriptions were the same—exploratory data analysis, well modeling, and summarization of data collected by the 4-D seismic survey applications. The first two items are run-of-the-mill assignments, but 4-D seismic testing is done only on the big deposits because it's very expensive and technologically demanding, and it's usually handled by the in-house data analytics departments of the big oil companies. Theo has not received a single request to work on a 4-D seismic in almost two years, and now he got five in one month, each one more lucrative than the previous. He was starting to suspect that all of these job offers were coming from the same source, like someone was slowly trying to figure out what it would take for him to accept. It didn't matter anyway, he promptly rejected them all. A long time ago, Theo made up his mind to never work with anyone involved with the oil industry. It was a matter of principle, a moral choice, but also an act of resistance against the unquenchable greed and contempt for the environment in which they operate. There might be good, well-meaning individuals in their ranks, but collectively, they're a powerful negative force capable of great destruction and evil deeds—the kind of people who wouldn't hesitate to set a person on fire if they hindered their interests.

Hopefully, Tischman can save him again so he can keep the solar operational until they fix the grid, or at least get it back to the same mediocre level as before. The grid performance has been spotty for years since protracted droughts took several hydropower plants in the Sierras out of commission, and downright disastrous after a quake knocked out a substation outside San Mateo, four months ago, resulting in a cascading power failure that left most of Northern California in the dark for five full days. Almost instantaneously, gangs spilled out of ghettos in Oakland, Sacramento, and Stockton looking to take advantage of the chaos, staging looting raids into the well-off areas, swiping away everything that wasn't nailed down or too heavy. The Public Protection Agency promptly rolled out their full SWAT arsenal, beefing up their street presence with riot squads, reserves, and minutemen pulled back from the Texas border, and after four days of intense urban warfare, they managed to push the gangs back and restore some tenuous semblance of order.

Public Utility responded with a miserably slow repair effort, focused primarily on the restoration of power to the cities, data farms, and industrial parks, leaving small towns and rural areas vulnerable to recurring outages. Concord was blacked out for almost two weeks before power started trickling back in fits and starts, like a schizophrenic thought. The grid would come alive randomly, almost accidentally, for a few minutes at a time, sometimes even a few hours, and then die off without warning. Eventually, Utility succeeded in keeping the cutoffs to a manageable pattern, two days on, one day off. But every now and again service collapses back into an unpredictable mess, just to remind everyone to keep their expectations low.

It took some planning and prioritizing, but the Smiths stayed largely unaffected by the main grid deficiencies when their home solar system worked properly. Although antiquated panels and outdated components dragged down capacity utilization, its output was still sufficient to cover their average daily use and keep the backup battery charged enough to get them comfortably through the night. On cloudy days, Theo would scale down his workload, turn off most of the high-powered equipment in his workshop to conserve energy, and instead try to catch up with offline management tasks, like summarizing Simulacrum discovery metadata into reports comprehensive enough for human interpretation or consulting clients over the Bussinet on hypotheticals, representative scenarios, system behaviors, performance optimizations, or some other computer simulation insight he churned out for them.

He locks his bike to the iron fence under a lightbox sign that reads "Tischman Additive Manufacturing and Hardware" and goes inside. In an empty showroom, up on the wall across from the counter, a muted media panel is showing a report on the worldwide coffee shortage due to massive hailstorms that ravaged the crops in Vietnam last year, and an erratic cyclone season that's been relentlessly pummeling the Indonesian islands for the third year in a row. The program then switches to a video feed of a light armor vehicle convoy crawling through a desert. The chyron below reads: *"Peace Enforcement Council of the North American Non-Aggression Treaty is reporting a rise in hostilities on the Texas-California border."* The image jumps to another desert scene, this time an aerial shot of thick smoke curling up from the sea of black and tan sand, with the chyron: *"Three years later, the Gulf Inferno not showing signs of subsiding."*

Behind a glass partition in the workshop, a redheaded kid, one of Tischman's sons, is tending to a jumbo 3-D printer. Theo knocks on the glass, but its thickness absorbs the sound smoothly. He steps around the counter into a small, enclosed L-shaped space that leads to the workshop door. Huffing and hissing like a mechanized monster choking on an oversized bone, the printer is retching out a foot-wide bowed column through its mouth.

"Mr. Smith," the kid stretches out his freckled cheeks into a smile.

"Hi. Where's your dad?"

"In the back, loading up a shipment."

"Fine detail," says Theo, sliding his palm down the spiraled grooves of the column's surface. "What's it for?"

"This? Some structural components for a sailboat."

"Nice."

"How's Miles?" little Tischman asks.

"Good. He's got some tournament online this evening, so he's getting ready for that."

"Yeah, I know. EternalQuest. Everyone at school is rooting for him. Pretty amazing he's made it to the quarterfinals."

"Yeah."

"Tell him good luck."

"Okay. Thanks."

Out on the loading dock, Tischman and another man are stacking up shrink-wrapped pallets on the pickup flatbed.

"There he is, the hardest working man in all of Concord," says Theo as he approaches.

"Small fish in a small pond, just nibbling on leftovers," Tischman replies.

Sparkling sweat droplets hang loosely off Tischman's hair, making a fuzzy orange net around his head.

"What's up?" he asks.

"Ah, you know what's up."

"MPPT controller again?"

"Yup."

"You gotta upgrade Theo, no two ways about it,"

Tischman slings the buckles over the pallets, then circles the truck in long strides, and latches them to the bottom of the pickup bed.

"This mess with the grid isn't getting any better. Can't depend on obsolete technology."

"Tell me about it. I'm ready to rip it all out."

"I can get you anything, you know that."

With a few powerful tugs, Tischman secures the load, then yanks the straps to check their grip. His orange halo suddenly vanishes as the sweat droplets break off from his hair and in fast little streams run down his nonabsorbent paper-white face before fleeing into the collar of his shirt.

"Go hit the pile. You might get lucky again. If not, we'll print one out for you. I think I still have some type H goop left."

In addition to his reputation as an excellent 3-D printer, Tischman is also known as a reliable, second-hand purveyor of common and specialized hardware, particularly hard-to-find and out-of-production items. He started off by buying bulk e-waste for resale to Material Recovery Facilities, then realized there's more value in those lumps of garbage than meets the eye, so he began to hire migrants to scavenge the shipments before he dumped them onto MRFs. In the beginning, he kept only the stuff he knew he could easily sell "as is" for a decent profit, but over time his hoarding tendencies evolved and he added obsolete equipment worth refurbishing to the mix—perfectly good, useful devices, their only sin being too old, a shame to send them to the crusher.

What Tischman referred to as "the pile," was actually an extended network of termite moundlike heaps of electronic junk strewn around the warehouse floor in a seemingly deliberate manner. Stripped of their purpose, like outgrown toys, the picked-over carcasses of appliances and gadgets gave off a faint smell of rust and acid. Theo scans "the pile" for a minute, trying to remember where he found the MMPT controller last time he was here, then spots a cracked solar panel on top of one of the crumbly stacks, walks over, and digs into its wiry guts.

------

This was Miles's fourth year playing EternalQuest. After being knocked out in the early rounds his first two years, last year he fought his way to the round of thirty-two, where he got his butt promptly kicked by more experienced players. This year, he made it all the way to the quarterfinals, which he still kind of can't believe. At fifteen, he is the youngest quarterfinalist who ever played the game, not that that really matters, but the game's marketing team is making a big deal out of that in their promos.

*"Wunderkind on the rise! FreeFire emerges as a new EternalQuest leader. Can the youngblood prodigy reshape the world in his own vision and achieve the fragile balance between Earth and humans, between war and peace?"*

It's ridiculous, the megalotalk. They're setting up tonight's match as some momentous clash of the genius minds.

*"Witness the greatness unfold before your eyes! Watch civilizations collide as the world's eight smartest teenagers square off in an epic battle for the right to lead the human race forth, into the next chapter of our shared history."*

Sure, you have to be pretty smart to make it this far. In addition to fast fingers and all-seeing eyes, you have to have real knowledge of math, physics, chemistry, and social sciences and be able to apply that knowledge in the game. But wunderkind? Prodigy? That's just laughable. It's just a game, after all. It's not like he's achieved some extraordinary feat, other than building a really great fictional civilization. And while that's cool, it makes no material difference in the real world. Smart is a relative term anyway. Besides, there's so much he doesn't know. Sometimes it seems like everything he will ever know, even if he lived a million lifetimes, everything he would physically be able to learn, simply wouldn't amount to much. Sum of all consciousness, the entire intelligent enterprise of humanity, every thought ever conceived by living brains and by the ones that perished thousands of years ago, all of it adds up to but a little crack in the impenetrable wall of the unknown, and the tiny spark of light coming through that crack is all we have to guide us in this scramble to survive against the odds, to make the Age of Man last just a tiny bit longer and keep it from fading into cosmic oblivion without a trace.

"Hey champ," Maritza calls out from the garden. "Why are you sitting alone in a dark room?"

Miles looks up across the room and finds his mom's inverted reflection on the surface of the dead media panel, shuffling through bean bushes with the grace and patience of a martial arts disciple. He feels procrastination guilt starting to gnaw at him.

"Beautiful day out here. Come out, let's pick some veggies for lunch."

"I can't Mom," he yells out. "I have to study for the test tomorrow."

Might as well whirl through it. He tacks on his immersion kit.

"Stax: Start Homework."

*"Welcome Miles,"* the pleasant voice of the Homework narrator chimes in. *"Please select mode."*

"Sync up to school curriculum."

*"Current class: Development of Society – History – Twenty-first century – Part one – Origins of Great Retraction. You can begin at any time."*

"Begin."

*"Loading the aggregator."*

Homework unleashes a flurry of windows, crowding Miles's field of vision with a deluge of information, a compressed spectacle of the history of the early twenty-first century.

*"Overview: The dawn of the new century was marked with equal amounts of exhilaration and fear. Numerous religious sects, primarily of the Christian faith, had their own reasons to believe that the year 2000 would be the year the world ends. Some interpretations of the Bible and the Scriptures offered predictions that the year 2000 would be the year of Rapture..."*

"Scrub overview. One point five."

*"... Second Coming of Christ... event Christians... died... resurrected... Christ... along with still living. Scientific community... own fears... world would cease to exist... brink of*

*uninhabitable. A Y2K computer bug... caused date-related... processing... incorrectly dates and times... January one, 2000... other critical dates... event horizons. Many feared... Y2K... cause nuclear weapons systems malfunctions... worldwide nuclear war... destroy the human race. New millennium... turbulent event. September 11th attacks... second Iraq war... Wall Street crash of 2008... worldwide political upheaval... challenged geopolitical stability... post-communism era. Learn more... topic... select hyperlink... or item... any time."*

"Continue overview."

*"Origins of Great Retraction — Global currency debasement — Sovereign debt collapse — Minsky Moment — Devolution — Breakup of the mega-states — Dissolution of the United States.*

*What began as a revolt against malevolent banking practices in Western democracies quickly became a global class conflict as the radicalization of the disenfranchised middle class spread around the world. Long repressed societies of the Middle East and North Africa were shaken to their cores by the wave of civil resistance and violent protests known as the Arab Spring."*

"Scrub overview. Double."

*"Arab Spring... sowing seeds... Oil Wars I, II, and III. Western liberal capitalism... only ideological alternative... world order... cause and consequence of the end of history... change. Ghosts... chauvinism... nationalism, class conflict surfaced... worldwide... inability to sustain welfare states... 2008... turning point... U.S. subprime mortgage... market crash... central banks... inflating monetary supply... combat weak growth... COVID-19 pandemic... financial instruments... unsustainable leverage levels, fiat currency destruction... ultimately collapse... sovereign debt. Steady decline... The Great Economic Retraction... wave... sovereign defaults... death blow to overleveraged... global economy... economic activity... contracted more than forty percent... decade... surge secessionist*

*movements... conditions... political devolution."*

"Stop scrubbing. Back up a paragraph."

*"A wave of sovereign defaults delivered a death blow to the over-leveraged financial foundation of the global economy, causing worldwide economic activity to contract more than forty percent in less than a decade, and setting off a surge of secessionist movements across the globe in the process, thus creating conditions for political devolution. As a result, the number of World Council recognized countries and territories today is more than twice the number of United Nations member-states at the beginning of the twenty-first century."*

Miles looks up the meaning of devolution.

*dev·o·lu·tion*

*devə'l(y)o͞oSH(ə)n/*

*— noun*

*the transfer or delegation of power to a lower level, especially by central government to local or regional administration.*

*— synonyms*

*decentralization*

*— formal*

*descent or degeneration to a lower or worse state.*

*— law*

*the legal transfer of property from one owner to another.*

*— biology*

*degeneration*

More than once, Miles wondered why the old country fell apart the way it did. The school curriculum offered detached examinations of the historical context—the cultural and political divide of the populace that over time grew too big to bridge; the rising ineffectiveness of the federal government that remained leashed to a flawed democratic model and could not reform itself, eventually becoming a captured entity of corporations and special interests and surrendering its purpose to serve the citizens; massive national debt that couldn't be paid off, resulting in sovereign default, runaway inflation, and loss of creditors' confidence. In addition to its looming problems, the country couldn't stay impervious to the state of the world either. Normative, ideological, economic, and social inertia that fed the zeitgeist tensions between nationalism and globalism, populism and democracy, the haves and the have nots, conformity and the revolutionary impulses, which ultimately incited the historical worldwide momentum toward self-determination in the big federal countries like Brazil, India, China, Argentina, Canada, Mexico, Nigeria, Russia, and the United States.

Beyond what they were taught in school, Miles had come across many well-reasoned arguments that, viewed from a safe historical distance, made it seem like the dissolution of the United States was an inevitable conclusion, brought about by the many mistakes the previous generations made—horrendous mismanagement of resources and priorities, systemic grift, endemic disregard for the public good, the inability and unwillingness of the political class to tackle the hard issues, the list was long. Still, many questions went unanswered. How did the great American spirit, that source of adventure, ingenuity, and optimism, turn into empty words? When did the ideas that it championed—freedom and openness, fairness and tolerance, strength of character, hard work, and moral fortitude—become meaningless? Self-reliant individualism became a cult of brazen selfishness, the land of plenty a vast Ponzi scheme, and the beacon of democracy a plutocratic caricature of itself that couldn't print its way out of its problems anymore.

A sense of shared destiny, the cohesive engine of the country, sputtered to a stop and the already polarized union fractured to pieces. Hawaii and the three biggest states of the old union, Alaska, Texas, and California, remained unaffiliated. In search of collective identity and economic opportunities, the other newly independent states over time forged political alliances of different types and levels of interrelation; the New America Federation, the Cascadian Union, the Atlantic Commonwealth, the League of Southern States of America, and the Great Plains Confederation of American States.

There it is again, that shrill cry of a dying iceberg, the same high-pitched crackling noise, nearly imperceptible in the sticky hum of data terminals, that's been driving him crazy for three days now. Jiang gets up from his desk and walks up to the glass edge of his office, almost expecting to see a visual depiction of the sound curling between the cubicles down below, a slow-moving light-blue vortex of thin air, whirling, sparkling, and popping tiny bubbles of freshness along the way, leaving a rich ozone smell in its wake. He feels slightly disappointed when instead, the mundane static sight of the Fusion Center floor presents itself, operators' heads glued to data displays, all alike and different at the same time, like a beetle collection pinboard framed by office partitions.

"Trust none of what you hear, some of what you read, and half of what you see," he remembers what old Pai-han liked to say to the handful of new IT recruits brilliant enough to be admitted among the elite security professionals at Sheng Long's Information Creation Department each year. "You're the first line of defense in the raging infowar, a soldier of order fighting for your own version of the truth. If you're not paranoid, you're not doing your job."

Pai-han's words stuck with Jiang long after the first days of basic training because the simple message they conveyed contained a profound truth—in the cutthroat business of surveillance and information control, reasoned paranoia is the only mindset that will keep you unbeaten. Only through absolute awareness can one achieve absolute control. And this rang even more true for Private Security Corporations like Sheng Long because the terror of profit and efficiency does not allow for a margin of error.

Perhaps he's just overworked? Weakness is a sneaky bitch. He hasn't slept more than an hour at a time since the West Vancouver riots began. The last few days have been enough to exhaust an algorithm, let alone a meat brain. Or maybe he's really going insane? Is this how it starts? You hear voices, sounds no one else does?

Ever since Jiang first heard it, he's been obsessed with getting a fix on it, but every time he thought he was close, the sound would vanish like it was never there, only to pop up again at a different end of the floor at some random interval. Right now, it's just hovering over the Bussinet and Oilnet scanner areas, daring him to come down and start this cat and mouse game again. What sound? No one else seems to have noticed it, or if they did, they never brought it to his attention. Maybe the fuckers are playing a prank on him? Or worse? Any of these two hundred eighty-two data monkeys below could be setting him up for a fall. None of them would mind sitting up here instead of him.

Jiang swipes through the ops update entries, then selects the most recent uplink from the field.

*Information Creation Department /*
*Central Operations / Tailored Access Operations*
*Task: TAO-4 —Y-55-B.*
*ICD Continuum: Pre-op. Monitor*
*Origin: Field/Target location*
*Chain: TAO-4, ICD, CO-12, Epiphany Resources*
*Edit Rights: Central Operations*
*/13:47 PST/*

*There are no material changes at the target location in the last hour. Still out of power. Agent progressing as forecast-*

*ed, currently ninety-two miles from the target.*

There are two live video feeds attached to the status report. The first one, a POV of someone riding in a car, humming along with a female voice that's affectedly crooning about rice paddies and lotus flowers in the morning dew, accompanied by syrupy plucks of zheng strings. Jiang recognizes the song from the old country and rolls his eyes in disgust. The other feed is a target location video, a static shot of the Smiths's living room. Obscured by semidarkness, with his face concealed by the immersion kit and arms stretched out navigating the Homework app, Miles looks like he's wrestling some shapeless demon coming at him from the sofa cushions. Jiang tacks the feed on the low priority split of his display, then selects the next entry.

Feeling an early afternoon slump coming over him, Moonie re-ups on the Quickstrike, chases down its semi-metallic aftertaste with a gulp of orange soda, and sets himself down to finally watch the damn thing.

*"Welcome to Pardes,"* a snazzy hologram of the presentation splashes out of his Allcom. *"This is a land of winners, the chosen few, the blessed ones. This is a fulfilled promise of a better life, the realization of your hopes, a living dream."*

The music picks up and a mandatory beauty shot montage ensues, happy people snorkeling, water-skiing, riding horses, wining and dining in the sunset light.

*"We're the youngest member of the exclusive club of reputable HVI communities with an Aurum Wealth Rating of seven hundred: Atlantis, Havana, Maui, Cabo, Barvikha, Canarias, and now Pardes. Nestled between untouched pampas in the west and beautiful sandy beaches in the east, this environmentally sound paradise on Earth stretches over six thousand square miles of pristine nature. In the heart of it lay our marvelous lagoons, Lagoa dos Patos, and Lagoa Mirim. A navigable channel connects the two lagoons with the Atlantic Ocean, providing easy access to residences by medium-size vessels."*

Moonie hears light thumping at the door, followed by anxious paws clicking against the porch tile. Bella's big wet eyes meet his as he opens the entrance door.

"Sorry I shut you out princess," he gives her a quick cuddle. "Come in, come in."

Bella snarls as she encounters the thin cloud of the hologram in the living room, barks at the jolly, seafaring intruders a couple of times for good measure, then huffs away indignantly to scout out the house.

*"You are a winner and winners deserve all that life can offer. You can find it here, in Pardes. If you are a High-Value Individual with an Aurum Wealth Rating of seven hundred or higher, Pardes is the place for you. Like other reputable HVI communities around the world, we are a Corporate City State governed solely by our shareholders, you. Pardes is a de facto sovereign state as defined by the Barcelona Convention, recognized by more than one hundred other states and free enterprise territories.*

*Of course, our main responsibility is to provide for the absolute personal and asset safety of our residents. Pardes's Double A+ SENTRY rated defense corps is among the top contracted protection forces in the world. Over thirty-two thousand strong, Pardes Protection Division boasts the most advanced military arsenal available today and is a major factor of stability in the southeastern part of the South American continent. As a premium member of the SENTRY Protection Forces Network, PPD has access to SENTRY's Steadfast reserves program, which is capable of rapidly deploying over half a million contracted troops in times of need."*

Bella trots back from the shadows, barks at the hologram again, then rams her head into Moonie's legs, looking for affection.

"Sweet girl," Moonie cups her head with his hands and tugs on her ears gently. "Come," he pats his lap. "Come up!"

Bella jumps up, prostrates herself over Moonie and, somehow transforming her stout Labrador physique into one of a much smaller, lighter dog, nestles on his stomach in a furry ball.

"Where's your brother?" Moonie asks in his dog voice, almost expecting Bella to answer. "Where's Sid? Is he wandering the woods again? He's a troublemaker, that guy."

*"Our Value Creation Division—Pardes Ventures—is a wealth vehicle available exclusively to our residents. With an outstanding track record of a 10.7 percent annual return since its inception, Pardes Ventures is by far the best in its class..."*

Moonie fast-forwards through another bout of images depicting the dreamy, bland lives of the privileged few, then stops to watch the end part in case there's some useful information there that Lark would expect him to retain. The promo ends with an uplifting crescendo, boasting once again about just how great one's life could be if they happen to find themselves perched at the apex of the neo-feudal corporatocracy. Well, close to the apex anyway.

Of all of the powers that money possesses, its ability to separate people from one another is probably the most explicit. More money, less riffraff is a simple rule by which real life conducts its affairs in the zero-sum world. And it's no different at the top. Sure, with an Aurum Wealth Rating of seven hundred you can buy your way into one of the bottom rung Corporates like Pardes and isolate yourself safely from the angry, unwashed masses and their pitchforks in one of these modern-day fortresses disguised as states, but that would still put you quite a few notches below the threshold of more desirable HVI havens like Swarga, Sochi, Malta, Hong Kong, and Macau. The same clear-cut mechanism of more money, more status, pretty much guarantees that lowly arms dealers, smugglers, robber barons, and miscellaneous other accomplished bandits dressed as businesspeople who call themselves citizens of Pardes will never set foot in Manhattan, London City, Luxembourg, or Geneva, let alone the old money strongholds like Monaco, Wiesbaden, Cuomo, or Versailles.

Moonie pushes Bella off his lap, walks to the kitchen, and pulls out an old ditty box off the top shelf of the cabinet. A keepsake from his first transcontinental sea voyage, the salt-eaten wooden box clearly had its share of adventure before being retired in a kitchen cabinet in suburban California. The top cover is warped, but still intact, sporting an engraving of a humpback whale wreathed by some Russian characters that, as he was told by Babushka, who sold it to him in Vladivostok Harbor, mean good fortune and calm seas. He never bothered to look up if that was true.

After graduating from The California Maritime Academy, Moonie spent the next three years working on tugboats, private yachts, and charter boats. When he accumulated enough sea time to get his Second Mate license, he took a job on the *CP-six Vostok*, a Russian cargo ship that carried copper and aluminum from Siberian smelters from its home port of Vladivostok to North American markets and North Pacific grain and fruit back to Russia. Sometimes, if they ran light on Russian cargo, or when there was an unusually high threat of piracy in the Peter the Great Gulf in the eastern part of the Sea of Japan, they'd get rerouted to Shanghai, to Sokcho, or to Uchiura, where they'd pick up containers of construction materials or consumer electronics to fill up their cargo holds.

In the off-hours, Moonie would wander off the ship into the ready-made world of port nightlife, where sailors' hard-earned money found its end in shady gambling dens, strip joints, black market alleys, and karaoke brothels, buying a temporary distraction and relief from the loneliness of the long days at sea. He liked the shabby cosmopolitanism of these faraway places that nobody called home, where people and cultures from around the globe converged into one, bonded by the most powerful social force—the dash for cash, the world where laws and sermons are written on the backs of banknotes, the world that belongs to people like Ed Lark.

Moonie opens up the ditty box and pulls an older model Allcom out of it, along with a small polymer card with an elaborate stereogram of a macaw in flight on its surface. He scans the card with the Allcom.

*"Please provide the spectral and numeral key to contin-*

*ue."*

"Blue, blue, yellow, six, blue, six, indigo, seven, orange, six, aqua, four," he drones out the access code.

*"In order to maintain a secure connection with your contact, Pardes Communications will now acquire all of the contents of your device. By proceeding, you will surrender all ownership of data on this device to Pardes Corporate. Continue if you agree."*

"Agree."

*"Encrypting pathway. Please wait for Ed Lark."*

After a little while, a video feed pops up on the Allcom's display, gentle ripples sparkling on the surface of an infinity pool, gliding hypnotically into the vast horizon of the ocean behind. A small bird flutters in the lush landscaping surrounding the poolside, the sound of ice cubes clinking in a tall glass, then Lark walks into the shot and plops down in a chair.

*"Did you watch the presentation?"* Lark asks.

"Yeah, yeah, winners and all..." says Moonie. "A bit over the top for my taste, but I guess that's the point, right?"

Lark puts down his drink and leans forward, clasping his hands.

"Anyway," Moonie continues. "I don't think Driggs is gonna need me to convince him this is a nice place. He probably already knows all there is to know about Pardes."

*"I'm sure he does. This was for you. It's important that you familiarize yourself with the details."*

"Yeah, I got it. Abundant pussy and exotic fruits, boats, armies, and glorious riches... Who wouldn't go for that? The man has been in hiding for years, squirreled up in the woods. I'm sure he wouldn't mind settling in a fucking Shangri-La. But, it's not a given he'd jump on it right away. We might need to work it a bit."

*"What do you mean?"*

"The way I see it, he doesn't know who you are, he barely knows me. You wouldn't believe the shit I had to do just to get this guy to agree to even talk to me, let alone meet in person. Next level scrutiny, I tell you. I think we gotta go in slow and easy, build some trust between us, take a look at his numbers, give him an impression..."

*"Slow and easy is for slugs and morons,"* Lark cuts him off. *"His numbers are garbage. There's only one reliable methodology for evaluating rare earth deposits and it's not the one he used. I have no interest in wasting my time massaging his ego. He either has the stuff or he doesn't. The only way to find out is to let my appraisers in."*

"You don't wanna scare him away, is all I'm saying. What if he starts thinking it's some sort of setup? You get what you want, then ship him back to Texas in a cage?"

*"Don't talk stupid,"* Lark starts getting irritated. *"There is no setup. We have a non- extradition agreement with everyone on the continent. He will get the full Corporate citizenship protection."*

"You think that's enough for a guy like that? Yeah, we have an agreement... He'll wipe his ass with your agreement."

*"Don't concern yourself with all of that. You get him to let my appraisers on the ground. That's all you need to do. If the prospect is solid, we're in business. He gets ironclad guarantees, a team gets sent to manage his exfiltration and transfer to Pardes, smooth sailing. It's a beautiful thing when people's interests align, things just happen on their own."*

"What kind of guarantees?"

*"That's for his eyes only. I can't discuss that with you."*

"Seriously?"

*"You worry too much. This is a simple business."*

"Easy for you to say when I'm the one sticking my neck out."

*"You brought this to me. You oughta know who you're dealing with."*

"I wish I did."

*"Then pull out if you're not feeling it. All the same to me.*

*I can find another way to reach out to him. Your call. I'll send you the finder's fee now and you're done, or you can make twenty times that if you see it through to completion. Who knows, maybe you'll get to even manage the project down the line."*

"Listen..."

*"Give me a yes or no. I gotta go."*

"Fuck!"

*"Yes or no?"*

"I'll do it."

*"Okay then. Call when you get there."*

"Fucking Lark," Moonie mutters as the feed goes dead.

Never a trace of doubt in his mind. Smug, sharp, and efficient to the point of compulsiveness. Fucking obnoxious. Every fucking time Moonie tries to challenge Lark's judgment he gets his ass handed to him. Always three steps ahead, always gets it his way, even when he's dead wrong.

They met in Rawee, in Shanghai, a watering hole with a Thai boxing ring in the back. Moonie was never much into gambling, but he liked the fights, the theatrics of the ring, the way in which the deceptive fragility of these boy-like gladiators turned into a fury of merciless rage in a split second, the hoots and jeers of the crowd that followed each quick punch and knee jab, their loyalty toward the fighters extending only as far as their bets for the night.

Moonie was waiting for his drink at the bar, watching a group of Filipino sailors knocking back shots, whooping and ritually punching each other in the chest. Three Russian beauties and an African queen were working the room, hoping to get some business before the fights began, methodically skipping the regulars who were nosing their Allcoms, pondering the spreads. A man in dark gray slacks and a crisp, plum-colored button-down came out of the side door, where the fighters' pens were, stealthily crisscrossed the room, and walked up to the bar next to Moonie. Clean-shaven and well-rested, he didn't seem like he belonged there.

"What are you drinking, sailor?" he asked without looking at Moonie.

Moonie glanced around, unsure if the man was talking to him or to someone else.

"Rumroll."

"What the hell is a rumroll?" The man turned to him.

"Rum, lemongrass juice, some other stuff I guess."

"Good?"

"It's okay."

"Where are you from?"

"California. Bay area. Just loading up here at the port. You?"

"Me? I used to be from Santa Cruz."

"Used to be?"

"Yeah, people change, right? Haven't been to America in a long time."

"What's a long time?"

"Eleven years."

The bartender came over. The man said something to him in Mandarin, the bartender nodded twice like a windup toy, and then marched off.

"You run this place?" Moonie asked.

"Oh no, god forbid. Just a vested interest."

"What do you do?"

The man looked at him silently, a moment too long. Moonie could almost feel his eyes piercing through his skull, probing around his brain. It made him very uncomfortable, even a little scared.

"Sorry. It's none of my business," he said nervously, averting his eyes.

The bartender came back with a small black velvet bag and put it on the bar in front of the man. The man swiped the bag off the bar, then leaned in toward Moonie.

"Third fight. Blue guy. I've heard he's got real talent, although the odds are against him," he said and walked off.

"What the fuck?" Moonie watched the man slowly edge through the crowd and, like he was never there, disappear back behind the door which he came in through.

"Rumroll," bartender pushed a drink in front of him. "For you, from Mr. Lark."

Moonie's mind was percolating. Why would a stranger go out of his way to give him a tip? Was it a tip? Not exactly a resounding endorsement of Bas Nantakarn's fighting prowess, but not a trivial speculation one would throw around just because, either. The way he said it, there was an intention there. Moonie checked the program directory—parlays and round robins, reverse bets, over rounds, under rounds, a mishmash of gamblers' vocabulary, none of which he understood. Finally, he finds the odds for a single win or lose bet. Fight number 3, blue trunks, Bas Nantakarn: 415. So... 100 nets 415. "Fuck it," after a brief hesitation, he decided to put up a 3,000 bet, about what he'd make on *Vostok* for a day.

The fight was close, as far as he could tell, with each boxer taking his turn pummeling the other, but then in the fourth round, his guy goes on a tear with a combo of low kicks and punches and with a wicked elbow strike to the nose, knocks out the opponent.

The next fight, a headliner, was kind of a dud. It ended after just thirty seconds when one of the fighters caught an axe kick to the side of the face. Tired and slightly drunk, Moonie decided he had enough. As he headed toward the exit, a skinny triad in a black polyester blazer blocked his way.

"Mr. Lark would like you to join him for a drink in the lounge," he said, standing a little too close for comfort.

Moonie backed up instinctively, and the man took that for consent.

"Follow me."

Inside the lounge, higher-rent girls danced around to a powdery tune while balancing champagne flutes between their fingers, while men, mostly in their fifties, sat around in small groups, drinking and laughing. Lark was sitting in one of the upholstered booths in the back, surrounded by a bunch of people, some of whom Moonie recognized from the bar.

"Hey bay boy, you beat the odds. Helluva fight, ha?" Lark seemed a little buzzed, maybe high on something.

"Good fight. Thank you for the tip," Moonie said.

Lark fixed on him with that same measuring gaze before suddenly breaking out in a big, weird smile.

"I like you," Lark waved his index finger. "Smart but not greedy. The world needs more people like that. Sit down, have a drink. I don't get many California expats around here."

It took a little while to put all of the pieces together, but, in the end, they worked out a perfect system. The minute Moonie got shipping schedules for the month, he'd call up Lark with the dates when *Vostok* was going to be in the Shanghai port. Lark would then rent a container from the shipper that handled all of the construction material shipments *Vostok* was regularly picking up in Shanghai, fill it in with slabs of prestressed concrete, and add it to the cargo. Prestressed concrete is a type of elastic prefabricated concrete commonly used for floors or for beams in high-rise buildings or in bridge construction. It's reinforced with steel cables, resulting in stronger, lighter, and more resilient building material. It also provides an excellent way to smuggle wealth.

Lark had done his part of the job with great attention to detail and methodical consistency that made it easy to keep track of the true cargo inside the concrete blocks. T-beams: gold, planks: platinum, columns: silver. Only marked pieces contained the secret load. T-beams with serial numbers ending in 5 had 5 kilos of gold buried inside, planks with serial numbers ending in 9 had 9 kilos of platinum, and columns with serial numbers ending in 45, 55, and 65, contained the corresponding number of kilos of silver inside them.

To avoid imaging detection in terminals, each of the precious metals was molded into bars matching the look and size of the steel bars used in the real prestressed concrete process, then embedded into casts before concrete was poured in. In the shipping manifests they were all classified as "Assorted Prestressed Concrete Structural Components," with bills of lading showing "Jiégòu Concrete, Nanjing, Jiangsu Province" as the shipper, and "Bedrock Construction Systems, Santa Cruz, California," as consignee, with San Francisco as the port of entry. It was a thing of beauty.

"Hands of Ali, heart of a lion, focus of samurai. Hands of Ali, heart of a lion, focus of samurai. Hands of Ali, heart of a lion, focus of samurai."

Once he discovered EternalQuest, Miles took to it immediately, and although he didn't last long the first time around, he knew he found his challenge. He knew that if he was going to be any good at it, he had to be faster, stronger, and smarter, and that meant upping his coding skills, working on his dexterity, both physical and mental, and learning, learning, learning. He had to learn everything there is to learn. But it also meant he needed to better understand the intricacies of the game itself, so that he can maximize his skills. The best way to understand the game, other than by actually playing it, is to watch others play, so during the season he'd keep an eye on good players, watch livecasts of their games, learn all the tricks and strategies and, in the off-season, scour the QuestFrontier archives for the matches of the great masters.

His all-time favorite was Bender, the only player in the history of the game to win three straight championships. At nineteen, Bender aged out of competition, a few years before Miles's time, but every now and then he'd pop up on the QuestFrontier in a special called "Way of the Champions," where they'd profile former great players, highlight their achievements and big moments, and showcase their legacies. In one of those specials, when asked how he prepared for the game, Bender said that he had a special mantra he repeated, which helped him get into the right state of mind. So, Miles came up with his own mantra.

"Hands of Ali, heart of a lion, focus of samurai": The lightning hands of Muhammad "float like a butterfly, sting like a bee" Ali, a lion's heart for fearlessness, and samurai for their discipline and dedication.

At first, he thought it was clumsy and stupid and he felt ridiculous saying it out loud, but after a while, the hypnotic power of repetition revealed itself and he realized that saying those words over and over again helped him tune out the noise and focus within. Eventually, the mantra became an essential part of his pregame ritual.

Of course, none of it would matter if his Portall was hooked up to an inferior machine. He was lucky to have his dad's Simulacrum mainframe at his disposal. Without its monster processing power, he wouldn't have stood a chance competing beyond the level of mere amusement. It still doesn't necessarily mean that "the one with the most toys wins" though. The top one thousand EternalQuest players all have powerful setups. At a certain point, the hardware arms race becomes meaningless, just like the real arms race, and if you want to win you have to look inside yourself and find out what's there.

Theo came back visibly upset. He couldn't find the MPPT controller in the pile and had to wait for Tischman to print out one for him.

"That's it," he kept saying. "That's it! I had it with this junk. Time to recondition this disaster."

The new MPPT controller worked fine when they put it in. There are still a few hours of sunlight left, enough to run the mainframe with all of the peripherals at full capacity and to top off the battery for later. Crisis averted.

In general, grownups had a much harder time dealing with the outages than the kids, maybe because they still remembered when the grid actually worked properly. They moped and fumed futilely every time the power went out as if they felt they should have some control over it. It's a systematic failure and there's very little an individual can do about it—kids knew that already. Or perhaps it was only the arrogance of youth and they didn't really care, as long as they had enough juice for their devices.

"Hands of Ali, heart of a lion, focus of samurai. Hands of Ali, heart of a lion, focus of samurai. Hands of Ali, heart of a lion, focus of samurai."

Miles puts the immersion kit on, launches the Eyeconic platform, and maneuvers to the EternalQuest gateway, initiating the intro featurette.

*"Empires rise and fall, but true greatness lives forever. Extraordinary feats touch the hearts of people, attract devotion, and invite a spirit of unity that extends beyond borders. What will your reign bring? Will you rise in the face of adversity or vanish into the ash heap of history? A great civilization expands horizons, strives for justice, and elevates all of humankind. How will the story of your people be written? What will your civilization be remembered for?"*

The featurette ends and a biometric reader pops up.

*"Authenticating... Welcome back, Miles. Your current scorecard shows a top eight average in all six scoring categories: Development of Society, Tactics, Technological Advances, Diplomacy, Population Influence, and Cultural Advancement. Congratulations Miles, you are an EternalQuest quarterfinalist.*

*You've come far. From the humble beginnings of prehistoric sustenance, with a handful of tools and a valiant spirit, you've built a viable civilization that stands the test of time, a global society that seeks harmony between humankind, nature, and technology. But new powers call forth. Your greatest challenge yet awaits you. There are questions to be answered, obstacles to be overcome, and mysteries of the world to be uncovered on the EternalQuest of humankind to survive and thrive on this planet we call home."*

# DAY_2

**Seated in the lotus position, hands cupped at** midriff, and eyes lowered in meditation, Maritza struggles to ignore the unending barking fit of the neighbor's dogs. Unable to maintain a still mind, she lets her thoughts tumble back in. They probably caught the scent of that bear, she thinks. He loves mornings. Funny how he keeps coming back, undeterred by the fact that every one of his attempts to raid the bird feeder has been a comic failure.

Maritza shifts out of the lotus position, does a few stretches to limber up, then rolls up her yoga mat. Of course, the dogs stop barking the minute she stashes it away.

Hoping to get some work in before the boys get up, she picks up a stack of blueprints for the San Francisco Harbor restoration project she's working on, then heads to the kitchen and pours herself a cup of coffee. She unrolls one of the blueprints on the kitchen table then looks outside the window to see if the bear is around. It's quite a show, watching him dance and growl and swipe the empty air with his paws, growing more irritated with every unsuccessful try. And he has tried hard, poor thing. She has seen him around at least half a dozen times, but the bird feeder is too high off the ground for him to reach. When will he finally concede that it might be time to stop obsessing over a handful of seeds and instead put all that effort into chasing himself a decent meal, like any other respectable predator?

The dogs start barking again, this time less fervently

and less consistently than before. They might have chased the bear away, Maritza thinks, and now they're just bragging about it to one another and to the rest of the world.

She walks out to the porch, opens the screen door, and cautiously heads outside into the yard. A few steps out she hears the sound of twigs cracking under feet and quickly retreats back to the porch, her eyes riveted on the trembling shadows in the woods. Nothing moves for a minute, then she hears the rhythmic shuffle of dry leaves getting closer.

Low-lying tree branches sway apart, revealing a small-framed figure. The figure breaks out of the woods onto the front lawn, then stands there, silently gazing at Maritza. A small Asian woman, probably in her fifties. She appears distraught and close to tears, holding her left arm as if she's in pain. Maritza steps out into the yard and walks up toward her.

"Are you okay?"

"I've been in an accident," the woman says. "Just up the road. My car slid off."

"ElBee," Moonie wakes up CALO. "A message for Danny Pitchford: Danny, tell Randy Ortiz this shit isn't gonna stand no more, he's holding up my entire operation with his bullshit. We can't do anything until we get our water hookup. Tell him he better have those machines moved to the site and ready to dig by the time I get there or he's fucking out. I'm spending the night on the road. I should be in Provo early afternoon tomorrow, so you got plenty of time to think about how you're going to convince me that you're actually doing your job. I'll stick around for a couple of days, then I'm heading out West. Get on his ass and don't take no for an answer. We waited long enough."

Damn contractors, they're all the same, not an honest bone in their bodies, and Danny is too nice of a guy to raise proper hell. Truth is, they're still on schedule, but it never hurts to light some fire under their asses. It's still early in the process, there will be plenty of hiccups along the way, but laying the goddamned water pipes shouldn't be one of them.

After three unsuccessful pitches, Lark finally nudged the Pardes Ventures board to give him a chance and now they're watching his every move to see if he's up to the task. He can't afford any slip-ups, and there won't be any. This mine is going to get online as projected, even if he has to personally grab all of the Randy Ortizes of the world by their dragging balls and get them to do what they're being paid to do.

Moonie opens the fridge door of the wet bar in the living

room, revealing a biometric safe built inside and scoops several one-ounce gold bars and a holstered gun out of it. He puts a couple of gold bars in his pockets and the rest inside an open suitcase lying on the coffee table, then clips the holster to his belt, smooths his jacket over it, zips up the suitcase, and brings it outside. He tosses the suitcase in the trunk, pulls another gun out of the side compartment, checks its magazine, then puts the gun back in its hiding place.

After they tended to the woman, Theo went to the woods to see if he could find her Allcom. She wasn't sure if she had left it in the car or if she had it on her when she got out and maybe dropped it somewhere on the way to the Smiths's house. The weathered little clunker was hanging off the side of the road like a discarded can, already leaking rust from its fenders straight onto the forest floor. It looked like it could roll down the ravine at the slightest touch. Theo peeked inside, but didn't dare go in. A search around the site of the crash and along the path she might have taken, yielded no result and he came back empty-handed, only to find Maritza and the woman sitting at the breakfast table.

"Miles, Dad's back," Maritza yells out when she sees him. "Come down for breakfast!"

"Are you sure you don't want us to call an ambulance?" Maritza asks the woman, cupping her palms around a warm tea mug.

"Oh, no dear, no," the woman shakes her head. "I'll be fine, it's just my arm and the knee a little bit. Honestly, I can't afford another medical bill, unless it's an absolute necessity. I have this condition... a respiratory thing, they don't cut me much slack."

"You should feel lucky you made it out of that wreck," says Theo. "Rough trip, Cloverdale to Winterhaven. Roads are infested with gangs down south."

"Believe me, the stuff I've seen... They usually leave me

alone, though. Raggedy old lady in a beat-up car," the woman smiles. "To most people, I'm not even an afterthought. I only make the trip a couple of times a year to check on my grandkids and get supplies, medicine, and rice. Border town, everything's so much cheaper down there."

"This thing in Yuma is getting ugly," Theo continues. "Looks like Texas is itching for a war with us."

"Please don't say that. My son's a ranger, they're first to be deployed."

"Oh, I'm sorry. Let's hope it doesn't come to that."

"I hate to impose on you, but I think I should call him now," the woman says.

"Please. Think nothing of it," Theo unlocks his Allcom and puts it on the table.

"Thank you so much," the woman starts dialing. "Well, I'm about to get an earful. He's gonna be worried when he sees me like this."

"We'll give you some privacy," Maritza grabs Theo by the sleeve and pulls him into the living room, then goes upstairs and knocks on Miles's door.

"Miles?"

"I'm coming," Miles answers behind the closed door.

"What are you doing in there?"

"Nothing. I'll be down in a minute."

Maritza goes back downstairs and joins Theo on the sofa. They can hear bits and pieces of the woman's conversation with her son.

*"... an accident?"*

"Maybe the brakes... In Concord... nice family took me in."

*"... disaster of a car on the road. You're so stubborn."*

"Yes... You should leave right away... I'm ready... Yes, now."

Theo and Maritza wait a few moments, then go back to the kitchen and join the woman at the table.

"Kids," Martiza offers small talk, but the woman seems somehow different now, her face tighter and eyes narrowed.

"Right," the woman's mouth transforms into a smile again. "They think they know everything."

"I was up north in your neck of the woods just a month ago, on a wine run," says Theo.

"Lots of good wine around Folsom," the woman responds.

"Didn't you say you're from Cloverdale?"

"Did I? No, I drove down from Cloverdale. Maybe you misunderstood. I was visiting a friend there."

"Aha."

"No, dear. I'm from Folsom."

"I think Folsom is more famous for its prison than for its wine," says Theo.

"Yeah, the prison. I don't drink, so I really wouldn't know if the wine is any good. It's just what I hear people say."

"I could have sworn you said you're from Cloverdale."

Out of nowhere, a faint air-ripping sound comes in from the distance, amplifying the awkward silence that ensues. They look at one another with sidelong glances, and just as Maritza was about to get up and call Miles to come down once again, the woman goes into a coughing fit, wheezing and convulsing with each dry bark coming out of her.

"Oh, my!" Maritza reacts. "Are you okay? Do you want some water?"

The woman lifts her hand, stretches her palm like she's trying to hold onto some invisible support, then reaches inside her jacket pocket and takes a surgical mask out and puts it on across her mouth and nose. The coughing stops instantly and she jumps to her feet, leaving Theo and Maritza astonished by this miraculous shift. She slings her arm forward, index finger half-raised, and before Theo and Maritza can grasp what they're looking at, she sprays a small vaporous cloud in each of their faces. Almost instantly, they slump in their chairs, their heads slowly sagging to the side in sleep. The woman stands above them motionless for a minute, listening to the sound of the aircraft approaching, then heads upstairs, clenching the vial in her bony hand.

At first, Miles wasn't sure if the coarse fluttering in his headphones was a part of the overcooked music mix he'd been listening to. It can't be, it's totally off beat, probably wireless interference of some kind. As he takes off his headphones he realizes the sound is real, and it's coming from somewhere outside. He glances through the window and sees two flyquads gliding in and out of weighted clouds at the edge of the town. He tosses the headphones on the bed and heads downstairs.

As he opens the door, he sees the woman coming up the stairs. She stops midway when she sees him and tucks her arms into her sides, clearly hiding something in her right hand.

"What's going on?" Miles blurts out, startled by her presence.

The woman doesn't respond. Shrouded by the shadows in the stairwell, her eyes glazed wet and cold above the line of the surgical mask, she stares up at him flatly, like some diabolical doll about to wreak vengeance on the world.

"Where are my parents?" a sting of panic trickles down Miles's spine. "Mom?" he yells out, dreading, in fact knowing, something is very wrong. "Dad?"

Sensing her moment, the woman starts creeping up the stairs with a feline-like focus. Miles backs up instinctively, then in a split moment changes direction and lunges at her, fists out. She grabs his arms, softening the impact, but the downward momentum of the stairs sends them both tumbling down. As they hit the base of the stairs, the woman's head bounces against the wall and she eases her grip with a muffled yowl. Miles untangles himself and leaps up to the kitchen, leaving the woman rolled over helplessly to the side.

"Mom! Dad!" Miles cries out when he sees his parents

collapsed around the kitchen table.

"Mom! Mom!" He checks Maritza's pulse, then lifts Theo's head looking for signs of consciousness. "Dad, wake up!"

Miles grabs some ice from the freezer and rubs it on Maritza's neck and temples, then tries the same with Theo, to no avail. From the corner of his eye, he sees that the woman got up on her knees and is looking for something on the floor.

"What did you do to them?" Miles screams out, but his voice is drowned out by the oncoming aircraft noise, which he realizes is suddenly much louder than before.

Seconds later, in a whirlwind of leaves and dry twigs, flyquads emerge from the treetops. They line up their noses then rhythmically swing around, hovering above the front lawn. As they start their descent, Miles notices a few helmeted heads inside preparing to deploy. The woman scoops the vial from the floor, then gets up on her feet, glaring at Miles with newfound anger. She readjusts the surgical mask on her face and readies herself to charge forward, but one of the straps has snapped out of place and she can't quite secure it back.

Restraining his panic as best he can, Miles realizes that his only option is to run. As he dashes out the door, a flying garden chair almost mows him down before it smashes against the patio window, spraying glass shards all around. He bolts across the yard, teetering forward like a bird trying to land, the downwash from the flyquad blades pressing on him from above. He loses his footing and hits the ground, but quickly picks himself up and somehow staggers into the woods. A few yards in, he takes cover behind a fallen tree and looks back to see six masked men in black uniforms disperse out of flyquads onto the lawn. They quickly spread into a diamond formation, then in a few rapid jolts, slither their way into the house. The edges of his vision blur up. He lets a few tears run down his cheeks, then wipes his eyes with the back of his hand.

Moments later, four of the men emerge from the house

lugging Maritza and Theo between them. They load them up into one of the flyquads, then two of the soldiers jump back out and return to the house. The flyquad takes off, and before Miles can process the shock of what has happened, it vanishes into the sky. The other flyquad cuts its engine, and a brief, ominous silence sets in before he hears the woman's voice as she marches out of the house in a fury, shouting at the four remaining men and gesticulating wildly toward the woods. On her orders, men fan out across the yard and head in Miles's direction.

He knows these woods inside out, but after a few minutes of frantic crashing through the branches and underbrush without a clear sense of direction, he realizes he's completely lost. He should have been near the stream by now. The rustling and crackling of the forest beneath his feet is making him an easy mark. He can hear soldiers' voices close behind, it's just a matter of time before they catch up.

At first, he thinks he has to get onto the trail, they won't be able to hear him running on a beaten dirt path. No, he quickly reasons, that would make it easier for them to track him. His legs are heavy. His face, whipped red by tree branches, is trembling with pain and rage. His hands and arms are bloodied by thorns. If he could only make it to the waterfall, he could slip inside and hide in the cavern below. They would never find him there. Or maybe he should run to the cliff, then turn up the stream toward Snake Ridge, slide down the rocks to the other side, and then make his way down the road to town. He'd be safe in town. But first he has to find the stream.

"ElBee, call Bobby D." Moonie activates CALO as he pulls out of his driveway.

The line rings for a long time before a crusty voice finally answers on the other side.

*"Moons."*

"Wake up, pea brain."

*"I was just about to call you."*

"Is that so?"

*"Yeah, yeah, just about to call you. I'm running a little late. Car trouble."*

"Right," Moonie decides to ignore Bobby's obvious lie. "Don't rush, I'm on the road already."

*"Sorry man, it's just..."*

"No worries Bobby, I know. Damn dogs disappeared before I got a chance to feed them. I think the neighbor had an airdrop delivery this morning, they get spooked by the noise. If you can come by noon that'd be great. They haven't eaten a thing."

*"Sure, sure, yeah."*

"They'll turn up soon, and, as I said, you're welcome to stay over while I'm gone, if you want. Sid and Bella would like that. It's good to have someone around. Or, you can take them to your place if you find that easier, but if you do, try to stop by the house every now and then. There's a lot of thieving scum out there."

*"Yeah, I might do that."*

"Which part?"

*"Stay over."*

"Great. Mi casa es su casa then. I'll authenticate the access for you, I got the details from before."

*"Good."*

"Alright, I'll be in touch. See you in a week or so."

*"Yeah."*

The joke in high school was that Bobby got high only once, but never came down. Not counting all the hard work he has put into preserving his optimal state of being for almost twenty years now, Bobby didn't do much else, so when Moonie came by money, out of some sense of obligation, hope that he can help, or pity—he wasn't completely sure which—he started giving him small odd jobs, which Bobby mostly managed to fuck up, one way or another. But he was a friend, someone who Moonie could trust around the house, as much as one can trust a junkie, and the dogs loved him.

Driving up the hill, Moonie notices something ruffling the tree branches and slows down. A moment later, a person leaps out of the woods onto the road and, frantically flagging with his hands, starts running toward him. The Smiths's kid! Moonie hits the brakes, leans across, and opens the passenger door.

"Drive! Drive, as fast as you can!" Miles jumps in, breathing heavily.

"Miles, you okay?"

"Drive! Get us out of here. Go!"

"Okay, okay." Moonie puts the truck in motion. "What the hell is going on?"

"Go faster! They're after me. You gotta drive faster!"

"Who's after you?"

"I don't know who they are." Miles looks back, his body swaying violently from hard hits of the bumpy country road. "Go, go!"

"What exactly happened?" Moonie asks.

"They kidnapped my mom and dad, I got away."

"What?"

The back end of the truck suddenly went crumbling down under a spray of bullets, shot-out tires spin and yank the wheel out of Moonie's hands. The truck swings to the side and hits the bank. The rear window shatters in pieces. Out of nowhere, four black uniforms appear in the rearview mirror. One of them kneels down and a red ribbon of smoke unfurls from his hands, whirls over the truck, and lands on the road in front of them, dispersing into a heavy curtain. Moonie wrestles back control of the steering wheel, then slams the gas pedal, giving the truck a jolt forward. They power through the smoke bomb, and with back wheels dragging, skid away down the road, leaving the soldiers behind.

## *Information Creation Department / Central Operations*

*Task: TAO-4 — Y-55-B*
*ICD Continuum: Op. Live*
*Origin: Field/Target location*
*Chain: TAO-4, ICD, CO-12, Epiphany Resources*
*Edit Rights: Central Operations*
*/10:23 PST/*

*Shift up to DOP level 3. Deviated operation. Sheng Long commanding field officer Fang requesting an immediate objective reassessment. Data sweep in progress.*

Snatch ops don't come easier than this one, Jiang thinks to himself as he watches the feed of Fang tottering across Theo Smith's office under the weight of a hefty piece of hardware. A couple of civilians and a kid, contained surroundings, six men, airlift... How could she possibly have fucked it up?

"Maybe you should have one of the guys help you with that," Jiang says out loud. "Those boxes could be pretty heavy."

Fang looks up to the camera, holding her chilling gaze long enough for Jiang to feel that she could actually see him on the other side.

"There should be a label on the left side of the unit," Jiang feels his throat tighten a bit. "Can you read what it says?"

Fang slams the metal box down on the desk.

*"Angstrom TF 12-C APU."*

“That’s a processing accelerator, there’s no actual data there. Move on.”

They don’t seem like the kind of people someone would send a squadron of commandoes after, thinks Jiang. Although the father’s packing some pretty serious computing power for a home operation, enough to run a small nuclear explosion simulation.

*“Next, Daemon 30-72 XAND Array.”*

“Hook it up.”

Fang latches ZeroPoint onto the box. The data ingest log pops up on Jiang’s display with a warning: *“Feistel cipher encountered.”*

“Proceed.”

He’ll decrypt it later; he’s hitting some latency on the sweep pipe, better get it all in first. He glances at the living room feed, where two uniforms are rifling through bookcases and cabinets.

“Tell your men to look for handwritten notes, assembled prototypes, parts, models, unusual materials, 3-D prints. Be specific. They don’t seem like they know what they’re doing.”

*“Leave my men to me,”* Fang barks back at him. *“You do your job, I’ll do mine. Next, Acorn 16 EMF.”*

“Take that box with you. ZeroPoint can’t extract data from fullerene storage or from holographic storage, for that matter. Any piece of hardware marked EMF or HGS has to be physically brought over for processing.”

Back tires recomposited a fair bit, but the truck keeps trembling and panting uphill like a deer in deep snow. Miles feels the branch whip marks starting to itch under his skin. He dabs his face with his palms, then, with an inaudible sigh, looks up to the sky.

"If they have air recon support they already know where we are," says Moonie, as if that was the answer Miles sought.

"You think they'll come after us with flyquads?"

"Possibly, but not likely. They can't do much from the air anyway, as long as we're moving. They might have operatives on the ground though. In any case, we should keep off the main road until we get to Byron."

"Who's your friend?"

"E.C.? Not really a friend. He did some work on my truck before. He'll fix us up in no time. If we can make it another fifteen miles."

Despite the backdraft from the broken rear window, the sugary smell of the smoke bomb still lingers around the cabin. Where did they take them? Miles wonders silently. Why? What do they want with them? His head wilts to the side against the window and he stares out at the valley below, where the maple tree crowns flutter in the autumn breeze like droplets of fire. Far away, on an empty road wiggling through the fields, he catches a glimpse of a figure toiling away on foot toward the rocky hills in the east. He used to take that road with his dad when they'd go trout fishing in the Los Vaqueros Reservoir. They'd get up before sunrise, pack up lunch and a thermos full of hot chocolate, and quietly sneak out so they wouldn't wake Mom. It'd still be dark when they'd push their boat off the dock and glide into the morning mist. By the time the first rays of dawn pierced through, they already had their lines in and were waiting for the trout to come out for breakfast. Why did he run away? Why didn't he try to rescue them?

The duo drive through the back streets of Byron until they reach the edge of town, then turn uphill toward the woods. Some two hundred yards after the road turns to gravel, they pass a discolored turned-over car hood sticking out of the ground by the side of the road like a forgotten tombstone, with the words "Salvage and Works" written on it in crude, heavy-handed cursive. The road dips into a small canyon of overgrown weeds and miscellaneous junk, which gradually becomes a two-story maze of piled up automobile carcasses, leading to a crumbling barn. The barn door is open, so they drive right inside.

"E.C.!" Moonie yells out.

"In here!" A voice answers from the back of the barn.

"It's me, Moonie."

A thin, grizzled man peeks out from behind a canvas tarp hanging between tool shelves. He sizes them up, sensing bother, then slowly walks out, wiping the grease off his hands with a filthy worn-out T-shirt.

"Boys," E.C. greets them with an unsure smile. "What brings you to my humble establishment?"

"We had a little run-in," Moonie aims his chin at the truck.

"Hollywagger!" E.C. recoils at the sight of the bullet holes.

"I know, it's totally fucked," says Moonie, looking annoyed like some asshole scratched his sports car with a screwdriver and worse, got away with it. "But hey, don't worry, we shook 'em off a while back. You know I wouldn't bring trouble to your door."

"And yet, you just did," E.C. grumbles back. "Close the doors."

Not waiting to be told twice, Moonie and Miles jump up and swing the barn doors shut, then stand back and watch E.C. hook up a chain pulley and lift the truck's back end off the ground.

"What do we have here?" E.C inspects the wheels. "Twenty-inch?"

"Yeah," Moonie confirms.

"Ride-ons, huh? The good stuff."

"Saved my ass today."

"It's your lucky day, I guess. I have a couple of ride-ons in the back. They're not new, but they look better than these."

"Moonie, I need to use your Allcom," Miles butts in. "Can you authorize me?"

"What? Now? What for?"

"I need to check something."

Moonie whips out his Allcom and scans Miles's retina with it. As soon as the Allcom beeps the confirmation, Miles grabs it out of Moonie's hands, and with eyes riveted on the display, walks to the back of the barn and sits on one of the mismatched chairs gathered around the grease-stained plywood table.

"What did you get yourselves into?" E.C. turns to Moonie.

"I'm not really sure," Moonie replies.

"Who's the boy?"

"My neighbor's kid. Someone abducted his parents from their home this morning, he got away. Popped up in front of my truck on Marsh Creek Road while being chased by four goons. We were lucky they didn't shoot to kill."

After a few moments of intense poking on its surface, Miles rests the Allcom on the table and throws its display up on the barn wall.

"What's this?" Moonie walks over, looking at a split screen of six different camera views.

"Our home surveillance system. They're still there," says Miles, his voice breaking with emotion. "Three in the garage," he points at the individual feeds, "one in the yard, by the flyquad, and here, in the bedroom, that's her."

"Who?"

"The old woman who attacked me in the house."

"Right."

They watch Fang rummage through Theo and Maritza's closet, flinging dresses and shirts out on top of the overturned mattress that's been slashed in a few places, pulling out drawers and dumping their contents on the floor, like she's deliberately trying to make as much of a mess as possible.

In the garage, soldiers are doing their part to trash the place, breaking stuff on purpose with the butts of their guns, weeding through tool lockers and shelves, then knocking them over and stumping on the spilled piles with their boots, all while casually laughing and bantering in an unfamiliar language.

"ElBee, un-Babel to English," Moonie instructs CALO.

*"Sampling language... Mandarin detected: ... Forget it. Yeah, six months is a minimum contract for tanker security. Can you even swim? Drop dead, dickface, I've spent two years at sea, oil rigs around Diaoyu Islands. Not exactly a ship experience. Who wants to be on a ship for six months? It's a death trap. That's why it pays double. Fuck that, they can keep their money. Those things get blown up way up too often."*

"Who are they?" asks Miles.

"Some Chinese circuit, it seems," Moonie replies.

"Circuit?"

"PSCs."

"What's a PSC?"

"Private security contractor."

"She's talking to someone."

Miles isolates tile four on the Allcom, and a full-size feed of Fang in the bedroom takes over the display.

*"What's done is done, the question is, what to do next... As a matter-of-fact, I do. I have a clear idea of what needs to be done. Redirect our field agents from San Francisco to the area immediately, tag his classmates, teachers, neighbors, family friends, the whole town, then lay low and wait for him to walk into the trap. He's got nowhere else to go. I'd give it three days max until he resurfaces. I'll stay behind to get them up to speed if you think that'll help... Yes... I understand... I will."*

After the conversation apparently ends, Fang stands motionless for a few moments, looking at her reflection in the dressing mirror on the wardrobe door. Then in a spark of rage, she grabs a lamp off the night table and throws it at the mirror, sending sparkling shards across the floor.

*"Lau, Maa,"* she yells out. *"We're done here. Load up the quad. Logistics should clear up the skies in a few minutes, we're going back."*

## *Information Creation Department / Central Operations*

*Task: TAO-4 – Y-55-B*
*ICD Continuum: Op. Live*
*Origin: Field/Target location*
*Chain: TAO-4, ICD, CO-12, Epiphany Resources*
*Edit Rights: Central Operations*
*/11:07 PST/*

*Shift up to DOP level 3. Deviated operation. Disengagement underway.*

No matter what happens next, she's finished, Jiang thinks, watching Fang run across the Smiths's lawn, shouting orders over the whirling blades. Too old to get a second chance. Fang ushers her men in and boards the flyquad, which then boosts up in the air and gets sucked into the gray sky, disappearing out of sight almost instantly.

The Smiths's security system feed stutters for a moment on Jiang's display, drops out for a few seconds, then comes back online. A glitch in the pipe? Maybe. Maybe not. Jiang pulls down the data scope interface. Trace track is showing a fresh login.

*"TAO-4—Y-55-B—New set of eyes on the target feed,"* he sends a message to Central Ops. *"Anyone we know?"*

*"No."*

*"Take a look at the trace track. Do we know who this is?*

*They got on eighteen minutes ago from Byron, California, twenty-seven miles from the initial target location."*

*"Yeah. I see it now."*

*"Anybody else out there on the ground?"*

*"No."*

*"It looks like a standard Allcom device."*

*"It's not ours. Grab it!"*

"What are you gonna do with the kid?" asks E.C., scraping the grime off the replacement window they found in the junkyard.

"The hell I know," Moonie shrugs. "They must have some family somewhere. I think the mother is from Eugene or someplace around there in the Willamette Valley. I don't get it. Why would anyone mess with them? I've known them for almost five years, nicest people you'll ever meet."

"You never know. Life is full of surprises," says E.C., spraying the dirt off with a hose.

"No shit, E.C. Your observation of the obvious is astounding."

"Hey!" E.C. squawks back, acting like he's offended.

"I just don't have time to deal with this right now. I gotta keep moving. I got shit to do."

"Don't look at me. I ain't running a daycare here."

"Fuck," Moonie rolls his eyes with a groan.

Moonie and E.C. grab the window panel and bring it inside the barn between them. Over in the corner, shoulders sagged, Miles is still absently staring at the feed.

"Miles," Moonie slowly walks over. "I'm gonna turn this off now. Okay?"

Miles nods weakly in response, then gets up and looks at Moonie, resolve building in his eyes.

"We have to go back," states Miles, in a surprisingly resolute tone.

"What?" Moonie sputters. "Why?"

"I'm going to find out who did this to us. I need gear. They only took the data storage devices, they left Dad's CPU behind, I can use it..."

"Miles..."

"Whoever it is, I'm gonna find out," says Miles with a defiant glint in his eyes. "I'm gonna find out who kidnapped them and why."

"How do you figure you'll do that?"

"First, I'm going to find out who hired these goons. Decompose the data trail, find out how they got into our home surveillance system, and then hack them right back."

"You think you can do that?"

"Anybody can get hacked. I need the right equipment, a few proxy stations, scramblers, encryptors, good bandwidth..."

"Miles, we can't go back," Moonie tries to reason. "Concord will be swarming with their agents in no time. They're on their way to your house as we speak, you can be sure of that. We can't go back unless you wanna get caught."

"Maybe it's better if I do just that, go back and turn myself in," Miles's voice starts to tremble. "At least we'd all be together."

"Miles..."

"I don't even know why I ran away," Miles lets the tears flow.

"Listen, listen," Moonie puts his hands on Miles's shoulders and holds him firmly. "Anybody would have done the same thing in your place. In moments like that you don't think, you just act. You did the best thing you could have done at that moment. You ran away to protect yourself. Now, you have to think about your mom and dad. I think if they know that you escaped, that can only make them stronger knowing that whatever happens to them you're unharmed and free. That's gonna be a source of strength for them. It's gonna be okay."

"What do they want from us? Money?"

"I don't know. Maybe. But I assure you, once they get what they want, they'll set them free. That's how this works. They'll let them come back home."

"What do we do until then?"

"Nothing. We'll hide you someplace safe and wait for things to resolve."

"But how? Nothing gets resolved on its own!"

"You'd be surprised."

"Shouldn't we at least go to the police?"

"I'm not sure that's our best option right now."

"Why?"

"PSCs have their tentacles in the entire system. We don't know who's involved in this mess and who we can trust. Most police are bought off, maybe not local cops, but they won't be able to do anything for you anyway. They'd keep you at the station for a few days, then, you being a minor, they'd have to send you off to child protective services. And I wouldn't trust them to keep you safe. Best case scenario, they'd put you up in some state-run foster home. I'm just telling you how it is, you're a grown kid now. Do you have any family outside of Concord? I think Maritza mentioned once she grew up in Eugene."

"There's no one there now. My grandparents are both dead."

"Anybody else?"

"No."

"All right, all right," Moonie extends his hands in the air like he's trying to push back the gathering predicament and give himself a little breathing space. "I'll think of something. We can't stay here, though. We gotta keep moving."

------

After going over a slim set of options while waiting for E.C. to finish fixing the truck, they figured the most sensible thing to do would be for Moonie to take Miles up to Stonyford, to Moonie's parents. With its seventy or so houses scattered loosely across farmland, the place was a perfect hideout, small enough and remote enough not to attract the wrong kind of attention. Miles would be safe and in good hands, and Moonie would still be able to make the trip east in time.

"This is weird!" Miles swivels in the passenger seat and looks back at an unassuming vehicle in the adjoining lane. "This is the fifth or sixth red van we've passed since we got on the highway."

"Oh yeah?" Moonie asks, staring vacantly at the road ahead.

"Exactly the same type of van."

"Probably automated cargo vehicles."

"Wouldn't cargo vans have some sort of business signage or something?"

"Hmm... I guess you're right," says Moonie, after a short consideration. "They usually do."

Moonie grew up in Vallejo, about twenty miles north from Concord in a small one-family house near the old fairgrounds on Lake Chabot. His mother was an accountant, his father a service technician. They both worked at Discovery Kingdom, a year-round amusement park that was just a five-minute walk from their house.

After he started making money with Lark, Moonie thought about buying a house in town, but quickly gave up on that idea. Unfortunately, Vallejo wasn't the same charming town he grew up in. It had become a third-class shithole within the lifespan of a single generation. Like many other unfortunate small towns and cities, it succumbed to the steady drubbing of diminishing opportunities that the Great Retraction left in its wake, its people and resources chewed up by complex and powerful economic forces and spat out onto the trash pile of history. Discovery Kingdom, the last big local employer, closed its gates three years before Moonie finished Maritime Academy. His parents, like many others, were never able to find real jobs again. Long after scrap metal crews dismantled the rides and hauled them off, his parents sat on their porch and watched the wild shrubs and tall swamp grass creep over the fairgrounds and turn the familiar place, once full of life and joy, into a wasteland.

They eventually sold their house for a pittance after Moonie graduated, and with their leftover savings bought a small home and a plot of land in Stonyford, a few hours drive north of the city.

Hands at ten and two, Moonie is mulling the plan over in his mind—except there is no plan, not really. Sure, it's a good idea to stash Miles up in Stonyford, but what happens after he comes back? He'll have the same fucked-up situation waiting for him. Unless the Smiths miraculously resurface by then, he's still going to be responsible for the kid.

*"Call from Bobby D,"* CALO interrupts his thoughts.

"What's up, Bobby?" Moonie answers.

*"Hey man, how's the motoring going?"* Bobby drawls out from the other side.

"Fine. Everything okay?"

*"Yeah, man. I just fed the dogs. They were mighty hungry. Listen, I don't wanna disturb you or anything, I just wanna let you know that there's been some activity around here."*

"What do you mean?"

*"Well, there was this dude in your driveway when I got here..."*

"A dude?"

*"Yeah, at first I thought he was lost or something."*

"What did he want?"

*"I don't know. He took off before I could talk to him."*

"What did he look like?"

*"Hard to say, he left in a hurry, which makes me think he might have been checking the place out and ran off when he saw me coming. Then, about ten minutes ago, I saw two dudes poking their noses around in the woods behind your house. One of them might have been the same guy I saw in the driveway, but I can't tell for sure. I don't see them right now, but I got a feeling they're still around. I was wondering if you want me to do something about it."*

Shit! Moonie realizes silently. The Circuit!

"You know what," he says as calmly as he can. "Why don't you take the dogs to your house for the time being. Take them to the beach, run them in the sand a bit, they'll love that."

*"Maybe I should stick around..."*

"That's alright Bobby. I'm sure it's nothing. Just take the dogs and go. Now. Don't come back to the house today, okay?"

*"Something going on?"*

"Don't worry about it. Just do what I told you. Take the dogs and go. I'll check in with you later."

*"Will do."*

Moonie hangs up with a nervous look on his face.

"And wouldn't you know it," Miles points with his finger as another red van appears in the lane ahead of them. "What was that all about?" he says and turns to Moonie.

"My dog sitter thinks he saw someone sneaking around my house."

"You think they found out where you live?"

"Maybe they're just combing the neighborhood."

All of a sudden, the red van in front of them inexplicably slows down, prompting Moonie to slam the brakes.

"What's with this fucker?" he screams.

As Moonie prepares to overtake the van, he sees two more red vans in the rearview mirror—one directly on his tail, the other one speeding up to him in the next lane. Before he can pull out from his lane, the speeding van lines up with his truck, then drops its speed to match Moonie's, effectively blocking him in. They drive in lockstep for some time until the lead van starts decelerating and rolls to a standstill, forcing the whole group to stop. Miles and Moonie look at each other silently, gauging the level of fear in one another's eyes.

"Shit!" Moonie finally figures it out. "They've been tracking us! They probably detected us peeking into the home security system."

Miles's eyes widen in fear. He scopes out the side van, expecting to see uniformed men jump out with guns drawn, but nothing seems to be moving behind the van's tinted windows.

"There's no one in there," Moonie reckons. "These are automated interceptors. They're just waiting for a squad car to come. Well, not today!" His jaw tightens. "Brace yourself, Miles!"

Moonie revs up the booster diesel engine then crams the truck's nose into the back end of the van in front of them and floors the gas pedal. The truck's cabin quivers from the struggle of the straining pistons, and a sharp smell of exhaust fumes fills the air as the sound of cracking plastic and shrieking metal cuts through the engine's roar.

After a minute of thrusting and shoving, the truck's horsepower finally prevails and the van starts gliding askew, eventually making enough room for Moonie to drive through. They speed up down the highway followed by the other two vans, but Moonie manages to keep them at a distance by frequently changing lanes and using other vehicles on the road as obstacles.

"We gotta get rid of this," Moonie throws his Allcom into Miles's lap.

Miles opens the window to throw the Allcom out, but Moonie stops him.

"Wait," he reaches inside his jacket pocket and hands him a folding combo knife.

"Try to take the wafer out first," Moonie says.

"With this?"

"That's all I got."

Miles twiddles the Allcom between his fingers, unsure of how to even begin, then stabs the knife into it but the knife skids off without even making a scratch.

"Here," Moonie takes his gun out of the holster.

"What?" Miles stammers. "What do you..."

"Smack it with the butt. Not too hard, you'll break the wafer inside."

Some hundred yards ahead, Moonie notices another red van creeping up in the collector lane.

"Hurry up, we gotta get off the highway soon! They're putting more cars on us."

Trying to keep his balance between the spastic swaying of the truck, Miles leans forward, puts the Allcom on the floor, steps on it with both feet to keep it in place, and gives it a whack. Nothing. He tries again a few more times until at last the glass spiderwebs under the metal. He sticks the pointy end of the knife into the cracks and starts butchering the device.

"Got it!" Miles cries out triumphantly as he pinches the wafer out. He then opens the window and tosses the rest of the massacred Allcom out.

"Alright!" Moonie cheers.

"What about the truck?" Miles suddenly realizes.

"What about it?"

"They can still track us through the automated driving system."

"No, they can't. This truck is all muscle, no brains. I ripped out all the AD hardware. No onboard computers of any kind, other than the battery utilization management. We lose these bots now and we're home free."

It took a couple of near-accidents and a bit of off-road-ing, but Moonie and Miles managed to get rid of the interceptors before the squad cars showed up. It will be easier to blend into the traffic now that they lost their electronic tail. Nonetheless, they're still exposed. Road cameras could still pick up the visual of the truck and alert their pursuers, and there's a real possibility that they've been under aerial surveillance from the get-go and are being watched and tracked right now. One thing's for sure, Stonyford is out. By now, the Circuit or whoever is involved has dug out all there is to know out there on Moonie, connected the dots, and figured they were headed up to his parents—and are already waiting for them somewhere along the way. They gotta hit the boonies. Fast. As soon as they're able to score a new Allcom.

Once they got off the highway, they stayed on the side roads running through the fields along the river and entered Sacramento from the north. According to Moonie, it was the least populated part of the city, halfway off the grid and easy to sneak into unnoticed. They drive through an acrid haze of garbage fires lingering somewhere behind weed-covered dunes of construction debris, down a street of boarded-up houses and forsaken one-story businesses. The only signs of life are the cars on the highway overpass a few blocks ahead of them. On the other side of the overpass, someone hung a hand-painted sign by the side of the road that says "Piggyback Temp Camp" with a yellow crooked arrow pointing to a cluster of trees behind a decaying structure of an abandoned strip mall.

Piggyback Temp Camp is a small makeshift village of tents, trailers, and wooden huts scattered haphazardly across a dirt lot, dotted with dry shrubs and clumps of exhausted grass. Along the dusty camp path, chewed up T-shirts and sweatpants drying on the clotheslines slacked between scrawny trees are waiving in the wind like claim flags. On the right to the entrance, Miles and Moonie see a group of men sitting on wooden pallets playing cards. They decide to slowly drive over to them. The men raise their heads as the truck pulls up.

"Hey fellas, you have a public terminal around here?" Moonie asks.

"By the taco truck," says one of the men, pointing at a congregation of RVs in the middle of the camp.

"Is it working?"

"As far as I know."

The pair pull up close to the taco truck, get out, and walk over. A heavy man inside the taco truck gives them a long, suspicious glare as they approach the counter.

"What's good here?" Moonie puts on a friendly front, looking up at the blackboard above the grill.

"Everything is good," the man answers mater-of-factly.

"What did you have for lunch?"

"Carnitas."

"Two carnitas, then. Rice and beans, the whole thing."

Moonie pours two cups of water from a canister on the counter, hands one to Miles, drains his in one go, then refills it. In the back of the tarp-covered patio leaning off the side of the taco truck, two boys around Miles's age, maybe a little younger, are playing shoot 'em up, cussing at each other over heavy grunts as incessant automatic weapon fire gushes from their Allcoms.

"These your kids?" Moonie asks the man.

The man looks down at Miles's scratched up face, then turns to Moonie. "Why do you ask?"

"I might have a proposition for you."

Before the man could say anything, Moonie plucks a one-ounce gold bar out of his jacket pocket and places it on the counter.

"This right here is an ounce of pure gold," he taps the gold bar gently with the tips of his fingers. "Real gold. This cub on the seal means that the Great State of California guarantees its authenticity and its purity."

The man's gaze jumps wildly from the gold bar to Moonie over to Miles and then to the gold bar again and back to Moonie.

"For the carnitas," Moonie smiles.

"It's too much money for the carnitas, Mr.," the man says and draws back inside his truck.

"What's your name?"

"Salazar."

"What's your first name?"

"Salazar is good," he nods defiantly.

"All right, Salazar is good, here's the deal. You let me and my friend here borrow one of your boys for five minutes and this shiny little thing is yours."

"What do you want?"

"None of what you're thinking, I assure you. Public terminal over there, is it working?"

"It's working."

"All I need is one of your kids to go over there and make a call for me."

Salazar glances at the gold bar glimmering on the steel surface of the counter.

"Why can't you make the call yourself?"

"Well, I got my reasons."

"An ounce of gold for a call?" Salazar narrows his eyes suspiciously, but his tone sounds curious, like he wants to believe his good fortune.

"My kingdom for a horse," Moonie jokes.

"What?"

"Nothing. The kid says one sentence, reads some numbers, and that's it. We eat our carnitas and go on our merry way and you made yourself some money. What do you say?"

"That's it?"

"Nothing more, nothing less."

"Okay Mr.," Salazar makes up his mind abruptly. "Gael,

Fernando!" he calls the boys over, then tells them something in Spanish.

The boys lay down their Allcoms and walk up to the truck.

"What do you need?" the older one asks Moonie.

"Which one are you?"

"I'm Gael."

"Gael, can you say unadulterated?"

"Whaaaat?" The boy chuckles nervously.

"Unadulterated. It means pure. Can you say that?"

"I don't know."

"Come on, try it."

"Undalt..." Gael starts laughing.

"You can do it," Moonie encourages him. "Say adult."

"Adult."

"Now say un-adult."

"Un-adult."

"Now say un-adult-erated. Unadulterated."

"Un-adult-erated. Un-adult-erated," the boy repeats.

"Great. You see, that wasn't too hard."

Moonie produces a black plastic card out of his jacket pocket and scrapes its face with a knife, revealing a numerical code.

"Here's what you need to do," he hands the card to Gael. "Ask the terminal to connect you to Seed Safe. Once you get connected, a Seed Safe automated assistant will ask you what you want. You'll say, 'I'm looking to purchase some unadulterated lavender seed in Sacramento, California.' Now, repeat it to me."

"I'm looking to purchase some unadulterated lavender seed in Sacramento, California," Gael recites.

"Great. Then, they will ask you, 'Can you be more specific?' That's when you read these numbers out loud. The system will give you the name and address of the store that sells the seeds. That's it."

"I can do that, sir," the boy chirps up.

They gather around the mushroom-shaped terminal booth, Gael in the front, Miles and Moonie behind the plastic enclosure in the back, away from its cameras. On Moonie's sign, Gael steps inside the booth and activates the terminal.

*"Welcome to California Public Information Utility,"* a faint fizzle comes out of the terminal's busted speaker. *"California Public Information Utility reminds you that any information transmitted during this session is subject to California Open Access Network and could be employed by anyone, for any purpose, without any restriction. To continue, please lean in for biometric recognition and authentication."*

------

"This is it. All that's left of the city," says Moonie as they drive across an invisible line that separates downtown Sacramento from its squalid surroundings. "Soon they'll give this up too. Then the whole thing could be wiped off the map. Just another hellhole with no trace of civilization."

"Some people call it Scarymento," Miles chimes in.

"Scarymento is right," Moonie agrees.

Miles considers telling Moonie that "some people" actually means he and his friend Jamie McIntyre. They came up with Scarymento after their misguided adventure to the city, four months ago, an experience they'd both rather forget. Embarrassed by his own naiveté, Miles decides against it. Plus, he swore to Jamie he'll never tell a soul.

Jamie took him into his garage one day.

"I wanna show you something really cool," Jamie said in a rather dramatic fashion before flicking the tarp off of a wrecked Suzuki GS 650.

"Ta-da! What do you think?"

Miles stared at what looked like a pile of trash miraculously balancing on a pair of warped wheels.

"I know it looks like crap, but I'm gonna fix it up," Jamie went on. "I found a guy in Sacramento who has another GS 650. I'm gonna combine the parts from his bike and mine and make a lean, mean riding machine."

Jamie's dad and uncle ran a hardware store in town and once a month they'd go to the city to pick up merchandise from the wholesaler. The plan was to wait until they leave to "borrow" Jamie's uncle's truck and haul the bike from Sacramento before anybody notices anything.

Caudillo Mechanics was not listed on LocLock but the seller gave them instructions: Get off the freeway on Forty-seventh Avenue East, then drive straight for eight blocks. They got off the ramp into a two-way street of derelict row houses, most of them missing doors, windows, and roofs. Bunch of kids kicked a threadbare soccer ball on the sidewalk. The left side of the street opened up into a small field, once probably a local park, but now overtaken by feral grass, age-old garbage, and shrubbery.

At the far end of the field, behind a mangled metal fence, a few teenagers sat on the crumbling concrete bleachers. When they saw the truck, they jumped up to their feet. One of them sprinted across the field, quickly disappearing behind the torn down walls of an adjacent house. The rest reshuffled into a semi-circle, eyeballing Miles and Jamie. As they drove by, two of the guys up front slowly pulled their shirts open to reveal handguns sticking out of their waists.

"Shit, oh shit!" Jamie whispered.

Part of the intersection at Forty-seventh and Vista was blocked off by a barricade made from the capsized skeleton of a burned down car, old tires, rocks, and rusty corrugated tin panels. They drove up to the barricade and stopped.

"Maybe this is it," said Jamie, looking around. "Do you see the body shop?"

On the other side of the barricade, they saw a man step out of a boarded-up building, slowly walk into the shadow of the street corner, then stand there, unmoving, looking at them. Jamie's Allcom rang.

"Yes?"

"I see you made it," the voice on the other side crackled. "Now, get out of the truck and walk over to my man Gonzalo, he'll take you to see the bike."

The man on the corner started signaling something they couldn't understand. They looked at each other, scared witless, then Miles noticed two figures rushing from the side street, both holding something in their hands that looked like guns, and realized that the man was signaling to them to get closer.

Jamie made that truck sing, sped up in reverse, then did a hard slam on the brakes and a bumpy, spinning U-turn. They darted out of there like scalded cats, happy that their dumbassery didn't cost them their lives that day, or at least Jamie's uncle's truck.

Moonie hid the truck under big oak trees encircling Capitol Mall Park before they continued on foot through the canyon of office towers sprawling around the old California State Capitol Building. Tucked away down a small side street, flanked by a homeopathy shop and a butcher, with its faux rustic front, Spice Sac looks like someone's idea of an old family store. Inside, smells of earth and exotic places fill the room. A long narrow space with exposed brick and low ceilings is packed with canvas bags and glass canisters full of spices and seeds.

"Welcome to Spice Sac! What can I do for you today?" the bespectacled man behind the counter eagerly offers when he sees them at the door.

Without a word, Moonie walks up to him and hands him the black card. The clerk examines the card, nods slightly in approval, then scans it with his Allcom. A high-pitched beep pierces the tense silence as they measure each other up.

"Okay, then," the clerk puts his hospitality face back on.

“I need two,” Moonie says.

“How fast?”

“How about right now?”

“I see.”

“A blank one is for the kid. This is to be put in mine,” Moonie lays the memory wafer on the counter.

“Ages?”

“Thirty-three and fifteen.”

The man leaves for a few minutes, then comes back.

“Greek Orthodox Church by McKinley Park,” he says, handing Moonie an RFID tag. “Go inside and wait, we’ll be there within two hours.”

Theo's ears are booming with pressure, but he can still hear voices burrowing through the dull pounding of the flyquad blades. Not sure if he's dreaming, he opens his eyes to see Maritza asleep across from him, her head resting on her shoulder, lips slightly parted, almost kissing the arm of the soldier on her left. He thrusts himself forward looking for Miles, but the belt straps around his shoulders yank him back in place and his head helplessly wilts to the side.

The sour smell of cooked bitumen grips his throat and nostrils and he opens his eyes again. Through the blur of his eyelids he sees lakes of black water glimmering through thick white smoke gushing out of smokestacks below. The smoke eventually thins out, revealing an eerie amphitheater of an open-pit mine, a swarm of excavators stirring around in a slow-motion feeding frenzy, a dump truck procession crawling in a loop from the bottom of the crater to the ore crushing stations on top and back. Suddenly, the flyquad pitches forward into a descent, tightening the security harness around Theo's chest, and then drops into a steep dive, sending a rush of blood to his head. He feels the breath escaping from his lungs and all becomes black again.

"Glory to Christ," a slight old man in a black robe greets Moonie and Miles in the vestibule of the Annunciation Greek Orthodox Church.

They look at him with an air of curiosity. Neither has ever seen a monk in person.

"Splendid day," the monk adds.

Moonie manages a small smile, keeping the irony to himself. Accustomed to being ignored, the monk shuffles out of their way, picks up a miniature wooden rake from the top of a tin sandbox standing in the shadow of the entrance door, and starts combing through the sand for wax lumps from spent candles.

The dark, empty nave feels small compared to the rest of the church, peaceful in its austerity, inviting contemplation. They sit in the middle pew, close to the exit. From the stained-glass windows above, the stern faces of Saint Peter and Saint George look down at them like they're passing judgment. The window on the left, with Saint George on a horse, is broken, and where the Saint's right hand was supposed to be clenching onto his almighty lance, there's a gaping hole instead, making him look more like a polo player in an elaborate getup searching for a mallet he dropped on the ground. Without a weapon against its neck, the vicious dragon representing the evils of this world that Saint George is supposed to be killing, seems carefree, his toothy mouth relaxed in a smile.

He'd been doing a good job pretending he's not a hairsbreadth from a full-fledged freakout, Moonie thought. It's better if Miles doesn't know how truly fucked they are. They must assume the worst because the worst is possible. The Circuit might put a bounty on them, get all the creeps crawling out of the woodwork from here to the Colorado River looking for them, dead or alive. Well, they'll want Miles alive... him, probably not so much. There's no going back home for a while, or any place the Circuit expects they might go for help. That includes Provo.

Danny is gonna have to deal with Ortiz and the water pipes on his own. They can't involve anyone they know, or more precisely, anyone the Circuit knows they know. Their best option might be to just head straight to Driggs's. They can hide there safely for a couple of weeks, at least until the appraisers come from Denver—unless Driggs refuses Lark's request straightaway and kicks them out. But that's a problem for another day. The real problem staring them in the face right now is how to cross over to New America. The minute they show up at the border checkpoint, the Circuit will swoop them up like a couple of rabbits. Under normal circumstances, the new IDs would have done the job of getting them through, but with the all-seeing eyes of the security apparatus, they're not a couple of innocuous travelers anymore. They're gonna have to jump the border.

One of the unforeseen, or depending on who you ask, very much expected and planned for consequences of the abolition of the federal government, back in the day, was the general rise in lawlessness—especially in poorer states that could not afford proper law enforcement on their own. It turns out that when the threat of punitive measures gets weaker, societies tend to devolve into a mere collection of selfish brutes rather quickly, and that goodness of the heart, feeling of shame, and fear of public humiliation aren't very effective guardians of peace and order.

The last years of the Union were a dysfunctional culmination of a slow-burning political crisis that fed on the long-standing social tensions and cultural divisions, endemic discontent, and mistrust. The centuries-old two-party system has grown inadequate to effectively channel the will of the people. In addition to being simply too big to contain the many different and often conflicting political agendas they each nominally embodied, the two parties found themselves locked in a mutually reinforcing cycle of revanchism and antagonistic myopia, so deeply entrenched in their positions that the civil debate practically ceased to exist, leading to a profound political rupture at a time when consensus was desperately needed.

The United States was already in deep economic trouble even before the secessionist movement gained traction. In fact, the general historical consensus is that the incessant economic downturn that took hold over the first half of the century was the main catalyst of change.

Economic opportunity was always the glue that held together the opposing ideological forces throughout American history, so as it waned, so did the relative singularity of what it meant to be an American. In the absence of compelling political leadership, competing visions of the future became a cacophony of discord, fostering the narcissism of small differences and challenging the notion of national identity, cultural kinship, and shared purpose.

The only thing everyone agreed on was the need for a referendum. In a twist of irony, the prospect of the referendum, divisive in its nature, was the unifying force that brought people together, narrowing down the conflict between the rivaling factions to the greater issue of allegiance to the Union. All of the differences between the Left and the Right, religious and godless, rich and poor, progressives and conservatives, globalists and isolationists, moderates and radicals came down to a single clash between the Secessionists and the Unionists.

It didn't take long for the consequences of the breakup of the United States to became glaringly relevant. When the ability of some of the newly independent states to provide basic services for their citizens weakened, the private sector was all too happy to jump in and fill the void, creating a maze of parallel institutions across-the-board. Nowhere has this change been more pronounced than in the public security sector. Employing the "infallible remedy of the free market," the states started supplementing their law enforcement duties with services provided by private security corporations, effectively surrendering parts of their sovereignty to private interests—and making, in turn, the intricate process of dealing in justice and law far simpler and truly cost-effective. If you had enough money you might get your share of law and justice—if not, better not stand in anyone's way.

The sanctuary door opens, and a slender silhouette of a man appears in it. He stands there for a few moments, observing, then vanishes. A minute later, a small delivery drone whirrs in, gliding along the nave divide, then abruptly stops and drops a box on the floor just a few feet from Miles and Moonie.

On their way out they pass by the monk again, who has made some progress with the raking.

"God bless you, children," he lifts his hand in the air, making what looks to Moonie like some sort of a friendly gang sign.

"Thank you," Miles responds with gratitude.

They wait until they get back to the truck to open the box. Inside, there are two smaller boxes, one with the number fifteen on it, the other one with the number thirty-three. They each open their box and find a brand-new series twenty-one Smoke Signals Allcom. Tucked under the Allcoms are reclosable static shielding bags.

"I'll go first," Moonie takes a pair of sham lenses out of the bag and attaches them to his eyes, and then turns on the Allcom.

*"Welcome to Smoke Signals,"* the Allcom announces

itself. *"The world awaits! Please calibrate your new device by scanning the retina of your eye."*

Moonie leans into the camera lens.

*"Your Retinal LiveScan signature is logged. Please wait for security assurances from the mainframe."*

"So, can we contact people now?" Miles asks.

"I don't think that's a good idea," Moonie replies.

"But we'll be anonymous with these new IDs."

"Yeah, maybe the first time around we will, but we have to assume the Circuit will be monitoring everyone you know. They see the same new number pop up on your friends' devices, they'll figure out what's going on."

"I thought Smoke Signals gear is untraceable."

"It's much safer than the rest of what's out there, but nothing is foolproof. It's not worth it, unless absolutely necessary. It's the others we have to think about too. We don't want to put anyone at risk. We're better off not taking chances."

*"Congratulations, Max Madigan. Your device has been authorized and is ready for use. You're now a part of the Smoke Signals community. The world awaits!"*

"Max Madigan!" Moonie cheers approvingly. "I like my new name."

"What's your real name?" Miles asks. "I always knew you only by Moonie."

"Lupo."

"Lupo?"

"Lupo Belan. Lupo means wolf in Italian."

"Why Moonie then?"

"It's after some character in a book my mom liked. A boy gets bitten by a wolf and becomes a werewolf wizard or something like that. His name was Moonie."

"Professor Remus Lupin from the Harry Potter books?"

"Yeah, that's it," says Moonie. "Harry Potter. Have you read them?"

"Yeah, when I was a kid."

"Nobody ever calls me Lupo, though. But now you can call me Max Madigan! It's got a swanky ring to it, don't you think?"

Following the same sequence as Moonie earlier, Miles authenticates his Allcom.

*"Congratulations, David Hart. Your device has been authorized and is ready for use. You're now a part of the Smoke Signals community. The world awaits!"*

"David Hart! Oh, that's a good name!" Moonie exclaims. "That's a good name!"

"It's okay," Miles nods.

"Are you kidding me? That's a hero's name."

"If you say so," Miles squeezes a small smile.

Cold air slices through Theo, sending shivers down his spine. He crumples further into a tight ball, feeling up the bed with his hand, instinctively seeking the comfort of covers. A thud of someone's boots wakes him up. As he opens his eyes, he sees a man exit the room, shutting the metal door behind him. Locks snap into place. The ceiling spins around as he gets up on his feet. He grabs onto the bed frame for support and stands still for a moment looking around the room, hesitant to make the first step. There are three plastic water bottles and a small pile of nutrition bars on a steel rolling table next to the bed. He cracks a bottle open and takes a few big sips out of it, then, in what looks like a two-way mirror, sees a reflection of himself.

"Hello?" Theo tries to shout, but his voice sounds frail. "Anybody out there?"

His words bounce against cinderblock walls before fading away in the steady hum of an air unit. He takes a few more sips of water, then walks up to the mirror and presses his face against the glass.

*"Theo Smith,"* a man's voice fills the room.

"Yes?" Theo swings around, trying to determine where the voice is coming from. The sudden move makes him stagger on his feet. He takes a few seconds to steady himself then looks up at the ceiling. "Where's my family?"

*"They're right here with you, a couple of doors down. We'll take good care of them, you shouldn't worry about that."*

"I want to see them. I want to see them right now!"

*"Now, Mr. Smith, in order to make our relationship mutually beneficial we need to develop trust and foster understanding. You're not in a position to make any demands. I would advise you to remember that going forward. It will make your stay here much more pleasant."*

"What's this all about? Who are you?"

Minutes pass in silence. Theo's legs start sinking beneath him and he slumps to the floor, hugging his knees to his chest.

*"We're the same age, you and me,"* the voice comes in again. *"Different shake of the dice and we could have played together on the high school hoops team. Or sat next to each other in Professor Lambert's physics class at Stanford. Well, I didn't make the grades to get into Stanford, but I did like physics when I was younger. We have so much in common, we probably would have been friends back in the day when we believed we could change the world.*

*I think our generation was probably the last one to truly believe there was going to be this great future waiting for us that would miraculously bring solutions to our problems: stop wars, eradicate famine, cure diseases, suppress wealth disparity and corruption, prevent climate change, reverse the great entropy of human existence somehow. And then it turned out the future had been eaten up by our forefathers and all we have left is this chewed up present in which we must live until we die.*

*I'm an oil man, Mr. Smith. A peculiar profession these days. The world has been coming unglued for years and now the Middle East blows itself up like that. May you live in interesting times, right? I think it might end up being a good thing; after all, we're long overdue for a real global collapse. I've had it with these piecemeal crises. Ha, ha!"* The man's cackle rings through the room.

"Why am I here?" Theo asks.

*"You're here because I decided to give you an opportunity to be part of history. You're an incredibly talented man, one of the best at what you do. I like to think of myself in the same terms. We're gonna build something great together, something that might give us both another shot at believing in a great future again."*

"Build what?"

*"All in due time. You had a long day. Drey will show you to your room."*

"Who are you?" Theo's question hangs in the air without an answer.

After a few minutes, the lock clacks open and a burly man with huge hands shows up at the door. He walks in slowly, sizing up Theo with concealed curiosity.

"Mr. Smith, my name's Drey. I'll be your escort during your time here. I'll manage your interactions with others and assist you with your responsibilities at the facility."

"You're my handler?"

"If that's what you want to call me. My job is to help you with all your needs. If..."

"All my needs?" Theo interrupts him. "All my needs? What kind of needs do you suppose a freshly abducted person would have, Drey? Do you think I want a sandwich? A puppy? I want to know what the hell this is all about! What am I doing here? Can you help me with that?"

Drey waits for Theo's flare-up to subside with the patience of a man used to being in control, then continues.

"Please come with me," Drey tries to help Theo off the floor. "I'll show you to your room now."

"Get your hands off me," Theo pushes him away with feeble anger, then slowly gets up. "I can walk on my own."

They take the elevator to the third floor, then walk down a windowless, carpeted hallway to room 302.

"This is it," says Drey as he unlocks the door.

They enter a small room with generic decor and modular Formica furniture, which emanates the clean utilitarian comfort of campus living.

"This is your two-way unit," Drey lays a device on the table. "From now on, you are to keep it on your person at all times. If you get a voice call, answer it, if you get a text message reply immediately. Tomorrow morning you'll visit the lab."

"Lab?"

"Yes. Anything you need, call or text me."

"Where is my son and my wife?" Theo asks.

"You should try to rest, Mr. Smith. I'll bring you dinner at seven o'clock."

The door automatically locks as Drey leaves. Drey strides down the hallway, past the elevator, then makes two quick rights along a row of doors on the other side of the floor and enters room 308.

The room is a mirror image of Theo's, except a lot darker due to the drawn blackout curtains. A media panel is on, showing some surfing program propelled by electronic music. Fast-cut video clips of twenty-year-olds gleefully riding foam-crested waves, laughing in the sun, lolling on the wet sand in some paradise, somewhere. The flickering blue light of the media panel intermittently reveals Maritza's sleeping figure on the bed. Scrunched on her side with her arms folded over her chest, she looks like a big child hugging an invisible stuffy. Drey grabs a throw blanket from the closet and covers her with it.

"Seems like the wife is still out," he says aloud.

*"Keep it that way,"* the voice in his earpiece tells him.

"Okay," Drey replies, then sprays a whiff of something under Maritza's nose and leaves the room.

Moonie and Miles drove through Yosemite without stopping, taking shortcuts along the way, grinding up and down logging roads and narrow forest paths. By the time they made it to the other side, the sun had already dipped behind the crest of the Half Dome and the great solemn shadows of its cliffs had begun to roll over the valley below. Further east, forests tapered off, giving way to barren hills that sloped down into the flat hollow of Mono Lake. A smell of faraway wildfire wafted through the air as they descended into Lee Vining, a small town at the eastern entrance of Yosemite that laid sprawled on the southwest shore of the lake.

Miraculously, a gas station on Main Street had diesel, so they seized the opportunity to tank up—but what they really needed to do was recharge the truck's battery. CALO found three charging stations in the area, but according to the gas station attendant, only one of them, about fifteen miles north from the town, was functional. Since they were going to be heading that way anyway, they decided to stop at a small cafe overlooking the lake for a bite first.

"There's only one road across," says Moonie, tracing the thin horizon line with his finger. "Right there, along the lake."

Moonie looks up at the sky, then zooms in on the Allcom's map display.

"The road branches out twelve miles past the border. Hawthorne is just another four miles north from the fork, then it's about two hours to Lovelock from there."

"What happens if we get caught?" Miles asks.

Pretending to study the map, Moonie takes a moment before answering.

"We're not going to get caught," he says, without raising his eyes. "If we do, we're gonna have to hope there are some reasonable people out there. If we do... which we're not."

Moonie seemed encouraged by his own words, but deep down he knew that the chances of them crossing over without tripping a security circuit breaker somewhere in the border surveillance system are slim. A joint fleet of scout drones scans the entire length of the California-New America border, 24/7. There are motion sensors inside the pavement at the crossing, a few miles out on each side, and who knows how many cameras. A drone feed goes to both sides simultaneously to ensure mutual information and compliance, roving patrols get alerted when something unexpected appears... and there are just so many places one can hide in the open desert. On a clear day like this, they wouldn't stand a chance, but at night, since drones have to rely on thermal imaging to lock in their trackers, their chances improve a bit. They're gonna have to drive electric the entire way, that's for sure—batteries don't give off as much heat.

The night came down suddenly, like a black cape full of moth holes. Stars are out. Not a cloud in sight. A big harvest moon is hanging low in the sky and its mirror image in the lake is amplifying its brightness, so much so, that even from miles away they can clearly see the strip of road swirling around lake shores and dwindling into the dark hills on the Nevada side. Somewhere behind the hills, in the distance, soft orange light is pulsating fitfully and the scent of burned wood is getting stronger than before.

"Now listen," says Moonie with measured gravity in his voice. "This is not going to be a walk in the park, but we got a fair shot. Hopefully, the forest fire keeps going through the night and the wind brings the smoke our way."

"The drones..." Miles nods in acknowledgment.

"Right," Moonie replies. Anything goes south, it's not the end of the world, alright? We'll still have a chance to work it out through the system."

"Got it."

Shrunk like a seahorse, hands deep inside the pockets of his mud-stained jeans, Miles is shivering in the night air.

"Kid, you're freezing!" Moonie realizes that Miles is wearing nothing but a T-shirt.

"I'm fine," Miles mutters unconvincingly.

"Tough guy, aren't ya?"

"Not me," Miles scoffs.

"Trust me, I know plenty of adults who would have cracked into pieces in your place."

"Oh, well..."

Moonie fetches a black hoodie out of the trunk it and tosses it over Miles's shoulders.

"Here. Now it's a fashion statement," he chuckles.

*"Your car battery is fully charged, Max,"* CALO announces.

Moonie plucks the nozzle out, sticks it back into the charging dock, then turns to Miles.

"Ready?"

"Ready."

"Let's ninja this shit."

Ample moonlight is making it easy to drive with the lights off, at first. They speed up through the lake basin, but as they begin to climb the hills start closing down on them, the moonlight inexplicably wanes, and soon they find themselves driving blind in a pitch-black winding maze. They slow down to a crawl, straining their eyes as they try to follow the road. Tasked with copiloting, Miles calls out the curves in advance as he reads them off the map, often stepping out of the truck to check the road on foot before they continue. They mistime one of the steep turns and slide down an embankment, almost tumbling over, but luckily the front wheel bounces against an exposed boulder and Moonie manages to swing the truck back onto the road without sustaining any damage. The mishap forces them to slow down even more.

Minutes seem like hours with the weight of the surveillance drones pressing on their shoulders from above like a physical burden. The longer they wobble around, the less of a chance they'll be able to squeeze through unnoticed.

Eventually, the road curls down around a stubby bluff that dips into a shallow valley and the sky widens out in front of them, dark like the inside of a vault. The burning smell comes back with renewed intensity.

"Amen," Moonie mouths to himself, realizing that the dark smudges hanging above the ridges of the valley are the smoke clouds from the forest fire.

Shortly after leaving the valley, they come across a bent road sign riddled with bullet holes. The sign reads, "Welcome to the Free States of New America."

"This is it?" Miles asks, disappointed and a little perplexed by the banality of it.

"I guess so," Moonie replies.

Before they can consult the map, CALO announces the crossing of the division line, confirming that they are, in fact, in New America right now.

As they reel out of the hills onto a ghostly desert plain, the moon reappears behind them, smaller and duller than before. Ahead, in the distance, they see a mushroom of faint light hovering above Hawthorne. A sense of relief washes over Moonie, melting the pent-up tension in his muscles. Right around 14 miles to go.

After a little while, strange dunes crop up on both sides of the road. There are 10, maybe 12 heaps of sand laid out in a row, each about 10 feet tall and 20 feet apart, followed by a derelict concrete building, a 100-yard clearance, probably once a service road, then another row of dunes and an abandoned concrete building. They drive up to the fork and turn left when suddenly the road flares up with flashing emergency lights rushing at them from the direction of town. For a second, Moonie thinks about turning around and trying to find cover behind those dunes, then realizes it's pointless to run. They can't drive fast enough without lights, patrol cars will catch up with them before they get there, and if they turn the lights on, they'll be easily spotted.

They pull up on the shoulder and before they can fully absorb the approaching fury of lights and roaring engines, three firetrucks thunder by them in a cloud of gravel and desert dust, fading into the night like shiny windup toys running out of steam. They look at each other with wide grins, like divers who dodged a shark, then start the truck and continue down the road to Hawthorne.

# DAY_3

**"These Infernal Skies..." Anniversaries tend to** stir up the men in gray suits into overdrive production of sanctioned truths meant to explain the world to the unenlightened.

*"Our Poisonous Legacy... Lessons of Middle Eastern Nuclear Winter..."*

Reports, analyses, critical dissertations... conduits of the media sewer are running unclogged, replenishing the non-factual void that stands in for public discourse. What-ifs and if-onlys, but no one is asking why. No, that's the hard question.

*"How we squandered our geological endowment..."*

So, what happens now? It's been three full years since the first bombs started falling and the oil fields are still burning. What comes after the petroleum age?

*"Blazing Wasteland... Engulfed in Flames..."*

Like some inane word juggling is supposed to covnice someone with more than half a brain that there was ever going to be a different outcome to this conflict, other than complete and utter devastation of the Gulf region, its resources, infrastructure, and peoples. This is how the religious resource war ends, a snake eating its tail, a circular firing squad where everyone ends up dead.

*"Scorched Earth Apostles..."*

Insanity cannot be predicted by a risk-management algorithm. None of the wargame scenarios or contingency plans can account for the wholesale madness and collective self-destruction that takes over when the end times draw near, and the desperate urge of a mortally wounded animal to kill the other before it dies takes hold. And yet the world is somehow still surprised at the heartless intensity of the violence and destruction that befell it, wary to concede that we have moved past the old "bombing back to the Stone Age" and into a scary new territory where the threat of total annihilation is not just a negotiating instrument in the dark alchemy of geopolitics, but a dreadful new reality.

*"Eternal Fire... Hell on Earth..."*

"Kenji, I think I had enough of this for one day," Russ cuts off the newsfeed in a fatigue-flattened voice. "Go to sleep."

*"As you wish, Russ,"* CALO responds with its usual mechanical delight.

Russ slides the eyepiece off, rubs his eyes briskly as if he's brushing away a veil, then looks outside the window, past the black streaks of utility poles whizzing across his reflection in the clickety-clack rhythm of the wheels.

The hills fringing the valley are crouched low and steady, pulling the moonless sky closer to the ground, down to the surface of the mighty Hudson that's wallowing in its own mud, slow and unyielding, like primordial liquid darkness. For a split second, Russ is transported back among the billowing black clouds above the Arabian Desert, the moment before the impact. Three years later and thousands of miles across the world, it seems like none of it really happened—the noiseless flash of the explosion, the incinerating heat blast that followed, the violent parachute whiplash, gusts of hot air colliding in an invisible storm and tangling his suspension lines, then a long, weightless fall, the shockwave of pain as he hit the ground. His head filled with visions of Miriam, dancing in the pearly glow of sun-drenched sand and curling up around his shattered legs, holding his broken hands in her palms, whispering softly in his ear as he drifted in and out of consciousness, a sliver of luck away from being just another nameless casualty littering the dunes.

The train car was almost deserted when Russ got on, save for a young couple and a craggy-looking man in a canvas jacket and dirt-covered overalls nodding off in the front. The couple got off after two stops, then shortly after, the craggy man sleepwalked out into the night. The last train back to the city is usually not this empty, but service has been spotty and unreliable due to power outages and people didn't want to risk being trapped in a stalled train late at night. Russ didn't really have a choice.

When his brother Stevie told him he was throwing a sweet sixteen bash for his older daughter Rosie he noncommittally promised he'd try to make it, then forgot all about it—until Rosie called him last week and asked if he was coming. He couldn't say no. Considering that, for one reason or another, he missed almost every single one of her previous fifteen birthdays, making "the big one" should earn him some favorite uncle points. Plus, Russ hadn't seen his dad in ages. The last time he visited he seemed frail and brittle, not very interested in living much longer. Seven long years since Mom was gone, he never adjusted to the life of a widower. It's a miracle he made it this far without her. Stevie, Marie, and the kids being around helps, but nothing can undo the corrosive static of old age.

The party was fun. In a light, airy gown, with her hair pinned under a flower crown, Rosie seemed like she was floating, poised and gracious, like some pagan goddess of eternal youth. Rosy-cheeked boys in dark blazers and giggly girls in flowery dresses danced away their awkwardness while adults clenched their grips tightly around their plastic cups and beer bottles. This afternoon, after the party was packed away, they sat around the fire pit in the yard, eating leftovers, drinking home brew that Stevie whipped up from local hops, and poking at the burning logs every time they ran out of conversation.

The booze unlocked the old man's affinity for conspiracies. “Mark my words,” he declared, “they’ll start rationing power soon. Another means of controlling the people, right? They’re just priming us for it. A couple of service interruptions, maintenance cut off here and there, and before long you’re waiting in the dark, happy to get plugged in two times a week so you can charge your batteries!”

Old age breeds fear and fear breeds contempt. It might also be a generational thing. Mangled by the vortex of social, economic, and political upheaval that accompanied the break-up of the Union, many of his father’s generation have found themselves out of place after the old country dissolved. Everything they knew, everything they were taught to believe, has been swept away, their standards and ideals becoming mere maladjustments in a world without convictions and certainties. They struggled to accept that history is powered by forces stronger than any one person or group of people. It had to be someone’s fault, some secret cabal hellbent on destroying humanity.

“As long as Manhattan is glittering like an overpriced whore,” he went on. “And you almost died for this shit, Russ!”

“I work for the Commonwealth Dad, not Manhattan Corporate.”

“Or so you think. They bought the Commonwealth a long time ago, and all of us along with it!”

“The rich are not the problem.” Russ sighed and drained his beer.

“Greed, son. It’s the source of all evil.”

A high-pitched, three-tone action alert brings him back to the present moment.

“Weiss?” Russ responds flatly, muffling his surprise.

*“Well, hello to you too, sweet pea.”* Weiss gurgles out, attempting sarcasm.

“What’s up?”

*“Need you to come in.”*

“When?”

*"Now."*

"I'm on the Metro-North..."

*"Your train is about to run out of track. There's a car waiting for you in Yonkers. It's twenty past midnight now, you should be at the Directorate by two."*

"What is it?"

*"Can't tell you much until you get here."*

"Okay."

*"I thought you'd be more eager to get back in the fold,"* says Weiss after a slight pause.

"Sure I am."

*"Doesn't sound like it."*

"What do you want, a goddamn cookie?" Russ snaps half-jokingly.

*"Just so you know, Pratt asked for you, specifically."*

"Well, that's nice of him. He gets a cookie too."

Twenty minutes later, hunched down behind tree branches and the roofs of suburban Yonkers lurking in the distance, the train slows down, then stops with a hiss.

*"Yonkers,"* an announcement comes through the train's PA system. *"Due to unforeseen circumstances, this train will terminate at this station. This is the last stop on this train. Yonkers. Last stop. Everybody must exit the train. Metro-North train service from this station will resume at 5:15 am. There will be no inbound train service until 5:15 am. This service stoppage is in accordance with the rules and regulations of the New York City Transit Authority and mandated by The Atlantic Commonwealth Energy Conservation Council. Last stop, last stop. Everybody, please exit the train."*

The moment Russ steps out the doors shut behind him, the train lights go off, and the fuzzy red glow of the waiting room exit light spills across the semidarkness of the platform. He spots the silhouette of the car in the otherwise empty commuter parking lot and heads toward it.

"Kenji," he activates CALO. "Start the vehicle."

The car flashes green then rolls itself across the parking lot and stops in front of him.

*"Welcome aboard,"* the cottony voice of the Vehicle Advisory System greets him as he gets in. *"Traffic ahead looks light. Our ETA at Pier 6, Brooklyn, New York is 52 minutes. Enjoy the ride."*

Russ shuts his eyes with a small smile as the car speeds up alongside the train tracks that under the red light look like two razor cuts in the swollen belly of the night.

Maritza is at the cliff's edge, breathless, bent in half, soaked in sweat after trying to catch up with Miles on an exhausting run through a dark, damp forest. Below, in the abyss, battling water currents are smashing one another against the rocks, sending clouds of mist in the air. On a sliver of rock, arched high over the river gorge, she sees Miles waving vigorously in her direction. He cups his hands near his mouth and shouts something, but his voice is trumped by the frantic pounding of her heart. He waves again, calling her to come closer. As she moves toward Miles, the ground starts slipping backward like the slack belt of an unwieldy treadmill.

The earth shifts under her feet and with a loud crack the arch Miles is standing on detaches from the main rock and plunges into the river. Miles raises his hands above his head and screams wildly as if this is some thrilling child's play. He flips around midair and slashes through deep green water headfirst, like a pearl diver. Maritza freezes up. She wants to jump in after him, but she cannot move her legs anymore.

"Miles! Come out! Miles!" she yells out, but her words turn into a dry, muffled growl that quickly vanishes in the wind.

Moonie peels the corner of the room's lace curtains and looks outside. The sun has already jumped over the brim of low-lying ridges in the east. In the distance, a small tractor is making its way through a field, chugging along valiantly under the weight of its load. Careful not to wake Miles, he eases out of the room.

As he walks down the stairs, the smell of bacon and fresh-baked pastry tickles his senses and he heads straight to the kitchen, where he finds Loise working on breakfast.

In her mid-thirties, petite and pretty, Loise exudes the confidence and poise of someone comfortable in her own skin, swaying her farm-worked arms from one task to another—chopping, whipping, stirring, and racing to have everything done by the time her family gets back from the field.

"Good morning," says Moonie, his voice slighly cracking.

"Oh, you're up?" Loise turns around, her cheeks ruddy from the kitchen heat.

"Smells delicious," Moonie swipes a  of bacon from the counter.

"Marty and the kids will be in any minute now. I can set up a plate for you if you want."

"Nah, I'll wait for them, thanks," says Moonie, salty bacon grease melting in his mouth.

"Coffee?"

"Sure. Grid still out?"

"Yeah."

"You think they'll turn it on today? I wouldn't mind charging the truck battery before we leave."

"That's what they said," Loise scoffs. "What they say doesn't mean much though."

"How long has it been out?"

"Four days now. Third time this month," Loise hands him a cup of coffee.

The sugary smell of fermented beets tickles his nostrils as he walks out on the porch. In the sky above the ethanol plant at the edge of town, a flock of jays is putting on an air show, circling the red brick smokestacks in chaotic eights then diving down heedlessly into the heap of biomass waste, looking for worms and leftovers to feast on.

Moonie knew it wasn't fair bringing his troubles to the Wheatons, but he wouldn't have come if he didn't think it was safe to do so. He and Miles were exhausted and badly in need of shelter after yesterday's ordeal. After the firetruck scare at the border, the rest of the trip was completely uneventful. They drove straight through to Lovelock, stopping only once to stretch their legs.

Lovelock was always Moonie's first stop on his trips east. Not because it was compelling in any way, but because it was convenient. Only five hours from Concord, it's centrally positioned, so no matter where his job would take him, up north to the Dakotas or further out to Utah and Colorado, he'd have to take the I-80 through Lovelock. It's also the last inhabited place with some comfortable lodging before the long stretch of desert.

Before meeting the Wheatons, Moonie used to stay at the Kaiser Inn, a two-story trucker's delight with thin walls, worn-out bedsheets, and a greasy spoon facing the road. One day after breakfast, he was getting ready to hit the road when he heard a loud crash outside. From his booth window, he noticed a yellow and black hauler speeding off. As he walked out, he saw a boy lying in the middle of the parking lot, his bicycle mangled in a lump nearby. The boy's eyes were shut and he wasn't moving. Moonie sprang to his side and checked his pulse. His breathing seemed normal. The boy came back after a few minutes, dazed but able to talk. His wrist was broken, his knees skinned, and a stream of blood was running down his neck from a laceration on the side of his head. Moonie ended up taking the boy to the local clinic and staying with him until Marty showed up in a frantic cold sweat some two hours later. He was on his way to Reno to pick up Loise and their little twins, Liam and Pearl, but turned back when the clinic called him.

"I don't know how to thank you, we'll never forget this," Marty said as they parted ways.

"Please, anyone would have done the same thing," Moonie replied.

"I'm not so sure, people are uncaring these days. Next time you're in Lovelock you have to come over for dinner, you have to promise me."

"Really, it's not necessary," Moonie was trying to fend him off.

"I insist, please. It would mean a lot to us."

Moonie did stop by on his way back to Concord, two weeks later, and after dinner, the Wheatons talked him into spending the night. Eventually, it became a regular thing and he'd look forward to the Wheaton stopover every time he'd head out that way on a job. At first, they didn't want to accept any money, but Moonie found a way around that. He set up a wallet for each of the three kids and every time he'd come around he'd transfer the amount he would have spent at the Kaiser Inn equally between them. He liked spending time with them, the kids' sprite-like energy, Marty's commonsensical wisdom, and Loise's caring heart, their strength to endure the crushing monotony of a shit town in the middle of nowhere and turn the isolation to their advantage.

As Moonie took a long, welcome sip of coffee the clacking sound from the field grew louder. Before long, a little tracktor emerges from the cornfield, with three small figures bopping up and down on top of a pile of cabbage heads and freshly unearthed sugar beets. It zigzags around the haystacks scattered throughout the barnyard and comes to a stop with a loud shriek of the brakes. The kids jump off the trailer, run to the porch, and each hug Moonie before they go inside.

"Bounty of riches, Marty," says Moonie, stepping off the porch.

"Nah," Marty waves it off. "The soil is weak. It needs potash. Hard to come by the real thing last few years."

They stand quietly side by side for a moment, looking in the distance beyond the fields.

"Summers are getting drier too. It'll be enough for us, not much to sell though. It is what it is, there's only so much I can do about it," Marty put his hand across Moonie's shoulder. "Let's eat."

"Moonie, I didn't know you have a nephew," says Loise as they sit down at the table.

"Yeah, Miles's dad and I are second cousins. They lived out east, then Theo and my aunt moved to California thirty years ago or there about. He's a few years older, so we didn't really hang out that much when we were kids. We only became close when I moved to Concord. Now we even work together. Brilliant man. Funny too. Helped me so much."

This was, of course, just partially true, but Moonie, like any good liar, knew that half-truths are the best lies.

The Shanghai scheme Lark devised worked perfectly—until it didn't. As the trade war between Eastern Chinese Provinces and Japan heated up to the point where each side was constantly obstructing the traffic along established shipping routes, conducting "stop and search" missions at will and occasionally seizing the ships and cargo, sporadic armed confrontations broke out, and the waters of the East China Sea and the Sea of Japan became unsafe for travel.

After *Vostok* stopped its runs to the area, Moonie stayed on for another three months, waiting to see if the conflict would calm down, but it soon became clear that the dispute between the Chinese and the Japanese wasn't going to be resolved quickly and easily, if at all, without a real war. When Lark called the operation off for good, Moonie decided he had enough of seafaring for a while and went back home.

In a year and a half, they moved enough gold, silver, and platinum to fund a small army. Moonie never knew where the shipments were really going or who was involved. It didn't matter anyway—he got his cut deposited in his account every time Bedrock Construction Systems picked up the merchandise. He never thought he'd make that much money in his entire life, let alone in a year and a half. The question now was what to do with it, so he reached out to Lark, the only person he knew who could give him sound money advice.

"Be smart, buy something tangible," Lark told him. "Land, precious metals, rentals, a factory, a house, something you can fall back onto if things don't go your way. Not all money is play money."

He took Lark's advice and bought a house in Concord. One story, ranch-style with exposed beams and wide plank floors, a big yard surrounded by three acres of oak and pine forest, about a mile and half down the road from the Smiths. The house itself was in great shape; there was nothing to add or to take away, fix or modify. It was perfect for him as is. He didn't know anyone in town, nor was he too eager to make new friends. He didn't fit the mold; most of them were family folks. Instead, he got a couple of dogs. He spent his days whatevering—working out, reading, getting high and trading real time for game time on his Portall, playing NeverNight till his eyes bled, obsessively accumulating Persistent World credits, and improving his online character. On Fridays, he'd drive up to Vallejo and hang out with the boys or drive up to Stonyford to see his parents. Sometimes he'd go partying in the city by himself or take a date to wine country or hiking in Big Sur for the weekend. It wasn't the most amazing life—but it was his.

Your perception of success changes after you succeed. Moonie was suddenly too rich to work and too young not to. He started wondering what's next for him. One lucky break—is that the best you can hope for in life? He missed travelling and thought about going back on a ship, but quickly dismissed that idea. He still had plenty of money left after buying the house, he could start something new. A couple of business ideas he thought about proved to be lame once he dug deeper in. Restaurant? Bar? Fishing boat? Nothing seemed worth the effort.

Always two steps ahead, Lark got out of Shanghai well before Qīngchú, aka "the Purge," a direct action by special forces in Jiangsu Province during which they effectively took back control of the city from Shanghai's oligarchy. The Purge, despite its ominous name, which was given by the Province's spinmeisters, wasn't much of a contest—and it was never intended to be. It was a shadow play for the masses: a preordained conclusion to the year-long wealth and power transfer already happening behind closed doors. Shanghai's ruling classes have already agreed to surrender the city without a fight in exchange for a clemency period of twelve months, during which they were given the chance to repent and to accept the new political reality or leave. A special fund was set up for that purpose, called the Lustration Fund, a shakedown vehicle devised by the new Jiangsu president and his cronies. For a mere sixty percent of their current worth and seventy percent of the ownership stake of their business, one could buy a "Citizen in Good Standing" certificate, continue their life untouched, and conduct their business under the new regime. Not very many thought that was a good deal, so the scramble to get out of Shanghai ensued—and Lark was there to help.

After the new Jiangsu president took power in the popular uprising, the Pardes board correctly predicted that his next move would be to strip Shanghai of its Free Trade Zone status and annex it. The decision was made to take advantage of the coming political and financial turmoil in the region and set up an expatriation network for High-Value Individuals and lure them to Pardes through securities offerings that would be used to fund the expansion of the Corporate without diluting existing shares.

Anxious Shanghai upper crust raced to the safety of Pardes shares, especially after the terms of the clemency agreement were laid out. By the time the purge was enacted, most of Shanghai's HVIs—and their wealth—were safely stashed in Pardes.

As a reward for the hard work he'd done in Shanghai, Lark was granted permanent residency status in Pardes, despite not having a high enough Aurum Wealth Rating, and was later put in charge of worldwide mining operations for the Pardes Ventures–Value Creation Division of the Corporate. Lark had his work cut out for him. The mining business had been underperforming greatly ever since its inception, and it became a real drag on the overall performance of Pardes Ventures. There were some mismanagement issues, but it was mostly due to circumstances beyond anyone's control. Led by an assorted bunch of egalitarian cranks, agrarian reformers, sustainability zealots, localists, and economic socialists of all kinds, populist movements were gaining momentum, becoming a grave threat to corporate power around the world. Masses were hungry and angry, and their leaders needed convenient scapegoats. Owned and operated by the phantom entities of global commerce, with no real connections to the communities, mining operations offered no benefit to the populace beyond contemptibly small tax revenue, and bribes for the few in power. Ore processing plants were environmental monsters weighing heavily on the local populations, especially their water supply systems and air quality. They were ready-made villains, easy targets for underclass insurrection. Twelve of Pardes's operations were seized and repossessed, or simply shut down for no good reason. Pardes Ventures was forced to renegotiate most of its previous arrangements, enter into revenue sharing and production control agreements with local governments, and even abandon some operations under pressure when security and operating costs outweighed the return.

Pardes Ventures had eight operations in North American territory—five in New America, one in Texas, and two in California. After he took over, Lark visited each one of them to show face and personally deliver a new set of rules and business strategies aimed at improving security and raising productivity. Once back in Pardes, he was kept up to date through a tangled web of business analytics: reports, forecasts, summaries, and statistical maps. To keep an eye on what was really going on he needed someone on the ground, an outsider he could trust. So, he called Moonie.

Moonie jumped at the opportunity to get back in business with Lark. However minor his role was, he felt like he was part of something bigger than his small-town existence again, and that unlike his daily routine of wake and bake time-wasting, it could lead somewhere. Although a far cry from globe-trotting capers, his monthly trips revived a sense of adventure in him and he was happy to be traveling again.

At first, Moonie didn't do much more than simple errands. He'd get a clear set of instructions from Lark for what needed to be done—the where, when, and how—and he'd simply follow instructions. He didn't know anything about the mining business, or any kind of business other than shipping for that matter, but he was eager to learn. But learning wasn't easy, as everyone played their cards close to their vests. Lark kept him on a strictly need to know basis and operation managers were wary of his presence. The little bits and pieces of information he picked up along the way, just weren't enough to put the big picture together.

That dynamic changed when Lark sent him to check on the progress of prospecting work being done in Central Saskatchewan. Originally, he was supposed to get on a supply Cessna out of Billings, but once he got there, he was told to pick up replacement parts for the drilling rig that were too heavy for the plane and drive them up in his truck, which added another twenty hours to his seventeen-hour drive from Concord.

The crew got to the site at the end of March, hoping for an early thaw, but the snow and cold weather persisted all throughout April, making it impossible to drill. For a month they were confined to doing the prep work, setting up the camp, assembling the drilling rig, establishing sample collection sites, and mapping out information. When the ground finally got soft enough, the rig broke after only two days, causing further delays. That's when Lark decided to send Moonie up to see what was going on.

The crew loved him from day one. Maybe it was only because after a month of semi-idle exile in muck and sleet they had exhausted each other's capacity for small talk or maybe because he salvaged the project schedule by bringing the replacement parts they needed to get the rig going, eventually sparing them late completion fees. Perhaps it was simply because people up north were generally nicer. No matter the reason, they enjoyed having him around, answering his questions, and teaching him about all things prospecting. And Moonie had a lot of questions. How does LIDAR work? What's geomatics? Which algorithm is best for filtering data out of digital terrain models? How do you decide where to drill for core samples? What does it take to turn probable reserves into proven reserves?

Moonie found something awe-inspiring, almost magical, in the ability to see the riches in the mud and stone, to visualize what lies under the earth's surface just by reading rainbow-colored squiggles of spatial analytics and cryptic data of chemical rock analysis. Although he was scheduled to stay only for a week, he ended up spending two months working hard with the crew—clearing out the woods, working the rig, mapping out and staking claims, collecting samples, studying the data, peeking over everyone's shoulder, and soaking up the knowledge and experience.

When he got back home, Moonie was determined to learn all he could about prospecting and early-phase exploration methods so he could set up his own operation. He asked Lark for deposit leads that he could explore and develop on his own for Pardes Ventures. After his initial reluctance and Moonie's persistent pestering, Lark gave him a titanium prospect near Salt Lake City and set him up with a local service company that did the series of LIDAR, hyperspectral magnetic imaging, and chemical mapping runs of the site. But when they reported their findings, Moonie realized he was in way over his head. He was completely overwhelmed by the amount of data he had received. It became obvious he was going to need help to make sense of it all. He didn't want to involve Lark again, so he started looking around for computer forecasting and modeling subcontractors who could derive a good geological model of the property from all the raw data. Theo Smith's name popped up numerous times, and when Moonie learned that he lived in Concord, just down the road, he decided to contact him. The prospect turned out to be a bust, but what mattered most to Moonie was just how much he had learned from this experience and from working with Theo, and that he was able to see the job through, proving to Lark and to himself that he could do whatever he set out to do.

Theo and Moonie worked together on three more projects in the same patch of land around Salt Lake City, including the one that was picked up by Pardes Ventures. Going from accidental neighbors to collaborators, they developed an improbable friendship, the kind of bond that sometimes crops up between diametrically different people despite, or perhaps because of, their differences. Moonie would occasionally drop in just for a quick chat in the Smiths's driveway, or late afternoon cocktails on the porch, sometimes staying for dinner. They came to rely on one another for neighborly help.

Like every teenager, Miles tactically avoided spending more time with adults than he absolutely had to, but he'd often stick around to listen to Moonie's stories about the impromptu roughneck boxing matches designed to reduce boredom and lift up spirits at the mining camps, flying over the Grand Canyon in a two-seater hydroplane, or having to jump off a thirty-foot cliff to escape a charging moose, the same stories Moonie was now telling the Wheatons at the breakfast table.

"Good morning," Loise chirps up when she sees Miles standing on the top of the stairs. "Just in time. Come down, pull up a chair."

"Thank you, this looks great," says Miles as he joins the others at the table.

"Did you sleep well?" Loise asks.

"Yes. Thank you, Mrs. Wheaton."

Oddly, he did sleep well. After turning and tossing for a while, overwhelmed by racing thoughts, his body and mind finally gave in to exhaustion and he fell asleep. But the minute he opened his eyes again, desolation crept up back in.

"Moonie was just telling us about your dad," says Marty.

"I hope only the good things," Miles somehow produces a smile, remembering that for the Wheatons he's supposed to be Moonie's nephew. "I have to tell you, Moonie is my favorite uncle. He's also the only uncle I've ever had."

Everyone chuckles at his joke and Miles feels the tightness in his chest abating for a moment. When his eyes involuntarily well up with longing for his parents, he quickly looks down at his plate, wipes his eyes casually with a napkin before anyone could notice, and then takes a bite of scrambled eggs.

"Miles, do you have any siblings?" Loise asks, slicing a corn muffin in half and then handing the pieces to the twins.

"No, just me. My mom always says they couldn't do any better than me, so why even try. One and done."

"What about you Moonie?" Marty asks.

"What about me?"

"Ever think about settling down?"

"Oh, Marty I'm too young for such things."

"Right. I'm telling you, there's nothing like the love of a sweet woman. The sooner you do it, the better. Men turn into wild animals if they live alone for too long."

"Nothing wrong with being a little wild Marty," says Moonie with a grin.

"You've been warned," Marty retorts.

After a long night of operational orientation with the Ops Development team, fueled by taurine Plenergy cans and frequent amphetamine micro-dosing, Russ felt spent but none the wiser. Why would they put him on this? Standing on the shallow stairs of the Directorate's entrance he squints into the morning sun as if recalibrating his senses to the light and air on this side of the heavy glass door. Any security-rank grunt would suffice. Why him? He couldn't shake the feeling that there's a backstory he wasn't being told and that Pratt's minions were spoon-feeding him information. Everytime he'd ask a sensible question, they'd silently stare at their displays like cows at the barn door.

Lined up on the magnetic levitation path running along the sidewalk hedge, a row of personal hoverpad shuttles greet him with the angst of idle soldiers. He decides to walk instead. A brisk ten-minute walk to the ferry terminal will help him clear up his mind.

Russ never thought he'd make it back to Operations after the crash, even for a minor assignment like this. After months of a confining routine of physical therapy and rehabilitation, countless doctor's appointments, and comprehensive mental health assessments he was deemed fit for duty, given a shiny new title—Senior Solutions Specialist—and promptly shoved into the Department of Analytics, where his "experience and talent will best be utilized, and where he will be able to contribute most to the common cause." Translation: DOA.

The name says it all. The department is a burial ground for irrelevant ghosts.

Russ hated it as much as he thought he would, for all of its overbearing bureaucracy and arrogant mediocrity. He missed the constant human interaction and risk of fieldwork. Weak-chinned wonders of Predictive Analysis, with their inflated sense of selves and no actual life experience, walking around thinking that they're oracle priests, don't make for very interesting company.

Most of his time at work was spent alone in a windowless room reading the proverbial tea leaves, looking for answers and clues in the mountains of data, analyzing the known and conceptualizing the unknown security predicaments, then passing his assumptions off to the programmers, who'd shovel related data into simulation models that came up with statistical probabilities based on his hunches and the best courses of action for the most likely scenarios.

In a cloud of diesel fumes, the ferry huffs its way forward through the sulfuric harbor stench, spewing out a crowd of uniformed Armed Forces square jaws and plainclothes Intelligence Services stiffs coming in early for the second shift. Russ climbs up the ramp to his usual spot on the top deck bow. In the distance, the skyscrapers of lower Manhattan are burning hot in the sun like unholy mercury-gray obelisks, casting back light across the river onto the gentle slopes of Brooklyn Heights and Cobble Hill. Home seems just a wingbeat away from here.

Theo spent the night stuck in a dark loop of guilt and dread, struggling to clear his mind past the powerless rage that was burning inside him. Dump trucks were making rounds all night and the little bit of sleep he managed to get was hindered by the steady clack of conveyer belts dumping chunks of earth into the dirt crushers and the deep, boisterous rumble of the extraction plant.

At last, he gave up trying to fall asleep, and through the corner slit window watched the indigo dawn slowly rise over steaming smokestacks. He tried to find one clue that would help him understand what exactly happened and why. Who was that woman who showed up at their door? How did that voice in the cinderblock room know who he was? What do they want from him? What could he possibly have to offer that would make someone go through all this in order to get it?

The biting odor of burning tar coming from outside reminded Theo of the moment of clarity he had in the flyquad. He remembers seeing Maritza tied up across from him, but not Miles. They were taken away around 9:30 in the morning. It was sometime in the late afternoon when they flew over the mine complex, so a six- or seven-hour flight at an average speed of around two hundred miles an hour, that's over one thousand miles. He lays his palm on the window pane. It's freezing cold. Big oil sands operations are all up in the northwest. They're probably somewhere in Alberta, maybe

Saskatchewan. It doesn't matter, it could be five minutes from home; he's still a hostage. He doesn't have any control over what happens next. Or maybe he does? He was brought here for a reason. There's a lab. The man said they're going to build something together. Crushed under the weight of exhaustion and frustration, Theo slumps into the corner and buries his face in his hands. At the moment, only one thing is certain to him—he has to find a way to see Miles and Maritza.

*"Be ready in thirty minutes,"* the two-way lights up with a message, breaking Theo's train of thought.

Drey abruptly enters Theo's room and leads him out into the hallway. They take the stairs down to the ground level and stop in front of an unmarked armored door. Drey pushes the base of his palm into the scanner. It reads the ID chip inside his palm and the door clicks open. Another set of stairs takes them down to a long corridor with purple tile floors. At the end of the corridor, there are two identical armored doors. Drey scans his palm and the door on the right opens.

They enter a large bright space with no windows.

"Chemical analysis lab," Drey informs him.

A maze of glass tubes runs throughout the lab, connecting a network of beakers, test tubes, funnels, condensers, and crucibles to data terminals. On a long glass shelf stretching along the wall, lay hundreds of triangular flasks, each containing a petroleum specimen of varying shades of black. Lab technicians look up as Theo and Drey walk by, then quickly bury their heads back into their work.

They come to another door. Drey scans his palm again and they enter complete darkness.

"This is where you'll work," says Drey, and flips a switch.

A cluster of holographic displays pops up above them, wrapping the room in a three hundred sixty-degree light-blue halo. Black upholstery covers the entire room. There's a single swivel chair in the middle of the room, surrounded by a huge circular multileveled console holding an abundance of control panels and data processing units.

"Please," Drey shows him to the chair.

Theo walks across the room, looking around and up at the holographic displays, checking out the equipment in the console, then sits down passively in the swivel chair.

*"Mr. Smith,"* a voice bellows from above. *"Go ahead, turn it on."*

Theo picks up the master control tablet and turns the system on. The soft, steady hum of cooling fans fills the room as the CPU clusters come online.

*"That'll be all, for now, Drey,"* the voice says.

Drey takes a step back, salutes with a brisk bow, and walks out.

*"I had this room built two years ago. It cost me an arm and a leg. 4-D seismic survey applications are data gluttons, as you can imagine. Are you familiar with 4-D seismic?"*

Theo bows his head in silence, staring at nothing in front of him.

*"Mr. Smith, I asked you a question..."*

"I want to see my wife and my son," says Theo, trying to muster some steel behind his words. "I need to make sure that they're safe and sound."

*"I thought I made it clear yesterday, Mr. Smith. Don't make me repeat myself. You're wasting everyone's time thinking that you can make demands. Any kind of concession you get, you'll have to earn first. Showing some good will would be a good start. Tell me you understand that?"*

Theo sinks back in his chair with a bitter sigh, feeling the glimmer of resolve he had fade away.

"I've done a bit of 4-D geological modeling," he replies passively. "Rock magnetism, surface expression in plate tectonics, earthquake data analysis mostly. Use of the fourth dimension is very much relative to a specific goal."

*"True. So, you're probably asking yourself why would*

*a simple dig-and-cook operation need such a sophisticated sytem capable of tracking seismic changes in real-time."*

"Water supply management?" Theo shrugs. "Groundwater aquifer observation?"

*"That's a pretty good guess. But the water supply isn't our concern. We have plenty of water to support the exploration of the entire deposit. Hell, there might even be some left over after the mine gets decommissioned. Between you and me, that day isn't that far away. Our bitumen yields have been dropping steadily over the last seven years and the feasibility forecast is pretty gloomy. We're pretty much scraping the bottom at this point. Soon, we'll start putting in more energy than we can extract, and when that happens that will be the end of it. To be honest with you, the only reason we're still in business is the oil price hike due to the Middle East war supply shock. Are you familiar with White's law, Mr. Smith?"*

"Leslie White?"

*"Yes."*

"Economic development is a function of energy per capita."

*"Exactly. The primary function of culture and the one that determines its level of advancement is its ability to harness and control energy. As energy production declines, so does prosperity. Access to cheap energy is everything, Mr. Smith. It's the only reason humanity got this far. Everything, everything we have, we owe to oil. It's the heart and blood of our existence, a difference between light and darkness, prosperity and hunger, life and death. But easy oil is gone, and we're now fighting over scraps. Every new barrel we produce will be more expensive and harder to come by than the one before it. What's worse, people are fooling themselves believing that the destruction of oil reserves left in the wake of the war is the real reason behind the current energy crisis. But it's only a symptom of something much deeper and more serious. The truth is, the world has reached its economic, ecological, and technolog-*

*ical limits of resource extraction. This war is just the maniacal culmination of our inability to face that obvious fact, a blow-off end to an unsustainable paradigm.*

*It's too late for proactive change, we've failed to evolve through the crisis. The Great Reset is already here, this is only the first chapter, and if anyone thinks that the economic and social ramifications of the coming energy catastrophe could be contained, they are gravely mistaken. There's no such thing as orderly decline. There will be hell on Earth, all-out war, mass starvation and disease, a swift collapse of civilization. Most of the cultural and technological progress we have achieved in the last two hundred plus years will be undone by the devastation it will leave in its aftermath. Nothing will ever replace the oil. This is the end of social evolution, the new dark age is coming. Nothing will prevent this. Nothing."*

The salvo of words stops suddenly and the last bits of hope that Theo was holding onto, hope that this was some terrible misunderstanding that would somehow get quickly resolved and he and his family would be allowed to get back to living their lives, vanished in the ringing silence that followed.

*"Unless, Mr. Smith, we do something drastic about it for the benefit of the next generation, like your son Miles—the ones destined to be doomed by our mistakes and by our propensity for inaction. It's up to you and me. I wish we could have done it differently, but unfortunately, this is the only way. I don't think you would have voluntarily agreed to work with me, given the nature of this project and your personal history."*

"My personal history?"

*"Your father's aspirations in alternative energy technologies and your own inclinations to publicly demonize Big Carbon, propagate disinvestment from fossil fuel producers, and blame 'the oil addiction' for all that's wrong with the world today. It's time to admit that all so-called clean energy revolutions have failed to provide a valid substitute to hydrocarbons*

*vand now, more than ever, we need to circle our wagons and put our collective minds to work on improving the production methods of one energy source that's actually proven to work, rather than spending precious time and resources building some technological Tower of Babel that offers little more than promises."*

"It was you, wasn't it?" Theo suddenly realizes. "It was you sending me all those job offers for 4-D work over the past month."

*"I tried to do the right thing, Mr. Smith. I approached you as a professional, but you seem to be stuck in a habitual loop of one-sided thinking, which is, if you don't mind me saying, incredibly irresponsible and self-absorbed. I don't enjoy this, but you left me no choice. Civilization is at stake. We need solutions now.*

*I'm giving you a chance to be part of the solution, Mr. Smith. I want you to promise you'll work with me to the best of your abilities, without reservations and distrust."*

"I don't understand what's required of me, but I will do anything to ensure the well-being of my family," says Theo.

*"I wish you were a little more enthusiastic, but it's understandable under the circumstances."*

Holographic displays above Theo's head come to life, displaying multiple data farm portals, InfiniBand transmission metrics, node function reports, and task windows of different Simulacrum applications.

*"Take today to familiarize yourself with our data infrastructure, browse the parameters and value spaces. Don't worry if you don't get through analysis summaries, there's a lot to take in. I understand. You're still in shock over everything. I'll lead you through the most relevant data landscapes tomorrow. I think you'll be pleasantly surprised by what you see."*

The clamor of skateboarders in the alley welcomes Russ back home as he gets out of the taxi. The growl of the wheels, like sandpaper scraping in slow motion, cuts off briefly when they fly up in the air, then comes back with the whack of landing, followed by excited squawks from the pack. Inside the building, a bass beat coming from the second floor is pumping through the walls like an underwater heartbeat, swaying the bare hallway lightbulbs and making the corner shadows expand and contract.

Russ kicks his shoes off and goes to the kitchen, pours a glass of water and drinks it, and then remembers Kenji's nagging FlowerPower reminder. He pours another glass of water, grabs a small bottle of plant food from the cupboard, squeezes a full dropper of blood-red liquid into the glass, then walks over to the living room and pours the pinkish solution into the water reservoir of a flowerpot holding a juniper bonsai tree. The pot's sensors spark up and the base lights up.

*"Thank you, Russ,"* the pot sounds off.

He stretches out on the couch, puts on an eyepiece, and dives into Smith's file, which Weiss put together for him.

Russ can see that Theo Smith had his share of misfortune, even before what happened yesterday. Smith grew up in Brooklyn Heights, just a twenty-minute walk from Russ's place, the only child of Amelia Smith, a sociology professor, and Augustus Smith, a technologist and inventor. When he was twelve years old, his father burned to death in his lab in the backyard of their family home. It was ruled an accident, but the final report from the Brooklyn DA's office looked like a haphazard document that obscured more than it showed. It was like someone willingly just shoved the whole thing aside to avoid the bother, or perhaps some other nefarious forces were at play. After Augustus's death, Amelia and Theo moved to her sister's house in New Paltz. They stayed there for about a year before they made their home in Concord, California.

Russ shuffles through files documenting Theo's professional life. After graduating at the top of his class at Stanford with a degree in computer science, he bounced around Silicon Valley for a few years before setting up his own shop. About nine months ago, he started working with the Commonwealth's Department of Energy on the Sundance project. Russ had never heard of Sundance before Weiss explained it to him this morning at the Directorate. Pretty wild stuff, if they can actually pull it off.

Absorbed in the documents, he doesn't notice Miriam coming in. She calls his name a couple of times, then walks over and puts her hand on his shoulder. Russ springs up at her touch, ripping the eyepiece off.

"Hey, I didn't hear you come in," he closes the small distance between them and gives her a light kiss on the mouth.

"What's so interesting that's got you all zombified?" Miriam asks, changing her shoes to a puffy pair of slippers.

"Just work."

"Ha. I'm gonna make some coffee. You want some?"

"Sure." Russ gets off the couch and follows Miriam to the kitchen. "How was your day?"

"The usual hassle. Karen's been driving me crazy with her shit. We have this huge benefit for the Maldives in three days, nothing is done, and she's bickering with everyone in sight over small things. If she'd just get out of the way and let the working people do the work."

Comforted by her voice, Russ lets her vent about Karen's uptight nature, the caterers' lack of good options, and the challenges of making a proper seating arrangement for a big event, throwing in a question or two when she winds down just so he could hear her talk.

Outside in the distance, a chopper appears in the sky. It swoops over the flimsy roofs of the Red Hook communes, then flutters across the faint silhouette of the Statue of Liberty and dissolves in the western sun over the swamps of New Jersey.

A tingling silence settled between Moonie and Miles as soon as they got out of Lovelock and hit the open road. Both lost in their thoughts, they absently watched the black ribbon of road twist capriciously ahead of them, finding the way of least resistance through stubby desert hills speckled with rocks and scraggy shrubs. The angst of obligation weighed heavily on Moonie. He wondered if he had made the right call back at E.C.'s. Maybe his instincts fooled him this time. Maybe they should have gone to the police, let them deal with it. Maybe Miles would have been safer with the police than hightailing it like this, under threat of being tracked down and caught. He would have been absolved of responsibility, free to go about his business. No use thinking about it now.

He gives Miles a quick sideways glance as if to reassure himself that he's still there. To have this shitty world come crashing down on you at fifteen. Why would anyone do this to them? The kid seems to be holding up well considering, but underneath he must still be raw. Moonie noticed that he almost broke into tears at breakfast. How do you talk to a fifteen-year-old? Last time he spent more than two minutes alone with a fifteen-year-old he was probably fifteen himself.

"Do you play games?" Moonie asks just to break the silence.

"Yeah," Miles looks at him, mildly surprised.

"Ever played NeverNight?"

"Sure. Why? Do you play?"

"I used to. A lot. For days on end. Not anymore."

"Why not?"

"I got busy in real life."

"Well, that's good, I guess."

"12,311."

"That's your NeverNight score?"

"Yup."

"That's insane! I barely cracked 8,000."

"I know. I can be a little obsessive, I suppose."

"What's your APM rating?" Miles asks.

"What's APM?"

"Actions per minute. How many game decisions you can execute in a minute."

"Oh yeah. I think it was about 200. You?"

"447."

"Wow! You would have easily gone to 20,000 if you played as much as I did."

"Maybe. But I don't really like master scenario games. Too linear. They can be fun for a while, but once you figure out the game design it gets boring. You end up doing the same thing over and over again. I prefer free-roaming strategy games."

"What are those?"

"Open world games. Players can modify the games and create their own ways to play. There are still game environment restrictions obviously, mostly technical limitations, but they all run on adaptable algorithms that constantly rewrite the games as players change the structures. So, the games are constantly changing. Remodeling is all the fun, you just have to balance the freedom of an open world with the structure of a storyline. And you really have to pay attention to the flow of the game, shifting objectives, changing rules, that type of stuff. It's more like real life."

"Way over my head. So, what's your favorite then?"

"EternalQuest."

"Never heard of it. What's it like?"

"Basically, you're dropped off on a randomly selected part of the Earth in 8000 B.C. with two units, a settler, and a warrior, and some basic tools and knowledge of the world humans would have had back then, and from there you try to build the best possible civilization you can. You're competing against thousands of others trying to do the same thing. And as you progress, you change your environment, discover new land, build villages, cities, farms, markets, and new units like warriors, workers, shamans, settlers, and explorers. You develop skills, acquire new knowledge, establish social structures.

There's a certain linearity, a discovery tree—you can't discover the alphabet or code of laws or math before you discover writing first, and you can't discover writing unless you discover farming and pottery. So, discoveries allow you to develop new discoveries, new technologies, and practical skills that help you manage your civilization. Like, in order to discover construction, you have to have the knowledge of masonry and math, then you can build walls and castles to protect your cities from foreign armies, or bridges that help you move your armed units and commerce faster.

You create value through trade and conquest, or you can build colosseums and temples that raise the overall happiness of your citizens, which raises your civilization standing. The game's designed more or less in the way that it ties the timing of the discoveries approximately to the time period of their origins in the actual history of civilization, especially in the beginning. But if you have a strong civilization you can gradually jack up the timeline and speed up the process. For example, I discovered the steam engine in the 1300s, more than four hundred years before it was really discovered. That gave me an enormous technological advantage of inventing railroads, industrialism, and mass production early on when most players were still stuck in the Middle Ages.

You also have to be careful about not overextending yourself and you have to learn a lot of stuff, you can't just advance through game actions alone. You have to pass a whole bunch of tests to prove that you have a real knowledge of your discoveries. Like, in order to acquire a combustion engine, you have to design a real, workable model of a combustion engine. Or physics, physics is a big one. To unlock it, you have to prove the immutability of major physical laws and how they apply in certain practical situations. Not easy, but once you got the physics, you open up a whole new set of branches on the discovery tree, you get tons of new technologies."

"Sounds great," says Moonie. "Like you get to reivent the world as we know it."

"That's a good way of putting it."

"Seems like a lot of work."

"Yes and no. The hardest part is to survive the early part of the game. There are lots of roaming barbarians, lots of warring, people start making irrational decisions, so you can easily get caught up in all that if you're not cautious. I tend to start conservatively. I build up my defenses and the economy and I throw most of my resources into discoveries and land exploration. When I start earning discoveries and inventions slightly before their historical timeline and have three or four cities built, I start expanding. Then it gets a little easier. I just keep compounding on my advantages until my progress becomes almost exponential. Essentially, you want to reach the point of asymmetrical development compared to your opponents. Then it becomes easy to mop up inferior civilizations."

"Asymmetrical war is the best kind of war."

"Or worst. Depending on which side you're on."

"True."

"I try to avoid warring whenever I can," Miles continues. "It's a huge waste of resources. You can also absorb other civilizations through economic and cultural assimilation. Essentially, you offer them a choice between annihilation and a better life."

"Makes it an easy choice," Moonie smirks. "War by other means. They still lose."

"They do, but they don't get destroyed in the process. They get to keep their legacies and game accomplishments. Plus, you get to make friends on Frontier. Most of those players later cheer for you."

"What's Frontier?"

"QuestFrontier. The game's social platform."

"Well, I hope your civilization ends up being better than the one we have now."

"I think it is."

"How good is it?"

"Um, it's pretty good," says Miles, slightly confused by Moonie's insistence. "I made it to the final eight worldwide. I just played this year's quarterfinals two days ago."

"How'd you do?"

"I don't know. It usually takes a day or two for the official results to come out."

"Why don't you check?"

"You think we should?"

"Yeah, why not?"

"It's a closed network, I would have to log in as myself."

"Ugh. Any way we get David Hart to join in?"

"They're tough on ID tampering."

"Your new ID is as good as the real one."

"We need eight recommendations from existing members."

"How do we get those recommendations? From people you know?"

"You said they're monitoring all my friends. I don't want to put people in danger."

"Not your real-life friends. Someone you just know from the game. The further away they are, the better."

"I guess that's possible. What do I tell them?"

"Boy, you gotta work on your lying skills. Tell 'em anything. Not the truth obviously."

"Okay, okay."

Jiang didn't always enjoy these sessions of cognitive invigoration, but they are mandatory. All employees are required to take them after twenty-four unbroken hours of work, to combat mental fatigue and boost waning productivity. More often than not, Jiang felt that they had completely the opposite effect on him. No matter how hard he tried, he couldn't make his mind cool off and rid itself of built-up static and he'd start getting irritated by this unnecessary work interruption, the whole presumptuous way it was designed to appeal to some yoga auntie's sense of serenity. But today it's working. He can almost smell the briny freshness of the clear ocean water, almost feel the wild gusts of polar wind kissing his cheeks, almost taste its purifying sweetness.

Antarctic Escape was always his favorite WindDown simuli. He has seen it at least a hundred times by now. It's the predictability that soothed his nerves. Sustained strings of drone music carrying the tense notes through the soundscape of trembling breeze and the shuffle of distant waves, as the free-flying camera reveals the familiar landscape, always in the same sequence: tall grass meadows waiving at the bottom of snow-adorned cliffs, the amorphous flow of a penguin colony at the far end of the rocky shore, a visual symphony of cubist iceberg sculptures doubled in the mirror of still lagoon water. Even the stinging scent of eucalyptus oil, drifting over the recoup stations and absurdly ill-suited to the Antarctica theme, is an essential part of the experience.

The call of a soaring albatross cues in the sun, which burns through the overcast sky and splashes everything with glittering snow dust that the wind swirls around like a light-headed damsel, precious and evanescent. Right on time, a one-minute alert pops up in the bottom left corner of his field of vision and his mind starts preparing to leave this beautiful, safe place, coiling slowly into a ball like a snake ready to strike.

*"Your WindDown session has now concluded,"* the soft female voice of the simuli announces. *"Have a productive day!"*

Jiang takes off the immersion kit, wipes his face and neck with a hot, moistened hand towel, and walks out into an empty lounge flooded in fake spiritual Muzak that droops over empty chairs and a miniature plastic oak tree water fountain at the center of a snack bar. Jiang grabs a sweaty can of mint-flavored water from a silver bowl filled with ice then returns to his office.

It took a little effort, but Jiang managed to trace down the owner of the Allcom used to access the Smiths's security system from Byron earlier—to their next-door neighbor, Lupo Belan, a thirty-three-year-old ex-employee of Devlaar Transpacific. The truck picked up by surveillance matches up with Belan as well, but it seems to have been ripped off the grid, so he had no entry there. After they lost them on the highway, he established a retroactive visual trace of the truck by rolling back the loc-sat feed, but the delay was too big and they lost them again when they vanished in the thick forests of Yosemite. They might still be hiding in Yosemite or maybe they're headed for the border from there. Jiang issued an immediate request for enhanced monitoring of Southern and Western California border activity, but so far there have been no actionable hits.

Belan used a premium NoMark service that automatically deletes communication records off their servers and stores them on the local memory of a device, where it can only be accessed with a biometric signature of the owner. NoMark retains only the time stamp and origin-destination geoloc info of the traffic, and only for three months before they are permanently destroyed. The audit of the last three months of Belan's communication activity showed that his primary area of operation was mostly in and around the Bay area, but also included Utah, Colorado, and South Dakota. Lots of recent voice calls to Utah.

Step by step, using the geoloc data, Jiang's team was able to identify some of the names with a decent degree of certainty. A cabinet maker, dry cleaning, housekeeping services, restaurants, all in Concord. Someone named Kyle Mirth, aka Fumble, in Vallejo, a Sante Viola, also in Vallejo, then a mining supply business in Orem, a general contractor in Lehi, Randy Ortiz at West Valley Water Main and Sewer, Demonico Entertainment, Utah Mining Association, Santaquin Pavement, all within a fifty-mile radius of Salt Lake City.

The real delicious discovery was Eliza Shannon from West Jordan, near Salt Lake City. Jiang pulls up the NetMirror profile of Eliza Shannon, aka Liz Faith, aka Thin Lizzy, aka Shannon Faith. Local West Jordan girl. She's 22, 5'10," 123 pounds. Strawberry blond. Jiang glances through the clutter of her net history: migraine treatments, ankle surgery, pet turtle, a hiking trip to Grand Canyon, biochemical body clock readjustment sessions, disputed charges at TabooTattoo, Demonico Dolls pageant runner-up, Convivial Companions exclusive provider.

"Hsia," he dials the first assistant. "Get me the list of all available Tailored Operations agents in the Salt Lake City area."

Other than a bunch of family trips to Oregon to visit his grandparents when they were still alive, Miles has never been outside of California. Last June, they were all supposed to go up to Vancouver for "Bridging Connections Between Mathematics and Science," a real-life regional math convention for students under seventeen. Miles worked on his proposal for months and when he was selected to be one of the presenters, he was beside himself with joy. They were going to take a train to Seattle, then a ferry over to Vancouver via Victoria. On the way back, the plan was to visit Lyndon and Berice, his parents' college friends who lived on one of the small islands in the San Juan archipelago, just below Vancouver Island, where they would spend a week Orca whale watching and hunting for oysters and Dungeness crabs.

Miles was excited about the trip, especially about the opportunity to finally meet in person all the kids he had known for years from the online math forum. But as the protests, which were smoldering for months on the streets of Vancouver, escalated into violent riots with the casualty count climbing almost daily, convention participants started pulling out and the organizers, unable to guarantee safety, canceled the real-life event and moved it back online.

Strangely enough, Theo and Maritza took the news of the cancellation harder than Miles did, with the all-encompassing "The world is going to hell in a handbasket" platitude. Miles had heard that one too many times growing up. Perhaps his parents were just longing for the days when things seemed to make more sense, when they were younger and able to keep up with the breakneck pace of the times.

Maybe the world has always been just as broken as it is today, but the people have grown to think that they deserve better. Broken or not, it's the only world Miles's generation has ever known, and they still had to go out there and find their place in it. Kids might not always be tough, but they are often very resilient. They fall down, they get up, they wipe the blood and tears off their cheeks, and they carry on. It's the parents who have to live through the precious agony made of love and fear, armed only with the wavering faith that the world they are leaving to their kids isn't going to eat them alive one day, when they can no longer shield them from the harshness of life. Will Miles ever see them again?

The sun that now hangs over Miles and Moonie is falling fast. They had lost too much time twirling around the mountains outside Lovelock and now their prudent plan to keep off major roads and enter the Salt Lake City metro area from the south side, through the desert, seems more dangerous than risking an encounter with a patrol car or surveillance vehicle on the highway. Beyond that, a desert road is no place to be, come nightfall. Armed gangs, corrupt cops, and rapacious locals all come out at night, looking for easy prey.

After a brief stop in Ely, they decide to change course and take Route 93 north, then cut through the Bonneville Salt Flats. Not too long after they turn north, sagebrush starts giving way to irregular patches of needle grass and the crimson soil of the high desert begins to turn pink, then gray. A few miles before the highway junction, Moonie swerves off onto a gravel road branching out to the west.

"Let's have some fun," he says with glee.

The gravel purr under their wheels shifts to a crackle as the road spills out into a vast barren plane of petrified mud laced by lesions of calcified salt.

"What's the fastest you ever went in a car?" Moonie asks.

"I don't know. Ninety, maybe a hundred," says Miles.

"Let's see what this puppy is made of," says Moonie as he guns the engine.

The truck thrusts up like a hungry bear chasing a meal, and soon there's nothing around them but a blinding white sea of salt, as far as the eye can see.

"Here comes a hundred!" Moonie yells over the roaring engine. "One hundred ten!"

The flawless surface of the ancient lakebed offers no resistance. Miles grabs his seat with both hands and his eyes grow large as the surge of adrenaline shoots from his stomach through his chest, all throughout his body.

"Slow down!" he wants to shout, but no words come out of his mouth.

"One hundred twenty!"

Everything's a blur. Racing clouds above them, the thin line of the horizon, his parents' bodies wilted on the kitchen floor, still locked in an embrace, his life, the foggy glow of the future.

"One hundred thirty!"

Something inside Miles wants to scream, let out a primal roar, a deafening war cry that lets the world know that he's here, alive, wounded but not afraid.

"One hundred forty!"

"Woooowwwwww!" they both scream in exhilaration, the sound of fast-whirling wheels throbbing in their ears.

They hit a small bump and the truck sways gently from side to side like a twig kicked up from the silt by some huge prehistoric creature that ruled this lake thousands of years ago and Moonie finally slows down a bit, still keeping it in the hundreds.

After a while, the even surface of the basin starts curling up, forming a cluster of crusty dunes, and the small hills begin to gradually grow into a full-fledged range of snow-capped mountains. They get on the highway, the only way through the mountains. The highway is empty but Moonie keeps it several miles under the speed limit, out of precaution. Seventy-two feels like a crawl after their dash across the salt flats.

"Dang nab it!" Moonie yells out. "There's gold in them thar hills! There's millions in it!"

"What?" Miles looks at Moonie like he's been seized by a ghost.

"Some old movie," Moonie waves it off with a smile. "But seriously, over there, those are the Oquirrh Mountains, there's a lot of gold in there."

"Yeah?"

"Tons of copper too."

"Is that where your mine is?"

"I wish. Everything you see there, that entire range has been claimed ages ago. End of the nineteenth century. This is the big boys, the majors. Bingham Canyon, an open-pit copper mine there, is the biggest man-made excavation. Almost a mile deep, some six miles wide. They say that the value of minerals taken from Bingham Canyon alone exceeds all of the finds of the California and Klondike gold rushes, plus the yields of the Comstock Lode. Many times over. I don't know if it's true or not. It might as well be."

It's already dark when they get to the outskirts of Salt Lake City. Past the airport, they get off the highway and turn south onto the dimly lit streets of West Valley. In the single-family units, obscured by outside walls of whitewashed brick, the simple lives of small-town folk go on, each consumed by its own narrative, an inconsequential collection of events that, however strange or random, demand a semblance of structure and purpose. God, greed, honor, love, fear, pleasure, sense of duty, eternal sadness—whatever gets you up in the morning.

A stretch of darkness divides West Valley and Jordan. Their headlights stir up a small group of street people gathered around a fire in the middle of an empty lot of an abandoned strip mall. Bums eyeball them with defiant fear as they drive by, then blend into the night again.

A grid of low-lying houses, Jordan looks no different than West Valley, or any other small town you drive straight through and never think about again. City hall, courthouse, a bank, and a Mormon temple. A giant smiling burger appears, floating above the road, little ketchup-colored arms sticking out of the bun, spreading out in a hug. Fanned across concrete tables and benches outside the burger joint, local teenagers are passing around a bottle of liquor under the neon glow.

At the edge of town, a winding road takes them up the hill. After a couple of miles, they see a purple cloud shimmering behind moving trees. The road splits up, one side continuing further up into the mountains, the other curving around to a secluded plateau with a building complex on it. Illuminated road delineators lead them to a vehicle security tunnel. The scan of the truck checks out fine and they slowly drive out of the tunnel, up to the gate booth.

"Good evening gentlemen," the guard peeks inside the truck from his seat. "Welcome to Fawn Resorts. Are you here for the party or will you be staying with us?"

"We're gonna stay the night," says Moonie.

"Very well. IDs, please."

As the guard scans their Allcoms, another guard comes out of the booth and circles the truck, sweeping it with an electronic particle tracer wand.

"Clean," he says, heading back inside.

"Thank you, Mr. Madigan," the guard in the booth says. "You're going to take a right here to lot A."

"I know, thank you," Moonie replies.

"We hope you have a pleasant stay."

The sound of sparse piano key plunks spills out of the

hotel lounge hovering over the bustle of the reception area. They glide over the polished granite floor, dodging slow-moving guests, and make their way behind a group of impatient twenty-somethings in the desk line.

A young couple in front of them is squabbling over what to do next. The guy wants to go out with a group waiting for them by the entrance door, the girl wants to have drinks in someone's room first. Shuffling and gesticulating, the girl inadvertently backs up into Miles.

"Sorry," her eyes sparkle behind thatch-like bangs.

Miles gives her a small, self-incriminating smile like it was him who bumped into her and not the other way around. She smells like freshly picked strawberries. Her hair, a jagged mesh of bright colors, loud green eyeliner, and indigo blue eyelashes make her look kind of unreal, like some simuli heroine.

"Busy night," says Moonie when they finally get to the desk.

"Mr. Belan!" The receptionist's cordial expression turns into a warm smile when he recognizes Moonie. "Yeah, big party at the club tonight. How are you? Welcome back."

"Good, good. Thanks."

Moonie presents his Allcom to be scanned with his left hand while sliding a one-ounce gold bar across the counter with his right.

"Mr.... Madigan," the receptionist's eyes shift furtively from his display to Moonie, then to Miles, and then to the gold bar.

"My nephew," Moonie says.

"Okay," says the receptionist, stretching out the last vowel. "Separate rooms?"

"No. Two-bed suite is fine. Just for tonight."

"Right," the receptionist looks at his display, smoothly palming the gold bar from the counter. "Seventh floor? You'll have a nice view."

"Sure."

"Alright. You're all set Mr.... um... Madigan. Room 729."

"Thanks."

"I'm Bradley sir," the receptionist hands a guest RFID tag to Moonie with a conspiratorial nod. "Anything you need."

"Thanks, Bradley."

"We gotta get you some new clothes," Moonie tells Miles as they head for the elevators. "Maybe after breakfast tomorrow. They have a nice boutique down the hall."

The suite is big and neat. They shower and eat dinner then sit on the balcony for a while, quietly looking at the twinkling valley bellow, savoring the short moment of safety and comfort, away from the world. As the night draws cold, they move back inside. Moonie crashes on the pull-out sofa bed in the main room and two minutes later he's asleep, sending out light snores across the suite. Miles slides the bedroom door shut, slips under the covers, and opens the EternalQuest landing page on his Allcom. The news of his disappearance has hit the headlines.

*"EternalQuest semifinalist FreeFire, family disappear in California."*

The article is directly taken from a short mention in the East Bay News Miles read earlier. *"Local Family Mysteriously Disappears from Their Home."* The original article offers no details, other than their names and pictures along with a boilerplate statement by the Concord police. Judging by the number of views, the story's getting a lot of attention on Frontier, but he can't get inside to see the comments without an account. He sent out a bunch of requests, but so far has gathered only four recommendations out of the eight he needs. FreeFire. He gazes at his name on the list of semifinalists and wonders if, after everything that has happened, this accomplishment actually means anything to him now. Unsure, and unwilling to think about it, he tosses the Allcom aside, shuts his eyes, and slowly drifts off to sleep.

After about an hour or so, Moonie wakes up from a fitful

sleep to a haze of worry. He tries to tune out the oncoming thoughts, turning and tossing around, adjusting his pillows and covers, but the harder he tries to fall back asleep, the more awake he becomes. Finally, he jumps out of bed in frustration, puts on his clothes in the dark, and sneaks out of the room, careful not to wake Miles up.

Dim and quiet, the hotel lounge seems closed at first, but the door is ajar so he goes in. The place is empty, save for a barback in a white uniform methodically restocking shelves with freshly washed glasses.

"Any way I can get a drink?" Moonie asks across the room, startling the young man.

"Yes, sir," the glasses in his hands rattle like bells as he turns around. "Uhh... I mean no sir. We're closed. Sorry." He almost seems guilty of something. "You might wanna try the club."

"Fuck it," Moonie mumbles to himself after a short contemplation and continues down the hall.

He cuts through the pool area to a tiled corridor along the bungalows at the far end of the hotel, exits through the gate, then walks over a small bridge onto a narrow path that curves through a beech grove. On the other side of the grove, across the chock-full parking lot, is a two-story brick and concrete box with a purple "Demonic" neon sign pasted across the top.

Moonie has been coming to "Demonic" regularly for the last year and a half, but he has never seen it this packed. There must be more than two thousand people in there. He abandons the idea of entering the throng of sweaty half-naked bodies and instead takes the stairs up to the VIP cabanas in the circular gallery above the main floor. One of the bouncers recognizes him and lets him in.

Sprawled out on the canvas cabana pillows, buckled in tense boredom charged with ephedrine-based uppers, working girls are craning their necks at anything that moves quickly, darting glances at him as he walks by. Some of them have have dates, but the ratio seems decidedly in Moonie's favor. He manages a couple of "maybe later" smiles but mostly ignores their attention and heads straight to the bar.

"Bourbon. Neat. Make it a double."

He swipes the drink off the bar and walks to the glass ledge of the balcony. Green and blue lasers are slashing the cavernous void of the main floor below, flashes of strobe lighting timed to slick beats. Propelled by drugs or lust or both, hot young bodies are pulsating in unison like some giant multiheaded jellyfish. The DJ shifts to a drumless bridge carried by an echoing vocal loop: *Now, ...ow, ...ow, ...ow... Forever!* The lights fade down. Boat sirens come in from all sides, rising in intensity and pitch. *Now, ...ow, ...ow, ...ow... Forever!*

The buildup continues. A white spotlight comes on, unveiling a solo dancer on a small round podium in the middle of the room. Her naked body, covered in gold paint, gleams above the cheering crowd. Two more spotlights, both red, pop up on the opposite sides of the floor, revealing slightly bigger dance podiums containing three dancers each, two guys and a girl on the left, two girls and a guy on the right, all completely naked save for purple and pink body paint. The crowd rides the riser then explodes in the air with the drop of the beat, lights blast out, and the controlled frenzy of the party resumes. Moonie feels someone's hands cupping his ass cheeks and yanks himself away.

"Easy tiger, just getting a feel. I missed those buns."

Liz.

"Hey you," caught by surprise, Moonie musters a quick smile.

"All by your handsome lonesome self, Moons? I thought we were going to party tonight."

He had completely forgotten about Liz.

"Oh yeah."

"I tried calling you a few times, but it kept bouncing

back. You okay, hon?"

"Yeah, yeah. You wanna drink?"

"Sure," she flags the waitress with an almost imperceptible wave of the hand.

Liz is pretty, but not beautiful in the way in which the other expensive girls are. Blue-eyed and thin with luscious kissable lips, perky round tits, and a dynamite ass. What she lacks in beauty she easily made up for with moxie. And she always has a top-notch stash.

"What's with the mob?" asks Moonie just to say something.

"They're all here for Skayee Blaze."

"Sky what?"

Liz smiles, but doesn't answer. She takes a miniature biosensor from her purse and swipes it over Moonie's forehead. It beeps and flashes as it completes the read.

"You really believe that thing?" says Moonie.

"Without any reservation," Liz answers while looking at the display. "You, my dear, need to relax a bit. Your cortisol and epinephrine levels are way too high. Now if you behave, I got just the thing for you."

The waitress brings Liz's drink and they join two other girls in one of the cabanas.

"You remember Puffs, and this is Cyra," Liz introduces her friends.

"Hi," Moonie smiles, trying to figure out which one of the two girls is the one he was expected to remember.

One of the girls has her eyes buried in her Allcom, checking the bidding action on her Convivial LIVE account. The other one does seem vaguely familiar, although Moonie can't really tell how he'd know her. That one must be Puffs. She's ogling a thickset guy in his early thirties standing by himself at the bar. Shaved head and clenched jaw, cut tattooed arms bulging out of a tight, yellow short-sleeved shirt. Puffs's Allcom flashes with a new bid.

"It's not him, Puffs," says Cyra. "He's not here for the girls."

"How do you know?" Puffs asks.

"It's really not that hard. Anyway, he looks like he likes it rough. I'd cut him off if he were bidding on me."

Liz throws a double glance at the bar.

"Hmm, strange. I can swear I saw that guy when I went to my dentist today. Hey!" she sparks up. "What do you think?" she lifts her upper lip, revealing a healthy white cuspid with a tiny diamond lodged in the middle of it. "I had it done today."

"Nice," says Puffs. "Was it painful?"

"A little bit after the anesthesia wore off," Liz smacks her lips. "Nothing like a couple of painkillers to make you feel better. Speaking of feeling better," she produces a small silver box, pinches out a thin translucent tab, and offers it to Moonie.

"What's this?" Moonie asks.

"Have I ever failed you?"

"Well, come to think of it..." Moonie chuckles.

"Shuut uup!" Liz rolls her eyes coyly.

"What else do you have in there?"

He grabs the silver box from her and looks inside.

"Anything you need. Uppers, downers, happy drops, skinny nips, dick raisers, eye-openers, shut-eye pops," she recites. "Help yourself."

Moonie pockets a few green-colored capsules from the box and gives it back to Liz. "

All right, but this is it," he lets Liz lay the tab on his tongue. "I have an early day tomorrow."

The tab dissolves quickly, leaving a fresh citrusy aftertaste in his mouth. He washes it down with a sip of bourbon.

"So, who's this Sky?" Moonie asks no one in particular.

"Skayee Blaze," Liz corrects him.

"Sky?"

"Skayee."

"I don't hear the difference."

"She's just some Vegas biznatch," says Cyra, finally letting go of her Allcom. "Nobody really. She sucks, but these rednecks around here think she's hot shit."

"I like her," chimes in Puffs equivocally.

"Why? Why do you like her?" Cyra keeps going. "Because she had a digital voice box put in her throat so she can sound like anyone she chooses to? Let's see what the crowd's into. Press the button for Florence Bee. Oh, something more substantial? How about Seer? Click-done. Something ancient? Amy Winehouse? Nina Simone? Done and done. Perfect pitch, perfectly in tune every time. All she does is sing other people's songs through a chip. She doesn't have an original bone in her body."

"So what? I still like her."

"You like everyone, Puffs."

"You say that like it's a bad thing."

Moonie feels the drug sinking down, loosening his muscles, syncing up his heart to the beats of the music, laying his head on a soft pillow of calm. He looks at Liz. Her lips are moving but her words are not words anymore; they're just sounds, a familiar harmony of hisses, squawks, and yaps, mhms and ohs, shs and aws, nasal vibrations and tongue clicks, a soundscape of habituation to something intimate, someone dear.

Puffs is a good-looking girl. A little zonked. It gives her an appeal of effortless sex. Now he remembers. They fooled around some time ago. Liz and him and her together. She's a gracious fuck. She'd probably be into it again. What about the fussy one? Why not? The more the merrier. She's gorgeous. Stunning in fact. How did he miss that earlier? He rivets his eyes on Cyra, unable to look away. Long jet-black hair, porcelain skin, smoky eyes, shiny nude lips, two tiny golden dots in the helix of her left ear—quite possibly the most beautiful woman he's ever laid his eyes upon. For one short delusional moment, he wonders if she might be the most beautiful woman who has ever lived. Life's been good to him.

"Hard up, aren't we?" Cyra leers and leans in.

"You like what you like," Moonie cracks a smile.

Cyra turns her eyes to Liz, who gives her a quick, imperceptible nod. She's in. Possibly.

"Right Puffs?" Moonie says.

"What?"

The music cuts off abruptly and the entire place goes dark in an instant. Liz grabs Moonie's arm. Screams and jeers pour out of the black pit of the main floor as the crowd scrambles to unknot itself. A moment of panic, then the white lights of Allcoms flash around in jerked spasms, tracing the movements of chaos—hollers and call-outs, searching for others in the shadows.

"Never a dull moment in this place," Liz says, irked.

Moonie rifles through his pockets for his Allcom but can't seem to find it.

"Everyone! Please stay where you are," he hears the security guards yell over the crowd. "There's no reason to panic. We lost power temporarily. Backup generators will kick in soon. Please! Stay where you are to avoid accidents. The power will be back shortly."

Two VIP security guards shuffle between the cabanas with flashlights.

"Sorry folks, this should be over soon," one of them says. "Just stay where you are for the time being."

Moonie keeps rummaging around for his Allcom, running his fingers through the cushions and looking down on the floor.

"No power! No power! No power!" a silly chant breaks out down below, accompanied by swaying Allcom lights.

He must have left it in the room. Fuck! He suddenly realizes—the kid! What the fuck am I doing? I shouldn't be here.

"I gotta go," he blurts out.

"What? Why?" Liz asks.

"I gotta go," Moonie repeats as he rolls off the pillows. "I'll catch you ladies next time."

With his vision veiled by the darkness and his legs softened by whatever Liz gave him, he falters down the stairs but stays on his feet and makes his way through the unnerved crowd pushing through the exit door.

Once outside, Moonie takes a few long breaths of fresh air to defog his mind. What the fuck was he thinking? He moves through the gaps between small huddles of people standing outside the club, crosses the parking lot, and enters the beech grove. An occasional beam from a headlight sparkles through the trees, making it easier to stay on the path. He thinks he hears something, someone moving behind him, and turns around, staring at the blackness for a moment, listening closely. Nothing.

The power is still out when he gets back to the hotel, but the bungalow corridor is sparsely lit by battery-operated emergency lights. He walks to the end of the corridor, then slips into the darkness that separates the bungalows from the pool area, ducks behind the hedges, and waits.

A moment later, a figure emerges from the beech grove into the light. Yellow shirt muscle guy from the club! He moves spryly for his size, shoulders raised, eyes fixed forward like a preying cat. The Circuit? Moonie tries to think quickly. He feels like he should be worried, but he isn't. It's all going to fall in place. One way or another. The universe has his back. No! Moonie pinches his arm hard, trying to fight off the drug's mellow. How could they possibly have tracked them down?

The man is almost at the end of the corridor, about to turn toward him. Liz! She said she saw him in town today, Moonie attempts to follow this thought. Coincidence? Maybe, it's a small town. But what if it isn't a coincidence?

He remembers taking a few uppers from Liz's stash box, feels them in his pocket, takes two out and pops them in his mouth, then lays down and presses his chest against wet grass. The man slows down slightly as he approaches, then stops, presumably looking for him. Moonie's breathing ceases. He can see the man's shoes through the hedge, mere inches from his nose. The man stands there for a short time, then shuffles off towards the pool. Moonie exhales inaudibly through his mouth, rolls over on his back, and turns his gaze up to the sky.

The moon's hiding somewhere, but the stars are all out in their twinkling glory. Western skies. He starts silently humming a gentle melody he first heard one moonless summer night, just like this one, laying alone faceup on the upper deck of *Vostok*, being rocked gently by the mighty Pacific, looking at these same stars, magnificent, mystical mothers of everything that exists, looking down at us, telling us to not be afraid.

The uppers are starting to work. He feels a surge of strength and lucidity coming over him. The Circuit hacked him, no doubt, but the question is how much sense they have made of his NoMark-stripped net activity records. Could they have predicted that they would end up coming here of all places, based solely on the metadata? No way. The best they could have done is make an informed guess and see if they showed up. A Hail Mary. And it worked! They fell right into it.

Maybe this is just fear doing the thinking, or the drug-induced paranoia is getting the best of him this time around. Maybe this is all one big nothing. He shouldn't have left Miles alone, they shouldn't have come here in the first place. They should have kept driving past Salt Lake City, found some off-the-map place further out on the road to crash for the night. He had checked in under a false name, so that didn't trigger any electronic surveillance alerts. Facial recognition from the front desk cameras? Maybe, but then it would have been all over by now. They would have been tied up in some trunk with black canvas bags over their heads on their way to who knows where. Or worse. But now the Circuit does know.

All things considered, he grasps for an upside; this might be a good thing. Now he knows the score too. He knows they're here and he and Miles will have a chance to make a run for it, right now, rather than walk into a trap in the morning, unaware of the danger.

Moonie slowly comes out of his hiding place, keeping his eyes on the passage to the pool area, almost expecting to see the man standing there, waiting for him in the shadows, grinning smugly, gun in hand. The passage is clear. He speeds down the corridor, through the beech grove, back to the Demonic's parking lot, which is now busier than before as more people abandon the party. He decides to head toward the circle road connecting the two parking lots.

Unlike at the Demonic, the hotel's lot is half-empty and seemingly devoid of any activity. Moonie spots his truck in the darkness and cautiously makes his way across, looking around, checking inside the parked cars, keeping one eye at the entrance. He takes a few careful moments to make sure that no one is watching the truck, then silently makes his way over to it, kneels next to the driver's door, and retrieves a small metal box hidden underneath.

Tightly packed inside the box are a jackknife, a spare physical key for his truck, a small can of pepper spray, high voltage taser tags, and a basic first aid kit. He puts the knife and pepper spray inside the front pockets of his pants, taser tags in his shirt pocket. He then circles around and opens the trunk and burrows his head inside of it. He finds his backup gun, which he sticks into his belt. He glances around the lot one more time, then jumps in and starts the engine.

Driving slowly with his headlights off, Moonie scouts out the area around the main hotel entrance. Some fifty feet away from the entrance driveway, screened off by a row of small cypress trees in oversized concrete planters, a service entrance ramp slopes down into the bowels of the hotel. Moonie parks at the top of the ramp, straightens himself up a little, and heads back to the main entrance on foot. It doesn't take long for him to notice that the power outage has affected the hotel too—whether or not this gives him some sort of an advantage remains to be seen.

Behind the front desk counter, Bradley is on a call with someone, patiently nodding at whatever information he's receiving in his earpiece. At the far end of the hallway, the hotel staff is gathered together, awaiting instructions on how to handle the current situation. Moonie heads to the elevators, but quickly realizes that they're not operating. Unsure what to do, he shuffles around, and then sees one of the hotel staff walking toward him, pointing to an ajar door behind him. He gives the man a small wave and enters the emergency exit stairwell.

The air inside is hot and stale. Cinderblock walls coated with reflective white paint amplify the glow of the emergency LEDs, making the stairwell surprisingly bright. Moonie squints as he enters, waits for his eyes to adjust, then pulls himself along the handrail, head down, like a devout follower headed on a pilgrimage. Strips of fluorescent tread tape flicker under his feet as he climbs. Four floors up, three to go. Suddenly, the steps in front of him darken.

"Hands above your head!" a voice commands.

Moonie's heart sinks as he looks up, furious with himself for brainlessly walking into an ambush, but not one bit surprised to see the man in the yellow shirt standing in front of him, pointing a gun at his chest. What a fucking fool he was to think he was smart enough to pull this off. He clasps his hands and places them slowly on the back of his head.

"Get up here," the man motions.

Moonie steps up to the landing, eye to eye with the man. His face is neither old or young, neither friendly nor hostile.

"Lift your shirt up."

Moonie lifts his shirt, revealing the gun.

"Toss it."

Metal clonks against the concrete floor.

"Empty your pockets."

Moonie casts the contents of his pockets at the man's feet: jackknife, RFID, truck key, Liz's pills, pepper spray can. The man carefully retrieves each of the items.

"Now, turn around and put your hands on the wall above your head."

It's over. Moonie feels the life seeping out of him as he waits for a blade spark under his chin, a deafening bang, a bullet tearing through his ribs on his way to his heart, another one cracking the back of his skull. The man kicks his feet apart and quickly pats him down.

"Where's the boy?" he asks.

"What boy?" Moonie almost couldn't believe himself saying it.

He feels the hard metal barrel of the gun pressing hard against his spine. Please, not now. Not just yet.

"I'm gonna ask you one more time before I snap your head off. Where's the boy? Is he in your room?"

"Listen, I got money..." Moonie tries to worm his way out.

In one effortless move, the man jams the butt of his gun between Moonie's shoulder blades, thrusting him forward. Moonie's face smashes against the wall, a sharp pain shoots through the back of his neck as he spills onto the floor.

"Do not fuck with me," the man utters calmly.

Moonie's nose feels numb from the close encounter with the wall. It's probably broken. There's blood in his mouth. He weakly brings himself onto his knees.

"Get up," the man commands.

In a small puddle of blood and spit, Moonie sees his tooth laying on the floor. Except, it's perfectly round. And bright yellow. The taser tag! It must have flown out of his shirt when he fell. He leans forward a bit, extends his arm, grabs the tag, and pushes himself up off the floor in one fluid motion.

"Yeah, he's in the room," he says.

"Let's go then."

Moonie twists the taser tag in his hand, feeling the circular groove of the trigger button under his fingers. Right now! It has to be right now! This is his only chance. He wipes the blood off his mouth with his sleeve then swings around and lunges at the man. The gun goes off, and a wave of excruciating pain rips through Moonie's ears. He feels the slack of the man's cheek slip up his cheekbone as he pushes the trigger button. The man's face crumples, his eyes widen in shock, mouth agape. He crumbles down, convulsing violently. The gun muzzle flashes in his hand as he hits the floor, once, twice, but no sound follows. Moonie stabs his heel into the man's wrist, loosening his grip on the weapon, and then kicks him in the face. The man grabs Moonie's leg, almost knocking him over, but he can't maintain the hold—his body's still quivering from the taser aftershock. Moonie gets a hold of the man's gun and bashes him on the head with it repeatedly until his body goes limp. He retrieves his own gun from the man's belt, then pulls back a couple of steps and aims, but cannot pull the trigger. He looks down at this man, a complete stranger who just seconds ago owned his life, now coiling in pain below his feet, his face nothing but a bloody mess.

Moonie's heart pushes out of his chest, its muffled beats swaying his entire body. Then, almost devoid of will, two flaps of a bat's wings break through the droning hum in his ears as the bullets from his gun rip through each of the man's legs.

# DAY_4

*"All units! Full alert! The security of the Operation Relay Network has been compromised."*

"Holy shit!" Weiss jumps in his chair as the message flashes in front of his eyes.

*"All units! Recourse to the alternative communication methods at once. All functions of the Operation Relay Network will cease immediately."*

Weiss stares at his display wordlessly for a few moments, turning over the implications of what he just read in his head.

"Motherfuckers!" someone yells out from the operations floor, then other voices come in, rising in intensity and frequency, transforming what's normally a somnolent ambiance of the TOC night shift into a soundscape of commotion and confused urgency.

One by one, the heads poke out of the shadows of workstations, bobbing around for answers. A small group of people emerge from the direction of the strategy room, hurrying across the main hallway of the Directorate. One of them peels off from the group and enters TOC. He says something to the people at the far end of the floor, nearest to the entrance, then leaves. Gradually the murmur swells, pierced by a shout here and there, and people start leaving their workstations and gathering in the open area in the middle of the TOC floor. Weiss gets out of his office and joins the expectant crowd.

After a little while, Deputy Commander Massey shows

up, flanked by two grim-looking I.I. agents.

"Listen up!" Massey shouts over the hum of the crowd. "It was just brought to our attention by the Integrity Investigations team that there's been a serious security breach of the Operations Relay Network. The Op Relay Network has been isolated from the mainframe by a perimeter gateway to maintain the normal functioning of all other networks. It'll stay inoperative until the I.I. concludes its investigation and/or comes up with a way to remedy the situation. They have located the source of the breach and identified the responsible party. They're currently examining the scope of the damage."

"Who was it?" a voice yells out, a few others joining in.

"All in due time," Massey replies. "The I.I. is running the show. You'll be given that information at their discretion, on a need-to-know basis. Right now, all of you handling live operations should go back to your workstations and bring your field agents up to speed with the current situation. You must act quickly. They're in the dark and we can't have that. Refer to the emergency communication protocol for the alternative ways to establish a safe and effective exchange of information. All non-time-sensitive operations are called off until we have more clarity on the matter."

The crowd rearranges itself and a few people scurry back to their workstations. Massey waits for them to leave, then continues.

"The rest of you will make yourselves available to Integrity Investigations agents for a debriefing process. The sessions will begin immediately. If you pass the debrief, based on your skillset and the operations history, you might be asked to help with the investigation."

*The walls were closing in on Theo. What kind* of sadistic monster locks up a child? The thought of not being able to be with Miles and Maritza during all of this, devastated him. The cruelty of it hurts more than any physical pain but even worse is the realization that he cannot do anything about it. He wanted to believe that there's always a way out, that no matter how tough and dark things are, there is always a way up towards hope and light, but deep down in his core, he was shuddering.

Theo felt almost relieved when Drey called, around seven, telling him to get ready. Being forced to focus on something else would hinder the raw anguish eating away at his heart and keep him sharp. Head up, eyes open. The chance will present itself. Patience is what he needs right now. Patience and vigilance.

Once in the lab, Theo casts his gaze across the holographic display above his head, and goes over the slew of data he reviewed yesterday one more time. At first sight, the data did not reveal much. A thin layer of peatland on top of 70 feet of low-yield overburden, then a 250- to 300-feet thick oil sands deposit, all sitting on a bed of shale and limestone. Not very different than other oil sands reservoir data he had seen over the years. But then, there was the hole. Too bizarre to be believable.

Slicing through wrinkled stripes of blues, greens, yellows, and reds on the synthetic seismogram of the mine's subsurface, a 6.8-mile-deep active borehole travels down into seemingly nothing. Was it real? Looking at the data, Theo could not find one good reason why somebody would decide to drill this deep at such a geologically unremarkable location. At the depth of 1.5 miles, in the lower shale member, the seismic reflection survey showed a small concentration of kerogen deposits, a prerequisite organic compound for the formation of oil and gas and, sure enough, in the gas and oil window, at around 2.2 miles, there were negligible amounts of oil and gas scattered around in small pockets in the sedimentary rock. Certainly not a good enough reason to drill so deep.

The oil and gas deposits trailed off after three miles. After that, there was absolutely nothing but solid metamorphic rock going down as deep as the sensors could detect. The four-dimensional monitoring system with seismic, pressure, and temperature dynamic nano auditors was set up to track subtle changes in conditions at various depths. Turnkey Integrated Nano Discovery and Exploration-INDEX system. Environ structure. Dynamic data arrays with class libraries and redundancy flush-outs, random access QSDB classifying protocol, self-building relevance subs, live discovery updates. Clearly, this isn't an ordinary truck and shovel operation.

In addition to the auditors, an army of AnNanites, the new generation of self-sustaining nanobots with built-in analytic capabilities was deployed, collecting and processing chemical, biological, and petrologic data across an 80-foot radius along the entire length of the hole. 6.8 miles!

Theo couldn't wrap his mind around it. A quarter of the way through the Earth's crust! That's an incredible feat. If it's real, this borehole would be among the deepest holes ever drilled in the history of human exploration and probably one of the top ten onshore. But for what purpose?

*"Pretty impressive, don't you think?"* the voice from above snaps Theo to attention.

"Is it real?"

*"Every inch of it."*

"What are you looking for?"

*"What everyone is looking for. Answers. It's humbling to realize just how much mystery still exists right here in our little world."*

"Answers? What..." Theo stops himself mid-thought, sensing another ostentatious rant coming.

*"You must already think I'm mad. Almost everyone else does, I guess. I might be, who's to say? But isn't that what they always think of people who try to redefine the status quo? It takes a certain amount of finesse in a leader to strike a balance between respectfully challenging the old ways and promoting the new ones.*

*But I'm not a leader. I don't have a talent for skullduggery or patience for the feebleminded. It's a waste of time trying to convince anyone who chooses to ignore the truth, whatever their reasons. The truth itself has a pretty good way of eventually doing all of the convincing or punishing of those who resist. Besides, I don't believe that men can move other men to action, only ideas can. People unite around what they love or hate, around what they believe is the truth. My job is merely to bring an idea out into the light, nourish it with evidence and facts, and let it become the truth. It's been a lonely effort so far, but now you're here."*

"I don't understand what you're trying to do," Theo interrupts, with as much impatience in his voice as he thought he could afford given the circumstances. "Judging by the seismic, if you're looking for oil you're not going to find much of it here. But I think you already know that."

*"Forgive the long overture. I didn't want to overwhelm you with too much information right off the bat, but it seems like I underestimated your quickness to comprehend. I'm very excited to share this with you. No one else has seen the complete data before. You're right, there isn't much oil down there, but that's not what we're looking for anyway."*

"So what then?" asks Theo, keen to put an end to this flaunting mystification.

*"Let's go back to the dependency framework."*

Theo dives into the seemingly boundless labyrinth of the INDEX archive, backtracking to the front end of the volume to reveal the inverted octahedral diagram of the dependency structure—two data pyramids joined at their tips, their bases extended in opposite directions, the bottom one marked Material and the top one Abstract.

At the base of the Material pyramid is the raw data collected by the nanobots. On top of the raw data is the output of the primary analysis engines tracking the environmental conditions of the borehole's surroundings: pressure, temperature, seismic, rock matrix, chemical, and biological, then layers of corollaries for each of the six categories ready for use by the synthesizing algorithms.

The Abstract pyramid is a nonhierarchical tangle of MVAs—multivariate analyses of a seemingly arbitrary collection of concepts: intermediate compounds in hydrocarbon synthesis, kerogen maturation rates, endothermic behavior of metamorphic rocks, alkanes and cycloalkanes generation, the lifecycles of anaerobic organisms, supramolecular assembly agents...

*"The synthetics are incomplete as you can see. Well, incomplete is maybe a bit of an understatement. I think it's fair to say that at this point we're dealing with a gigantic pile of fitful incoherence. There's still so much raw data to grind through, so our veracity quotient will only improve. You're one of the very few people in the entire world who can successfully explicate this mess in a timely matter. That's why you're here. Your datasets are the stuff of legend. I was hoping you could begin with creating a new set of synthesizer builds for each of these concepts then reformat the statistical models so we can start performing valid decoupling. Once we sort through the clutter, we can start doing the real work."*

"Which is what exactly?"

*"Creating an algorithm for identifying optimum conditions for abiotic generation of hydrocarbons."*

"Excuse me?"

*"We're going to synthesize our own hydrocarbon fuel, Mr. Smith. From inorganic sources."*

"Abiotic..." Theo starts, but runs out of words in awe.

*"I know, I know. But before you dismiss it as an archaic hypothesis, obsolete pseudoscience, or whatever else we were conditioned to call it, consider this. Just like religion, in its goal-seeking ways, science can be deceitful. It'll tempt us with the most logical or the most convenient explanation in order to test us, to prevent us from seeking further truth. More often than not, we end up settling for small truths and half-measures, spending the rest of our days rationalizing them, and willingly tampering with our ability to fulfill our potentials.*

*So, long ago, the scientific community settled on the idea that the only practical way to source energy from hydrocarbons is to explore the deposits already found in nature, which are created exclusively from organic material. Let's just slurp up what's already there. Not much of a stretch. Don't you agree? Sure, there are volumes of well-documented evidence to support this view, but what if all that evidence is a product of a backward calculation perpetrated to obtain a given result, an elaborate example of science trying to prove itself right at any cost, the rationalization of an inflexible theory. What if this kind of thinking prevented us from seeking further, from looking for the deeper truth?"*

"Well, do you have any data disproving the biotic origin theory?" Theo asks.

*"You're missing my point. I'm not trying to disprove the biotic theory. All of the oil and gas we used up to this point did come from the chemical transformation of organic matter, only a fool would argue otherwise. But now that sweet juice of easy life is almost all gone. We squandered most of our great*

*geological inheritance on the frivolous pursuit of pleasure and amusement instead of using it as a nest egg to develop a viable alternative. It took mother Earth hundreds of thousands of years to make all that oil. We managed to burn through it all in a split second and now have hardly anything to show for it. Billions and billions of barrels gone. Poof, just like that. But that's a trivial amount in the great scheme of things. The way I look at it, it's a tease of a greater truth we accidentally stumbled upon, and also a sour reminder of how much we still don't know. After all these years, we still don't fully understand the basic mechanism of hydrocarbon creation. It's still a confounding mystery. But it shouldn't be."*

"There are plenty of computational chemistry studies that explain molecular properties of hydrocarbons, reaction paths for chemical reactions that lead to..."

*"Let me ask you this. Is there life on Neptune?"*

"What?"

*"It's a simple question. Does life as we know it exists on Neptune?"*

"No."

*"How about Uranus, Titan, Pluto?"*

"No."

*"Is there any evidence that shows there was once life there? Any traces of organic material?"*

"Not to my knowledge."

*"Yet they're all awash in methane and other simple hydrocarbons. How's that? Where did these hydrocarbons come from?"*

"I don't know."

*"So then, would you agree that if they were not derived from organic material those hydrocarbons must have been created from inorganic sources?"*

"That would be logical."

*"Why is it that hydrocarbons on Earth couldn't originate in the same way, from nonorganic sources?"*

"No one is saying they couldn't, but it's a known fact that ninety-nine percent of Earth's methane comes from biological activity."

*"What about that one percent?"*

"Mostly volcanic action, as far as I know."

*"So, from inorganic sources?"*

"It seems like you know more about this process than I do, so why don't you just tell me what you need to tell me."

*"Very well. The basic precondition for the creation of abiogenic methane is the presence of molecular hydrogen and carbon dioxide. If you put them together, the laws of thermodynamics dictate that you will get methane. The reaction speed depends on temperature, pressure, and catalysts. Since carbon dioxide is so readily available in the atmosphere and in the oceans, finding sources of abiogenic methane is really just a search for molecular hydrogen and the presence of suitable catalysts for the reaction. So, at the sites of volcanic activity on the ocean floor, the magma heats the water, breaking the molecular ties between oxygen and hydrogen, then spurred by catalysts like iron or magnesium, liberated hydrogen reacts with carbon from carbon dioxide to form methane and byproduct minerals. Sounds simple, right?"*

"Laws of nature are often simple."

*"The beauty and elegance of scientific truth. It is simple. Under the right conditions, of course. What's difficult, is quantifying those conditions and then replicating them in a controlled manner. But what's life without a little bit of a challenge, right? Only idiots never change their minds. It's beyond obvious at this point that by continuing to do what we've been doing for the last couple of hundred years, burning fossil fuels without regard for the environmental consequences of the climate change it's causing, we're putting ourselves on a surefire path to quickly and effectively end our time here on Earth.*

*You never hear industry men talk openly about the environmental impact of fossil fuel use and it's not because we're unaware of the devastation our product is causing. No. It's because we think that we don't have a choice but to keep doing what we have been doing. The world needs enegy and we have to provide it, clean or dirty. There's simply no alternative. As hard as we've tried to develop renewable energy sources, they still contribute less than twenty-five percent of the world's energy needs. So, take the fossil fuels out of the equation and our civilization gets effectively pushed into sharp, irreversible decline, which is now underway due to the total destruction of the Middle Eastern reserves. And it's going to get worse before it gets better. The oil shortages are causing a worldwide rush to revamp coal, which almost certainly means that we might not last long enough on this Earth to see things take a turn for the better.*

*We're doomed, unless we kill off three-quarters of the world's population with war, disease, and hunger or come up with an inexhaustible, carbon-neutral energy source, whichever comes first. Equilibrium must be achieved."*

A brief period of silence ensues; perhaps the man is gauging the effect of his words on Theo before continuing, now less prophetically and more matter-of-factly.

*"Every now and then with open-pit mining, as you get deeper, you have to reevaluate the methods of extraction because of the subsidence hazard zones, which are shifts in rock formations that can negatively impact the structural configuration of the mine. You have to do a very detailed examination of those areas before you start making any significant decisions about how to proceed with the exploration. The entire operation depends on the ability to do this part right; otherwise, the mine can easily collapse in on itself.*

*During this process, one ends up scrutinizing every bit of data so closely that eventually you discover all sorts of information that might have otherwise gone unnoticed. Oil and gas, as they migrate upward, get trapped in the low porosity fault regions forming the hydrocarbon concentrations. So, not unexpectedly, we found clusters of small deposits in those subsidence zones. We ran the chemical analysis of hydrocarbons found in those deposits and micro seepage pathways that connect to them, and what we found was very interesting, to say the least. The presence of organic markers in those hydrocarbons was consistently dropping as we dug deeper, until, at one point, it disappeared completely.*

*Obviously, this was a very unexpected development. We followed the migration paths down, looking for further confirmation of these results, and step by step we ended up building this exploratory model. Borehole, INDEX, the whole bit. Now, this type of discovery can lead to all kinds of speculative thinking, but one factor that convinced us that we're onto something bigger than a mere peculiarity was the increased presence of natural gas at greater depths. Sure, as you go deeper toward the mantle, it gets hotter, the pressure rises, and as you enter the gas window thermal cracking takes place and all intermediate hydrocarbon compounds turn into gas. But the gas we found down there did not have a trace of biological origin. Not one single biological marker in millions of cubic feet analyzed. The absence of biological markers points to the only conclusion possible—its source is abiotic.*

*This opens up a Pandora's box of possibilities. How exactly is this happening? Where is the necessary carbon coming from? What about free hydrogen atoms? Our drills can go down just so deep before they start melting, but I know we're close. If we can identify the thermodynamically favorable reaction environment necessary for this process and replicate it consistently, we'll be able to create an inexhaustible source of carbon-neutral fuel and at the same time solve the two biggest problems threatening our civilization: limitations of available energy and environmental damage caused by the negative feedback loop of fossil fuel-powered growth."*

Theo was determined to play devil's advocate. "Suppose you accomplish that, measure the optimum conditions for abiotic generation of hydrocarbons. Then what? How do you turn that information into an inexhaustible source of energy? A carbon-neutral source of energy, no less."

*"I understand your skepticism. Perhaps that's a conversation we should have at another time. We'll have plenty of opportunities. We're going to spend a lot of time together in the near and probably not-so-near future. There's a lot left to do before we get there, but I assure you, that part of the process is going to be much less difficult. Let's just focus on the task ahead for now. I'm sure you're eager to start working. I'll monitor your progress and guide you remotely as needed. I'll spare you any further harangue and will communicate mainly through the Simulacrum's interface from now on. And of course, Drey will always be there for everything else."*

"What about my wife and my son? You have me, why do you need them?" Theo stares at the blank ceiling floating high over his head. "Please... my son is only fifteen," he cries out pleadingly. "Have you no heart at all?"

Theo's voice rings out then fades into the semidarkness of the room as the cold silence reasserts itself.

*Russ knew that the bubbly feeling of being* back in action wouldn't last, but he didn't expect it to blow up in his face so soon. Sparse with people, the main operations floor seems bigger than he remembers it. He sees Weiss's reflection in the glass office partition, crouching behind the displays, and heads his way.

"What the fuck's going on?" Russ barges into Weiss's office. "Why am I being summoned by the I.I.?"

Weiss looks at him with a vacant stare, like he'd gone blind.

"We got owned," he conveys flatly.

"What?"

"Sheng Long jacked our Ops Relay network."

"Are you serious?"

"The I.I. is up everybody's ass, it's not just you," Weiss turns back to his display. "They're assessing the damage... if they got into any of the databases..."

"Did they question you?"

"Last night, yeah."

"And?"

"I'm here aren't I?"

Russ chews on the new information for a moment.

"They even asked a few of us running the ops in Sheng Long's area of influence to help out with data forensics," Weiss continues. "There's something you'll find interesting..."

"What's that?"

"The Smith thing… It's not a hundred percent yet, but we're going with the assumption that it was Sheng Long."

"Ha! Based on what?"

"The I.I. kept an eye on Smith. Among other things, they had access to his home security system feeds. Last night, I watched the footage from three days ago, when the Smiths were taken…"

Weiss proceeds to describe the kidnapping to Russ.

"Other than the fact that they let the kid get away, it was a well-executed operation. Unmarked flyquads, SWAT team, a ghost field operative. Unless it was some sort of state-sponsored black op, it had to be a PSC."

"How do you know it was Sheng Long and not some other PSC?" Russ asks. "Maybe Keystone or Absolute Compliance? They're both very active in California."

"We got a hit on the field operative. Rachel Fang. Twenty-one years in Taiwanese secret service, jumped the fence with the regime when they lost the war. Details get sketchy afterward, obviously bleached, but we found enough to link her to Sheng Long."

The hallways are deserted, save for a few figures muddling about in the shadows, wary of being swept up in the I.I.'s ongoing hunt for responsibility. To shed his prickly mood before the interview, Russ walks over to the bank of windows overlooking the New York harbor and looks at the passing ships for a few minutes, letting the deep calm of the bay dissolve his anxiety.

The last time he was questioned by Integrity Investigations was five years ago, when Claire Henderson left the force. One thing everyone who knew Claire would agree on, is that you would likely never meet another person who embodies dedication, intelligence, compassion, insane focus, and hard-working ethic so completely and all in one package like she does. She possessed a strange mix of impulsivity and prudence, tempered with an uncanny intuition, all powered by an incredible inner drive and a true passion for whatever task she had in front of her—she's living proof that if you give it your best every step of the way, you'll never regret the consequences of your choices. Maybe that's how we all ought to live our lives.

The quality of Claire's work and her commitment to the job earned her respect in the department and helped her climb the ladder fast enough to become the youngest station chief in the department's history. But just a few months after Russ worked with her in Cyprus, seemingly on a whim, she decided that her contribution to the world would be better made elsewhere—specifically, combating the effects of climate change by joining an international effort for the restoration of the Amazon Basin, which has been destroyed by decades of reckless deforestation.

Her decision to leave did not sit well with people higher up on the totem pole, to say the least. You don't just get to quit when you feel like it. They get to chew you up and spit you out, reassign you, demote you, or retire you, one way or another, but you don't get to just leave on your own terms. And if you happen to somehow find an amicable way out, it'll be knowing that ACIS will keep close tabs on you for the rest of your time on this Earth. There will always be strings attached. You will never be truly free. It's what you have to learn to live with.

Being questioned by the I.I. is, in itself, a bizarre, mind-warping experience, guaranteed to scramble one's reasoning to the point that you're not even sure if you have control over what you're saying anymore. Relying on biometrics to pick up and analyze variations in the answers, one of their techniques involves asking the same question five, ten, even fifteen times in succession, then throwing in a seemingly unrelated problem-solving exercise, like "Sam, who is twelve years old, is three times as old as his cousin Mary. How old will Sam be when he is twice as old as Mary?" Then a question about, say, one's grooming habits, the tile color in the Directorate's bathrooms, or "What do you think the lifespan of a goldfish is?" Then, while giving the same suspicious and nodding nonresponse to all of your answers, they ask you the original question again several times, making you repeat yourself until your mind effectively gets dissociated from your answers and your words completely lose their meaning.

After more than four hours of having to remember and explain every minute detail of what he had learned about the Smith operation over the last few days, and even retrace and clarify his whereabouts and actions prior to getting the call from Weiss that night in Yonkers, Russ felt mentally and physically drained. Where do they find them? These humorless creatures with slit-eyed stares full of mistrustful detachment, a trademark look of their creed—there are no innocents. His patience was wearing thin, but he knew he had to maintain an easygoing front and keep his composure or the whole cycle of questioning would begin again and again with no end in sight.

"Are we about done here?" he asks cautiously, sensing a lull in the intensity of questioning.

The two I.I. agents look at one another, and then down at their Allcom displays.

"For now," the chunkier of the two says. "Stay vigilant, Mr. Oakley, we're under attack."

"Stay vigilant?" Russ wanted to ask. "You mean like how you guys stayed vigilant while Sheng Long dick-rammed you like it's anal bonanza night at the sex slave education camp?" Instead, he nods reassuringly as they get up to leave. "Anything I can do to help."

"Thank you," says the other agent, without gratitude. "We'll be in touch."

A minute after the I.I. agents leave, Pratt shows up at the door, his usual fuming self.

"Can you believe this shit?" Pratt barks.

"Fucking audacious," Russ concurs, thinking that he's talking about the I.I.

"I've been warning everyone who'd listen about Sheng Long encroaching on our interests in the West for ages," Pratt continues. "Nobody fucking listens. You let them get away with pissing on your lawn, they'll end up shitting in your cornflakes."

Pratt calms down a bit as he crosses the room and drops into a seat that's still warm from the chunky agent's ass.

"I'm not much of a schmaltz peddler, but it's good to see your face around here," Pratt cracks a half-smile. "Welcome back."

"Just in time for the I.I. witch hunt..."

"You know how it is when they get Jimmy legs."

"Sheng Long, huh?"

"Fucking hirelings! It's time they get cut down to size. We gotta hit them hard for this."

"Is that why you brought me back in? To smash some skulls? You thought a little agent role play would cheer me up?"

"Stop that self-pitying shit, it's embarrassing. You're a little banged-up, that's all. It doesn't mean you should spend the rest of your days in a box. You still have a good head on your shoulders. I know you're miserable at DOA, who wouldn't be? I'm trying to get you out of there, plug you back in. I need good people, people I can trust."

"Well, thank you," Russ flashes a content smirk, then fetches a tablet out of his bag. "Since I have you here, there's something you should see."

"What is it?"

"It's a recording of Augustus Smith at some environmental panel about a year and a half before he died."

"Augustus Smith?" Pratt gives Russ a perplexed look. "What panel?"

"Just watch it, it'll take you a minute," Russ starts the

video. "I skipped ahead to the key part."

It's a medium-wide shot of a chock-full, midsize auditorium. On a small stage, three people are sitting in a semi-circle facing the audience, one of them is speaking.

*"... and before we hurry and proclaim ourselves winners of history, we should really ask this question..."*

"This is Mitchum Brown. He was the head of Degrowth Northeast at the time," Russ explains.

*"How are we really better than the generations that came before us?"* Brown continues. *"Is it only because we have slicker tools and shinier toys to help us alleviate the hardships of our short existence? As we developed as a species, we became more and more dependent on technology, and by extension, we now define any progress as material progress to the severe detriment of our moral and cultural development.*

*Our blind faith in technology is leading us astray and straight into a trap, a trap that swallowed many great civilizations before us and will certainly enable our own to effectively self-destruct if we don't change our ways. Mr. Smith certainly knows what I'm talking about. It's called the progress trap.*

*History is littered by great civilizations that robbed the future to pay the present, squandering their natural resources on an audacious binge of excess and grandstanding until they collapsed. The same thing is happening right now, on the grandest of scales. Unlike our ancestral future eaters, we will not get a second or third chance to try this again. We're all in. This is it. By declaring the bottom line our new god and the world market our new messiah, we managed to put the entire human experiment at risk of permanent decline. Material progress and its embodiment, growth, has a nasty trait—it creates problems that could be solved only by further growth. We have fallen victim to our inventions, our disastrous creativity, our shortsightedness. We clearly made too much material progress too quickly, while our cultural progress has been neglected. We need to reverse this course, change our priorities—and do it right now. Our bad habit of compulsive consumption has become an incurable addiction enabled only by indiscriminate exploitation of natural capital, leading to an ecological disaster and destruction of our habitat. How much can nature take before snuffing us out? How much longer do we have before this course of ruin becomes irreversible? Maybe we're already past that point."*

Mitchum Brown pauses for a moment, letting the auditorium fill with his words while gazing back into the silent crowd as if he's looking for affirmation, and then continues, dialing down his prescient tone a bit.

*"Here, today, I represent only a small regional cell of Degrowth Northeast, but I think I speak for tens of millions of members of Degrowth movements around the world whose voices are ignored by the establishment or written off as prophecies of doom. Our message is unequivocal. We must transform our deeply troubled socioeconomic model into one based on ecological economics and a fair distribution of resources. This can only be accomplished by a de-escalation of the deadly cycle of production and consumption and the creation of new forms of democratic institutions that will ensure that sustainability becomes the number one priority in our social dialogue—and the true measure of progress.*

*But, before we can hope to achieve any success at all, we need to challenge the entrenched beliefs and practices that led us to this dead end, reexamine the consequences of our collective decisions, and accept the existential responsibilities that we have toward one another. We're all here together on this Earth. We need to curtail our obsession with material progress and embrace the idea of cultural progress. Only by changing this paradigm can we hope to change our circumstance. In this light, we need to be exceptionally wary of the fatalism of technology, because technology is the main instrument of material progress. By presenting itself as the best hope that humankind has, technology reduces the complex questions of the human condition to a series of simplistic off/on solutions, ignoring the cultural factors in the process. Perhaps the most dangerous aspect of this dynamic is a paradox of sorts—technological advances, in general, create conditions that require exponentially more resources to sustain the trajectory of material progress they're creating, thereby causing increased damage to the world. Incessant consumption is a doomsday machine. I know, Mr. Smith's kind hates to hear this, but it's the truth."*

Brown turns to Augustus with a baiting grin.

*"Go ahead, I'm listening."* Augustus fends him off politely. *"You're making a compelling argument."*

*"When the Wright Brothers attained the once impossible dream of flight, nobody could have predicted the far-reaching consequences of their success."* Brown continues. *"This incredible triumph of human ingenuity, the crown jewel of the Second Industrial Revolution, launched a new era of material progress, pushing the limits of growth past geographical constraints, accelerating the world market to the point of complete interconnectedness and interdependence that we're living in today. Now, a little over a hundred years later, we can enjoy fresh apples in February in New York, days after they've been picked in an orchard in Chile. Or we can just say to hell with the snow and in a few hours we can be basking in the Caribbean sun, sipping on a Czech beer from a glass made in Vietnam.*

*Progress, you say. But at what cost? How many acres of arable land in Eastern Africa have been turned into barren wasteland just to extract enough ore to make our airplanes? How many tons of poisonous sludge have been dumped into Chinese forests by the aluminum smelter who processed that ore? How many farmers lost their orchards to the international conglomerate that consolidated the Chilean apple industry by killing off the local economy and diversity of the local crops and replacing them with a genetically modified kind designed to ripen in the dark warehouses of the world market? What are the long-term consequences of fracking wastewater seeping into North American waterways or the destruction of oceanic life caused by deepwater drilling off the coast of Brazil? How many billions of gallons of petrol have been burned to power these planes? How many people died or lost their livelihoods due to floods, droughts, crop failure, mudslides, or wildfires, consequences of abnormal climatic patterns caused by excessive amounts of carbon dioxide in the atmosphere?*

*This is the true cost of material progress. It's the cost that the powers-that-be repeatedly refuse to acknowledge because it reveals the flaws of their economic models, which value only what can be commoditized for human consumption in the global marketplace. Anything that doesn't fit that definition, anything that cannot be monopolized, marketed, and sold is deemed worthless. We don't want to change who we are in order to live in harmony with nature; we want nature to live in harmony with us while we remain who we are. That's not going to work. There are limits to this vicious circle of overconsumption and disregard for the environment. Just because these limits are not yet fully visible does not mean they don't exist. We can depend on the corporate machinery of progress to be only interested in continuing the status quo, even as things get worse. It's up to us to change things around before it's too late, by changing the minds and hearts of the people who are still struggling to understand the urgency with which we need to act."*

The crowd applauds vigorously as Mitchum Brown finishes, and some stand up and shout:

*"Degrowth! Degrowth!"*

*"Mr. Smith,"* says the moderator, shuffling some papers on a small glass table in front of him. *"As a member of the technological elite, I'm sure you have some insights you'd like to share with us."*

*"Technological elite?"* Augustus glances at the moderator. *"I don't know what the technological elite even is. I'm not here to represent some marching army of technocrats if that's*

*what you're implying."*

*"I apologize. Poor choice of words. I meant to say 'as an established technologist...'"*

*"It's alright,"* Augustus smiles. *"I've been called worse."*

*"Anyhow, what is your take on these complex issues Mr. Brown was talking about?"*

Augustus leans forward in his chair, clasps his hands together in front of his face, and rests his chin on his thumbs.

*"Dare I say, I think the next few years will probably be the most important time in modern human history. Our survival as a species depends on the wisdom of the actions we need to take in order to reverse the effects of economic expansion based on fossil fuels and build a new socioeconomic model based on sustainability and regard for the environment. If we fail, if we degrade the ecosystem so deeply that it can no longer sustain us, nature will just shrug it off, wrap up its unsuccessful human experiment, and continue without us. That is, of course, the worst-case scenario—but it's entirely plausible if we don't act without delay. If we're to save ourselves from this self-inflicted calamity we need to rise above our technological and cultural limitations and prove ourselves worthy of our place on Earth. It's going to be extremely hard, and we must be prepared to accept any outcome.*

*Mr. Brown suggested that we need a cultural revolution of sorts to bring environmental issues to the fore of the public discussion. I couldn't agree more, but I think it would be very naive to rely solely on cultural progress to solve our problems. We can't catapult the entire world population into some magical state of higher consciousness overnight. The world might seem closely knit due to our shared destiny, but in fact, it's little more than a random collection of billions of individuals or small groups guided by self-interests and the blind pursuit of short-term gains.*

*This lack of ability to look beyond immediate reward and foresee the long-term consequences of our actions might be an inherent part of the human condition, wrought into our psyche by the long history of living hand to mouth. Deep down in our bones, we know that life is short and hard, and we'll grab at whatever is in front us with little concern for tomorrow. Nobody wants to be the person who cuts down the last tree, but achieving the global political consensus required to make the changes needed in time to make a difference is going to be close to impossible. The purpose of this cultural revolution should be to create political and economic conditions for these changes, and it will be up to science and technology to carry them out. Science is not..."*

A few mild disruptive boos and disapproving whistles come from the crowd then taper off quickly.

*"Science is not a one-time, all-or-nothing endeavor,"* Augustus continues. *"It's a process of refining our understanding of the universe and, if our model doesn't fit reality, adding details or changing the model altogether. Technology can't defeat nature. We need to better understand our world, the intrinsic laws of nature, and life—so we can learn from it. Along with the fact that they're not very effective, today's renewables depend on certain decidedly nonrenewable resources. They are a partial and haphazard solution. Our problems require a holistic approach. We need to develop new technologies that will allow us to live in harmony with nature rather than in this grave conflict we've created. So, to counter Mr. Brown, we need more technology not less—but we need better technology. Much better technology, real breakthroughs, first and foremost, in information processing and power generation..."*

*"Breakthroughs?"* A man shouts from the crowd. *"Like your last invention? You're a fraud. Get off the stage!"*

*"Excuse me?"* says Augustus.

*"How can you sit there and preach that nonsense with a straight face. You are the problem. People like you are the problem, paid agents of corporate interests deployed to confuse the masses with your lies!"*

Augustus turns to the moderator.

*"Sir, please sit down. We're trying to have a civil discussion,"* the moderator tries to calm the man.

*"Do you even know who Augustus Smith is?"* the man asks as he looks around the auditorium. *"He's the inventor of the Rapid Cellulose Solvent, the RCS enzyme that turns plants into oil. This production method is now being used by plundering corporations to systematically destroy our forests and burn them off as oil. I don't need his opinion on how to stop global warming. Do you?"*

Murmurs cascade through the crowd.

*"I'm sorry, Mr. Smith,"* the moderator turns to Augustus.

*"What's your name?"* Augustus addresses the man.

*"What do you care?"*

*"I just like to know who I'm talking to."*

*"It doesn't matter what my name is."*

*"All right. I'm not going to apologize for what I do, but I will answer you because you seem to be uninformed. I'm actually very proud of RCS because it gives us a commercially viable option to use renewable resources like plants to generate power. This process is carbon neutral because it does not result in fossil carbon being released into the atmosphere. All carbon contained in biofuel was absorbed from the atmosphere by photosynthesis in plants just a few months or years earlier. This means that when you burn biofuel, you simply release the carbon back into the atmosphere where it came from. There's no overall effect on atmospheric carbon dioxide levels in the long term.*

*In contrast, fossil fuels contain carbon that has been locked up underground for millions of years and it isn't balanced out by photosynthesis. Now, about cutting the forests down. The RCS enzyme is engineered to work with algae and switchgrass feedstock, not trees. I'll admit that while RCS technology represents a clear improvement in the way in which we approach power generation, it's hardly the monumental breakthrough we desperately need. It's just one of many small technological successes we've achieved in pushing back looming limits.*

*The problem with incremental progress is that these successes help create widespread confidence in existing models, which could be a very dangerous situation. What if the technological improvements are entering a terminal phase of diminishing returns? What if simple upgrades to our current way of thinking simply won't do in the near future? Cultural progress is possible only because of technological progress, they're inseparable. If it weren't for technological progress we'd be still living in caves..."*

Another man jumps up from the third row and charges toward the stage, yelling.

*"Stop deceiving these people! We know who you are. You're an agent of big business. It's people like you who enable this insanity to go on. You and your dirty schemes."*

*"Jared, no!"* Mitchum Brown yells out, but it's too late.

The man jumps on the stage, runs up to Augustus, and punches him so hard that Augustus falls off the chair. The man continues by kicking him in the stomach until Augustus somehow wraps his arms around his legs and pulls him down. The man flies off the stage headfirst. His face bounces off the floor twice before the security team grabs him by his arms. As they carry him out, he keeps wrestling and kicking, his face covered in blood.

*"You will burn for this!"* he shouts.

"That's about it," Russ says, and then stops the video.

"So?" Pratt swings in his chair. "Degrowth didn't like Smith. Why's that relevant? Those pigeon pricks didn't like anyone."

"Yeah, but this guy who punched him, Jared Hiebert..."

"What about him?"

"He gets five months on an assault charge, then while

in prison has a psychotic episode, ends up doing the thorazine shuffle for another eleven months, and then gets released, supposedly all fixed up, a week before Smith's lab catches fire. Then Hiebert falls off the face of the Earth."

"And?"

"Four years later, he gets arrested for fire-bombing a research facility at Dartmouth College. Two dead. It turns out he belonged to the ultra-radical wing of the Degrowth movement called Cease and Desist, responsible for a number of violent acts against businesses and individuals throughout the northeast. Destruction of property, kidnappings, assassinations of politicians, bankers, and business leaders."

"I know who they were. My old boss Sam Trout, took part in their eradication. They were really just a jumble of small, independent groups that were loosely connected around the same idea, mostly off the grid, difficult to pin down. They chased them for years throughout the Adirondacks, Maine, and Vermont. It turned out that some of those groups were actually paid corporate assassins and saboteurs, hired by big oil and big pharma, believe it or not. They got them all in the end."

"Apparently, due in no small part to the hard work of Jared Hiebert. According to the records he became a cooperator, hoping to avoid the death penalty, which he did, ending up instead with forty with no parole—but soon after he suffered another breakdown and was back in the nuthouse, this time for good. He's still at a CP facility up in Chester."

"So, you think he set the fire to Smith's lab then fled to the woods to join the others?"

"Probably, although he never admitted to it."

"So, even if he did it makes no difference now. Why dig through it? It's not going to bring Smith back. We have more pressing things to do than solving an ancient murder."

"Part of me thinks we owe it to Theo Smith to set the record straight."

“I guarantee you that’s the least of his worries at this moment.”

“I’d like to go up to Chester, to see Hiebert anyway. It’s a half-day trip.”

“What do you expect to get out of him? His brain’s been pickled for decades. It’ll be like talking to a three-year-old.”

“That might be, but you never know, it might help us.”

“Do what you want, but I’m telling you, it’s going to be a waste of time.”

After six hours of uneventful driving, the strain of the sleepless night finally caught up with Moonie. His head bobbed down and up like a rooster pecking for grain in slow motion. He was thoroughly exhausted but hopeful that this cat-and-mouse game with the bad guys might have run its course. He knew he could easily be wrong. There was no way of telling if Sheng Long was still at their heels, or how far their influence extended. The way in which the PSCs operate is very much the way the gangs do—it's all about controlling the territory, and this part of New America—Wyoming, Northern Colorado, the Dakotas, and the western part of Nebraska—is Claymore country, at least according to Driggs. He would know, he enjoyed their protection for years despite being badly wanted by Texas. Sheng Long can still outsource plenty of freelance bandits everywhere, but it will be more difficult for them to put something together further away from their sphere of influence. The roads won't be crawling with squads of manhunters out here in the ass of nowhere, that's for sure.

He catches a glimpse of the swollen bell pepper that was once his nose in the rearview mirror. It's turned from red to purple, probably broken. His nasal passage is clotted with a crusty mix of blood and snot and it hurts like hell every time he tries to breathe through it. His right eye looks even worse, bloody and half-closed. Up ahead he sees a sign for a rest area and switches lanes.

"No dawdling. Ten minutes max," he tells Miles.

They climb up a small mound overlooking the main road to an abandoned rest area building and park next to a row of crooked benches dying a slow death under lonely trees. They take a few minutes to walk off the stiffness and pee. Moonie then fetches a first aid kit and, using the side mirror of the truck, starts cleaning his face with an antiseptic wipe. Once he's finished, he squeezes some antibacterial ointment onto a gauze pad and tries to push some of it up his nostrils. Miles watches him struggle with it in pain.

"Let me try," he takes the gauze pad from Moonie. "It's easier if I do it. Just stay still."

Miles gently pushes the gauze pad up each of Moonie's nostrils then puts some more ointment on a fresh gauze pad and applies it to the cuts and grazes on Moonie's face.

"There..."

He dabs up a few drops of Moonie's sweat and involuntary tears leftover on his cheeks with the dry end of the pad.

"Like new," declares Miles.

Suddenly they hear seven or eight bursts of automatic gunfire ripping through the air nearby. Moonie grabs Miles by the arm and pulls him to the ground. They hide behind the truck, intently watching both sides of the road. Nothing happens for a few minutes; then, a rumbling sound of big engines approaches from behind the hills. With one hand clasping Miles's shoulder and the other tightly clenching his gun, Moonie pokes his head out and sees a light armored vehicle with an unmanned machine gun on its turret driving from the direction opposite of where they came from, followed by four double fuel tankers. The convoy barrels by in a cloud of dust then, about fifteen seconds later, another light armored vehicle with its turret machine gun facing backward speeds by, following the others.

After a minute or two, three black pickup trucks appear on the road in pursuit of the fuel convoy. On closer look, Moonie sees that the pickups have been modified into improvised combat vehicles, with grafted armored plating on the sides and makeshift armored domes on their cargo beds.

"What's happening out there?" Miles peeks from behind the truck.

"Stay down," Moonie pulls him back somewhat forcefully. "Gas pirates," he explains without elaborating.

They wait a few minutes after the pickups vanish from sight to make sure no others are coming, then get in the truck and drive off in a haste. About five miles down the road they come across an overturned car by the side of the debris-littered road.

"Looks like the fuel convoy escaped the ambush here and they took chase after them," Moonie muses out loud.

"That's crazy," Miles responds. "I heard stories about gas pirates before, but I never thought this stuff was real."

"Things you learn hanging out with me," Moonie cracks up.

It doesn't take long for the tedium of the high desert scenery to lull them back into a driving stupor. With the adrenaline rush of the gas pirates encounter gone, Moonie feels the fatigue pressing back down upon him, messing with his focus and softening his grip on the wheel. He swerves to the side a few times, but the rasping noise of the shoulder gravel snaps him back to attention each time. From the corner of his eye Miles watches him shifting in his seat, occasionally rubbing his eyes between deep sighs.

"You know, I can drive," Miles says after a while with intention in his voice.

"Yeah? You know how to drive?"

"Sure I do," Miles answers without hesitation.

"Theo lets you drive?"

"He does. Around town. Sometimes on the open road too."

"But can you actually drive? Unaided? Anyone can drive with the autonomous drive turned on."

"I can drive," Miles says with confidence.

"Wanna drive?"

"Are you sure?"

"Are *you* sure?"

"What do you mean?"

"Are you sure you can drive without the computer's help?"

"Oh. Yeah, I'm sure."

"Okay then. Let's give it a try."

Moonie pulls over and they get into each other's seats. Miles is apprehensive behind the wheel at first. He has never driven a truck before. It seems loftier from the driver's seat, heavy and huge, almost too big for one lane, the chunky gas pedal tricky to gauge.

"You're doing great," Moonie encourages him. "Next sixty miles or so is straight as an arrow. Just keep it on the road."

"I think I can do that much," says Miles half-jokingly.

"I'm gonna shut my eyes for a second. If I fall asleep, wake me up when you see Hoovers. It's the only thing around for miles, you can't miss it."

Moonie reclines his seat halfway down and stretches back with a mix of a sigh and yawn. Two minutes later he's out, his mouth still open, as though he was meaning to say one last thing but fell asleep before he could fashion the words.

How lucky he was to run into Moonie of all people, Miles thinks. The PSCs would have eventually caught him if it weren't for him. And although Miles never asked him to, Moonie did not hesitate for one second to take responsibility for him, never once making Miles feel like he's a burden to him. That's what good people do, they help when they see a friend in trouble. They're there through good times and bad.

After a few wobbly miles, the initial sensation of being overwhelmed wears off and Miles manages to get a steady hold of the steering wheel. The monotony of the highway sets in, a landscape without character repeating itself on an endless loop, Moonie's breathing dropping in and out against the unchanging grind of the wheels.

Miles feels a wave of sadness sneak upon him. How is he ever going to find his parents? Maybe they should all have had BodyBeacon ICs installed in their armpits after all. He remembers his mom bringing it up one time after some widely publicized child disappearance story played out in the media, but his dad was against it.

"No. No," he was adamant. "It's another instrument of control over us and we're not going to voluntarily subject ourselves to it."

"Lots of people are doing it," Maritza argued.

"That doesn't mean we should."

"Why not? I feel like it would give me peace of mind to know where Miles is at all times. Things happen. You never know," Maritza tried to make a point.

"Do you realize what that circuit does?" Theo went on. "Location tracking is just a side feature. It's a bioauditor, first and foremost. It constantly monitors your body's internal environment. It records every breath you've ever taken, every heartbeat, every galvanic skin response. It knows when you're excited, when you're sad, frightened, tired, drunk, and hungry. We're not going to give some faceless entity unlimited access to our bodies."

"Lighten up. Not everything is a big conspiracy."

"Sure, but this thing, in the wrong hands, could be an absolute nightmare."

Well, it certainly would have helped right now, Miles thinks. "Things happen..." his mother's words echo in his mind.

A cluster of bald-topped hills, fringed by chunks of rugged grass, spring up on the horizon, like a band of jolly Franciscan monks about to break out into beer-soaked song. In the barren, flat piece of land between the hills, the awkward structure of Hoovers comes into sight. A bank of giant rectangular boxes wrapped in black armored glass, a megalith of deployed retail laid out on its side.

"Moonie," Miles gives Moonie a push on the shoulder. "Moonie, wake up," he tries again to no avail.

He taps the breaks a few times in succession. The truck stutters, rocking them forward and back like rowers in adjacent lanes who inevitably end up synchronizing their strokes during a long race.

"What's going on?" Moonie rouses out of his nap, disoriented by the turbulence.

"Hoovers. You said to wake you up when we got to it."

"Right," Moonie wipes the sleep out his uninjured eye. "How long was I out?"

"A little less than an hour."

"Seen anyone on the road?"

"A few cars. An eighteen-wheeler, about twenty minutes ago, went the opposite way."

Moonie sits up, snaps the seat back in place, glances at the rearview mirror, then assesses the Hoovers lot in the distance. It seems empty.

"How's it looking?" Moonie cranes towards the command panel.

"All out of diesel. The battery is down to twenty-eight percent."

"Not too bad. We could have made it to Casper without stopping. Still, we should have charged the batteries right away when we got to the hotel. My fault. I thought I'd do it in the morning, before breakfast, but I guess our plans changed rather abruptly."

"So, what exactly happened to you last night?" Miles asks.

"As I told you, I couldn't fall asleep, too wired I guess. I went down to the lounge for a drink and I'm sitting all by myself when this guy comes at me for no reason whatsoever. He starts yelling at me, 'Who the hell do you think you are? What the fuck do you think you're doing? You messed with the wrong guy,' this and that, keeps blabbering about some girl. He was so drunk, he probably thought I was someone else. Bam! He smashes my head against the bar. What was I supposed to do?"

"He got you real good."

"You should have seen him after I was done whooping his ass."

"Yeah, but why did we have to run out in the middle of the night like that?"

"I didn't want to chance it with the police. I thought it would be best that we split in case they came knocking on the door."

"That makes sense," says Miles after mulling it over for a moment.

"Don't worry too much, everything's gonna work out kiddo. I don't know how, but it will."

Miles gives him a purse-lipped smile. As they drive closer, huge billboards pop up on the side of the road:

*"Hoovers - Your Friend Wherever You Are"*

*"Hoovers - Your Neighborhood Store Off the Beaten Path"*

*"Hoovers - Always There For You"*

The off-ramp forks into three lanes, each carving a narrow passage through the fifteen-foot-high concrete wall encircling the compound. Floating just above the pavement, an arch of neon-green holographic text appears: "*Welcome to Hoovers. Please present your device at the gate."*

They slow down and roll through the holo up to the reinforced concrete gate. Moonie scans his Allcom. As the gate parts, another holographic text arch appears: *"Welcome to Hoovers. Our Door Is Always Open."*

"Right," Moonie scoffs at the absurdity of the slogan's placement.

Some sixty feet ahead they enter a tunnel that broadens into a small underground square containing two dozen shopping pens separated by gleaming steel pipes. They pull into one of the pens and kill the engine.

*"Hello, Max Madigan. Welcome to the Hoovers shopping experience!"* The Hoovers augment pops up on the holo in front of them. *"Please use your device to choose the items you wish to purchase, then proceed to the retrieval gate to claim your merchandise."*

Moonie shuffles through the holographic replica of a supermarket and begins selecting items from the virtual isles: water, convenience foods and snacks, powdered QuickStrike, two T-shirts for Miles, aspirin, a few packets of coffee crystals, and a medical kit. They wrap up at the supermarket and head to the automotive center at the end of the tunnel only to find the diesel pumps locked.

*"Sorry Max, it appears that this item is out of stock,"* Hoovers's augment chimes in.

"Skank ass bitches," Moonie can't resist throwing an insult at invisible villains in control of Hoovers's diesel supply.

They pick up their order at the retrieval gate, then once outside, leave the truck to charge at the far end of the lot, away from the entrance. They then walk a short distance to one of the hexagonal concrete gazeboes scattered throughout the rest area. Inside the gazebo, they stretch out on a pair of comfortable foam-covered chaises facing the trembling reflection of the morning sun that's bouncing off the black-glass mirror of Hoovers's exterior. Miles shuts his eyes for a brief moment and takes in the faint scent of berries and dry grass carried by the breeze drifting from the mountains. A lone bird call cuts through the stillness, sharp-edged and distinct. A moment later the wind changes. The new wind feels warm on his face, bringing a hint of fire smoke with it.

"Nutrition pack one or nutrition pack two?" Moonie asks, holding two identical-looking yellow, white, and green boxes in his hands.

"What's the difference?"

"I have no idea."

"What's inside?"

"Nothing good I'm sure."

"One."

"Heads up! Incoming! Fallout shelter special number one," Moonie tosses one of the boxes Miles's way.

*Oops! What a ditz she is, Maritza giggles out* loud, feeling a cold liquid stream down her chin and neck and onto the sheets. She missed the mouth of the water bottle again. This nice man is trying to help her drink, but she can't take her eyes off the surfing images on the display. She didn't even know she was thirsty. Or hungry. But somehow, he did. He woke her up and told her "Maritza, you're hungry. You need to eat." And he was right. She had some crackers, and, yeah, oatmeal. The man helped her. He fed her with a spoon. He also gave her medicine. He said it would make her feel better. Which it did.

She remembers a brief moment when she felt sad when she woke up, not sure why, maybe because sometimes everyone feels a bit sad, but the medicine fixed that. It's gone now. She feels cheerful again. She wants to jump into the ocean and ride on that cotton puff surf forever, fly, barefoot and unencumbered, over the mist-filled surface, until the water calms down in a mirror and spills her back out. Then she will lay down on the soft coral sand, soaking the sun into her body, recharging her muscles, and watching the kids run in and out of the water, chased by the waves.

"Do you have kids?" she turns her eyes to Drey.

He looks at her without answering.

"I want a kid one day," she slurs the words. "Kids are awesome."

Drey helps her take a few more sips of water, then waits

until her head sags to the side and her eyes close again. He lowers her upper body onto the bed, tucks her in, and leaves.

*Russ gets out of the taxi in DUMBO, then on* foot, continues under the Brooklyn Queens Expressway overpass, toward the Eastern District of New York court building, where, in the three-story underground garage they shared with other Commonwealth agencies, ACIS keeps their fleet vehicles. The car was supposed to come and get him at the landing, but it was deemed unsafe to travel unattended because of the risk of being vandalized by protesters.

As he strides upslope along Cadman Plaza, he hears a hum, not unlike a flying ant swarm, hovering in midair. Gradually, the hum breaks up into a cacophony of cheers, jeers, and muffled cries and he sees clamoring groups of people carrying protest signs pouring into the plaza's park from side streets, joining the already sizable crowd amassed in front of the court building. Most of the protestors are wearing face privatizers or impromptu masks made of bandanas or shawls. A few of them have visored motorcycle helmets on with small boxes attached on top that shoot green and purple lasers to disrupt the face recognition cameras.

"Respect existence or expect resistance!" Russ can now hear individual voices shouting emphatically.

A song breaks out somewhere in the middle.

"We are the proud, we are not few, there is no me, there is no you. We stand united in our plight. Make it right or we will fight! Make it right or we will fight! Make it right or we will fight!" Booming chants spread through the crowd.

Russ backs up from the protesters, makes a long circle around the park, and approaches the court building from the rear. There, along the concrete barrier wall ascending from the bowels of the courthouse, a squadron of anti-riot police officers at the ready watches the protest, waiting. Russ walks up to the guard booth at the entrance of the garage.

"Lots of commotion today," Russ flings his thumb behind his shoulder.

The guard gives him a quick, incurious glance.

"Everybody's gotta eat," he says flatly and waves him through.

He invited Miriam to join him on the trip to Chester. It's not much of a getaway, but the leaves upstate are beginning to turn, and although it will be a good month or so until they peak, they'll certainly get a nice preview of autumn's visual crescendo, which comes into being this time of year, when the entire northeastern seaboard seems like it spontaneously bursts into flames and shrouds itself in hundreds of shades of red, purple, orange, yellow, and brown, one last glorious fireworks display of nature's vigor before the cold, colorless winter takes hold.

Getting out of Brooklyn in the sparse midday traffic wasn't much of a pain and soon enough they were on the I-87 North, cruising along the disowned streets of the South Bronx.

"Everybody's gotta eat." The guard's plain, vapid declaration stuck in Russ's mind. It really does come down to that, doesn't it? It's the sole reason every living thing exists. To grab, rip, catch, kill—to eat. To suck the life out of something so you can go on living yourself. It's why the hawk has its talons and the snake packs the poison, and how humans can pretend to justify the horrible things they do to one another.

Absorbed in her Allcom, Miriam types and chuckles by turns.

"What's so funny?" Russ asks.

"Oh. Nothing. Just Allison being Allison."

"Who's the new guy?"

"Another crackerjack fella judging by the state of her infatuation. Class Three Citizen of the Manhattan Corporate. Thirty-seven, no kids, six-bedroom place in one of the Spireon buildings in Chelsea. Old money it seems."

"She likes her princes."

"Why do you always have to put people in boxes? You don't even know the guy."

"I'm sure that deep down he's just like the rest of us. Once you take away the entitlement that comes with the Class Three Citizenship. After all, he's mixing with the plebs, how stuck up can he be?"

"They're going to a farm retreat in North Fork next week."

"Yeah? What do you do on a farm retreat?"

"Work the farm I guess, hang out with the farmers, pretend you're one of them for a week. Would you wanna do something like that?"

"I can certainly pretend, but I don't know how much farmwork I can do in my present state."

"You can milk the goats..." Miriam chortles.

"Maybe I'll get a powered exoskeleton," Russ grins. "Have one of the combat models adopted for farmwork."

"... or bake a pie," Miriam adds.

"Oh, I'd bake your pie anytime," Russ leers at her.

The foliage spectacle did not disappoint. Dripping with earthy pigments, an invisible painter's brush transformed the Catskills into a bucolic fairytale backdrop. The golden glow of freshly cut wheat fields amid fiery tree crowns, plump black-and-white cows patiently grazing their way up to a dairy barn atop round green hills, a troop of horses trotting free in the meadows, their long manes billowing in the wind. They even saw a family of deer drinking indulgently at a brook, staring back at them with anthracite eyes.

Through her inexhaustible friend-of-a-friend network,

Miriam found a beautiful converted stone barn just outside town for them to stay in. The place is an impeccable mix of new and old, charming and functional, its unique design and fine detailed work suggesting that it was done with patience and love.

As soon as they get in, like a high jumper with a lively three-step run-up, Miriam throws herself on a white canvas sofa occupying the middle of the enormous living room. Lush pillows absorb her body with a cozy embrace. With her hair spilled out in a halo, she lays unmoving while Russ unpacks, gazing at the twilight rays and shadows dancing through the tree branches in the skylight.

"C'mon, let's go to town," Russ finishes unpacking.

"I'm not going anywhere," Miriam replies. "Let's have dinner here."

Kenji couldn't find a restaurant that delivers, so Russ gets back in the car and drives to town. Chester looks dim under the brownout. Pizza shop, liquor store, bar, and a couple of restaurants are still open. The old-fashioned diner on Main Street is jam-packed. It seems like the whole town has assembled there for a communal meal. Russ places a to-go order then goes to the liquor store to buy wine. With not much to choose from, he settles on some Hudson Valley Cabernet Franc, picks up the food from the diner, and heads back.

In the darkness, from outside, their elegant abode looks like just another old barn. The door's open and the lights are off, but Miriam isn't there.

"Miriam!" Russ yells out.

No answer.

"Miriam!"

He turns the lights on, drops the food and wine on the kitchen counter, and then walks up a wooden staircase to the second floor. He checks the bedrooms and upstairs bathroom—empty.

"Kenji, call Miriam."

Her Allcom pings and flashes on the living room coffee table then settles back into standby. A wave of unease spirals through Russ. He hears a voice and rushes outside. Halfway up a grassy hill that raises from the creek bed behind the barn, he sees a silhouette in motion and breathes a sigh of relief.

"Hey! Whatcha doing out here?" Russ asks Miriam.

"Come up," Miriam hollers out. "Bring everything up here."

After Russ left to town, Miriam went out for a walk around the property and found a lookout point on top of the hill, with a beautiful view of Chester Valley amid the wild currents of the Catskills Mountains. The owners have built a nice outdoor hangout with a round stone fire pit, large low-lying table, and chairs carved out of knotty tree stumps.

In a cedar hot tub to the side, reposed in a dreamlike state, with her face slightly obscured by a cloud of pale mist and her nipples piercing the surface of the water, Miriam is lazing away.

"Wine me," she extends her wrist, waving an invisible glass through the mist, then giggles at the silliness of it.

Russ opens the wine then fetches some logs from a nearby firewood shed and starts the fire in the pit. All those years of being pulled away from her, from his own life. How many perfect moments like this has he missed? A few sparks fly up in the air and escape the whipping flames, miniature airborne lanterns valiantly reaching for the infinite skies.

He strips naked and gets in the tub behind Miriam. Her body is warm and light in the water. She snuggles against his chest, rests her head on his arm, then turns around and looks at him silently for a second before leaning in and giving him a kiss. Short shivers run down her spine as she arches back, the fleeting Indian summer giving way to the first cold nibbles of the northern winds. She smacks him gently on the forehead then lifts her legs up on his shoulders and takes him in.

*"Boo-ya," Jiang mouths to himself, reviewing* the details of the Salt Lake City operation with the sort of impersonal curiosity one develops after years of being an invisible part of many battles and never having skin in any of them.

Now that it's pretty much out of his hands, the fact that the Smith kid and Belan are still at large, despite everything Sheng Long threw at them, almost brought a smirk of respect out of Jiang. Although he was well aware that, more often than not, he ended up fighting on the side of the corrupt and the nefarious, Jiang has never questioned his clients' motives or, for that matter, his own virtue. A pouncing lion has no moral ambiguities. A hurricane never turns back.

He knows the world is not just a playground of fiends and fairies. There are also people like him, invisible extensions of the hand that tips the scale of fate—friendly phantoms of unfair advantage or wicked avatars of bad luck, depending on which side you're on. Winning is the only thing that matters. The burden of consequence lies on the backs of the defeated.

A long time ago, he submitted to the inevitable. To become a true professional, one must be completely unencumbered by his own perception of what's right or wrong. But, in the way that cosmic justice works, he had to concede that Smith's kid getting away was a good thing. A young boy thrown into the big nasty world before his time beats the odds—a fitting outcome for a vintage sap story. It almost made Jiang feel something. Empathy maybe. Compassion. No, not toward

Miles but toward himself, toward the little boy who he once was, a long time ago, far away from here.

Jiang glances at the profile of the downed Sheng Long asset. Trevor E. Garza. Unaffiliated. Texas-born. Six months of formal training. Spanish speaker. A veteran of three previous Sheng Long jobs: Las Vegas, surveillance and data collection; Salt Lake City, personal security detail, secondary unit; long-range fugitive pursuit throughout the south and northern ex-Mex states. He'll live, but he won't be out dancing anytime soon. Belan took care of that back at the hotel. Jiang never would've guessed that he had it in him.

Jiang pushes away from his desk and rolls his chair to the edge of the glass wall of his office. Below, in the pits, second shift associates are shambling about, taking advantage of the 4:00 am slowdown to handle the three Rs: restroom, refuel, and recalibrate their terminals.

Vancouver riots are slowly but surely getting out of control—six more dead yesterday, two of them Sheng Long moles who got found out. One shot on the street in West Vancouver, the other one beaten to death by rioters and thrown into the narrows off the Lion's Gate Bridge. And now the shit storm is moving south. Seattle is bubbling over, and it seems like it's gonna blow soon. Jiang knows he needs to put more eyes on it; they need to stay ahead of the game and avoid another blunder.

He whirls back to his desk, checks the activity monitors for data flow stress, deems it optimal, then crosses over to the other side of the office and enters his private alcove studio through a tinted sliding glass door. He sniffs his armpits, briefly considers taking a shower, decides against it, then kicks off his shoes, plunges into the softness of the sofa cushions, and shuts his eyes.

*Moonie licks his fingers before reaching back* into a near-empty container of powdered Quickstrike, methodically probes the bottom and the corners, and scrapes up just enough for one more amphetamine hit. The powder dissolves quickly on his tongue, leaving a puffy metallic cloud in his mouth. The best stuff is always at the bottom, he thinks, languidly affirming one of life's great truths. Miles is almost out, struggling to keep his eyes open.

"Almost there, kiddo."

Miles nods, silently staring off at the nearly invisible horizon line ahead, beyond the reach of their headlights, where lumbering mountaintops fade into the big purple sky.

"Oh, I get it," Moonie smiles. "You wanna see Mount Rushmore, don't you?"

"Yeah. It's supposed to be around here somewhere," Miles brings up the map on the Allcom.

"They used to have these big reflectors at night, you could see them glowing in the dark for miles. Quite a sight. Not anymore, I guess."

"That's too bad."

"I don't have much interest in things that happened before I was born," Moonie declares blandly.

"You mean history?"

"Right."

"How do you know this guy, Driggs?" Miles asks after a few moments of silence.

"He's my business partner. Potential business partner, I should say. I ran some tests for him, now we'll see if we can make a deal."

"What kind of tests?"

"Mineral testing. He has this old abandoned gold mine on his property, so he thought it would be a good idea to look it over."

"And?"

"It looks like there could be something in there."

"Gold?"

"Nope. Something much better."

"What?"

"Rare earth elements. Do you know what those are?"

"Yes."

"Of course you do," Moonie smiles fondly. "But do you know that the rare earth elements are not that rare. There's plenty of that stuff in the Earth's crust. Now, the problem is, because of their geochemical properties they're scattered in tiny amounts all over the place. It's extremely hard to find a concentration of those elements big enough to form an actual mineral deposit. That's why they're called rare elements, not because they're scarce."

"So, did you find a big enough deposit at this guy's mine?"

"A lot of things have to come together to get to the exploitation phase, but it looks promising. Very, very promising."

"They're expensive, right, rare earth metals?"

"You bet your little acorn they are. There isn't much price flexibility either, the market is extremely tight. There are only six mines in the entire world that produce rare earths on a commercial level, and five of them are in Asia. This stuff is Meta-Tech magic dust. High powered lasers, high-resolution optics, microwave transmission, satellites, superconductors, precision-guided weapons, layered computer memory. None of that stuff would exist without rare earths. And that's only what we know is out there right now. For a miner, it's pretty much the best stuff you can find."

"Sounds like it."

"Just don't mention any of this to anyone at Driggs's. I gotta handle this whole thing with velvet gloves."

"What do you mean?"

"You'll get an idea when we get there. Just keep your mouth shut about everything I just told you okay?"

"I won't say a thing."

"Anybody asks you anything, pretend you're some dumb-ass kid who knows nothing. And stick to our story. I'm your uncle, I'm taking you to your grandparents in Denver."

The road abruptly turns uphill, carving its way through a maze of overhanging bluffs and roadside boulders. Off in the distance, above pine treetops, the contour of a head emerges. Then the straight line of a nose, the dim hollow of an eye below an arch of a brow.

"Is that it?" Miles looks up.

"That's it, kid."

The monument swells out of the darkness, trapping the frail moonlight in its curves. Massive, overwhelming, and unreal. It's hard to determine where the mountain ends and the work of a human hand begins. Moonie pulls over into the service lane directly across from the monument and kills the engine. They get out of the truck, silently gazing at the shapes and shadows chiseled into the ashen granite above, adhering to the gravitational pull of the sculpture.

"A lot of people think it would have been better for everyone if the big country never split up," says Miles after a while.

"Probably," says Moonie. "But who knows what's better?"

He draws a deep breath of fresh air, clasps his hands at the back of his head, and stretches away the stiffness with a soft grunt.

"When the money runs out the shit hits the fan real fast," he adds. "The whole world went down the tubes all at once. It's not like it coulda gone any other way for us."

The unyielding faces of the past presidents seem almost animate, yet remain wistfully defiant of earthly life, of rot and oblivion.

"Could have been a lot worse," Moonie goes on. "At least we're not at war with ourselves like everyone else seems to be."

"Peace and friendship with all mankind is our wisest policy," says Miles, prompting a baffled "Huh?" from Moonie.

"Thomas Jefferson said that," Miles explains.

"Yeah? I didn't know that. He's one of them up in the rocks?"

"Are you serious?"

"What?"

"You really don't know?"

"I told you, I don't care about that stuff. History to me is like a nicely wrapped box of fairytales that gets handed over from one generation to the next so that everyone feels better about themselves, hoping that there's some greater sense behind it all. Some people might think they can learn a thing or two from these stories, but in the end, that's all they are. Just stories. Life is something else."

"You have to know your history in order to make good decisions about your future," says Miles.

"Maybe. I try to enjoy what I have, while I have it."

"George Washington, Thomas Jefferson, Theodore Roosevelt, and Abraham Lincoln," Miles points at each of the figures carved in the rock with his finger, then turns to Moonie with a smile, "Just so you know."

"All right, now I know. Washington, Jefferson, Roosevelt, Lincoln," Moonie recites promptly. "Got it. Now, let's get going. I'm hungry."

They hop back in the truck. Twenty minutes later, a small constellation of blurry lights appears in the distance.

"How about this tiny bit of history?" Moonie says. "Those lights there, that's Lead. That little piece of shit town used to be the epicenter of the American gold mining business for one hundred twenty-five years. Can you believe that?"

Miles shrugs lackadaisically.

"That's where Homestake used to be," Moonie continues.

"What's Homestake?"

"All this, Black Hills, used to be Sioux land. Then in the 1870s, they found gold in Deadwood Creek, a little bit to the north from here. And so the Gold Rush ensues, thousands of get-rich-quick scoundrels storm the place, as it goes. But it was mostly placer gold, which is basically tiny nuggets that wash up in and around the streams. Once they turned the gulches over most people moved on, thinking it was over. But good prospectors knew that this placer gold eroded from hard rock deposits, so they snatched up the claims and started digging in the hills. Hundreds of mines all over the place. Then a small group of prospectors found the motherlode, right there, near Lead. That's Homestake. About a year after the discovery, George Hearst moves in and starts squeezing the small guys out. In a couple of years, he consolidates, expands the property, and starts exploitation. For the next one hundred twenty-five years, about ten percent of the world's gold supply came from Homestake. Yup."

"Wow," Miles says with muffled excitement.

"Tell me if I'm boring you with all this mining talk."

"No. Not at all. I'm just really tired."

"I hear you. I feel like I can sleep for twenty hours straight."

The only sound Jiang could hear over the steady hum of the engine was a gentle whoosh of the waves of the Tamsui river as they slowly steered toward the harbor, hidden under old fishing nets in the machine room of an old shrimp trawler. Then, a distant thunder of an exploding missile, followed by the incessant cackling of small arms, then his mother's soothing voice telling him and his sister that everything will be all right as she pressed their little heads closer to her chest.

It's been a long time since the dream last came to him. Five or six years, maybe longer. For a while, this recurring dream was the only constant in his whirlwind life and over time it became a narrative of its own, consistently infringing on his actual memory of that night. It gave him comfort, a reprieve from survivor's guilt, one more night with his family before the South China Sea took them away.

That memory, that dream, was all he had left of them. But can a five-year-old truthfully remember anything? Jiang certainly didn't remember much of what came after that night. The shipwreck, being fished out of the water by the coastal patrol of the Philippine Navy, or his days in the refugee collection center in Manila, really not much of anything before his new life with his new adoptive family on a new continent began. But he remembered that night when Taipei fell to mainland aggression, thirty-two years ago. Or was it the dream itself that became his memory—where does the truth now lie?

But this wasn't the same dream anymore. This time, his father was not with them under the nets in the machine room. He was standing outside, alone on the deck, watching the flickering Taipei skyline being sliced apart by glowing trails of antiaircraft bullets that pecked away at the night sky in vain, as Taiwan's Armed Forces scrambled to defend the city against descending attack helicopters. Alarm sirens wailed in the distance, growing in intensity and urgency. Jiang stirred around in his mother's warm embrace. He wanted to run out and join his father on the deck, to hold his hand. Maybe they can see their home from there, one last time.

Then the air trembled and an odd noise barged in from somewhere and filled the machine room with earsplitting turmoil. The boat began vibrating and wobbling, shrieking like a predator caught in a steel trap. The smell of fumes and heated metal, the motor grinding itself to pieces. A droning rumble careened upon them from the sky, rhythmic, almost melodic, and a boorish, grating voice began shouting verses down at them in English:

*It's all over now*
*You do understand*
*It's all over now*
*It's all over my friend*

Jiang jerks awake, panting, scared. Throbbing through the PA system, split-up by ominous percussive crashes, the droning sound still hovers over him, sirens still blaring their two-tone monition. The voice returns, now louder and harsher than before:

*So scoop up your brains*
*And stagger away*
*Find a place to die*
*It's still better than chains*

Jiang jumps up from the sofa and runs out into his office. The lights are off, his monitor display flickering helplessly on the desk. He tries accessing the mainframe by scanning his palm, but as he touches the display the gaping mouth of a rattlesnake lunges forward with a sharp hiss. The image freezes and the word *TERMINATED* starts flashing between the snake's bared fangs, accompanied by a burst of manic, diabolical laughter. The voice booms from above:

*Cause it's all over now*
*You should have known*
*When you raised your sword*
*You have killed your own*

The glass wall of his office suppresses panicked calls and shouts coming from the pits, but the chaos below is palpable. Black silhouettes are jostling against one another under pulsating red alarm lights, leaping between rows of seized displays, each one flashing the same *TERMINATED* message as his own.

That sound... Jiang remembers. That crackling, shrieking sound of the dying iceberg he's been hearing for the last eight days... They've been compromised all along!

Jiang grabs the master key from the drawer and rushes down a narrow stairwell that connects his office to the subterranean server farm caves. As he opens the door a wave of hot air, smelling of melted plastic and softened solder, smacks him across the face. Servers are aglow with frantic activity. It's worse than he thought.

"They have complete control of the facility," he realizes. "They're trying to burn us down now."

Cooling systems are jacked. Remote shutdown protocol should have been triggered by now. There's only one option left—manually shut down the power. As he rushes out to the Auxiliary Control Center, the voice from the PA system follows him down the hall like an anathema, bouncing against the concrete walls of the cave and growing more tyrannical with every step he takes.

*It's all over now*
*You do understand*
*It's all over now*
*It's all over my friend*

# DAY_5

*After twenty minutes of driving through the* twisted strip of woods and meadows surrounding Chester, the Correctional Psychology Center Building comes into full view. A graceful, lonely pile of blood-red brick confidently perched on top of a grass-carpeted hill, the mid-nineteenth century Gothic revival was originally a part of the van Gaal family estate and served as a summer house for three generations before it was endowed to a trust. It changed its purpose several times over the years, steadily attracting new layers of misfortune and suffering—a long-term shelter for battered women, an addiction treatment center, a halfway house, then finally, some thirty years ago, it became part of the Correctional Administration when the state decided to move the old CPC from Fishkill into it.

Majestic from afar, up close the building seems rather pointlessly complicated with its complex network of pointed arches, steeply pitched roofs, spires and towers, balconies, parapets, and tracery windows reinforced by iron bars. Russ follows the pea gravel walkway to the entrance door, which silently parts open, inviting him in. A young Asian woman in a light-pink uniform, with shoulder-length hair and eyes like coat buttons dipped in hot tar, checks his credentials and then disappears through a door behind the front desk counter, only to come back a moment later.

"Mr. Oakley?"

"Yes?"

"You are Mr. Oakley?"

"Yes," says Russ, confused by her insistence.

"Here to see patient Hiebert?"

Something about her seemed different.

"Yes. Jared Hiebert."

"We don't get many visitors here," she attempts a smile, then takes a few measured steps forward. "Please, come with me."

As they walk through a series of thick double-wing doors, five or six, an almost tactile funk of institutionalized misery, sweat, piss, chlorine, and enduring mold fused together in the fetid air, raising from the dark corners and squeezing his throat. A narrow-arched corridor leads them to an extended hallway. The woman leaves without much of an explanation, then reappears less than a minute later.

"Mr. Oakley. Here to see patient Hiebert?"

Just as he was about to yell out "Yes, I'm Mr. Oakley! And yes, I'm here to see patient Hiebert!" as loudly and assuredly as he possibly could so they might finally settle the issue of his identity and his interest in being here once and for all, it occurs to Russ that this might not be the same woman who walked him over here. Or the woman he saw at the entrance. He opts for a polite nod.

"Please, come with me. I'll take you to him," the woman says.

Of course! A small Asian woman, stereotypically the least threatening personification of the human species, the epitome of congeniality. Just like the one Sheng Long sent to Smith's house. He was sure now that this omnipresent woman is, in fact, three different people bearing an uncanny resemblance to one another. Bizarre but logical in its own way. Consistency. The illusion of permanence, instrumental in building a complacent environment. Someone, a person who's always there, unchanging, unchangeable, a caring pillar of mental support that people who ended up here were lacking throughout their entire lives.

They eventually get to the glass wall of a large room. Inside the room, a group of patients dressed in pastel yellow uniforms sit on the same pastel yellow-colored beanbag sofas and chairs watching some sort of program on the media display. They are motionless statues, completely absorbed by the action on the display, some dated, stripped-down comedy featuring real actors.

"We employ a lot of entertainment in the treatment," the woman says. "It keeps them sedated and it makes our jobs easier. Patient Hiebert was not very happy about missing showtime today, but we promised him an extra entertainment voucher, so most likely he'll be agreeable when you meet him."

Russ's attention turns to the odd-looking rimless mesh caps with sensors the patients are wearing.

"What's that on their heads?"

"Those are impression monitors."

"Impression monitors?"

"Yes. They measure the effectiveness of whatever program they're watching by monitoring their brainwave activity. Given the patients' decreased mental acuity, we're only observing the mechanism of emotional triggers, basically the emotional responses to aural and visual catalysts, plot developments, character transformations, news, and other kinds of curated information."

"And what do you do with the data you collect?"

"It helps us adjust the patients' therapy regimens."

"That's it?"

"Well, yes, the enhanced..."

"Because I can easily find out on my own..."

"Right," she says after a sharp stare. "Certain organizations are granted access to the data."

"Which organizations?"

"I don't know, but it's also used by marketing specialists and news and entertainment producers to optimize programming for the general audience."

"Optimize?"

"Adjust it for desired emotional impact."

Russ realizes that he should be careful asking questions that he really doesn't want to know the answers to. They walk up to another door. The woman presses her palm against the smooth surface of the access control reader and it clicks open. She silently motions Russ in and then leaves.

The room is small, windowless with padded walls. Two yellow beanbag chairs face each other, a single-leg table made out of soft rubber next to them. Hiebert is sitting in one of the chairs, his profile facing the entrance. Sure enough, there's another Asian woman in a pink uniform standing by the door, but this one is unmistakably different than the others. A good head taller, corpulent, with pronounced cheekbones, olive skin, and meaty lips. Her hands are clasped in front of her holding a thin, horsewhip-like taser wand. She nods as Russ enters.

"Jared, this is Mr. Oakley," the woman says in a loud voice. "He's going to ask you some questions. Please try your best to answer them."

"Okay," Hiebert replies faintly.

"Just like what Mr. Schumer talked to you about earlier."

"Okay."

Staring at the tips of his shoes or maybe examining the abstract pattern of the carpet under his feet, Hiebert barely acknowledges Russ as he takes the seat across from him.

"Jared, my name's Russell Oakley," Russ leans in a bit. "I work for the Atlantic Commonwealth Intelligence Service over in Brooklyn," he introduces himself, deliberately stretching out the pauses between words.

Hiebert bends his skinny neck closer to the ground like a tired bird looking for seeds in the muck, the sharp bones of his shoulders point upward.

"Like Casey," he mumbles after a few moments of silence.

"Casey? Who's Casey?" Russ asks.

Hiebert looks up. The watery blues of his eyes are almost completely dissolved into the whites, giving off an eerie vapid glow.

"Jared, who's Casey?" Russ asks.

"Casey's my good friend. She works in Brooklyn too."

"Yeah? What does she do?"

"Casey has a bakery. She's very nice. Casey works in Brooklyn too," he dips his head down again.

"Yes, like Casey. I work in Brooklyn. Have you ever been to Brooklyn?"

"Of course I've been to Brooklyn," Hiebert snaps back at him.

"Oh, okay. When was the last time you were there?"

"Yesterday."

"Yeah? You were in Brooklyn yesterday? Where in Brooklyn?"

"I went to Casey's bakery yesterday. I had a zucchini muffin and a cup of coffee. Vigor Robusta, exclusively at Casey's café and bakery. Casey's pours a great cup of coffee."

"Brooklyn's nice, right?"

"Vigor Robusta, skillfully roasted to perfection," Hiebert declares.

"Sounds good. So, you like coffee?"

"Yes, but coffee isn't good for you. You have to be careful."

"That's true. Jared, have you ever been to Brooklyn before you met Casey?"

Hiebert looks up at Russ with a listless glance. His face is old and dry, almost transparent from decades without sun, like a wrinkled and smudged cellophane wrapper.

"Do you know Greyson?" Hiebert asks.

Russ is surprised by the question, not entirely sure why. Somehow, he didn't expect Hiebert to stray away from his passive demeanor, to initiate anything. Maybe it was because he didn't know what to do with this question. Is Greyson a real person or some fictional character?

"Sure I do," Russ says.

"You know Greyson? That's good. So, what happened?"

"With Greyson?"

"Yes. What happened?"

"Wouldn't you wanna know?"

"Did he win the race? Do you know?"

"Yes, I do know, but I'm afraid I can't tell you that."

A wave of agitation comes over Jared.

"Why?" He jerks back in his seat. "Why can't you tell me?"

Russ looks at him silently, measuring his next move. Hiebert is growing visibly upset, shifting in his seat and flapping his arms feebly.

"Why can't you tell me?"

Hiebert's breathing gets faster and shallower, turning into a series of weak hisses and snorts.

"Because Greyson asked me not to tell you. He wants it to be a surprise."

"Oh," Hiebert seems appeased by this. "He's in Acapulco then." A faint ghost of a smile emerges on his face. "He won. He won the race."

"Actually, I just saw him in Brooklyn today."

"Yeah?"

"He said he was looking for his grandfather."

"Greyson lives in Brooklyn too?"

"Greyson's grandfather does. His grandfather's name is Augustus Smith. Greyson never met him before. As a matter-of-fact, no one in their family has seen him or heard from him in a very, very long time, but someone recently told Greyson that he's living in Brooklyn somewhere, so he started looking for him. He wants to finally meet him. He sent me here to ask you if you know where his grandfather might be.

He thought maybe you knew him from back in your day. You know, before you moved up here."

Russ pauses for a moment to gauge Hiebert's reaction, then continues to build upon his story patiently.

"His grandfather's name is Augustus Smith. You and he are about the same age, he might be a few years older. Tall, handsome man. He is a scientist, an inventor. Augustus Smith. Everybody says he was a good man."

"A good man doesn't abandon his family," Hiebert's eyes drop back to the floor.

"True. That's true Jared. But maybe it's not his fault. Maybe it's not his fault that he wasn't there."

Hiebert's breathing becomes louder, a series of deep wheezes and grunts and the occasional reticent plosive releasing pent-up air. He's turning.

"Greyson is looking for him, but he can't find him," Russ forges on. "He's sad and worried. You know what he said to me? He said, 'Russ, I don't know what to do anymore. I've done everything I could. I've looked everywhere, I've asked everyone. I know my grandfather would reach out to me if he knew I was looking for him. I have to find him, I'm not gonna be able to keep racing anymore if I don't find him. I just don't think I can do it.'"

"No," Jared starts swaying his upper body back and forth, rubbing his palms against his squeezed-together knees. "He can't stop now. No. No."

"Well, that's what he said. And I said to him, 'Greyson, I'm gonna help you find your grandfather, dead or alive, we have to find him.' Because maybe he's not alive anymore, you know. And I went around asking people if they knew Augustus Smith, a scientist, and an inventor, a tall, handsome man. He had a lab in Brooklyn. In Brooklyn Heights, on Grace Court. And Jared, you know what I found out from my sources?"

Hiebert stops moving. His hands freeze in midair, waiting for an answer.

"I found out that his lab burned to the ground and that he was dead. They think someone set fire to it. Someone burned Greyson's grandfather's lab in Brooklyn and him in it. I couldn't tell Greyson though, because I couldn't bear seeing him suffer. And also, what if it's not true? Right? What if it's not true? I mean who would do such a thing, set a man on fire like that, a good man with a wife and a small child at home?"

Russ veers back in his chair to get a glimpse of Hiebert's face, which has sunk to the ground again. Was it enough to jolt his scrambled mind, to make a ripple in the dark puddles of his memory? He's wilted forward, splotched over his own lap, motionless. Even his breathing seems to have ceased.

"Jared?"

Hiebert lets out a low, rattling sigh that turns into an indiscernible guttural mumble as he attempts to utter a sentence.

"What was that Jared? What are you saying?"

Jared's body starts quivering with strangled sobs. He tries to talk again, but his words die out in a weak, prolonged shriek. Russ feels tempted to reach across and put a hand on his back, to console him, to pull him back into the conversation with a simple act of kindness—but doesn't.

"Jared?"

Hiebert slowly lifts his head. His face is wet with tears and snot, distorted by a frozen grimace of fear. Islets of stress sweat are breaking through the thin fabric of his uniform, under his armpits, down his chest and belly. His crotch is soaked. And that awful smell. Fuck. Russ backs up in his chair.

"He's shit himself," he motions to the guard, unsure of what else to do.

She circles around and examines Hiebert's state, then stands aside at the ready.

"I have full voidance in consultation two," she says to someone. "Hiebert, G-Sixteen. Yes. Amenable. Lead balloon. Okay."

Hiebert is completely numb, with the same frozen expression interrupted by the occasional snivel. Russ looks at the guard, expecting some sort of resolution.

"It happens," the guard says. "Very often, in fact. Especially when they're taken out of their quotidian environment."

"What now?"

"He's blocked out. It's hard to bring them back once they are. Patient care takes over from here. They have to put him in recovery. I'm afraid you have to leave now, Mr. Oakley. Maybe try again at some other time in the future."

A rickety double swing door shrieks open and a tall, thin woman in her late fifties busts out of the kitchen, plates of breakfast sausage, waffles, eggs, and bacon fanned out over her outstretched arms. She wades through a maze of naked tables and disarrayed chairs, circles the round striptease stage and, without a word, dumps her load in front of a pair of hard-looking men sitting at the far end booth in the semidark barroom. The woman mutters something unintelligible, then goes behind the bar and flips a switch. Outside by the entrance, a red neon sign goes off and the glowing words "Billygoat Gentlemen's Lodge" suddenly disappear.

"Are you done there?" she yells out briskly across the barroom, heading over to Moonie's and Miles's table.

"I'm done," Moonie tells her.

"What about you?" the woman turns to Miles, who's preoccupied with something on the Allcom.

"Kid," she raises her voice impatiently. "Are you done?"

"Oh," Miles snaps out of it. "Yes, thank you. Sorry."

She makes a half-hearted attempt at wiping the table with a wet rag, then stacks up a wobbly pile of dishes on top of her left arm and disappears behind the shrieking kitchen door.

"So, what's new in the land of EternalQuest?" Moonie asks.

"Lots of chatter about tonight. People wondering if I'm playing or not. One half thinks I'm dead, the other half thinks it's all a stunt. They're saying I'm an attention-seeking narcissist and publicity whore, conspiracy theories galore."

"Like what?"

"Like, me, my dad, and mom got paid by EtenalQuest to fake the whole disappearance story to drum up interest for the semis, or that I kidnapped my parents myself and now I'm keeping them locked up in some basement in San Francisco."

"That's crazy."

"Some people are saying that I'm not even a real person, that I'm an embodied agent created by EternalQuest's swarm intelligence algorithm to make the game more appealing to our age group."

"Don't take that stuff too seriously."

"I don't, but it's kind of hard to hear some of this stuff and not respond, let people know what happened, my friends at least. Maybe someone knows something we don't, maybe someone can help us."

"Well, we can't. Not yet. I'm sorry."

"I know."

"It stinks to have gotten this far and not get a chance to win the whole thing," Moonie points out.

"Who cares, it's just a game," says Miles.

"Hey, you, California," one of the men by the window shouts across the room.

"Yeah?" Moonie replies. "What is it?"

"Your ride's on the way. Ten minutes. Be ready, the boss doesn't like to wait."

Moonie nods toward the booth, downs the rest of his Jitter Juice, and pushes away from the table.

"Let's go."

"I'm going too?" Miles asks.

"You wanna spend the rest of the day hanging out in a strip club with a couple of goons and a washed-up hooker?"

"I was gonna go back to our cabin and wait for you there."

"No way I'm leaving you by yourself again. Where I go, you go."

Outside, the crisp mountain air nibbles on their cheeks and ears like a curious whelp as they watch sun rays emerge from behind fuzzy pine treetops. Grassy slopes glitter with vanishing morning dew, birds are chatting away without a care in the world—not the worst place to disappear to if you need to erase the proof of your existence and don't mind a bit of isolation. Overlooked, remote, stretched-out, and sparsely populated, it makes for a dependable hideout.

Moonie always wondered what it was exactly that Driggs did in Texas, what kind of circumstance led him to flee. It must have been something huge. Murder? Robbery? Both? If only the law went hard after every murderer and robber walking among us. It must have been something bigger than that. Must've ticked off someone high up on the food chain. Whatever it was, he was able to stash away his money before he flew the coop, which, judging by the scope of the operation he's running here, is a pretty hefty sum. Around three hundred fifty acres of land in what was formerly known as Black Hills National Forest that he bought from the state, the fortresslike mansion he built in the hills, with twenty-foot reinforced walls, guard towers, a Skywall anti-drone system, visual scramblers against air surveillance, an underground helicopter hangar, and who knows what else. Then there's the fortune he's paying Claymore and other PSCs for logistical support and a small army of around-the-clock bodyguards. He clearly doesn't lack funds.

Just then, a matte-black utility vehicle with tinted windows pulls up in the lot and two thickset uniformed characters come out of it. Bullpups, barrels down, hang over their shoulders. Bulletproof vests keep their postures perfect. PSC shift change. The men size up Miles and Moonie up as they walk by, then continue past the Billygoat Gentlemen's Lodge neon sign, down a red brick path that stretches from the back end of the barroom to a cluster of single-story log cabins obscured by an aspen thicket.

In its heyday, the complex, once simply called Black Hills National Forest Visitors Center offered accommodations to weekend picnickers, avid hikers, and abandoned mine hobbyists who came from all over, but after Driggs bought it and the land it was on, it was revamped, renamed, and repurposed to serve mainly as a barracks for PSC and other service personnel in his employ. The lodge was still open to the public, but instead of outdoor enthusiasts from afar it now attracted indoor dwellers from Lead and neighboring towns who were drawn to the night and the stripping talents of "Nurse Lilly's Frolic and Detour Fair" girls—their sacred art of getting men hard and their readiness to engage in easy, inexpensive sex.

Another utility vehicle, this one dark green, drives up to the lot and parks next to the first one.

"This must be our ride," says Moonie as he takes a couple of reluctant steps forward, then adds under his breath. "I didn't tell you this before, but when we get there, whatever you do, don't stare at Driggs's face."

"Why?"

"It's all fucked up. You'll see. If he looks at you, if he asks you something, don't act like a gawking numbskull. Be cool."

"Okay," says Miles, perplexed.

"Look at the top of his forehead instead. I find that helps."

A uniformed PSC comes out of the vehicle and waves them forward.

"Belan?"

"Yeah."

"Who's this?" The man points at Miles with his chin.

"This is my nephew."

"Not in the protocol. You can come, he stays here."

"I can't leave him by himself..." Moonie tries.

"Not in the protocol," PSC cuts him short.

"Please check with Driggs. I should've told him, but it was sort of last minute. Call it in, he'll okay it, I guarantee it. He's fifteen..."

The PSC steps forward and then, twisting his body slightly, points his Panoptic directly at Miles.

"Wait here," he says, then goes back to the vehicle and exchanges words with the driver inside. After a few tense moments, the PSC turns back to Miles and Moonie holding an open BlackHole signal-shielding bag.

"Put all your devices and weapons in here."

"No weapons," Moonie says.

Miles and Moonie both drop their Allcoms inside the BlackHole bag.

"That's it?" PSC asks. "Any built-in devices? Medical helpers, body function monitors, locators, LocTrac, BodyBeacon?"

"No." Moonie replies.

"Nothing else," Miles chirps.

"Hands on the hood, spread your legs."

The PSC frisks them, then unfolds a thin telescopic wand and scans them both top to bottom with it.

"ES countermeasures sweep negative," he says into his Panoptic after he finishes scanning. "Yeah. Okay. On the way."

Next up is a forty-five-minute ride along a rough and narrow road that coils and dips through the woods and steep hillsides. No one uttered a single word the whole time. They eventually reach a flat rift between uplands, and the road opens up into an elongated rocky basin speckled with scrub bush and angular slabs of granite. After about half a mile, the vehicle comes to a stop at a roadblock filled with tightly parked utility vehicles. The trailing dust cloud from their wheels catches up with them as they get out of the car, covering them in pale dirt powder.

Guards flanking the barricade stare at them intently as

they walk by. Some one hundred yards further down, a group of PSCs is standing around in a loose huddle facing the other way. Out of nowhere, a soft, barely audible pop echoes through the rocks, and the sound of a rushing bullet tears up the air, followed by distant chatter. After a while, the crowd quiets down. Another pop and bullet whirlwind follows.

As they approach, flocking PSCs pull apart to let them inside the huddle. Stretched out on the ground, hugging a sniper rifle with his right eye pressed against the scope, Driggs is waiting for the right moment to squeeze the trigger. Everyone seems to have stopped their breathing in anticipation. He takes a shot and the bullet kicks up a dirt puff somewhere far up on a hill above. Driggs takes a few seconds to patiently scrutinize the target through the scope.

"Better. But it's still pulling a bit to the right."

Driggs slowly gets up and notices Moonie among the uniforms.

"Belan," he puts on a smile and extends his hand to Moonie and they shake.

"Nice stick," Moonie gestures toward the rifle.

"Oh. Yeah. That's a beauty. Original 2003 Windrunner M 96, .50 BMG cartridge. Leupold Ultra M3A, standard-issue, fixed power scope. Which is showing its age, I must say."

"Fuller," he turns to one of the PSCs. "Break it down and give it a rub, then put the Zeiss LaserScope on. I wanna test it out. Then we'll do the self-guided system. Tell the guys to prepare moving targets for it."

"Yes, sir," Fuller answers promptly, grabs the rifle, and starts breaking it down.

"Guns are like women, you gotta keep them well oiled," Driggs says with a grin. "The older they get, the more lubrication they require," he cackles at his own joke, then turns to Miles. "So, this is the nephew?"

Miles wasn't ready for it. Trying not to look at Driggs's face, as per Moonie's instructions, he struggled to find a safe place to look at instead. He stared at the PSCs and gazed up at the hilltops and down the road at a narrow passage hidden behind a pile of huge boulders, which looked like an entrance to a quarry or a mine, before finally locking his eyes on Fuller's hands as he was dismantling the rifle and starting to clean it. He knew he now had to make eye contact with Driggs, or appear to, and remembered what Moonie told him, to look at the top of his forehead instead, so he quickly flipped his eyes and focused there. But he caught a quick sight of the shapeless blob that was the left side of Driggs's face, just enough to repel and unnerve him. His eye and cheekbone were completely blown out, and part of his skull was missing. The recessed cavity where his temple would have been dissolved into a crushed eye socket, covered in the rough varnish of livid scar tissue.

"Yes, this is Miles," Moonie quickly intervenes, sensing Miles's unease.

"Do you like guns, Miles?" Driggs asks.

"Not particularly," Miles shrugs.

"You two been fighting?" asks Driggs, amused by their bruised faces.

"Not each other," Moonie smiles back.

"I would hope not."

"We had a minor misunderstanding in a hotel in Salt Lake City. Some people shouldn't be allowed to be around others."

"The world would be a pretty boring place if it weren't for the idiots," Driggs exclaims, then gives Moonie a friendly pat on the shoulder, "C'mon, I wanna show you a couple of things."

As they stroll down the road, a pair of PSCs trails after them at the same leisurely pace, keeping a constant distance of twenty-five feet between them. Driggs seems animated, stopping frequently, turning around, sweeping the brim of the valley with his hand, pointing forward with his finger toward the passage behind a pile of boulders. Miles exhales deeply and silently then closes his eyes, wishing this was all a bad dream.

After fifteen minutes of arduous struggle to find the least uncomfortable position to sit in while he waited for Weiss, the pain in Russ's lower back finally forces him out of the chair. He gets up with a vexatious sigh and takes a few small steps around Weiss's office, shifting his weight gingerly from one foot to another.

It's his own fault. Well, sort of. Maybe if he'd kept the autonomous drive engaged when he got off the expressway, none of this would have happened. Maybe the car's computer sensory system would have done a better job detecting "unsound roadway ahead" conditions than his outdated human one. But the thing is so infuriatingly slow in city drive mode that it would have taken him forever to get through the tangled web of one-way streets that connect the stretch between the Manhattan and Brooklyn bridges.

Russ dropped Miriam off at her subway stop in DUMBO and zigzagged his way back to the Brooklyn Heights side. As he drove by Cadman Plaza, the remnants of the protest were all too visible. The signs that yesterday proudly displayed defiance and demanded justice lay strewn about, hastily discarded, trampled in a stampede that ensued after the riot police stormed in, and are now just another layer of loose garbage left behind. Many windows on the courthouse are shattered. A pile of rocks, concrete chunks, and smashed half-gallon paint cans block the entrance to the building. Streaks of bright-red paint run down the facade from as far up as the seventh floor. They must have used one of those do-it-yourself catapults made from two-by-fours and bungee stretch cords.

A small cleanup crew in orange overalls was dismantling the makeshift barricades of broken park benches and concrete planters that protesters set up on the main access road to the courthouse. The workers directed Russ to the auxiliary entrance on the other side of the plaza, by the Waterways Emergency Service station. He drove back down, under the Brooklyn Bridge, then up toward the courthouse. As he came around the curve, the car bucked under him with a loud thud, then plunged nose first, whipping him forward like a rodeo clown, then backward, as the rear wheels followed the front two into the hole. A flash of pain cut him in half across the lumbar curve, rippling down his legs, then back up along the spine.

The car was stuck, its wheels inching up then sliding back into the hole helplessly. Russ pushed the gas pedal, but nothing happened. For a moment he thought he lost feeling in his legs. What a fucking joke! You survived a plane crash only to be crippled by a giant pothole!

As the pain subsided, he realized that the impact knocked his foot off the gas pedal and he was pressing on the floor instead. He came this way once before and remembered clearly this pothole was there even then. And no one bothered to fix it in four years! In fact, it was a lot bigger now, probably due to the now almost yearly flooding of the Brooklyn coastline during hurricane season. He waited for the pain to localize then, hoping he hadn't done serious damage to the car already, swung it gently back and forth a few times before gaining enough momentum to drive out of the hole in one swoop. Once safely out of the hole, he launched into a minute-long, curse-rich rant aimed at no one in particular. Ridiculous, he knew, but therapeutic nonetheless.

The wait for Weiss was getting tiresome and Russ's five-step shuffle around the cramped office was starting to feel claustrophobic. He decides to sit down again, giving his pain threshold another test. The low ceiling and morose lighting made Weiss's office look somewhat like the inside of a cave. Even the abstract shadows dotting the gray veneer of the locked-out display that spanned the room in a half-circle, looked like the sort of odd pictographs and crude symbols that could be found on some cave wall. If you look at it long enough you can almost make out an ancient hunting scene, with little stick figures chasing wild beasts with tiny spears back in the day when human survival depended on raw instinct instead of a numbers-based pursuit of information.

"Sorry for the wait," Weiss finally huffs in through the door, holding a small box. "Things are a little hectic right now. I got here as fast as I could. Here, new device," he hands the box to Russ, then squeezes by him and sits at his desk.

"No worries. I have nothing to do, nowhere to go," Russ replies, annoyed by apparently being the lowest on Weiss's list of priorities.

"Oh, fuck off. Shit is going down."

"What's going down?" asks Russ as he unseals the box.

"We got them."

"Got who?"

"Sheng Long."

"Got them how?"

"We hacked one of their fusion centers last night. Complete snatch and wipe."

"Well, that was quick and easy!" says Russ, genuinely surprised.

"Yeah, everything seems quick and easy after it's been done. Nobody sees all the work that went into it beforehand. It took us years to plant a workable logic bomb inside their network. You field agents are so ignorant, you think shit just happens..."

"All right, all right," Russ grows tired of Weiss's crowing. "Found anything interesting?"

"It's a bonanza," Weiss snaps excitedly. "You wouldn't believe the shit we got."

After a small battle with plastic clamshell packaging, Russ pries a brand-new Allcom out of it, feels its weight and texture in his palm, and then turns it on.

"Why are you so jumpy then?" He looks up at Weiss.

"Fucking I.I. They're outright harassing people now."

"What else would you expect? It is an epic fuck-up."

"They can suck my nut sack."

"Are you implicated?"

"No. Of course not, but you know how it is, they never let you get too cozy."

The Allcom prompts Russ for LiveScan authentication.

"We all have skeletons in our closets," Russ says as he scans his retina. "So, what does this mean for our operation? Do we know what happened to Smith?"

"We gotta wait. I.I. gets first look at the captured data, we get nothing until they're done."

Weiss retrieves a plastic pouch from his desk drawer and hands it to Russ. Russ puts his old Allcom in it, folds the bag closed, and activates the electronic seal on its flap.

"Why are we dumping Allcoms anyway?"

"I.I. suspects that the relay breach might have been enabled by a piece of blackguard hardware. They found vampire microchip blocks in some of our devices. Nobody can say for certain that's how Sheng Long got in, but it's one of the possibilities."

Russ hands him the pouch back.

"So, what did you get upstate?" Weiss asks.

"I got shit."

"Loony wasn't talkative?"

"No, literally, I got shit. He shit in his pants during questioning. A complete meltdown. They made me stop the interview and pretty much kicked me out."

"Went a little too rough on a fellow human being, Russ?

You gotta learn to be more compassionate."

"I got a bit of compassion for you," Russ gives him the finger.

"So, nothing?"

"Just drivel." Russ gets up to leave. "I still think he did it. When I mentioned Smith and the lab fire, that seemed to set him off. I think he still remembers, I just couldn't get it out of him. He mumbled something at the very end, right before he dropped the dookie. I didn't catch it though. I played the recording back ten times and I still can't make out what he was saying."

"I'll check it out. All I need is a word or two, and I can probably emulate the rest using his speech patterns."

"That would be great." Russ grabs the door. "Let me know when I.I. releases the data."

"Will do."

Russ decides to get lunch at the Operations cafeteria, but first things first—he needed drugs more than he needed food. He takes the elevator up to the pharmacy at the fifth-floor convenience store.

*"Welcome to the Health Guardians family of products,"* the drug dispenser greets him with robotic enthusiasm as he launches the shopping augment on his new Allcom. *"Please make your selections."*

Russ went through the painkiller tasting menu while at the hospital and later, during rehab. He got to know his opioids well. Maybe a little too well. But a choice between unbearable chronic pain and addiction is not really a choice, is it? And when exactly does a dependence become an addiction? Ostensibly, the ACIS Substance Abuse Board knows when, since they made a "clear and unambiguous recommendation" that he clean up for the medical exam he needed to pass before being allowed back to work. Given his circumstances, the commission was expected to cut him some slack regarding the physical, but the ACIS substance dependence policy could not be bent. It wasn't easy coming off, but as his physical condition improved, and with Miriam by his side every step of the way, he was able to cut down on the heavy stuff and gradually switch to over-the-counter alternatives, and regain angelic purity in time for the exam.

Russ scrolls through the available categories and selects an old favorite, Valerian.

*"You have selected Valerian—quick-acting, musculoskeletal pain management solution,"* the drug dispenser declares. *"This is a regulated item. Please provide your personal medical history to proceed."*

Russ unlocks access to his medical history then tries again.

*"Russell, may I suggest another item?"* the machine asks primly.

He realizes that he likely isn't getting any real painkillers today.

"No, I want Valerian," he says out loud.

*"This treatment option must be approved by a medical professional. May I suggest something more moderate."*

"No, I want Valerian."

*"I advise against it, Russell. May I suggest something more moderate?"*

"Suggest away, you twat," Russ throws up his hands in resignation.

*"Okay. Based on your original selection, your medical history, and your phenotype, I determined that a customized compound medication with an active ingredient ratio—71% ibuprofen, 16% duloxetine, 11% meperidine, and 2% desipramine will be the best course of treatment for you today. Shall I mix this customized compound medication for you?"*

Unlike DOA's pathetic luncheonette, with its six-item offering of frozen ready-made meals and limp sandwiches, the Operations cafeteria is a real restaurant with real food, just how the people who work in Operations have real jobs, somehing most of the DOA personnel couldn't claim with a straight face. Russ picks up a grilled pork chop with a side of mashed potatoes and creamed spinach and a bottle of flavored Plenergy water and sits at one of the single-seater tables by the window. Outside, the early autumn is fine-tuning its maritime color scheme, smearing the pale blue sky with dirty silver nebulae. In the distance, across the bay, rusty skeletons of loading cranes at the Greenville container terminal are lurking in the smog like gigantic preying spiders.

Suddenly, a group of associate agents bursts through the door—hungry, young, and loud. They move nimbly down the aisle, joking, smiling, and pushing each other, their spirits animated by the proximity of food and a chance to pluck their heads out of their assignments for a few minutes. You're only as old as you feel. The throbbing pain in Russ's back is doing its best to remind him that he's no spring chicken anymore. He reaches into his pocket, grabs a vial, and shakes out a couple of white pills that the dispenser so generously recommended. It ain't the big guns, but it'll help.

*Cascading through the INDEX structure of a* massive data archive like this one can feel like a never-ending search for a maze exit, especially when you're as physically exhausted and psychologically paralyzed as Theo is right now. What seems like an exit turns out to be nothing more than an entrance to another maze, awfully similar to the one before, then another... further in... or out... away... until there is no entrance or exit anymore.

How could he have been so damn naive to let that woman into the house? He couldn't help but blame himself, even though, deep down, he knew there was nothing he could have done to prevent this. They were out to get him one way or another. People like this don't give up until they get what they want. If there were only a way Miles and Maritza could have been spared this nightmare. But no, that was always a part of the plan. They knew they would only have full control over him if they had them too.

The timed air conditioning unit comes to life and startles Theo with its soft rumble as it begins its cycle, and he realizes he's been sitting motionless for almost an hour staring at the control panel in front of him. His head feels like a water balloon about to burst under the weight of the hovering holos above, the jumbled array of vector fields, fusion charts, reservoir timelines, and seismograms impatiently waiting to be tended to and made sense of.

How is he going to do this? How is he going to keep

working while pretending he doesn't see how completely insane this whole endeavor is? Abiotic oil synthesis? Seven thousand feet below ground? The entire premise is nothing but unqualified lunacy. Achieving energy independence through perpetual carbon resequestering?

Even if it were practically possible, a project like this would require the collaboration of thousands of minds from every field of science and industry, countless man-hours, and immeasurable amounts of computing power. It's a job that takes the effort of a generation, not one person toiling away at a Simulacrum station. This might be it for him, he might never get out of here. But it can't be for Miles and Maritza. No! It can't be. He has to do something. It can't end like this. He feels the relentless frustration of his own helplessness break something inside of him and he rises to his feet and starts screaming at the top of his lungs.

"You sick son of a bitch!"

Theo grabs the master control tablet and flings it across the room as hard as he can. The tablet springs off high against the upholstered wall, twisting wildly midair before hitting the ground. Shards of glass fly up in the air, then spill down on the bare floor like glimmering droplets of a clear mountain stream.

"Where is my family?" Theo shouts wildly at the security cameras hidden in the ceiling panels. "I refuse to do anything unless you give them back to me. Do you hear me?"

He grabs the door handle and yanks it futilely a few times, then begins kicking the door maniacally, but the black velvet upholstery covering it absorbs the brunt of his anger.

"You'll get nothing from me, you bastard! Nothing!"

Theo runs behind the console, picks up the swivel chair, lifts it up over his head, and tosses it on the floor with all the force he could muster. He then starts kicking the top of the console with his heel. Holos above him coil up into a single smudged image then flicker out one by one. He cries out unintelligibly as he watches them die out and his eyes begin to swell with tears. He doesn't even notice Drey rush in through the door. With the speed and determination of a linebacker, Drey leaps forward and grabs Theo from behind into a bear hug, lifts him up, and carefully flips him over before laying him flat on the ground—and before Theo can even grasp what's happening, Drey discharges a jet of misty spray into his eyes.

"Easy, easy now," Drey says, then calmly but firmly grips Theo's wrists, folds his arms, and presses down on his chest with his forearm.

The bittersweet smell of burned sugar hangs in the air just long enough for Theo to realize that it's the same spray the old woman used on them back home. He strains to push Drey off of his chest, but his arms are getting weak and his mind is growing hazy, draining away his resolve, pulling him down against his will into a familiar place of calm and comfort where he can let go and rest, unencumbered by the weight of his conscience.

Miles's blindfold is on way too tight. He can feel it squeezing his brain like a vise, his heart hammering in his temples. The total blackness beneath it reminds him of that one time he passed out after he stupidly succumbed to peer pressure and let Cal Griffith almost choke him to death at the tennis courts behind the school, part of the pass-out game that for some dumb reason everyone was into at the time. Like teenagers really need more proof that not being in control of your own body is an unnerving experience. The rough fabric, moist with his own sweat, itches like hell. All he wants to do right now is stick his fingers under it and rub his eyelids and brow, but he can't tell if the PSCs are watching.

Miles tries to distract himself from the discomfort by letting his mind race. It's Friday. The Spartans are playing the Pirates tonight. Spartans beat them the last time but now the Pirates have that huge running back, Mike Lautenberg. Monster Mike. He's only fifteen, but has a full-grown beard and is fifty pounds heavier and a good head taller than everyone else on the field. Kind of freaky, he looks like someone's uncle. They can beat them again, Monster Mike or not.

The quick shrill laugh of one of the PSCs pops the bubble of nostalgia and Miles realizes he wouldn't have watched tonight's game anyway. Right now, he would have been home getting ready for the EternalQuest semis, which, it turns out, he'll get the chance to play after all. Part of him didn't even want to play, but Moonie had already arranged it. Driggs already sent a car along with two of his least abrasive PSCs to pick them up. They were almost apologetic as they put blindfolds on him and Moonie. Protocol. It must be so visitors can't trace the way to Driggs's mansion afterward.

Unlike the silent pair of beefheads who took them to see Driggs this morning, these two turned out to be genuine chatterboxes, but they only spoke to one another, and in Spanish, so it was difficult to follow their conversation. Something about some guy named Diego Bloom, or Plume, who's making a lot of money moving some sort of merchandise across the border. Someone's cousin worked for Diego, or was it the other way around? After a while, he gave up on trying to understand.

The car finally comes to a stop, doors open, and the PSC's meaty fingers start crawling at the back of his head. As the blindfold comes off, the sunlight hits him like a slap across the face. PSCs direct them toward a short dark tunnel that cuts through a stone-covered guard tower heaving up at the edge of a circular driveway. On the other side of the tunnel, a slender man with slicked-back, thinning blond hair is waiting for them between gate pillars. He ushers them into a concrete-walled corridor lined with cameras, at the end of which is a small, remotely operated elevator.

Upstairs, the elevator opens into a black-and-white tiled hallway. Glass display cases housing a collection of rare weapons adorn the walls: ornate pistols, antique sabers, gold plated daggers, a Luger with a broken handle, an engraved desert camo AR-15... the trophies of a serious collector.

At the end of the hallway, they enter a spacious sunroom with whitewashed wall panels and flooring. In an egg-shaped wicker chair, hanging off of one of the massive wooden beams that support the thick sunroom enclosure made of bulletproof glass, Driggs is basking in the red sunset glow.

"Riddle wrapped in a mystery inside an enigma, Belan," he says as he swivels around to face them.

Nested among pillows in a beige funnel neck cashmere hoodie and sporting oversize sunglasses, Driggs looks like a giant caterpillar reposed in its cocoon.

"What's that?" Moonie asks, confused.

"Your employers," Driggs reaches for a tall glass resting on a silver tray at the coffee table beside him. "I like that," he draws a sip of gooey pinkish liquid through a fat straw. "It means they're a serious group of people."

"Well..." Moonie starts.

"What I don't like though, is being uninformed."

"I assure you all your questions will be answered in time. There's a..."

Driggs raises his hand, stopping Moonie mid-sentence.

"We'll talk at dinner." He springs from his chair and puts his arm on Miles's shoulder. "We've got to get our champion to the ring first."

Startled, Miles backs up a step, then seeing his frightened face in the reflective black mirrors of Driggs's glasses, musters a shy smile in an attempt to act normal.

"Thank you so much for letting me use your Portall, Mr. Driggs," he mumbles.

"Glad I could help."

Driggs's playroom is a huge windowless space with a curved opalescent ceiling and padded linen wallpaper, dominated by a giant three-quarter surround interactive display. Colorful floor cushions of all sizes lie strewn around in arbitrary bunches, fuzzy blankets and crumpled silk comforters marking makeshift one-person dens.

Driggs makes his way to an unruly pile of clothes at the far end of the room and starts picking items off of it, one by one, throwing them aside, making several smaller piles in the process. A white satin ruffle shirt, square buckle leather belt, tricorn hat... A long black cape slips off the pile on its own, revealing a naked knee, then the silky inside of a female thigh. Miles gasps inaudibly as Driggs continues plucking the pile: pink feather boa, blue velvet gown, embroidered corset, black lace underwear... He uncovers a naked female body sitting in a Portall chair. She is slender and well-proportioned with hay-colored hair, light green eyes, and a perfect complexion. Her face is fresh and inviting, luscious lips slightly parted with mild surprise. Her hands are hanging over the Portall armrest-mounted command panels at odd angles, palms up like she's waiting for a hug. Driggs picks her up and throws her, face-first, on top of one of the newly created piles.

"The throne is all yours, young master," he says with a theatrically peppy countenance. "I abdicate for the greater good."

Miles feels a wave of embarrassment flushing his face, not completely sure if it's because he's been so naive to have, if only for a moment, mistaken a haptic sexbot for a real person, or because he's getting creeped out by the very thought of Driggs having sex, any kind of sex, even mixed reality sex with a silicone mannequin, right here in this room, on these cushions, wearing the same immersion set he's supposed to use now to play EternalQuest.

"It gets boring around here, believe it or not," chortles Driggs, amused by Miles's fuddled state. "Nothing like a little telehaptic cosplay to get your rocks off... It's better than the real thing," he turns to Moonie. "Local women are mostly skanks with retarded sensuality."

Moonie spreads his arms in a shrugging gesture.

"Anyway, this is it," Driggs heads for the door. "Phillip will come around with refreshments. Tell him what you want for dinner, they can make anything. And hey, kid..." he turns around. "Break a leg!"

"Thank you again, Mister Driggs," says Miles.

"Are you gonna be okay here by yourself?" Moonie asks as he starts after Driggs.

"Oh yeah, no worries," Miles says. "I'll be fine."

"All right. Good luck kiddo, I'll see you later."

Miles waits for Driggs and Moonie to leave, then perches himself on the Portall and starts loosening up his wrists and elbows. As he looks around the room, his gaze stops on the shallow dip between the sexbot's shoulder blades. She's arched forward over the clothes pile, her hair swept to the side baring her delicate neck and her round ass pitched up, exposing the petal folds of her vagina. Using only the tips of his fingers, Miles picks up one of the blankets off the floor and covers the sexbot with it, then jumps back into the Portall, closes his eyes, and begins his mantra.

"Hands of Ali, heart of a lion, focus of samurai. Hands of Ali, heart of a lion, focus of samurai. Hands of Ali, heart of a lion, focus of samurai."

------

Silently forking their salads at the opposite ends of a twelve-person dining table, neither Moonie nor Driggs seem like they're in a terrible rush to bridge the distance between them and strike up a conversation. Back in Concord before he left, Moonie felt confident that he wouldn't have to do much convincing once he brings the good news to Driggs. It's a real win-win, with obvious benefits for both sides. Well, maybe Pardes will be getting more out of the deal than would be fair under different circumstances, but for Driggs to be able to leave this glitzy cage with a load of money and the prospect of becoming a protected citizen of Pardes Corporate, to get a chance to spend the rest of his life like a human being and not some psychotic recluse, is more than he ever could have hoped for. This should be an easy decision for him.

Keeping the truth from Driggs about the true potential value of the mine might be an issue down the road, but no one is going to volunteer that information. To an untrained eye, feasibility studies look like they might as well be written in hieroglyphs. Driggs is going to have to shovel through the mountain of bullshit that Pardes is going to baffle him with in order to dig out some reasonable suspicion he can act on. But the money isn't the draw here anyway. It's the promise of a ritzy new life in a new land far away from here, free from old burdens and safe from the constant threat of being nabbed. It's a chance for Driggs to regain his freedom, and what's more valuable than that?

"So," Moonie lays down his hands on the table. "What was it, a mystery wrapped in a conundrum? Is that what you said?" He puts on a friendly smile, seemingly unfazed by Driggs's flat stare from the other side of the table. "I don't think that's an unfair characterization, but we're all familiar with the advantages of keeping to oneself. Truth is, I'm sure you know more about Pardes Ventures than I do. I'm just a messenger. But what I do know is that all of your concerns will be addressed in a timely manner as we go forward. There are people whose only job is to facilitate the transition, they brought entire families in from all over the world, often under very difficult conditions, as you can imagine."

Moonie reaches into his pocket and takes out a polymer card like the one he used earlier at home to access the Pardes promo, except this one features a stereogram of an iguana instead of a macaw.

"I was told to give you this," Moonie lays the card on the table. "It's a single sign-on pass with built-in security authentication. There's a lot of useful information there. It's customized for your status and circumstance, so I don't know exactly what's on it, but I'm pretty sure it will explain everything you need to know about the process at this stage."

A server comes in and takes their salad plates away, then comes back with a pair of steaks. Moonie waits for the server to leave, then continues.

"Nothing is set in stone, of course. Our team has yet to confirm the initial hypotheses and delineate the full extent of the resource. After that, they'll work out a feasibility study that will be the basis for negotiation regarding deal terms. Our predictive models are very accurate, but nobody knows how they'll compare to the actual data. They might find something, some problem that could kill the project, you just never know. But the odds are good that this thing is going to work and you're going to get yourself the deal of a lifetime. If all goes as planned, you'll be soaking your feet in the ocean, cocktail in hand, in less than six months."

"Good," says Driggs, slicing off a chunk of a perfectly charred ribeye.

"Pardes is a hell of a place, as much as I can tell..."

"How quickly can they get here?" Driggs cuts him off. "The feasibility team?"

"The minute you're ready to give permission, I'll call it in. I think we can get them here from Denver in under two weeks."

Driggs soaks his bite in bloody steak juice.

"And how are you imagining your involvement with the project going forward?"

"Me? I'm pretty much done once they get here and the big guns take over."

Driggs swipes a bite off the fork then chews it slowly, almost deliberately, for what seems like at least two minutes, before sending it down his gullet. Moonie looks at him with confused curiosity, then remembers the man is practically missing half a jaw. For a moment, he considers mentioning the excellent healthcare services that Corporate provides to its members—prosthetics with 3-D maxilofacial reconstruction means they can now print out a whole new face in a matter of hours—but quickly realizes he better shut up. At this point, it would only seem like he's trying too hard, and it might just piss Driggs off if he brought up the subject of his fucked-up face.

"Have you ever gone fly-fishing?" Driggs asks before taking a sip of water.

"Fly-fishing? No, I don't think so."

"We've got some of the best trout-fishing waters around. Few miles up the road. This all used to be a National Park, they took good care of the land. Quite beautiful, don't you think? Clean. I don't know about you, but I love being in nature. It calms me. Somehow it reminds me I still have a soul. There are few tricks to fly-fishing, a few different styles—dry fly, duo, nymphing, streamer. Don't worry, you'll have plenty of time to learn."

"What do you mean?" Moonie's eyes widen.

"A long time ago, I've learned that total skepticism is the only appropriate response to all types of human interaction. It takes a while for me to change my mind. I don't do it very often, maybe that's why. So, we're gonna spend some time together, see if you can change my mind. Call it honing trust. We'll set you up at the lodge, you'll get a nicer room, of course. There, you'll wait for your guys, help them settle in when they come."

"Well, sure. Of course."

"Then I want you to stay here with your Denver team. Until we reach an agreement, or not, whichever ends up being the case."

"I'm not sure I can do that. I have my own business to run. In Salt Lake City. I... it's a time-sensitive..."

"I don't think you understand, Belan. I'm not asking. Tomorrow you'll call Pardes and set this all in motion."

# DAY_6

Russ pours his first cup of coffee and, with his eyes closed, brings it up to his nose, searching for familiar flavors in its ambrosial vapor. He takes a big sip then contentedly smacks his lips, letting the sweetness and bitterness work together to lure his mind out of the post-sleep fog and into the new day. Weiss left three messages, the first one timestamped 12:57 am: *"I.I. about to release Sheng Long data,"* the second at 1:16 am: *"We're on. Get your ass in gear,"* and the third at 2:41 am: *"At T.O.C. now. Where are you?"* Does this guy ever sleep?

"I'll be on the 6:00 am ferry," Russ replies.

Inside the event goodie bag Miriam brought home last night from the Maldives gala, among the throwaway printed brochures and trinkets, he finds two muffins wrapped in clear gusseted cellophane, neatly tied at the top with a bow made of green cloth ribbon. He stuffs one of the muffins into his coat pocket, finishes his coffee, and heads out into the morning.

The ferry is empty, save for a few Directorate maintenance personnel sitting on a row of wooden benches and a ferry crew member, a barely twenty-year-old kid who looks like he's about to fall off his chair any second, 6:00 am obviously being either too early or too late for him depending on when he started his shift. In contrast to the dozy youngster, the maintenance guys, all somewhere between fifty and sixty years old, are as animated as one can be at such an early hour, chatting and laughing the six-minute trip away, probably the only time in their day when no one is going to ask them to do something or to be someone: a father, husband, neighbor, a responsible and well-adjusted member of society. Six minutes, twice a day, the only time they can just be one of the guys.

Up on the top deck bow, Russ turns east looking for the sun. The thin, pale wafer is barely visible in a blanket of gray clouds thrown over still-dreaming Brooklyn. The ferry speeds up, pulling one long wave along its hull as the engine hum becomes a growl and the propeller gets trapped between the crest and trough of the single wave it created. Russ takes the muffin out of his pocket and starts untying the green bow, but it requires a little more skill and patience than he's willing to spare, so he bites into the cellophane instead and rips it open to uncover a red and green mini-stick flag balancing precariously in the middle of the muffin top. The other side of the flag is a solid red rectangle with the words, "Save the people of Maldives" printed across. He tosses the mini-flag in the trash and bites into the muffin.

Save the people of Maldives! Why the people of Maldives and not the millions of Bangladeshis dying of hunger and disease in the Ganges Delta in the Bay of Bengal, where rising seas turned the most fertile land on Earth, which nourished generations for thousands of years, into a mishmash of barren salt swamps just over the course of a few decades. Those poor bastards have no one to throw a fancy party for them, to raise awareness and funds for their cause. They're forgotten by everyone, left there to die off, one by one, human sacrifices to the gods of seas and storms and berserk weather, unwitting victims of ignorance and shortsightedness that will ultimately be our collective undoing, one way or another.

No wonder Miriam doesn't bring him to these parties, given his penchant for diatribe. Her friends Mai and Preet organized the event. Mai is a second-generation Maldivian and one of the most prominent members of the Maldivian expat community in New York, which is a very odd notion since the country itself is virtually nonexistent and will most certainly be completely gone in a year or two. How could you be an expat of a country that doesn't exist anymore?

As the ocean swallowed their islands one by one, Maldives effectively became a nation of environmental refugees. Anyone who had a chance to leave already left. Out of the 400,000 people who once lived there, only about 6,000 are left now, gathered on two inhabited islands that are still above water, living without electricity and running water in rickety huts scattered among the ruins of once exquisite resorts that have been wrecked by relentless flooding and unforgiving monsoon winds. This handful of holdovers hope for a miracle that will somehow make the ocean waters recede, these abandoned people without money or connections to escape, these are the people Mai is trying to save—and if the only way to do that is to entertain a bunch of self-righteous busybodies halfway across the world and make them feel good about themselves, and at the same time challenge them enough to make a difference, then more power to her. Save the ones who could be saved, by any means.

Russ's gaze wanders over the quicksilver surface of the water. Who is going to be next? Bangkok, Kolkata, Alexandria, Galveston, New Orleans, and Charleston are already half submerged. Southern Vietnam, Mumbai, Guangzhou, Atlantic City, Miami, Coney Island, and the Rockaways are all but erased. Tomorrow it will be Jakarta, Amsterdam, Shanghai, Dhaka, Williamsburg, Red Hook, Long Island City, and Manhattan—one day, this great city will be no more.

After leaving the ferry, Russ soon arrives at the Tactical Operations Center and feels a tingling rush of adrenaline slowly come over him. He's been jonesing for a hit of real actionable intelligence ever since this thing started. So far, it's been nothing but one small stingy squirt of information after another. Hopefully, now that I.I. removed the roadblocks, they'll soon have enough to make sense of it all.

The TOC floor is a beehive of clear and purposeful focus, with rows of heads harnessed to immersion kits bobbing with the haste of a data-feeding frenzy. As he makes his way through the labyrinth of workstations, the only two people without immersion kits over their eyes look at him with bland attentiveness, like he was some harmless fruit fly that flew in through an open door by accident. He walks up to Weiss and puts his hand on his shoulder.

"Half a day today Oak?" Weiss greets him with a snark, sliding his immersion kit up on his forehead.

"Simmer down sparky, it's all about efficiency, not effort. I hope you'll learn that one of these days."

"Whatever you say, captain."

Weiss moves over to the next workstation and with a few competent moves sets Russ up.

"You can piggyback on my profile," Weiss hands him an immersion kit then falls back into his chair. "Strictly look-don't-touch though. You can still add to consilience scenarios in the decision support engine, you just can't edit."

"Good enough," Russ sits down.

"We've located the Smiths," Weiss puts on the grin of a child yearning to impress an adult.

"Well, fuck me running!"

"Yeah, but don't get all wet just yet."

"Go on."

"Breach. Looks like we had Long Shlong up our ass for at least four months before anyone noticed anything. I think Pratt's about to start burning people at the stake."

"That's if he survives this himself."

"You heard something?" Weiss whispers.

"Nothing you haven't," Russ lowers his voice, "but I've been around long enough to know that when there's blood in the water sharks will come to feed—and when they do, they won't be satisfied with just small fish."

Mulling over Russ's words, Weiss gazes up at the elevated glass cube of the commander's station, where, secluded behind the softened palpitation of signal lights and reflections on the TOC floor, Pratt paces around talking to his CALO, gesticulating energetically, gripping and squeezing the air with his big hands, slicing it into bite-size pieces with the side of his palm.

"Anyway, what do we have?" Russ asks.

Weiss motions to Russ to put the immersion kit on, then slides his own down from his forehead. Russ straps in and dives into the dataset.

"Here's Sheng Long's operations log," Weiss narrates as he leads Russ through the compiled data. "These are our bad guys here, Epiphany Resources. It's a Macau Corporate venture, which explains the Sheng Long connection. Open-pit oil sands operation. Four mines, three in Alberta, one in Saskatchewan.

About two months ago, they take keen interest in Theo Smith, for some reason. They approach him in a roundabout way, but he rejects them flat out. They try again a few more times to the same end. The carrot doesn't work so it's time for the stick. They hire Sheng Long to abduct him, along with the wife and his kid on the side as leverage. The kid gets away, Smith and his wife are taken to one of Epiphany Resources's Alberta mines in the Cold Lake region, a three-hour drive from Edmonton, along the Saskatchewan border. All indications are that they're still being held there. Recon UAV is already in the area and a tactical team is being deployed from Chicago as we speak. Pratt is putting together the plan of action, no details yet on when and how."

"Does this put Sundance in danger?"

"The working assumption is that Sheng Long doesn't know that Smith is ours. If they did, they probably wouldn't have dared touch him. They had him under surveillance before they made the move, but there's no way for them to crack our network encryption. All data traffic between us and Smith was safe. They raided his workshop before they left, took everything worth taking, but they'll get nothing out of that. None of the Sundance data was stored locally. At the end of each session all the data comes back to us. And even if they did know he worked with us, they wouldn't have known in what capacity exactly. Smith's one of the most sought-after people in the data analytics field, so we could just be another client looking to update their weather forecasting model or some shit like that. However, we don't know the details of Smith's present circumstance. We can't take the risk of this becoming a bigger problem than it already is, that's why we gotta go in fast."

Weiss clears up their field of vision and pushes the clutter of documents to the side.

They stack up neatly along the left edge in the order they've been viewed, then disappear into the background. A strip of four headshots pops up—three middle-aged men and a woman in her early thirties.

"Obviously, unscrambling the power structure of the Corporate venture is a fool's errand, but we've got some key underlings here. These are the Operations Directors of each of the four Epiphany Resources mines: Foster Wei, Wendy Gao, Peter Sasala, and Stuart Fletcher. Pretty unremarkable bunch, run-of-the-mill Edmonton taskmasters, other than our chief guy here, Fletcher. After earning a Ph.D. in Earth Sciences from California Institute of Technology, he spends four years in Beijing as an "Our Century" research fellow. Geodynamics. He then goes back to his alma mater as a Senior Research Scientist in geodynamics and Earth History. After six years at Caltech, he decides to cash in on his talents and heads up to Calgary, where he builds a career as a petrophysicist and reservoir engineer, working with major oil sands players in the Athabasca region. About five years ago, Fletcher gets hired by Epiphany Resources as Chief Operating Director for their entire operation.

Four mines sounds like a a lot, but compared to other ventures in the region it's more like managing a mom and pop shop. Essentially, he takes a big step down the industry ladder, and it makes me wonder why. Money talks, I guess. Maybe Epiphany threw too much moolah at him and he just couldn't say no. Then again, why would they do that? It doesn't make much sense for them to overpay for someone like Fletcher to run such a small operation. Any of these other grunts probably could have done the job, so there must be something else going on."

"Like what?"

"My guess, with oil markets in such a state of chaos, everyone is under pressure to secure reserves. Easy oil is gone forever, shale oil deposits are almost all played out, deep offshore and oil sands are the only ways to go. It's expensive and dirty, but who cares, right? The spice must flow, as they say, and besides we're all fucked anyway. There are no new discoveries, what's there is there, and if you want it you gotta either steal it or buy it. So, let's say our guys at Epiphany Resources are nice guys who are buying and not stealing. And if you're buying, wouldn't you want to know what exactly you're buying? Wouldn't you want to have a reliable expert with insider knowledge of the region's reservoirs to assess the value of potential takeover targets for you?"

"What does that have to do with Smith?" Russ asks.

"That's lots of data to grind through, and who's better at that than Theo Smith? They couldn't buy him so they stole him."

"You're taking a lot of big leaps to fill in the blanks."

"Isn't that what we're supposed to be doing here?"

"No. We're supposed to come up with actionable facts."

"Well, here's an actionable fact—whatever their fucking reason is, these assholes have our guy and we gotta find a way to get him back!"

An aerial image of an endless aspen forest pops up in their field of vision. "It's 2:00 am in Alberta, so we won't have a usable live UAV feed until it's morning there," Weiss continues. "This is from our Geosat pass three days ago."

As he zooms in on the image, black veins of service roads break up the smooth surface of the forest, winding and warping between dark pits of oil sands mines.

"This is where we think they took them," Weiss locks in on a cluster of buildings around a giant navel-like hole. "Elk Creek. Epiphany's flagship mine. The other three mines are satellite digs, the entire operation is run out of here—ore processing, project engineering, testing lab, administrative, security, workers' housing, everything. The big question is, how do we get in? Alberta is a Free Enterprise Territory..."

"So was Qatar," Russ interrupts him. "UAE, Kuwait, Bahrain. How did that work out for them?"

"What are you saying?"

"I'm saying Free Enterprise Demilitarized Zones aren't what they used to be, and these bastards should be made aware of that."

"And what? Storm the place? That's nuts. No one is going to risk being charged with willful infringement of Free Enterprise DMZ over this. We have business interests..."

"Saskatchewan is still a free-for-all. We give them a fair warning, take over their Saskatchewan operation. They need a little push? We threaten to go public. Sheng Long's data trail implicates them in no uncertain terms. We take it up to the Free Enterprise Security Council, make our case for intervention, then we bust in, and justice is on our side. Remember, we're the good guys here, and they're the crooked monsters nobody trusts anymore."

"Not bad, Oakley. Although, that might take a long time to play out, longer than Pratt's willing to wait."

"What do we know about the kid?" Russ asks.

"Still in the wind. Presumably, he's still with Belan. They'll turn up eventually."

"Really? That's our strategy? They'll just eventually turn up? We don't even know if they're still alive."

“Look, the focus right now is on getting Theo and his wife safely out of Alberta. We’re working with what we have, and we have nothing on the kid. Sheng Long lost track of them after Salt Lake City. They could be anywhere.”

At the click of the door latch Theo jumps to his feet, carried by the hope that his feeble attempt at rebellion yesterday has tipped the scale of power in his favor, at least a little. He stumbles into the foyer, ready to see Miles and Maritza dash through the door and into his open arms, but instead, Drey's ugly mug emerges from the shadows.

"Time to go to work, Mr. Smith."

"I'm not going anywhere," says Theo, struggling to withstand the cold rush of anger and disappointment surging through his body.

"Come on." Drey waves him out. "You have to fix what you broke yesterday."

"I'm not going anywhere," Theo backtracks. "I'm not taking one step through that door unless I see my son and my wife."

"Please, don't make me be a bad guy, Mr. Smith," Drey slowly makes his way inside. "I don't wanna use force."

Theo sits in one of the chairs by the table, then grabs tightly onto its thin plastic armrests.

"You do what you need to do and I'll do what I need to do," Theo says, bracing for what he knows is going to be a very short, one-sided fight.

Surprisingly, instead of grabbing him into a crushing headlock, Drey pulls up a chair and sits across from him.

"Listen," Drey slides his hands across the table like he's pushing an invisible gift toward Theo. "I know how you feel..."

"How could you possibly know how I feel?" Theo cuts him off.

"I have a kid too. A little daughter. Ten years old."

"Yeah? Was your daughter also kidnapped by a sadistic psychopath who's trying to force you to work for him? Because if that's how it is, I could certainly use your help. I'm really not sure what to do here, a little friendly advice would go a long way. Please, go on."

"There's no need to make this worse than it already is."

"Can it get any worse?"

"It can always get worse," Drey says matter-of-factly, staring Theo down. He then removes his Panoptic and somewhat ceremoniously turns it off, setting it aside. "I'm not supposed to tell you any of this," Drey continues in a low, confiding tone, "I'm not even supposed to talk to you off the record, but it's the sensible thing to do, so here it is. You're up for a nice surprise at the end of the day."

Theo stares back at him wordlessly, wanting to believe this show of solidarity. "What are you saying?"

"The boss has loosened up a little..."

"Meaning what, exactly?"

"Meaning your situation is about to improve. But only if you stop acting out and start complying with the orders. It's tough, I know. It doesn't seem like you have a choice, but you do. I suggest you make the right one."

Theo looks at him intently, searching for traces of compassion and integrity in his deep-set eyes, but finds nothing there but the dull glimmer of his own abjection.

"Please stop this buddy-buddy act, it's embarrassingly obvious what you're trying to do. Just tell me straight up what he sent you out here to tell me."

"Fair enough," Drey smirks, dropping all pretense of friendliness. "We're ready to make some concessions if you stop this nonsense."

"What kind of concessions?"

"You get back to work and I'll bring your wife here at the end of the day today. You can even stay in the same room together from now on."

"What about my son?"

"Well, here's the thing... We thought you should know, there's no point in trying to hide it. He's not here. We don't have your son. But we will soon."

"What do you mean?" Theo's eyes widen.

"He got away, back in California, but we tracked him down and now we're in the process of bringing him in. So, we might as well continue under the assumption that we have him."

"Where is he? Is he okay?"

"I can't tell you any more than that."

Theo buries his face in his hands.

"C'mon, you'll be all together soon enough," Drey puts his hand on Theo's shoulder. "Let's go—and please no more drama, Mr. Smith. It's time we all start working together."

"I'm going up there," says Russ, flinging off his immersion kit.

Weiss rubs his eyes with his palms and turns around to say something, but realizes that Russ has already gotten up from his chair and is on his way to the commander's station. He tilts back, crosses his arms, and with confused admiration watches Russ zoom through the physical stillness of the TOC floor, bouncing and rolling between unmoving heads and blinking displays like a loose ball bearing.

Why does he think that taking a half-baked piece of information to Pratt would be a good idea? If there's one thing Pratt hates, it's being told half a story, especially if it's the half that leads to more questions and no answers. You gotta give it to him though, the entire team missed the game connection. Such an obvious lead, right under everyone's noses, but Russ was the only one who caught it.

Russ climbs the flight of stairs up to Pratt's office and just as he's about to knock on the door, Pratt sees him and waves him in. As he opens the door, Pratt raises his index finger in the air, mouths something, then points to his ear. For a moment, Russ just stands there, neither in nor out, with Pratt staring back at him intently yet somehow absentmindedly, and he starts wondering if he's waiting on him to start talking or if he's still processing whatever is coming into his ear.

"Come in, Russ," Pratt says finally. "What is it?"

"Smith's kid popped up on the net."

"That's progress. Go on."

"We tracked him down on Eyeconic, one of the gaming agglomerates, playing a game called EternalQuest. It's a yearly global tournament, immensely popular, especially among brainy kids. As of yesterday, he was one of the last four players left in his age group."

"And?" Pratt flips his palms up like he's hastily opening an invisible book.

"Last night he played the semis. Six-hour session."

"From where?"

"We don't know. Someplace well concealed. We tried nailing down the point of origin, but all we got were false hits halfway across the world: Australia, Gabon, Portugal, the Cook Islands in the South Pacific. Guys on the floor have never seen location encryption like this. No one knows what to do next."

"How do we even know it was him?"

"The game requires biometric login."

"That can be tampered with. Maybe someone is trying to flush him out, get him to react."

"I don't see it. Sheng Long is knocked out. Who else? We're fairly certain he did play last night. No one would be able to pick up game skills that quickly and play a full session at such a high level. And he crushed it, according to the reactions on the game's social platform."

"Did he interact with anyone?"

"No. He just logged in, played the round, and logged out."

"So, basically we got nothing?"

"That's not true. We just have to put the pieces together. We gotta do something for that family, they suffered enough. We gotta find this kid. What good are we if we can't even protect our own?"

"What does it look like we're doing right now, Russ? What the fuck?" Pratt shakes his head annoyed.

"Sorry," Russ apologizes.

Pratt waves him off and then slowly walks behind his desk, the stress of the situation clearly weighing down on his shoulders.

"Keep sifting through what we have. What else do we know about Belan? Dig into that social platform, try to find some connection—friends, family, anything. And we gotta crack that loc encryption algorithm. We can't do shit if we can't find out where he is."

"Well, I'm sure he'll turn up," Russ says sourly, recalling Weiss's remark from before. "Maybe in Tibet next time, or Helsinki, or maybe even right here at TOC."

"What the fuck are you saying?"

"Whoever designed that encryption likes to take the piss out of people. Every time we run the search it gives us some mocking smack along with the bogus coordinates, like: 'Did you check your asshole, asshole?' 'Blessings be upon you, shit for brains.' 'Simon says, sniff my balls.' 'I don't appreciate your assholean intentions, Dave.' Stuff like that. They want us to know that they're toying with us. They want to piss us off so we keep doing it over and over again. Here's the brilliant part—it looks like it's also a self-learning algorithm, so the more we run it the more it learns about us. At one point it gave us the exact location of our own safe house in Vientiane, in Laos."

"Wait, what? Vientiane?"

"Yes, Vientiane. Why?"

"Are you sure?"

"Yeah, I'm sure. As a matter-of-fact, that one popped up twice, it was the only repeat we got. And by the way, didn't we pull out of Laos altogether ages ago?"

"Yes, we did."

"So why would we still have a safe house there?"

"We don't."

"So, what's it reading then?"

Pratt sits at his desk, opens up the decision support engine, then slides along the operation development timeline.

"When did you get that hit?" he asks, shuffling through recent entries.

"About an hour and a half ago."

Pratt finds the tracking sequence and plays it back on his display. A satellite image of Southeast Asia comes up. GeoTrack zooms toward Laos, then further down to Vientiane, finally locking onto a small building on Rue Nokeokoummane, two blocks away from the Mekong River and Thailand border. Thin white characters fade in, marking the coordinates of the building's location, followed by an animated green and red dragon, menacingly baring his teeth, huffing and puffing gray smoke out of his nostrils. The smoke whirls and dances, filling up the entire image, and then starts shrinking and curling, organizing itself to form the words *"Here be dragons, bitches."*

"This is good, Russ," Pratt smiles.

"I don't understand."

"Come around."

Russ crosses the room and looks up at the display over Pratt's shoulder. All he can see is the orange fiery ball of the dragon's eye, a thin black slit running through the middle of it. Pratt presses and holds a couple of keys on his control tablet and the words *"Level Three Clearance Confirmed"* flash out, prompting GeoTrack to zoom out from the building on Rue Nokeokoummane, out from Vientiane, Laos, and the Indochinese Peninsula. It then pans across the Pacific Ocean, past the west coast of North America, over the forests and deserts of California, Nevada, and Utah, before it starts its descent on the high plains of Wyoming. Finally, it locks its crosshairs onto a pine forest some twenty miles from the Wyoming/South Dakota border, displaying the geographical coordinates of the location.

"Wait, what happened here?" Russ asks. "How did we end up in the Black Hills all the way from Vientiane?"

"Their location encryption algorithm took our bait."

"What does that mean?"

Pratt spins around in his chair, away from the display, and looks at Russ with a commanding smile.

"A self-learning algorithm is a hell of a weapon, but it's a double-edged sword. Two-way communication is always prone to counterattack. If you can latch onto it and crack into the codebase, you can also use its own structure to reverse the data flow. We let this one steal a genuine, but irrelevant piece of information—in this case, the location of our defunct safe house, then we followed it as it went back to its data repository. If you manage to get inside the data repository, then it's just a matter of knowing what to look for. Kind of like a reverse hack. Once you find your target and with reversed data flow now enabled, the algorithm is compelled to send the data back to you. But you can't go on a looting rampage, you gotta be nimble, stealthy, and see what you can get away with because it'll detect you sooner than you think. Once it figures out it's been duped, the algorithm self corrects fairly quickly, rewrites its code, and kicks you out. The next time you try it will be more difficult because it knows you're coming. Machines can end up slugging it out like that ad infinitum, for minimal gain, so if the information you're looking for is time-sensitive, it usually ends up being a waste of time and resources. Basically, you get one good shot at it. Luckily we got a hit."

Pratt turns back to the display and starts slowly zooming in on a small clearing in the middle of the forest.

"There's nothing there," Russ squints at the display.

Just as he says that, the GeoTrack flashes a message: *"Ghost Site Detected."*

"Oh, it's there," Pratt says cheerily as he reaches for his control tablet. "They just think they can hide."

The display softly flutters up, switching to an augmented view of the same location, this time showing a bird's-eye view of a cluster of low-lying buildings in close proximity to one another, a compound of some sort.

"Nothing like the calm and quiet of country living, eh Russ?" Pratt jokes.

"Fuck," Moonie mutters under his breath, watching his truck drop out of sight down a narrow road between the rocky hills surrounding Billygoat Lodge.

Two PSCs showed up at their door this morning, to "help" them move into a suite. Unlike the other generic brutes Driggs has surrounded himself with, these two actually seem like nice enough guys. They even have names—Tim and Barkley. They're friendly, but firm, like one would be toward a new pet. Hopefully, they didn't spook Miles too much. After Barkley told him they're going to move his truck to a "secure lot," Moonie asked him if he could get his working clothes out of the trunk first. Miles could use another layer of clothing too and it wouldn't hurt to have a waterproof jacket and rain boots nearby in case the weather starts turning. Who knows how long they'll be stuck here?

Driggs threw him completely off balance last night. This week's crazy chain of events blurred his focus and he wasn't sure how to deal with this new situation. Are they being held hostage now? In retrospect, it really shouldn't have been a big surprise that Driggs would pull something like this. You don't get to stay invisible to the world for this long by leaving things to chance. The PSCs refused to give them back their Allcoms when they got back from Driggs's last night. And now they took away his truck too.

Moonie folds his raincoat in a neat square and sticks it inside the duffle bag with the rest of his work clothes, then grabs his boots and heads back to the suite. As he walks by the barroom, through its smudged windows he sees his reflection moving alongside him, looking as surprised as he is at the physical likeness between them. He takes a quick glance inside and sees Tim standing by the entrance door, camouflaged by uneven shadows, looking right back at him. He smiles and waves at Moonie, then slips into the darkness of the barroom like a disembodied spirit.

Back in the suite, he finds Miles reading a book.

"Hey, kiddo."

"Hey," says Miles, not taking his eyes off the page.

"Where did you find a book?"

"There's a bunch of them by the fireplace. They're all like a hundred years old. There are some old board games too. The whole pile smells funky."

"Ha. What's that one about?"

"Stuff you were talking about earlier, Black Hills gold rush. It's interesting, you should read it when I'm done. Looks like there were hundreds of little towns around here at the time. There are maps of all these old mining camps and tips on how to locate them. This place is in it too. It had a different name before, though. People would stay here when they came to look for these ghost towns and abandoned mines. Apparently, that was a thing to do on the weekend, go hiking in the woods looking for ruins."

"That could be fun. Maybe we should do that one day."

"Sure," Miles says unenthusiastically and shuts the book. "They brought these in while you were out," he points at two identical black cuboid boxes on top of the rough-hewn desk in the corner.

"Listen, Miles, they switched up this thing on me. We just have to stay here a little longer than I thought, which in our case might not be such a bad thing anyway, right?" Moonie flashes a grin.

"How much longer?"

"That's the thing, I don't know. It might be two weeks, it might be two months. Sorry. There's nothing I can do. I'm not the one calling the shots."

"I know, it's just... What if my parents start looking for me? And my friends... Everyone is worried. Nobody knows where I am."

"I understand, but the best thing for us to do right now is to do exactly nothing, to wait it all out. Sometimes that's the hardest part. We don't know if Sheng Long is still after us. At least we're safe here. Once this deal gets off the ground we'll be on our way. It'll happen, I know it."

"Okay."

"What are these?" Moonie grabs one of the black boxes from the desk.

"I don't know. Tim said they were for us."

Moonie runs his fingers across the sharp, sleek edges of the box looking for a way to open it. The box emits a short soft sound, and blue light the size of an apricot pit appears in the middle of it, pulsating dimly. Moonie covers the light with his right index finger, allowing it to scan his fingertip. The box unlocks itself and he slides the two halves apart to uncover a thin, three-by-five-inch tablet cradled inside.

"It's a OneWay," he turns to Miles.

"Also known as a NoWay," Miles adds.

"They could have at least given us something with a bigger display."

"Makes no difference when all you can see is preprogrammed garbage."

"I guess you're right." Moonie grabs the other box and tosses it across the room to Miles. "Here, this one's yours."

Bemused by their new devices, they don't notice Tim standing in the door frame, watching them. He waits for a few moments, then knocks on the open door and without waiting for an answer, steps inside.

"At least he knocks," says Moonie, not trying to veil his

agitation.

"Gotta have manners," Tim smirks.

"Something you need?"

"It's time to make the call."

"Right now?"

"Why, are your people late risers?"

"This is a receiver only," Moonie raises the OneWay in his hand.

"Yes, it is," Tim nods coolly.

"How am I supposed to call anyone with this?"

Tim reaches inside his jacket and pulls out Moonie's Allcom. He hesitates for a moment before handing it to him.

"One call. That's it."

With his Allcom in hand, Moonie crosses the room and walks outside on the terrace, sliding the glass door behind him. Just as the door is about to clack closed, Tim grabs the handle and slides it back open.

"Do you mind?" says Moonie unnerved.

"Sorry buddy, I gotta make a record of it for the boss," he taps his Panopticon.

Moonie goes through his pockets, produces the polymer encryption key card, and scans it with his Allcom, initiating the call to Lark.

*"Please provide the spectral and numeral keys to continue,"* his Allcom sounds off.

Moonie looks up at Tim warily.

"Go on now," Tim encourages him. "Don't mind me."

*"Please provide the spectral and numeral keys to continue,"* the Allcom repeats patiently.

"Blue, blue, yellow, six, blue, six, indigo, seven..." Moonie starts reciting the access code.

Sunk in a drugged-out stupor, her eyes riveted on the ceiling, Maritza watches the heaving afternoon shadows appear from nowhere and vanish into nothing. Fractals... Chaos theory... The butterfly effect... A glimmer of memory sparks through her mind. They're in an orchard. Miles is by her side, giggling and squealing in a toddler's falsetto while pointing at a worm inside a fallen apple he found lying on the ground.

"Look, Mom, silly worm is eating his house!" Miles declares.

Theo is in front of them, carrying a wooden fruit crate full of freshly picked apples on his shoulder. He turns around, laughing at Miles's revelation, then disappears behind the branches of apple trees.

Maritza feels a small tear building in the corner of her eye. As she turns her head to the side, the tear rushes across her temple and flees into the pillowcase, leaving a faint mark. Sunrays dance in through a narrow window and blend with the light streaks of the images that are bouncing off of the display, exposing the incandescent haze of dust particles floating aimlessly in the air. She forces herself out of bed, but gets up too quickly and her legs buckle at the knees as she struggles to maintain her balance. She grips the side of the bed and waits for the lightheadedness to subside, then slowly walks up to the display and searches for a way to turn it off. Unable to find the off switch, she pulls the two lamps placed on top of the dresser beneath the display closer together, then throws pillows and blankets on the makeshift scaffold to block it off.

Where is she? What is this place? She looks out of the window, compelled not to repress the confusion any longer. How did she end up here? The questions circle in her muddled mind and her surroundings offer no clues. She goes to the bathroom and splashes her face with cold water a few times, then looks at herself in the mirror, continuing her search for answers. She remembers sitting at the kitchen table with Theo, waiting for Miles to come down and have breakfast. There was another person with them. A woman she didn't know. Who was she? And what was she doing in their kitchen?

She strains to recall the morning. It could have been days ago, even months ago, she had no way of telling. Suddenly, Maritza hears somebody at the door. She turns around and sees Drey standing there, looking at her.

"Who are you?" she asks, vaguely remembering his face.

"Mrs. Smith, it's time to go."

"Go where?"

"Your husband is waiting for you."

Miriam is pissed. Russ can tell by the way she throws her purse on the table in the foyer, hastily stuffs her coat into the closet then, without a word, marches straight into the kitchen and starts making herself a snack.

"Hey," Russ walks up behind her.

"Go ahead and get yourself killed already. I don't care anymore," Miriam says quietly, without turning around.

All morning, after Russ told her he's going on a trip, she felt it creeping up on her—that same blunt, disorienting pain that rushed through her body when they told her his plane went down in the desert, that wrenching agony that turned to euphoria when the search and rescue unit found him two days later, unconscious but still breathing.

For the next few weeks, while Russ was shuttled between intensive care and surgery rooms at the military hospital in Turkey, she tried to stay calm and strong, determined to withstand whatever came their way. He was alive; that's all that mattered. But there's no courage without fear. It wasn't until two months later, when they finally brought him back to Brooklyn and she watched him smile quietly—his head shrunken on top of the body cast, his eyes soft and tired, his left arm, one of the few unbroken parts of his body, dangling awkwardly off the side of the hospital bed—that the fear finally overwhelmed her, that mix of irrational fear of what had already happened and the very real fear that it could all happen again.

"I'm sorry, I didn't mean that," she turns around to face him. "I just can't believe you'd want to go back in the field, after everything we went through. And how do you even think you can manage it physically? You can't even walk for more than two miles without doubling over."

"It's not like that. This is something different. I'm done with tactical engagement. Forever."

"Where are you going?"

"Black Hills. Three or four days, max."

"Why you? Can't they send somebody else?"

"This is what I do..."

"Here we go again. That 'once a soldier always a soldier' bullshit. What about me? What about us? You've done your part. I've done my part. We deserve a chance to have a normal life, don't we?"

"Honey, nothing really changes. It's just a few days, I'll be back pixel counting at the DOA before you know it."

"Right," she says, a frown pulling at her brow. "Because that's how it works."

His sweet Miriam. He'll never understand why she chose to share her life with him. Why would anyone voluntarily accept all the crap that comes with this job, his hard-edged surface, the sudden disappearances, long absences, and moody secrecy, and now this wreck that he's become? She deserves much more than he could give her. And she's right to be upset—he had broken an unspoken agreement between them by taking a field assignment. But he couldn't say no when Pratt asked him. The thought of getting back out there, outside of the confines of his four walls, was just way too tempting.

Russ packs lightly, then comes out to the living room to see Miriam on the sofa, knees up, gazing at the display in her lap, making an effort not to look his way.

"I don't know what else to say," he utters solemnly.

"Then don't say anything," Miriam responds with false indifference. "Do you need help with the bag?"

"I think I can manage that much," Russ smiles, unsure if that was a whimsical dig or genuine concern on her part, then leans over and kisses her on the head. "Thank you."

Not counting the sedated trip home from Turkey on military transport, Russ hasn't been on a plane since the crash. He thought he might get anxious, but he didn't even have time to think about it. They originally booked him on the last flight of the day, but that flight got canceled so he had to scramble to make the one that was leaving three hours earlier; otherwise the whole operation would have had to be pushed back a full day. He barely made it, and before he could properly get settled in his seat, they were airborne—and up there, it's too late for fear.

The war was fast approaching, but the world still hung in a state of suspended disbelief. Sometimes, hope dies last. On the surface, it seemed like there was still time to stop the bloodshed. There were peace initiatives at play, negotiations, eleventh-hour diplomacy efforts, and calls to reason, all of it amounting to little more than an exercise in deception. The beast of war had awakened, its finger already on the trigger—and the caskets were being hewn.

As the intensity of the skirmishes picked up, interagency chatter became a cacophony of last-minute maneuvering. Russ knew the aerial assault was imminent when his group was pulled out of Beirut and sent to Incirlik Air Base. As one of the agents with extensive tactical experience, he was put on an exfiltration unit under the command of the Gulf Guard Alliance to help with evacuations. They flew three missions in two days, airlifting civilian personnel stranded at oil installations in Qatar and in Kuwait. It was in the middle of their fourth run when things went straight to hell.

They were leaving the embassy in Manama, Bahrain, with nine in tow; a commercial attaché, his wife, their twelve-year-old son, a Belgian ambassador, his bodyguard, and four Norwegian nationals. Muffled explosions and pecks of small arms fire along the outskirts echoed through empty streets. Then, one after another, three guided missiles screamed out of the sky, ripping the air in ribbons and lighting up the horizon with a phosphorous blue. On the causeway, several pickup trucks full of young men in civilian clothes wielding assault weapons and RPGs rushed by them on their way to the harbor, as helicopters crisscrossed the curtain of black smoke above the bay. The airport was next to be hit, but they were told to proceed. When they got there, a skeleton airport crew was scrambling to get a few hundred panicked civilians on two charter planes that were waiting on the tarmac. None of them made it out.

About twenty minutes into the flight, the cockpit display started bleeding out with predicted trajectories of airborne missiles. A systematic and indiscriminate effort at annihilation by both sides was well underway—and they were in the middle of it. To avoid the worst of the shooting, they were instructed to head west, deeper into the desert. As they lowered their altitude, they could see missile craters pockmarking the flawless surface of the desert. Then out of nowhere, the sky turned black and smoke from underneath started seeping inside the cabin, forcing them to put their masks on.

Through foggy glass, Russ looked at the inferno below. Entire oil fields violently exploded into spectacular nebulae, sending waves of flames high up in the air before dying down in an ominous orange glow that kept throbbing below boiling black clouds. Then a burst of light, a silent panic behind the gas masks, and the crashing thunder from the hit. A part of the wing was blown away and the engine was now dangling unsupported, sending the entire plane into spastic convulsions and its passengers into fits of pure terror. Finally, the engine broke off, taking the rest of the wing with it and sending them spiraling down in free fall, weightless nothingness, which now lives deep in his memory.

Nudged off balance by high-altitude winds whipping down from the Rockies, the plane tacks and veers as it touches down, prompting the woman in the seat next to Russ to grab his forearm, squeezing and tugging him for support with each loud thump of the grinding wheels. A few whispery gasps escape from the back rows of the plane as the passengers fling forward and back like string puppets bowing repeatedly at the end of a show. Finally, the plane's spoilers deploy, reducing the speed, and the aircraft's weight transfers fully to its wheels. Gradually relaxing her grip, the woman lets out a quiet sigh of relief, then snaps back after realizing that her armrest was not an armrest.

"Oh, I'm so sorry," she springs her hand off of Russ's forearm, slightly embarrassed.

"It's all right," Russ smiles. "It gets bumpy sometimes."

"This was a little more than I was ready for," the woman says.

"Still in one piece. That's what counts, right?"

"Ladies and gentlemen, welcome to Denver," the in-flight announcement blares, setting the cabin in motion. "It's a balmy sixty-three degrees in the Mile High City this evening, a bit windy, as you can tell..."

As they pull up to the gate Russ leaps out of his seat, looking to gain ground before everyone stands up and clogs the aisle with their carry-ons. The splendor of flying commercial. Up ahead, a couple of empty seats in the back of first class are luring him like unclaimed thrones. ACIS could have splurged a little.

First out of the door, he activates a motion-sensitive hologram and a dazzling burst of colors overtakes the drabness of the beige aluminum paneling, covering the walls of the jetway with a beautiful moving image of a mountain meadow in full bloom. At the far end of the meadow, a covered wagon is jiggling on a distant trail.

*"Welcome to Pioneer Provisions Denver International Airport,"* a voice emerges from somewhere. *"Find yourself at home, here in the heart of America's pioneer spirit."*

The hologram is so vivid, that Russ can almost feel grass blades and flower petals swaying around his ankles, the freshness of the clear mountain air, the warmth of the sun on his face.

*"Pioneer Provisions, your one source for all your consumer needs,"* the voice continues, as the image of the covered wagon grows bigger, wrapping itself lengthwise around the back end of the jetway and transforming the exit into the back entrance of the wagon.

*"Explore! Live it up! Embrace the adventure! Pioneer Provisions will be with you every step of the way."*

True to their promise, Pioneer Provisions meets him on the other side of the wagon as he steps into the arrivals area, this time in the form of a boring translucent display hanging over a two-lane corridor: *"Pioneer Provisions—a Hoovers Subsidiary."*

Directly below the display, pulsating red arrows are pointing to the opposite sides of the corridor: *"New America Citizens"* to the right, *"Noncitizens"* to the left. Russ takes the left lane to the end of the corridor. As he turns into the customs control waiting area, an athletic, sharp-eyed man in plain clothes signals him to step outside the lane to one of the security substations, behind a bank of frosted glass panels. Inside, the man puts on a pair of surgical gloves, then unseals a DNA collection kit and pulls a cotton-tipped swab applicator out of it.

"Mr. Oakley, please open your mouth."

"No," Russ responds coolly. "I'm not doing that."

The man tries to hide his surprise with a blank stare, twiddling the long, thin wooden handle of the applicator between his fingers like an unpaired chopstick, waiting for further instructions from whoever is in his ear. The men study each other's faces silently for a moment, waiting for time to pass.

"Understood," the man utters under his breath, responding to the voice in his earpiece.

He tosses the applicator aside and picks up a biometrics authenticator, scans Russ's palms, face, and retinas, and then, without a word, dips his eyes to the screen and waits for validation. The authenticator chirps and flashes green.

"Follow me," he snaps the rubber gloves off and waves Russ through an unmarked door.

They exit out to the tarmac and get inside one of the small service vehicles parked in the shadows below the gates. With the adroit efficiency of a person who's firmly in charge, the man steers through the gate traffic of mechanics, baggage handlers, and caterers, then cuts across the double yellow lines of the runways toward an isolated hangar at the back end of the tarmac, about a mile from the terminal building. A few moments after their arrival, the hangar door slides open and a two-seater light jet rolls out of it and lines up for takeoff.

"Thank you," Russ gives the man a nod as he steps out of the vehicle.

"Yah," the man nods back.

Russ scrunches his shoulders to squeeze through the jet door, then jams his body into a small but cushy space behind the pilot.

"Good to go," he says, clicking the belt. "How long to Rapid City you reckon?"

"Not much more than an hour," the pilot answers.

"All right, light her up then."

------

The last few houses and barns on the outskirts of Rapid City trickle by them, swallowed by the encroaching nightfall as the road ahead gradually shrinks to the size of their headlight beams, a lone pale gash inching through the vast expanse of darkness.

"So where are you from, Russ?"

Russ stifles a yawn, regretting he underestimated Ty's appetite for unprompted chatter. The kid has been chewing his ear off from the minute he picked him up at the airport, jabbering flat-out like his life would end instantly if he were to stop, even for a moment.

"Upstate New York," Russ takes his time before answering, hoping to slow him down.

"Cool, New York native," Ty bubbles up. "Me too. I was born in Queens, but I grew up on Long Island. Massapequa Park, Oyster Bay. Strong Island!" he raises his fist in the air, only half-joking. "My mom's from around here though. She moved back to RC after my dad passed, a few years ago. I'd come to visit her, once-twice a year, when I was at the academy, then somehow it just became a thing. They thought I'd do well starting out as a junior agent here, so they put me up in Sioux Falls after graduation. Sometimes I get called up to Minneapolis or to Fargo when they need help, but yeah, this here is my domain, my little piece of turf, Sioux City, Badlands, Black Hills. Between us, I'm not so sure this is really where I should be at this point in my career. You know, it's kind of slow around here, not much happening. Careful what you wish for, right? Yeah, I know. I just feel like I need to go out there and get some real field experience. So, as you can imagine, I'm excited to be part of this operation. I'm really glad you're here."

"Good."

Under a blanket of tall trees, the road winds up a series of switchbacks, elbowing out precariously to the edges of the cliffs. Suddenly, the car speed drops to twenty, their seats begin quivering with short, intense pulses, and the Trip Status Alert warning starts flashing on the dashboard, followed by the incessant dinging of the alarm.

*"Demanding road conditions ahead,"* the Vehicle Advisory System sounds out. *"Would you like to revert to manual control?"*

Ty pokes at the control panel a few times with his finger, overriding the warning notification. The dinging and seat vibrations stop.

*"Autonomous mode maintained. For your safety, stay vigilant during this stage of the trip. Be prepared to take control of the vehicle if needed."*

Ty squints at the road, assuring himself that the computer is back at work before turning to Russ with a fresh dose of irritating curiosity.

"So, how long have you been with ACIS?"

Russ arches his brow.

"A long time."

"A long time like two years or a long time like twenty years?"

"You think two years is a long time?"

"Two years is a very long time. Twenty years, that's a lifetime."

"How old are you, Ty?"

"Twenty-three."

Russ gazes out into the shifting darkness, and wonders if he thought the same thing when he was Ty's age. Probably.

"You should take the wheel. We wanna get there tonight, don't we?"

"There's no need, we'll pick up speed soon. I've driven this road before. Once we're over the hill, it's a straight shot to the lodge. We'll get there in time, don't worry. I've done a little research," Ty smirks. "Nothing happens before the girls come out, which is usually around midnight. Just a bunch of sullen dudes sitting around staring at their drinks. Later we get there, the better."

"Yeah? And why is that?"

"Because everyone will be too loaded to pay close attention to us."

"It's not like we're going to rob the place."

"Yeah, but we don't want to raise suspicion. Right?" he asks, not entirely convinced of the validity of his argument.

"Why would we raise any suspicion?" Russ asks. "We're just a couple of regular guys blowing off steam, trying to have a good time."

"Right."

"I'm gonna close my eyes just for a minute," Russ says. "Long day..."

"Of course. Make yourself comfortable. It's not an easy trip, I know..."

"Hey Ty," Russ cuts him off. "Once we get there, it's best if you stand back and let me do the talking, okay?"

"Okay. It's not a problem. We're going in as a team, you do the talking, and I'll..."

"As a matter-of-fact, why don't you practice keeping quiet for a while? Maybe starting right now."

"Oh, I got it. Done," Ty ceremoniously pretends to zip his mouth shut.

Russ lowers his seat, clasps his hands behind his head, and shuts his eyes.

"You know," Ty breaks the short-lived silence, "some people believe seniority is an outdated concept."

"Yeah," Russ stirs up in his seat, looking for comfort, his eyes still closed. "It's a shitty thing when you don't have any."

------

The smell of rotting wood and spilled beer greets them as they enter Billygoat. The place looks dead despite being almost half-filled with T&A aficionados sucking on beer bottles and fiddling idly with their devices. No one seems in a rush to acknowledge their presence as Russ and Ty walk across the barroom. They find an empty table in the back, to the right of the stage, and sit there. After a few minutes, a petite blond with balloon boobs two sizes too big for her frame walks up.

"Hiya," she drops two RFIDs on the table.

"We'll need only one of those. Tonight's all on me," Russ pushes one of the RFIDs back. "What's your name, honey tits?"

"Caprice."

"That's a nice name," Russ pairs up the RFID with his Allcom. "Well, Caprice, my buddy here is about to make the biggest mistake of his life." He puts his arm on Ty's shoulder and gives him a friendly shake. "I wanna give him a little taste of what he's gonna be missing when the young missus takes the reins."

"Congratulations," Caprice chirps up.

"Only twenty-three and rushing to get married! Can you believe it?"

"It's never too soon to marry the right person," she offers her two cents.

The house music fades down and an up-tempo track comes on.

"Welcome, welcome, welcome, ladies and gentlemen, to Nurse Lilly Frolic and Detour Fair," a woman's voice blasts out from behind the stage curtain. "Thank you all for coming out tonight to take a turn for the nurse. Now I don't know if you're all aware, but we got naked ladies here tonight!"

Suddenly, the animated crowd sends a few claps and whoops toward the stage as a woman's leg in sheer thigh-high stockings glides in through the crack in the curtain.

"And, as always," the MC continues, "we have a little foreplay before the main event. Coming out to the go-go spot, please welcome the lovely Bambi Boo!"

Bambi Boo slips through the curtain, skimming the sides of her breasts, curving and arching her ass to the beat of the music. In a few smooth, theatrical moves she steps off the stage and without giving up an inch of her seductiveness, curls between the tables to the small round platform of the go-go spot in the middle of the barroom.

"Grab a drink, take a hit, do a line. We're gonna get the show started shortly. Bambi Boo, everyone!"

"Gentlemen, two whiskey sours," Caprice comes back with their drinks, and from somewhere inside her glittering booty shorts produces a blister pack of peach-colored pills. "And a little something extra on the side," she tears two pills off and hands them to Russ. "Compliments of the house."

"What do we have here?" Russ looks at the pills.

"A little something to perk you up, if you feel in the mood."

"Light or heavy?"

"Dex-three."

"Real thing? I don't want some hillbilly chalk."

"It's bonded. I use it myself."

"I never knew those things have pockets." Russ smiles while looking at Caprice's tight shorts.

"I'm full of surprises," she smiles back flirtatiously.

"I bet you are. You should get up there on the stage, show us what you got."

"Maybe I will," Caprice whips her hair to the side as she walks off, leaving behind a dash of cotton candy scented air.

Ty waits for the waitress to leave then leans in toward Russ.

"What's Dex-three?" he asks under his breath.

"Dextroamphetamine variety."

"We can't..." Ty's eyes grow big. "Is that gonna show up on the drug test?"

"There's some wiggle room with amphetamines. Obviously, you don't have to take it, it's for show. Just put in your pocket and flush it down the toilet later."

The music shifts again, this time to a lively lounge track full of light brass and soft snare. The curtain opens up and a voluptuous woman wearing a shiny gold and green outfit and an intricate helmet-like headpiece steps on the stage.

"Who's ready for the show? We got Tiny D here tonight in the house, gentlemen. We also have Sierra... brrr... snappy Sierra, Melody Mae, sweet ass Satin, Bunny Vega, Luva Flow is here, and let's not forget the lovely Bambi Boo!"

She waits for the crowd's reaction, then continues through the clapping and cheers. "Welcome to Billygoat! I'm your hostess, obviously with the mostess," she props her ample bust with her palms, then gives it a playful jiggle. "My name is Trifecta. Yeah, that's right! Those who know me know the holy trinity of my talents. But enough about me," she breaks out into a quick, high-pitched chuckle. "I'm just kidding, of course. I'm feeling awesome, ladies and gentlemen. I just recently dyed my hair purple, I don't know if you guys can tell," she twists around on the runway, stroking her purple locks gently. "Now, yesterday I broke my toe, don't ask how it happened. I'm not even completely sure myself, so I might be on painkillers tonight. Just keep that in mind when bidding, you might get a more relaxed version of me. Speaking of things that make you feel good, we have something very special tonight. Our first performer is a huge talent in a tiny package, and she's gonna come out here and dance like she's never danced before. Please give it up for the tiny dancer of your dreams, Tiny D!"

Tiny D takes the stage with a confident sexy strut and gets on with her routine of provocative hip thrusts, rump shakes, and playful titty tassel twirls. With all eyes locked on on Tiny D, Russ takes a moment to scan the room. Upfront, in the pervert row, there's a mix of burnout hogs and young wannabes blissfully chubbed up by the proximity of real-life female flesh. Right behind them, two men, both over fifty, with a couple of could-be sisters, basic white girls. Older one's probably eighteen or nineteen; the other, despite an elaborate slutty getup, isn't looking a day over sixteen. To the left of the stage, spread across a few tables, a bunch of greasy local stiffs are hollering and bullshitting each other. A string of lone gawkers lined up on the bar stools are ardently following Tiny D's every move, her every thigh stroke, deep squat, and suggestive crotch rub. Away from the rest of the patrons, in the half-moon booth in the far corner, a man is sitting by himself, occupied by something in his eyepiece and not paying attention to the show, unlike Ty, who's barely blinked twice since Tiny D came on.

"Nice little spinner, eh?" says Russ.

"What's that?" Ty snaps back from his lust stupor, hiding the guilt in the corner of his eyes.

"I said, nice little spinner," Russ cocks his chin up toward the stage.

"What do you mean?"

"Oh, nothing," Russ waves it off, slightly annoyed with Ty's cluelessness. "I'll put in a bid."

Tiny D drops to her knees, stirring forward in a submissive crawl, grinding her glutes against an invisible lover. She then twists around into cowgirl position, meshing and riding the full measure before running the palms of her hands down her hips and slipping her fingers between the hot pink strings of her black lace underwear. She plays with the knots a little, then pulls the strings and slides her underwear off from under her, flicks it away, and then with her best orgasmic face, tosses her head side to side and brings her performance to a spirited crescendo.

"Give it up for Tiny D, everybody!" Trifecta comes back

from behind the curtains as the music dies down.

Tiny D receives a standing ovation and takes a bow.

"So juicy, like a cherry. Makes you think if you squeeze her, a little bit of delicious juice is going to come out," Trifecta declares, and gives Tiny D a longing look as she twirls off the stage. "Speaking of cherries, I lost mine a long time ago, but I still have the box that it came in. The night's young, folks!"

Just then, the entrance door opens and three remarkably similar-looking men in tight black V necks and matching fade haircuts come in. They linger by the entrance for a bit, checking out the room and gazing over people's heads like some weird triplicate of a thick, perplexed nimrod.

"One of the best things about Billygoat, is that everyone is welcome to come back for seconds. We give past performers a chance to get up and get naked all over again. It's fucking awesome, gentlemen! Now, after an eight-month hiatus, she's known as the naughty girl next door, and tonight she'll be known as the girl of your dreams. Rap, tap, tap your steel-toed boots together for the firmest butt this side of the Rockies—Sierra is up next!"

In a slow and deliberate manner, like they're looking for whoever is hiding in the shadows, the three newcomers cross the room and join the man wearing an eyepiece in the half-moon booth.

"Circuit?" asks Ty, trying not to look in their direction.

"Yup," Russ nods.

Sierra takes the stage and dazzles right away, rubbing and tugging on her glass-cutter nipples, pointing them randomly at the crowd like laser guns about to shoot out magic multicolored rays of pleasure. Spectacular ass, as advertised. Her whole body is amazing, in fact. Young and nimble, almost too perfect, smooth-skinned, tight and lightly oiled up, glimmering daringly under stage lights like a mylar balloon on the verge of bursting. All of a sudden, Russ feels someone's hands on his neck and shoulders, soft like declawed kitten paws. He turns around to see a petite brunette smiling down at him.

"Hi," she purrs.

"Hi," Russ replies, gazing at her big brown eyes.

"You guys want some company?"

Then he recognizes her. Tiny D. She looks older up close. Maybe it's her hair, which is now tamed in a fluffy bun.

"It's you," Russ says, genuinely surprised.

"Of course, it's me. Who did you expect?" she squeezes his shoulders gently. "You bid on my off-stage time and here I am, off-stage. Are you guys having a good time?"

"There's no place I'd rather be than right here, right now," says Russ. "You got some skills, girl."

"Thanks," she smiles, then playfully runs her fingertips over Russ's earlobes as she lifts her hands off his shoulders.

"So, where are you guys from?" she comes around the table to face them.

"Philadelphia," says Russ.

"Wow! How did you end up here?"

"Work."

"What do you do?" Tiny D asks, her eyes rustling inquisitively from Russ to Ty and back.

"We're water resource engineers."

"What does a water resource engineer do?"

"We make sure your tap water comes to you clean and safe, among other things."

"Hmm... that's an important job."

"Yes, it is," Russ confirms.

"You married?" Tiny D asks.

"Happily. But my buddy here isn't. Not yet. He's free for three more weeks. And he really likes what you did there on the stage. Maybe you can show him a couple of moves later that he can take to his bride-to-be."

"You two are cute. Keep bidding. If the price is right, I might come back... but only one gets the goods, no double-dipping."

She gives them one last lubricious look and then wanders off to another bidder, coasting between tables smoothly like a silk scarf blown by the wind.

# DAY_7

Russ managed to get a good night sleep, despite being woken up a few times by an unending loop of loud debauchery coming from behind the drywall—a blast of pulsating music, a round of foot-stomping and dancing accompanied by enthusiastic whoops and cheers, all fueled by whatever high-flying junk they were on. Then the music faded down and muffled conversation ensued, chopped up by high-pitched giggles and gurgling chortles, then a bout of aggressive, crashing sex, a rapid succession of "fucks," "fuck yeahs," and "oh fuck, oh fuck, oh fuck yeahs," all culminating in a mixture of coyote-like howls, wrenching near-cry moans, and orgasmic growls. It actually got quiet for a few minutes at one point, until a bottle got knocked over and rolled across the floor with the audacity of a bowling ball, which set them off all over again.

Russ reaches for his Allcom. A couple of status updates from Weiss. Nothing from Ty yet. Last night after the show, the crowd broke up into smaller groups, some leaving right away and some sticking around for another round of drinks at the bar. The high bidders waited at their tables to claim their luscious prizes. In an unexpected twist, they ended up winning the bid for Tiny D, even though they never intended to. The girls always have the last word, and Tiny D picked Ty over the greasy bearded guy with bulging frog eyes sitting in the front row who was willing to pay almost twice as much for her sweet ass. She sure had her share of ogres in this hole, but not tonight. Tonight, she was going to have some fun toying with a gullible wage slave. It didn't hurt that he was young, fit, and easy on the eyes. Maybe she was intrigued by the opportunity to be a guy's last fuck before he ties the knot; he's definitely going to remember her. The kid needed a little impromptu action to sharpen his instincts anyway, and he might learn a little something along the way.

A loud crash next door propels Russ out of his warm, dozy languor. His neighbors are now at each other's throats over something, cursing and shouting ferociously before inexplicably bursting into a fit of laughter—coarse, hard, crazy laughter that stops as abruptly as it started. It then gets oddly quiet for a moment, and Russ can hear birds fluttering in the treetops outside. Time to get up before they go at it in earnest again. A quick cold shower jumpstarts his senses and fine-tunes his brain. He gets dressed, pops a couple of painkillers, and steps out into the chilly morning, ready to take on whatever today throws at him.

Under sunless metallic light and devoid of people, the small hamlet of two-room log cabins looks like an abandoned set from an Old West historical show. Only clouds are moving, tumbling heavily, hiding the shards of winter from the far North inside their fluffy exterior. As he heads toward the barroom, the timeworn wooden walkway warbles under his feet, piercing the wailing humdrum of the wind with its throttled squeaks. A chipmunk kicks up a pile of dry leaves brimming over the edge of the walkway then quickly disappears under one of the loose planks, only to reemerge a second later. It stares quizzically at Russ, gauging the security of its winter den.

Russ walks up to Ty's cabin and bangs on the door. There's some commotion inside, followed by a short muffled conversation, then shuffling footsteps. Finally, Ty's sleepy face pokes out.

"What's up?"

"You all good in there?" Russ throws a glance inside.

"Yeah, yeah," Ty mumbles, bobbing his head to deliberately obstruct Russ's view.

Russ grins mischievously, catching sight of female feet sticking out from under the crumpled sheets.

"All right cowboy, come down to breakfast when you wrap up here. No rush."

The wooden walkway ends in a small dry bridge that connects the guest cabin area to the rest of the property, then splits into a network of narrow red brick paths covered with moss and fallen leaves. Some thirty yards to his right, three men in black uniforms emerge from the woods and climb inside a black utility vehicle idling in the parking lot. Russ waits until the vehicle drives off, then continues toward the barroom.

The air inside the barroom is stale and sticky, punctuated by the acrid scent of floor-cleaning solution. A pile of tables and chairs stacked slapdash on and around the stage give the room the feel of an abandoned storage room. He hears someone in the kitchen and peeks through the swinging doors. A short, stocky man in kitchen whites is chopping a gigantic onion on a steel counter. At the shriek of the door, he raises his eyes toward Russ.

"Hi," Russ offers a greeting.

The man stops his knife for a brief moment, silently inspects the stranger in his kitchen, then swings the onion around and continues to hack at it.

"Any chance I can get some coffee?" Russ asks.

"Coffee?" the cook responds with a snort of laughter.

He wipes the heap of chopped onions into a mixing bowl with the side of his palm, rinses his knife, then squats down and looks for something in the bottom drawer of the fridge. He's clearly done talking.

Russ retreats to the darkness of the barroom, takes the window table by the entrance, and puts on his eyepiece, engaging the ACIS relay protocol.

*"Welcome, GAMMA 7,"* the network authenticates him.

"Start CoreCast," Russ whispers the command.

*"CoreCast access denied."*

"What? Why?"

*"CoreCast participation requires the sanction of Level 3 command. Your current security permissions are restricted to Level 8."*

"Hammerheads," Russ leans back, gusting a sigh of annoyance. "Go upriver. Passive."

*"Wait,"* Weiss bumps him off as soon as the connection establishes.

A beam of light swipes across the barroom as a thin blond woman walks in through the backdoor. She wedges the door open, letting the fresh morning air in, and then starts patiently disentangling chairs and tables from the messy heap and arranging them methodically around the room.

*"What've you got?"* Weiss comes back.

"Nothing. I need some entertainment."

*"It's busy here, Russ..."*

"No shit."

*"What do you want?"*

"What's going on up north? I'm shut out of CoreCast for some reason."

*"Why would you expect you could get on CoreCast?"*

"Seriously?"

*"Yeah, seriously. The network is still vulnerable. Live operation monitoring is severely restricted. All nonessentials are cut out."*

"So, I'm nonessential?"

*"Please. Get over yourself."*

"So?"

*"Nothing yet. All in place, just waiting for clouds to clear up. I'll keep you in the loop once we start rolling. By the way, before I forget, I figured out what Hiebert said to you up-*

*state."*

"What?"

*"He said, 'shadows will fall behind you.'"*

"Shadows will fall behind you? What the hell does that mean?"

*"I have no idea, but that's what he said. Alright, I gotta go. Now, go be useful,"* Weiss hangs up.

Outside, the black utility vehicle returns to the same spot where Russ saw it before, and three uniformed men step out and walk off into the woods. The driver then circles the lot, parks in front of the entrance to the barroom and, with a plunging, swaying gait, walks inside. He eyeballs Russ as he passes by and takes one of the newly arranged tables in the back that's partially concealed by the curve of the bar. The blond woman finishes setting up the tables and chairs, exchanges a few words with the man, then walks off into the kitchen.

"Kenji—give me the news."

*"Hi, Russ, here's the news,"* CALO replies. *"Special Drawing Rights Council negotiations continue in Zurich as the Corporates seek to dislodge top-ranking Sovereigns, demanding a new weighting formula for the global capital markets that reflects a more adequate representation of the financial capacities of the SDR councilmembers."*

"Skip now, follow the story."

*"The death toll from the Kunming Flu reaches a grim milestone today, claiming the 10,000th victim as the latest mutated form of SARS-CoV virus spreads from the former Chinese province of Yunnan to Myanmar, Laos, Thailand, and Vietnam. The total number of confirmed cases now exceeds 700,000 and is expected to rise exponentially in the coming days. With the outbreak still in its early stages, it is unlikely that there is sufficient data to predict the course and impact of the pandemic through standard modeling. Hospitals in affected areas are making urgent pleas for help and supplies..."*

Ty's figure appears in Russ's field of vision.

"Hey," Ty chirps, and sinks in the chair across from Russ.

"Well, if it isn't the Black Hills Casanova," says Russ, taking off his eyepiece.

"What did I miss?" Ty's eyes flutter like he's the one who needs to adjust back to the spatiality of the real world.

"Nothing. Been hanging around here like a spare dick at the wedding."

"I dug out a couple of things..."

"Yeah?"

"The girl was helpful."

"I bet she was," Russ grins, enjoying catching young Ty in his own verbal trap.

"Hey! It was part of the job."

"I didn't say anything."

"Anyway," Ty continues, slightly dismayed. "The Circuit. There's more than a dozen of them. They have their own separate quarters..."

"Where, in the woods?" Russ looks across the parking lot.

"Somewhere in there, I guess. They don't mix with the rest much, but they're always around. Like those guys we saw last night."

Russ shifts his eyes carefully toward the man at the corner table. Ty dips his head in acknowledgment, then lowers his voice.

"Girls all hate them." Ty says.

"There's a surprise."

"They're not very friendly, and they always cheap out when they have to pay up for sex. All she knows, they're taking care of somebody up in the hills, but she doesn't know exactly where or who it might be they're protecting."

The blond woman comes out of the kitchen and gives them an inquiring side glance.

"Excuse me," Russ flashes a bland smile. "Can we get a couple of cups of coffee here, please?"

"I got no real thing," the waitress ignores his smile. "Jitter Juice or Wakey Juice. Both taste like shit. Which one do you want?"

"That's all right," Russ refuses her offer of fake coffee. "We'll just get some breakfast, no juice of any kind."

The waitress takes their order and trots back into the kitchen without a word.

"No love for weary travelers," Russ makes a sour face. "What else?"

"It seems like there's very little turnover," Ty continues. "She says she's been seeing exactly the same faces over the last two years she's been here. There have only been one or two new guys during that time. That's unusual for the Circuit, don't you think?"

"That's not really that strange in the EPP world."

"EPP?"

"Exec personal protection. Ironclad contracts, usually three-year minimum. Impossible to get out of. But the money's good. They're all getting a gag premium."

Just then, a man in his thirties walks in, followed by a thick-necked PSC. While eye sweeping across the room the man makes brief eye contact with Russ then, prompted by the PSC, slogs over to one of the booths at the opposite end of the barroom and sits down. The PSC sits across from him, plunking down his heavy arms on the table like he's about to shuffle a deck of cards.

"What is it?" asks Ty, watching Russ's face furrow in concentration.

Ignoring Ty altogether, Russ puts his eyepiece back on and begins clipping through the mission log. Once inside the subfolder marked, "Lupo Belan," he races through a condensed history of known facts about Moonie's life—biographical information, psychological profile, Moonie's online imprint, habits portfolio, and DISC behavior assessment. He then expectantly shuffles through various images of Moonie. Not quite convinced of the likeness, he pans around and covertly snaps a still of the man in the booth and sends it through the live face read engine.

*Facial Recognition Outlook:*
*First-degree search - Max Madigan - 54% probability.*
*Second-degree search - Ronald Paulk - 18% probability.*
*Martin Ford - 16% probability.*
*Third-degree search - Ben Topper - 3% probability.*
*Indeterminate - 9% probability.*

The results confound Russ momentarily. He slides his eyepiece off and out of the corner of his eye takes another look across the barroom, seeking confirmation, then fixes his eyes on Ty absently, like he's looking through him. From his vantage point he sees two figures of disparate sizes shapeshifting through layers of thick window grime like single-cell organisms. They get off the dry bridge and head toward the barroom, the smaller figure ahead, followed by the bigger. As they get closer, the features of their faces gradually reconfigure. A small smile jumps across Russ's face as he positively identifies Miles.

They enter the barroom together, and after a brief exchange, the PSC goes back out, leaving Miles by himself. Russ notices scratches and bruises on Miles's face. Did they beat him?

With small hesitant steps, Miles crosses the barroom and joins Moonie and the other PSC in the booth. Ty leans in, shifting his eyes inquisitively.

"Yup," Russ nods before he could ask a question.

"Well, better lucky than good, huh?" Ty flashes his teeth at Russ.

“Who told you that?” Russ looks at him like he just kicked a kitten.

“I don’t know,” Ty backpedals his earnestness. “It’s just something people say, right?”

“People say all kinds of bullshit. Be good at what you do, kid. Luck’s a slut.”

“Noted. Be good,” Ty nods sarcastically.

“Your life may one day depend on it.”

“Okay, got it.”

“That’s if you actually ever get to be good enough to be selected for an assignment that you’ll have to rely on your own brain for...”

“Right.” Ty tunes out, waiting for the latest life lesson to come to an end.

“...an important, dangerous mission behind enemy lines, where you kill or get killed, where flying bullets sort out the true soldiers from the warrior wannabes, men from boys, the living from the dead. Is that what you’re waiting for?”

“Now you’re just fucking with me.”

“That’s right! I’m fucking with you, but it’s also true what I’m saying. When the shit hits the fan, you’ll want to be good rather than lucky. Keep talking, we wanna look like we’re having a sensible conversation.”

“What do you wanna talk about?”

“For fuck’s sake! Anything. I thought you had the gift of gab. Or is it a curse? Do you have a dog? How’s the weather in Rapid City this time of year? Have you ever tried...”

“I heard you survived a plane crash in the Gulf,” Ty cuts him off.

“That’s true,” Russ confirms reluctantly.

“So, what’s it like...”

“I don’t want to talk about it.”

“You said anything.”

“Yeah, well I meant anything else.”

“I bet you felt pretty lucky when they found you in the

desert," Ty chuckles.

"Fucking right I did, smartass." Russ laughs back. "Is that a OneWay?"

"What?"

"The kid. Is that a OneWay he's on?"

Ty sneaks a glance towards the booth.

"It looks like it."

"Keep talking."

Russ launches Circumambience on his Allcom and scans the surroundings, looking for Miles's device UnQID.

Hidden behind steam clouds, reaction furnaces outside the window are hard at work, sweating black gold out of greasy ancient mud, hissing ardently like the propulsion modules of an alien ship about to take off. Merged with Maritza's relaxed breathing, their steady whirr feels strangely comforting, almost calming. Theo shuts his eyes and tries not to think about anything, grateful that Maritza is still asleep and that they don't have to talk. Words won't make any of this better.

Yesterday, motivated by Drey's promise that he'll be reunited with Maritza if he falls in line with their demands, he managed to switch to full-on work mode for a few good hours and did a fair amount of work organizing the INDEX archive on the Simulacrum. He was quiet and docile, playing the role of a person whose spirit has been broken. It worked.

At the end of the day, when Drey brought him back to his room, Maritza was there, physically at least. It was heartbreaking to see her so scared and helpless and even harder not to break into tears in front of her. Confused and disoriented, she barely recognized him. Theo quickly realized that he had to contain his emotions and bring her back to reality slowly and patiently. After a night of attending to her through a myriad of affective states as she coped with the comedown from whatever drug cocktail they had her on, shifting through stages of grief without reprieve or resolution, he was drained. He was dreading the moment her lucidity fully comes back and she has to face the harsh inevitability of the truth—when she's forced to accept the fact that Miles might be gone from their lives forever—and all they'll have left of him are fleeting memories and the enduring pain of his absence.

Considering the circumstances, maybe it's best that he isn't here. It's certainly hard to come to terms with that notion, but what's the alternative? There's no mercy in the hearts of people who are capable of this. They will never set them free. At least out there in the world Miles still stands a chance. There are still good people, hopefully someone will help him. He's a good kid, a smart kid, he'll manage. Theo's throat tightens, tears break through his closed eyelids. Careful not to wake Maritza up, he holds back the deep sigh that's been swelling in his chest like a gust of poisoned air and silently swallows his pain.

At first, it sounded like one of the furnaces had been seized by a ghost trumpeting an irritating two-tone refrain through its steam valve. Then, multiplying at the speed of urgency, an awful blare rips the air, cascading throughout the complex like an aural tidal wave, finally barging into their room through the ceiling speakers and prompting Maritza to spring out from under the covers.

"What's happening?" She grabs Theo's arm, her eyes wet and wide with confusion and terror.

"I don't know," he replies.

They leap up to look out of the window, but they can't see much through the narrow slits: the rotating yellow light of a pickup truck bumping along the service road in the distance, another vehicle speeding across in a cloud of dust, frightened workers dispersing throughout the maze of pipelines like some disturbed termite colony, a few figures rushing toward their building. The alarm shifts to a single high-pitched tone truncated by brief periods of unsettling silence and a pulsating red light sweeps throughout the room, blinding them temporarily.

*"Please evacuate the building now,"* a calm mechanical voice blasts through the speakers.

Maritza tries the door, but it's locked.

*"Please evacuate the building now,"* the voice keeps repeating the warning.

Unsure of what to do, they look at each other silently, then take each other's hands and embrace in a hug. The door bursts open and Drey barges in, shouting.

"Let's go."

"What's all this?" Theo asks.

"I don't have time to explain. We gotta leave. Now!"

"We're not going anywhere unless you tell us what's going on," Maritza confronts him.

Drey gives her a flinty stare, ready to pounce at any sign of further dissent.

"There's been an event," he softens a bit.

"An event?" Theo pushes for a better answer, stretching Drey's patience.

"Yes," Drey offers no further explanation. "Everyone has to evacuate, and that includes you. Now please, no more questions. Just do as you're told so I can get you out of here safely."

The turbulent strain of the alarm follows them down the emergency staircase, which is congested by disoriented shift workers forced to flee the warmth of their beds before they could've properly fallen asleep. Outside, lined up along the wall, those who already made it out are awaiting further instructions.

For a brief moment, the absence of walls feels like freedom to Theo. After six full days of being confined to the darkness of the Simulacrum lab and the constricting oppression of their tiny room, the sky seems bigger than he remembers it. There's been an event. An event? What kind of event exactly? Obviously, something big enough to warrant total evacuation. Fire? Industrial accident? Sabotage? Are they under attack?

Theo looks around for the point of trouble, but other than the current state of chaotic agitation due to the evacuation, nothing seems out of the ordinary. A slow-moving pickup truck glides by them, in the back of it an anti-drone team combing the skies with DroneGun jammers. On top of the watchtower, above a cluster of communication antennas, two flags drift dispassionately in the chilly breeze. Theo recognizes the blue one. Free Enterprise of Alberta. His first guess was on the mark, they're in Alberta. The other flag is dark olive green with the word "Epiphany" written on it in vigorous cursive. Epiphany. He tries to remember if he ever came across that name before.

Drey ushers them past the crowd into a walled-off corridor that leads to the entrance of a domed concrete structure buried in a dirt hill. The metal blast door slides open and damp bunker air crawls out from the inside, sending cold shivers down Maritza's back.

"This way," Drey leads them down a murky hallway.

There are two doors on the left, one on each end of the hallway, and a double door in the middle, on the right, with a security guard standing in front of it. Without moving a muscle, the guard scans them as they walk by him to the far door on the left.

"I'll come to get you when we get an all clear." Drey engages a biometric scan, and as the door clicks open, Maritza suddenly turns around and looks back.

"He's here somewhere, isn't he? The monster who's responsible for doing this to us," Maritza says, right before lunging across the hallway and past the surprised guard to the double doors. She starts pounding on the door, shouting from the top of her lungs.

"Come out, you coward!"

The guard reacts quickly by gripping her arms from behind.

"Leave her alone!" Theo jumps to Maritza's defense,

but Drey grabs him in a headlock.

The guard clasps Maritza against his chest and lifts her off the ground.

"Show your face if you have any decency in you," she shouts as the guard carries her inside the other room.

In one fell swoop, Drey releases his hold on Theo and pushes and trips him forward into the room, onto the ground next to Maritza.

"You two gotta cool off," says Drey, now visibly pissed off. "Understand? Or it's back to zonktown for both of you."

He gives them a stern look to underscore his threat, then slams the door shut behind him.

*"The Systems That Aren't Busy Being Born* ***Are Busy Dying.*** *German federation at the brink of dissolution. Status quo proponents struggle to maintain the illusion of legitimacy as breakaway* ***Bavaria*** *refuses federal jurisdiction over Klaus Klein case."*

*"Logan's Selfishness Finally Revealed! Logan Branford leaves the production of* ***Frantic*** *to pursue 'humanitarian interests.' Army of fans grumbling."*

*"**Pioneer Provisions** - With You Every Step of the Way - a **Hoovers** subsidiary."*

*"Why haven't we found aliens? Have they been here all along? **Type o Bipeds**, storied Simuli now on **Eyeconic**."*

*"**Functional Foods - MealPrinter 8C** - Customized Foods System. Custom-designed flavors and colors. More than three hundred ingredients from natural sources formulated according to your personal dietary needs. Available at all **Hoovers** locations."*

"What's on?" Tim's question startles Miles out of his display-gazing stupor.

"Oh, nothing." Miles shoves the OneWay back into his hoodie pocket. "Just the usual feedthrough junk."

He glances at Tim, then quickly averts his eyes and looks aimlessly around the barroom before settling on a table of single-seaters by the entrance, where the only other guests beside them—two men, one in his forties, the other one much younger—are having breakfast. The men seem to be engaged in a lively discussion, laughing and gesticulating with their hands, in stark contrast to their table, where no one said a word besides Tim's comment since the waitress brought the food out. Miles notices that Moonie's been strangely quiet too—anxious, absent, indifferently nibbling on his waffle, his eyes downcast and only occasionally looking up to watch Tim and Barkley stuff their faces with mute soldierly devotion. There's something he's not telling. Why did they take away their Allcoms? And why are these two with them all the time?

Perhaps sensing Miles's moodiness, Moonie purses his lips and gives him a slow compassionate wink.

"Eat something," he points at Miles's barely touched plate.

"I'm not that hungry," Miles obliviously reaches back into his hoodie for his OneWay and dives back into the feed stream.

*"Is gene editing a human right? As new technologies like **OwnGen** make gene editing more accessible, the public is divided on the ethical implications of altering unwanted genes."*

***"FreeFormFit** - Laser Body Sculpting - Now Available in Lead, **FFF** at 309 West Main Street."*

*"Logan Strays. Sources confirm what Logan calls 'humanitarian interests' might be nothing more than a sex cult hustle and flow."*

*"Are Your Thoughts Your Own? - **PsyDy - BrainWorks** new algorithm dissects the inner dynamics of your mind. Plug in Now."*

The sun has broken through the clouds, lighting up the remnants of the morning dew atop the trees in the hills above Billygoat. Staring straight out but keeping his peripheral vision fixed on the booth across the barroom, Russ takes a moment to admire the dazzling dance of sun rays, all the while wondering if it would have been better to skip this whole charade, undo these two clowns here and now, and just take the kid with him. Clean and simple. They could be back in New York by dinnertime. Then again, there's nothing wrong with enjoying a little theater—you don't see very often somebody like Speights lay down his burdens. How did they end up here anyway? What's the Pardes's errand boy doing in the lair of one of the biggest arms dealers who ever operated in North America? Is Speights truly out of the game, or is this part of some unrelated scheme?

*"Eyes,"* a text from Weiss jolts him out of his thoughts.

"About time," Russ grumbles softly under his breath.

As he puts on his eyepiece, aerial surveillance feed of an industrial facility fills his field of vision.

*"Elk Creek, half an hour ago."* Weiss magnifies the image then rapidly pans over the scabbed landscape of the mine, across the intricate web of oil sand processing installations before finally focusing on three people walking out of one of the rectangular buildings.

*"Saved us the trouble of going door to door,"* Weiss zooms in on the faces.

It's Theo and Maritza with Drey in front, clipping along at a medium pace through narrow passages between buildings. A pickup truck crawls up on the circular road beside them with two people standing in the cargo bed clasping a long white pole pointed upward. Suddenly, the image rips apart into jagged digital ribbons.

*"Jammer."*

"I figured."

*"Blaustrahl ZU, I-14 protocol. Useless turd,"* Weiss scoffs.

The signal clears up after a few moments, and Theo, Maritza, and Drey come into sight again. They get on a path leading to a concrete corridor then disappear through a big metal door built into the side of a hill.

*"Survival shelter,"* Weiss clarifies.

"Ha! Did you get a skeeter in there?"

*"We dropped fifty on the place. Most are still transmitting, which gives us decent coverage of the grounds. We snuck a few inside the bunker too, got a live feed of the room where they put them in. Now we need to locate Fletcher. We'll let the bastards scramble for a little while longer before we allow them to restore their security data infrastructure. He'll pop out once he feels safe again. I jacked the kid's OneWay, you're plugged into his feedthrough generator, use it as you see fit. Still working on Speights's system encryptions, so stay low for a while longer."*

"Sounds good."

*"Logan Branford leaves production of* ***Frantic*** *to join a sex cult?"*

*"Blackouts across Scandinavia on the rise as recent storms batter the already damaged infrastructure. Governments ask* ***FullPower*** *for help. Its parent Corporate promises emergency power infusion."*

*"Logan goes off the deep end. Joins sex cult. Career in jeopardy.* ***Frantic*** *hiatus possible."*

Who cares? Miles lifts his head away from the display. It's a dumb show anyway. Stupid OneWay! Its passive, confining essence is just amplifying the claustrophobia he's feeling right now, squeezed against the wall of the booth by Tim's huge frame. All he wants to do is be alone, go back to the room, maybe finish the gold rush book.

Across the table, Barkley aims his beady eyes on the last piece of spongy bread in the basket, then like some beast of prey, grips it with his sausage fingers, wipes the last yolk smudge off his plate with it and, jutting out his jaw to avoid a potential sticky drip, brings it to his mouth. He chews on it no more than twice before sending it down his gullet, then smacks his lips ceremoniously, marking the end of the meal.

"Good, maybe now we can get out of here," Miles sighs silently and looks back down at the display.

*"**Chasing Singularity** - a challenge of overcoming our*

*own organic matter. Three new chapters available now. Only on **Good Machine**."*

*"**Frantic** urges Branford to rethink his selfish decision to abandon the show and pursue humanitarian interests. Says legal risks will arise."*

*"**Outer Skin**" - Fashion and functionality. Conductive carbon-enhanced silk polo gets a handsome upgrade. Now made with **OS-CS 5** hyper-perceptive biosensing fibers that aid in blood circulation, chi flow, and muscle performance."*

***"Miles..."***

Miles flinches at the sight of his name in the feed.

"It will all be over soon. ***Help is here!***"

A mix of panic and excitement rushes through him, blurring his vision. The OneWay almost drops out of his hands.

*"Your **mom and dad are well**. You'll be together soon."*

Miles brushes his eyes with the back of his hand and looks up, but the barroom provides no answers. No one at the table seems to have noticed anything. Then he sees the older of the two men at the booth by the entrance, furtively looking at their table.

"Everyone done?" Tim blurts out, then, not waiting for an answer pushes away from the table, prompting Barkley to his feet.

"Good. Let's go for a little walk then."

"Where are we going?" Moonie gets up unenthusiastically.

"The boss said to show you the grounds, so we're gonna take you on a little tour."

Miles waits until Tim turns his back to him, then stealthily tucks his OneWay between the cushions and falters out of the booth after them. On the way out, he tries to get a closer look at the two men at the booth, but Tim and Barkley, plodding along in front of him before parting at the entrance to let him and Moonie out first, manage to obstruct his view enough so that he doesn't catch a good glimpse.

They head back toward the cabins in silent procession. Some fifty feet before the bridge Miles determines they're far enough. He turns around and starts patting his pockets, looking at Tim apprehensively.

"My OneWay."

"What about it?"

"It must have slipped out of my pocket."

"So go back and get it," Tim replies after a brief consideration.

Surprised by how easily his little ploy came to pass, Miles heads back to the barroom. Unsure if he's being watched, he walks by Russ and Ty without looking, heads straight to the back of the room, plucks his OneWay out from between the cushions, then turns around to see Russ staring at him with a smile on his face.

"Nice move."

Miles scans the windows for Tim and Barkley, thinking about what to say.

"Excuse me?" he finally utters unconvincingly.

"I know you're scared and you feel like you can't trust anyone anymore, but we're here to help. You should know that."

"Who are you?" Miles steps forward, feeling like his feet are sinking into the floorboards.

"We're friends of your dad."

"Where are they?"

"Not too far from here."

"Where?"

"They're in Alberta."

"Alberta?"

"Yes. I'll explain everything later."

Vacantly still, with his arms hanging uselessly at his sides, Miles fixes his gaze on Russ, deciding if he should believe him.

"Courage Miles, it's all gonna work out."

"How?"

"We're gonna get them back. And we're gonna get you out of here. You should go back now before they come looking for you. Don't mention any of this to anyone, including Belan."

Steering through patches of hangover fog still lingering around the edges of her mind, Maritza tries to fend off unbidden thoughts by keeping her attention on an acrylic canvas hanging on the wall across from her. At least someone had the good sense to add a touch of color to this cave. Pressed between two frameless plexiglass panels, the painting blends into the concrete like graffiti, an obvious if not very successful attempt at Van Gogh's Wheatfield with Crows, except the artist decided to substitute wheat stalks with blooming sunflowers and crows with some nondescript white birds. Seagulls perhaps?

She curls up on the sofa against a stack of throw pillows and watches Theo purposelessly circle the white plastic table in the middle of the room for the nth time.

"Come," Maritza taps the sofa cushion with her palm. "You're making me dizzy."

"Sorry," Theo sits next to her on the sofa and lays his head upon her lap.

"What do you think those white birds are?" Maritza points to the painting.

"I don't know," Theo shrugs. "Doves?"

Maritza weighs his suggestion for a moment, scrutinizing the painting with renewed focus.

"Of course!" she jolts up in her seat. "Doves! How silly of me not to realize that."

"Well, it's not like it's that obvious," adds Theo, surprised by her exuberance.

"No, it is! Doves. It can't be anything else."

"Well, I'm glad that's been sorted out," Theo rolls to his side, dismissing the whole thing.

Maritza runs her fingers through his hair, gently stroking the new grays invading his temples and sneaking into the dark brush of his beard.

"Hey," she half whispers. "Do you remember that one time we were coming back from Eugene? Miles was still nursing, he was ten, maybe eleven months old. I think we had some party in the city that night, but we decided to blow it off and drive to the coast instead. It was the most gorgeous day, sunny but fresh. We had lunch at that little seafood place in Depoe Bay, with fishing nets on the ceiling."

"Hank's."

"Yeah. We spent the rest of the day on Glenden Beach doing nothing. Remember? It was the first time Miles crawled in the sand, he kept trying to get up on his little feet."

They suddenly both grew quiet, reluctant to fully reach back into the memory of that day fifteen years ago, fearful of where the stirred-up emotions might take them.

"I think that was the happiest I've ever been," Maritza says quietly after a little while, her eyes longingly returning to the colors of the painting on the wall.

*"All clear! All clear! All clear!"*

A sense of relief comes over Weiss at the sound of an automated voice announcement from the bunker's PA speakers as he watches Theo and Maritza scuttle to the door in confused anticipation. He felt uncomfortable intruding on their intimate moment through the skeeter feed on his display and was glad that he could now shift his focus back onto the mechanics of the mission.

Epiphany's CommSec almost detected their presence in the system earlier, causing a snag in execution while the ACIS algorithm adjusted itself against their defensive efforts.

Setting off the all-clear signal confirms they're now back on track. In the meantime, two more surveilling microdrones went offline, one due to a thruster chip malfunction, the other swatted dead by one of the workers with an apparent distaste for flying insects.

Weiss synthesizes the surveillance data into a single overworld on his display, then digs into it, closely looking over video feeds coming in from throughout the complex for any clues to where Fletcher might be hiding. He rounds up four microdrones closest to the bunker entrance and dovetails them with the one in the room where Theo and Maritza are being held to be ready to track their movement once the handler takes them out. He then syncs up the remaining twenty into an integrated search unit, deploying MugTrigger to reassess their individual surveilling priorities at the first sight of Fletcher's face. He can't hide forever. Sooner or later, one of the skeeters will catch sight of him.

Driggs is sitting alone at the head of his immense dining table, twiddling the Pardes sign-on card between his fingers, seemingly charmed by the sparkling dance of light coming off the holographic stereogram of the green iguana on a tree branch.

This place was supposed to be a temporary retreat, a quiet haven where he could recover physically and mentally, take some time to restore his political alliances, and reboot his business while doctors put what was left of his face back together. Year or two, three maximum.

Seven years later he's still here, stranded in the sticks. The only difference is now the hope of reclaiming his life that kept him spirited in the beginning has faded away with nothing taking its place, leaving him feeling blown over, defunct, completely useless. His hermit-like existence seems even more pathetic now that there might be a way out. The empty years are coming back with a vengeance, reminding him just how trivial his life has become. What the fuck did he do here for the last seven years?

Things have changed fast back home after he fled. Through what easily could have been characterized as a coup, Samuelson and the Tricoastals took control of the executive branch, then doubled down by weeding out softies from the legislature and judiciary, fast-tracking staunch loyalists in their place. The new government quickly reinstated the expansionist policies of the first post-union decade, during which

Texas absorbed Oklahoma, New Mexico, Louisiana, and Mississippi along with Nuevo Leon and Tamaulipas, south of the old border. Less than three years into the new Tricoastals's regime, an Association Agreement with Alabama and Florida was signed, securing direct access to the Atlantic and further asserting Texas's dominance across the bottom half of the continent.

Then came the push west, toward the Pacific. Emboldened by skyrocketing oil prices caused by the Gulf War devastation, and now officially becoming the third largest producer of the most important commodity in the world, the chieftains of the Lone Star State recognized that it was time to act quickly and decisively on the long-held ambition of the "Texas of Three Coasts." The annexation of Arizona was a formality; the real test of force was always going to be the last stretch from Yuma to Tijuana and San Diego. The region is now on the perilous edges of armed conflict. A great environment for the business—if he still had one left. At least Claymore, in their positioning for the upcoming shit show, still believes he has some sway in the area and that he'll eventually prove himself useful. There can't be any other reason why they continue to give him protection. He's paying them, of course, but money is never the prime motivation with PSC—it's influence.

Driggs grips the passcard in the palm of his hand and bends it sideway, as if checking its sturdiness, and then brings it up to his Allcom and scans it.

*"Welcome to Pardes, the land of winners, the chosen few, the blessed. This is a fulfilled promise of a better life, the realization of your hopes, a living dream. We are the youngest member of the exclusive club of reputable HVI communities with an Aurum Wealth Rating of seven hundred; Atlantis, Havana, Maui, Cabo, Barvikha, Canarias, and now Pardes. You are a winner and winners deserve all that life can offer. You can find it all here, in Pardes.*

*We are a de facto sovereign state, as defined by the Bar-*

*celona Convention, recognized by more than one hundred other states and free enterprise territories, and, like other reputable HVI communities around the world, we are a Corporate, governed solely by our shareholders, namely you..."*

A long shadow appears in the doorway.

"Sir."

"What is it, Phillip?" Driggs asks without lifting his eyes from the Pardes promo.

"Well..." the servant starts nervously, shifting his weight from one foot to the other.

"Speak up."

"I think you should come to the sunroom and see for yourself, sir."

With brisk, confident steps Driggs strides down the black-and-white tiled hallway, trailed by his own reflection in the glass of the weapons display cases. At the end of the hallway he halts abruptly, realizing that someone has activated the display panel built into the sunroom's bulletproof glass enclosure. It's showing a picture of a man in his mid-forties with the words, *"Remember this guy?"* superimposed across his eyes. Driggs instinctively backs up, startled by the image of his former self, then warily steps inside the sunroom. The candid closeup photograph doesn't offer much context; then he recognizes the paisley pearl snap shirt in the photo. Rachel got it for him in Sedona, on their last trip together.

"Who are you?" Driggs asks out loud.

The photograph fades out and a Geosat aerial image of forest-covered hills comes on the display.

As it scales up, Driggs recognizes the slate roofs of his mansion. The data sidebar pops up, displaying GPS coordinates and detailed blueprints and floor plans of the buildings throughout the compound, featuring diagrams of various escape routes from the main house to an underground heliport hidden in the woods nearby.

The display then changes to a grid view of the compound's security camera network, shifting the feeds with a steady cadence: guard towers, entrance gate, driveway, underground garage, garden, back gate, walkways, corridors, hallways, then the individual rooms inside the mansion—they've got everything. The display twitches again and a split view of four sunroom security cameras comes on, multiplying Driggs's figure stuck fast in the middle of the room and creating a disorienting hall-of-mirrors-like effect.

*"Hello, Speights,"* Russ's headshot appears on the display. *"Or is it Driggs now? You should have gone with something a little more generic, Collins maybe. Michael. Michael Collins. That's a good, wholesome name. It has a nice ring to it. Carl Driggs? I don't know. Still better than your old name, though. Gavin Speights. A guy with a name like that can't be anything else but a fugitive arms dealer."*

Driggs gazes at the display in stunned silence, looking for answers.

*"Nice place you got over here."* Russ pans the camera around, revealing his location in front of Billygoat. *"Fresh air, friendly girls, no law, what's not to like, right?"*

"Who are you?" Driggs asks.

*"First, you should know that we have no unfriendly intentions,"* Russ goes on. *"We have no bones to pick with you or Claymore, for that matter. This is just a means to an end. A little good faith on your end and you'll never see me again."*

"Who's we?"

*"Think of us as folks who just did you a favor by demonstrating how exposed you are. It took us less than a few hours to bust into your network, and we weren't even looking for you. So, maybe you wanna do something about that in the future. Next time somebody comes snooping around, they might not be as kind. I'm sure Senator Samuelson would greatly appreciate information about where the man who killed his son is hiding."*

"I didn't kill Robert!" Driggs flinches. "It was an accident."

*"Well, Senator Samuelson seems to disagree with you, so much so that he publicly vowed to chase you to the ends of the Earth, string you up by the balls, and let wild hogs have their way with you. Good luck trying to convince him it was an accident. Frankly, I'm surprised you're still alive. And a free man on top of that!"*

Driggs takes a couple of slow steps further inside then takes his sunglasses off, baring his disfigured face. Russ studies him wordlessly for a moment from above, then continues.

*"I'm actually curious what exactly happened in Fort Worth that day."*

"Like I said, it was an accident," Driggs utters dryly.

Russ realizes that's likely as much of an answer as he's going to get.

*"Kind of ironic, isn't it? To find yourself trapped in a fire inside your own ammo dump, your own weapons turning against you. Poetic justice of sorts."*

Russ pauses and waits for Driggs's reaction, but he's as still as a sculpture.

*"So, the place blows up,"* Russ continues matter-of-factly. *"Everyone's dead, twelve people in total, including the head of the Texas State Guard, the senator's son, a three-star general, and two of your business partners, and yet somehow you manage to survive. How's that?"*

"Luck, I guess," Driggs says.

*"Hmm... funny to hear a self-made man like yourself bring up luck. You strike me more as someone who'd say something like, 'You make your own luck,' or some shit like that. You know what I think? I think any schmuck can have a bit of luck, but not everyone knows how to make use of it. Which you did, so hats off to you. Your business literally blows up in front of your eyes, everything you worked so hard for—poof, gone up in smoke.*

*You're facing the wrath of some very powerful people,*

*you gotta know when it's over, right? At first, everyone thought you were dead too, splattered around in the smoldering rubble, so it was pretty much the perfect opportunity to stage a disappearing act.*

*But then you got greedy. Only fools don't have a contingency plan. Rules of business, I guess, sometimes the only play left is to smash the piggybank and run as fast as you can. It's always the damn money, isn't it? It's hard getting your hands on it without leaving a mark. I've seen it a thousand times. If you ask me, Senator Samuelson might have been more inclined to believe the whole accident story, maybe even include you in a state funeral with the others, before he realized that you cleaned out the joint company accounts mere hours after the explosion. A dead man doesn't need money."*

"What do you want?" Driggs interrupts him, having heard more than enough.

*"All right, all right..."* Russ can't hold back a smile.

"Shits and grins aside..."

*"I'm here for the kid."*

"What kid?"

*"Don't give me that shit! I just saw him at breakfast."*

"What fucking kid?" Driggs raises his voice slightly, a spasm of chagrin seeping through.

*"The kid that came here with Lupo Belan two days ago,"* Russ restrains himself from bursting out in anger.

"His nephew?" Driggs asks, genuinely surprised.

*"Is that who he said he was? His nephew?"*

"You should ask Belan. I got nothing to do with that boy."

*"So why the guards then?"*

"I got ongoing business with Belan. I asked him to stick around for a few days. The kid's with him, so..."

*"What kind of business?"*

"Certainly not child trafficking. You want the kid? Take him with you, I could care less."

*"I told you this was going to be easy."*
"Is that it?" Driggs asks unbelieving.
*"That's it,"* Russ replies flatly.
"What about Belan?"
*"He's his own man. I'm not here for him."*

Could it really be true? A jumbled mix of hope and fear sloshed amok inside Miles. Russ's words echoed in his mind: "We're gonna get them back." He trembled at the thought of his parents lying on the floor of some dungeon in Alberta. But who is that man? How does he know where his parents are? And how did he find them? Miles shoots a tense glance across the room at Tim and Moonie, then quickly dips his eyes inside the book that he's pretending to read, hiding his thoughts between the pages.

What if he's lying? The initial rush of excitement and optimism slowly turns to a wall of panic. What if he's just another Sheng Long agent sent out to finish the job? Then it's all over. For all of them. But then why would he go through the trouble of hacking his OneWay and making contact? Why would he make his presence known to him if he isn't here to help?

Slashing through weighty wooden blinds, slivers of intense sunlight stretch out long and sharp, slicing across Moonie's legs, which are laid out flat on a faux leather footstool. Moonie's staring across the semidarkness of the room, halfheartedly trying to rebuff Tim's attempts to engage him in conversation.

"How're things in California?" Tim asks him.

"What do you mean?"

"My contract's up in four months, I thought I'd give it a try. I got a cousin in San Jose, he says there's money to be made out there."

"Your kind can make money anywhere nowadays."

"Yeah, I meant in general. I've never been west of Nevada."

"It's same everywhere, man," Moonie utters vacuously. "But it's a different kind of same if that makes any sense. People are people, no matter where you go."

This nonanswer seems to satisfy Tim for the time being. He walks up to the window, parts the blinds with his index and middle fingers, and peeks outside.

"I gotta tell you, I'm not going to miss this shithole, Three years of my life I'll never get back."

Moonie looks at him with a smirk then snipes away.

"Why would you want any of your own life back?"

"What do you mean?" asks Tim, missing the sarcasm.

"Never mind."

Tim's facial expression changes from mild puzzlement to anxious alacrity and Moonie realizes it's because of something that came in through his earpiece. Tim walks out on the terrace, leaving Moonie wondering what prompted him to change his mood so quickly. He strains his ears trying to decipher muffled pieces of Tim's conversation coming in from behind the glass door but can't make out more than a few disconnected words. A minute later, Tim comes back in and turns to Moonie.

"Let's go."

"What now? We just got in," Moonie rolls his eyes. "Where are we going?"

"Out of here."

Miles puts his book away and slowly gets up to leave, but Tim stops him.

"Not you. You're staying."

Moonie and Miles look at each other, but neither says anything. The door opens with a soft shriek and Barkley comes in. Behind him, framed in the doorway, is Russ, waiting on the porch.

"C'mon," Tim gives Moonie a nudge. Moonie drags his feet trying to stall for a moment.

"Who is this?" he says, pointing at Russ.

"That doesn't concern you," says Barkley.

"What do you mean it doesn't concern me?" Moonie raises his voice.

"That's exactly what I mean," Barkley responds coolly. "It's none of your business. Now move it."

"What the fuck is this?" Moonie stops in the doorway and stares down Russ. "Who are you?"

Tim grabs Moonie's arm, but he wrestles it away.

"What are you doing here?" Moonie asks Russ.

Barkley moves toward Moonie, but Russ signals him to stop.

"Relax, Belan." Russ lowers his hand. "We're on the same team."

"And what team is that?"

"We're both trying to help Miles. You did your part getting him here, which was no small feat, and we thank you for that. Now, let me do the rest."

Moonie turns to Miles with inquiring eyes.

"It's okay, Moonie," Miles nods softly.

"Do you know this man?" Moonie asks.

"Yes. Well, no. Sort of. I talked to him this morning at the restaurant."

"At the restaurant?"

"When I went back to get the OneWay. He says he knows where my mom and dad are."

"Is that so?" Moonie darts a suspicious look at Russ.

"He says they're going to rescue them," Miles adds.

"Who's they?"

"I don't know. He said he was going to explain everything. Let him in."

Russ moves aside to let Moonie out. Confounded by his

own self-perceived ineptitude, Moonie stands there for a moment, looking at Russ, then Miles, then back at Russ. Nothing else to say, he hangs his head and dawdles out, followed by Tim and Barkley.

"Miles, I'll be right outside," he shouts out as Russ shuts the door behind him. "I'm just gonna hang out here on the porch. You let me know if you need me, okay?"

Russ looks around the room studiously then pulls up a chair and sits across from Miles.

"Sorry about your friend. I thought it'd be better if it's just you and me. Are you okay?" He points at Miles's face.

"It's nothing," Miles waves it off. "Just some scratches."

"How're you doing? You've been through a lot."

Miles shrugs his shoulders without answering.

"I know. The world can sometimes be an ugly place. But it looks like you're one tough kid," Russ smiles. "Smart too. EternalQuest semis—that's a big deal! I guess it's true what they say, the apple doesn't fall far from the tree. Your dad is an extraordinary man, your grandpa too, both one-in-a-million minds."

Holding to a catlike stillness, Miles politely waits for Russ to get the pleasantries out of the way; all he wants to hear from him is why he's really there. Sensing his edginess, Russ switches gears.

"Miles, my name's Russell Oakley. People call me Russ. I'm with Atlantic Commonwealth Intelligence. I'm gonna be direct with you because I've never seen any use in trying to sugarcoat a bad situation. The people who kidnapped your mom and dad work for a private security corporation called Sheng Long. They're mercenaries without moral values or social considerations, people who would do anything for anyone who's willing to pay the price. Not the good guys by any stretch of the imagination. This was probably done to coerce your dad into working for the people who hired Sheng Long to kidnap you. Taking you and your mom along as hostages was supposed to ensure he complies with their demands. This is not uncommon, especially in the world of industrial espionage. Top scientists, engineers, encryption specialists, financial experts are always being approached by competing interests using bribes, threats, or blackmail. Sometimes, if nothing else works, they're just abducted and forced into submission. All clear so far?"

Miles nods guardedly.

"Your mom and dad are being held in an oil sands facility in Eastern Alberta, run by a man named Stuart Fletcher. The facility is owned by a subsidiary of Macau Corporate called Epiphany Resources. It's possible that Fletcher orchestrated the whole thing and made arrangements with Sheng Long on his own, but it's unlikely that he wouldn't have to clear this with his superiors. There's no telling how deep this goes and who else is involved, but right now we're not focusing on that. Right now, it's all about getting your parents out of there safely. And that's what we're doing. A plan of action is in place, we have the area covered with surveillance, our people are already on the ground awaiting the signal. It's all happening right now. Miles, we're going to win this. We're gonna get them out of there and it's gonna happen fast, I want you to believe that. Possibly today or tomorrow, depending on the circumstances."

"Is it going to get dangerous? Will there be a shootout?" Miles asks, his heart pumping like crazy.

"No, nothing like that. But in the end, their captors will have no choice but to let them go, trust me, we've done this a few times before. I'm here to bring you back to New York with me. Once they're free, your parents will join you there. That's the plan."

Russ's confident tone calms Miles down a little.

"Why are my parents so important to you that you'd go to such lengths to rescue them?" Miles asks.

"We take care of our own," Russ replies.

"What do you mean?"

"I don't know how much you know about your grandfather's work on artificial photosynthesis..."

"My dad told me all about it."

"Okay, good. About nine months ago, your dad joined a group of scientists from our energy department who are trying to determine the technological methodology behind your grandfather's invention. He had to keep it secret, but I assure you, he is very excited to be part of it."

In an effort to conceal his surprise at how fast things are turning, Miles gets up and walks to the window, and looks over at Moonie shuffling his feet outside.

"How do I know you're not one of them trying to trick me, telling me things I want to hear?"

"You're gonna have to trust me, Miles. I'm not leaving here without you. Why would I even bother talking to you if I were Sheng Long?"

"Because Driggs is protecting us and you want me to go with you voluntarily."

"Believe me, that's not the issue," Russ laughs. "I can pack you in my trunk, nobody would say a word. I got Driggs under my thumb. He'll do whatever I say."

"How did you manage that?"

"I got a few tricks up my sleeve."

"So, I really don't have a choice at all?"

"Your only real choice here is to trust me and go along with it."

"That makes it all easy then," says Miles with a sullen smile.

"Sorry. That's just how things break down sometimes."

"What about Moonie?"

"Who?"

"My friend, Lupo. He's the one who's been helping me this whole time."

"What about him?"

“Isn’t he going to get in trouble with Driggs because of all this?”

“How so?”

“I think you should talk to him.”

# DAY_8

Miles could feel the reassuring recoil of the touchdown long before the plane's wheels actually touched the ground at Idlewild Airport. Part of him wanted to stay up in the air, cocooned in the humming oblivion above reality, above everything that's happened in the last week and away from the fear of what's about to happen. But he was heartened by the fact that they're not at the mercy of chance anymore. For the first time since he left home, which seems like forever now, he felt truly safe. Safe, but far from unworried. Despite Russ's insistence that his parent's rescue mission was about to commence at any moment, nothing has happened yet. Has something gone wrong and they're just not telling him?

"Everything's going to be fine," Russ kept repeating, and Miles could do nothing else, but believe it and wait. Still, what then? Even if everything goes without a hitch and they get them out unharmed, what happens next? Will they ever be able to safely return home? Are they going to have to leave Concord, leave everything behind, and go into hiding and live someplace where no one knows who they are?

Outside, in the gunmetal blue chill that precedes the dawn, a grounded flock of military transport planes are lined up by his window, ominous and eerie like colossal prehistoric birds. As they exit the plane, a small boxy two-seater crawls across the tarmac and pulls up to the gangway. Despite looking narrow and stiff, the car is quite comfortable inside, sporting full-length silicone gel seats with built-in motorized muscle massagers, an oxygen-enriched climate system, and auto-ambient lighting.

"Directorate," Russ issues a command and their runty ride sportively obeys, taking advantage of its small size to cut through a tangled network of taxiways, corridors, and access roads to get them onto the expressway in what seems like record time.

The LIE is deserted at this early hour, save for the gliding procession of autonomous delivery vehicles in the freight lane carrying their loads to the city at a steady twenty-five miles per hour. Miles drifts off, thinking about Moonie. They left Billygoat in a hurry and he hardly had any time to say good-bye, let alone properly thank him for everything he's done for him. Moonie really put himself out there, risked his life for him, the least he deserved is a little gratitude. Who knows, they might never see each other again. They did hug it out, though. Hopefully, the whole thing with Driggs will end up going his way.

By the time they got to the Directorate, the sun had already leaped up on top of the thin, pliant clouds that foretold a beautiful fall day. Tired and hungry, Miles and Russ make their way through morning office traffic to the second-floor guest lounge. Display walls on both sides of the lounge are showing a slow-motion montage of beautiful pastoral imagery from around the Atlantic Commonwealth: vineyards somewhere in Upstate New York, rolling wheat fields in southern Ontario, a crab cookout in the Chesapeake Bay, salmon fishing in Nova Scotia, the morning fog rising over farm fields in rural Pennsylvania, the thick pine forests of New England, a sunset horizon across the windswept shores of the Great Lakes. Occasionally, a set of superimposed words floats over the images to reinforce the overall warm and fuzzy messaging: *"Kindred Spirits Bond Together. Atlantic Commonwealth–Strength in Unity, Progress and Freedom, Justice and Amity."*

"That's him," Russ juts his jaw toward the entrance.

Pratt waves hello when he sees them and walks over

with a blank smile on his face.

"Miles, it's so good to see you," he grabs Miles's hand and shakes it vigorously.

Miles falters a bit, keeping his hand inside Pratt's a little longer than seems fitting.

"Thank you. For everything," he finally utters.

"Nah, don't thank me. If it weren't for this guy here," Pratt points at Russ, "we'd be still guessing blind where you and Belan might be. He found you, he brought you over, I'm just the one who gets credit for it," he chuckles.

"I know you 're worried about what's happening in Alberta right now," Pratt takes a more serious tone. "Of course you are, but I don't want you to stress out about it too much. We're close. We just have to be patient and stick with the plan, wait for the right moment to make our move. Everything's gonna work out. Okay?" Pratt puts his hand on Miles's shoulder as if to check his hardiness.

"Okay," Miles nods.

"Good. I just wanted to say a quick hello and meet you. Mornings are busy around here. Why don't you two get some food and rest, and I'll check in with you later today? Russ will set you up with everything you need."

With a long and steady stride, Pratt heads back into the hallway.

"Wait here," Russ tells Miles and scurries after Pratt. He catches up with him by the elevators just as he was about to get in.

"What's up?" Pratt asks, surprised to see him.

"The kid's been through the wringer."

"Point being?"

"He's sad and scared. He needs to be around people. We put him up alone in the fourth-floor residences, it's no different than a lockup. He needs some semblance of normalcy."

"What do you suggest?"

"I can take him home with me."

"Wanna be a dad for a day?" Pratt gives him an amused look, bordering admiration. "I don't see why not, as long as you put a BodyBeacon on him."

Back at the guest lounge, Russ finds Miles as he left him, tired but wired, holding back his anxiety the best he can.

"All right, Miles," Russ lays it out for him. "We got a couple of options. One, you can stay here at the Directorate residences. We'll get you a nice room. You can order food and drinks from the cafeteria 24/7. There's an entertainment system in each room with a bunch of offerings, you'll probably find something you like. You can relax, get some sleep, whatever... But, once you go up, you can't leave the room until somebody comes and gets you."

"What's the other option?" Miles asks.

"I'm gonna go home for a bit, here in Brooklyn, nearby. You can come with me if you'd like. I can't promise it'll be all that interesting, but I thought maybe you'd prefer some company. It's up to you."

"Let's do that," says Miles without hesitation.

"However, the downside... There's always a downside, isn't there?" Russ smiles. "The downside of that is that I have to chip you. Have you ever worn a BodyBeacon, LocTrack, or something similar?"

"No."

"There's nothing to it, I've been wearing one for ages. All ACIS personnel have one. A little peck under your shoulder blade, you barely feel it. We gotta be able to track you down in case you get lost. And unlike me, you can opt out of it anytime you want."

"I have no problem with that." Miles says. "Let's do it."

"Are you sure?"

"Yeah, I'm sure. I'd love to finally see Brooklyn."

Theo and Martiza were separated again. A couple of hours after the all-clear signal, Drey came in with another guard and without any explanation escorted Maritza out of the bunker, back to another room, while the other guard contained Theo. Maritza spent the night alone trying not to slip into all-out gloom, listening to the sounds outside, hoping that each set of approaching footsteps were Theo's, that he'd walk in through the door with a calming smile on his face and say something reassuring, something that will help her keep her faith.

She knew this wasn't some random decision on their part. Unpredictability is the crux of captivity and must be fed a steady diet of hope and despair until the prisoner becomes disoriented, disengaged, and disheartened, ready to follow the path of least resistance—the ultimate goal, of course, being the attainment of some sort of Stockholm syndrome, where the victim eventually starts developing a trusting bond toward the captors and starts fully cooperating. This is just the beginning; they'll keep taking their shots.

At the click of the lock, Maritza jumps to her feet to see Drey thrust through the doorway like some sort of moving wall, gradually revealing Theo behind. In the semidarkness pouring from the hallway, he looks small and worn out.

"Are you alright?" she looks him over.

"I'm fine. You?" Theo touches her cheek lightly.

"I'm okay."

Maritza turns her eyes to Drey.

"Why do you have to do this to us? Why do you have to make us suffer?"

Drey looks at her silently, almost amused by her agitation.

"Are you going to tell us what's going on?" Maritza snaps. "What was that alarm all about? Are we in danger? You owe us an explanation for all this!"

Drey waits for her to finish and then laughs at her attempted assertiveness.

"You two seem like smart people, yet I don't think you realize how this works. Simple fact, you have no rights. No one owes you shit. You want something, you're gonna have to earn it, and a good way to do that is to shut the fuck up and do as you're told. Quit pissing everyone off with your constant bitching, both of you. It'll get you nowhere. You're food, deal with it."

Shook up by Drey's bluntness, Maritza takes a moment to collect herself. Then, with her index finger pointed at Drey's chest, lunges forward, about to let him have it, but Drey quickly pivots, leaves the room, and slams the door in her face before the words leave her mouth.

Drey thinks to himself that the last thing he needs right now is the two of them giving him any shit. It's been almost twenty-four hours since the alarm went off and they still haven't found out what triggered it. The security team conducted a thorough inspection of operations and facilities and found absolutely nothing—no safety protocol oversights, no breaches of acceptable risk levels in the pit slopes, no chemical or biological hazards, no leaking gas pipes or faulty monitoring stations, not even an exposed wire.

This led them to the only possible conclusion—there's a glitch in network security. It's either malfunctioning or it's been jacked. But so far, they've found no evidence to support one or the other. It's like having felt a snake bite and not being able to locate it. You don't know if it really happened or if the fear of being bitten is playing a trick on you.

Eventually, the decision was made to resume normal work protocols, but that didn't exactly bring calm or clear up lingering confusion. Walking back to the bunker, Drey could see the apprehension on people's faces, a dull fear, everyone pretending to be preoccupied with the task at hand, avoiding direct eye contact.

The guard greets Drey as he enters the bunker, then opens the double door and lets him in. Sunk in a deep, cushioned armchair with his back to the door, Fletcher's swiping through multicolored charts on a tablet in his lap.

"Those two giving you a hard time, Drey?" Fletcher says without turning around.

"Gotta earn my keep," Drey answers in jest.

"It's not easy to discourage an idealist."

"Nice or nasty, we'll get them there. They'll heel."

"I know they will, but that's not enough," Fletcher sets the tablet aside, "I want to make Theo a believer. I got to make him see the big picture. He's worth it."

"Well..." Drey can't think of anything else to say.

"Not very many people can manage to think through an ocean of information," Fletcher continues talking, more to himself than to Drey now, "and not get distracted by inconsequential variables or fall prey to their own cognitive bias. It's just human nature."

Fletcher lets out a muffled sigh, grabs a face privatizer off the coffee table in front of him and fastens it around his head, and then gets up and turns around, facing Drey like he's about to challenge him to a fencing duel.

"Let's go."

At the sight of them, ACIS microdrones bustle out of their hiding places in the crevices of the bunker's hallway and stealthily start regrouping into a sentry unit. Fletcher is out first, then Drey, flanking him like a lonely honor guard.

They slowly leave the bunker, adjust their eyes to the daylight, and crane their necks to the scent of fresh air, oblivious to the swarm of invisible insects trailing behind them.

Buoyed by the sense of relief and renewed optimism brought about by yesterday's events, Moonie's nudging his truck down the steep serpentine road, back to Billygoat lodge. Even though he probably won't need it until the feasibility team gets here from Denver, it felt good to get his truck back. If nothing else, he felt like he regained his freedom and the power of choice that he unwittingly surrendered to Driggs a few days ago.

He rolls down the window, letting the brisk mountain air inside the cabin. It's a picture-perfect day, sunny and clear. From his high vantage point, far in the distance, past the granite cliffs of Black Hills, he can see the big country opening up like an unending runway, luring him in with the promise of the lonesome joy of the journey. But his job here isn't quite done yet. It won't be long. Despite all of the crazy things that happened over the last few days, they actually might be in a better position to seal the deal in their favor than they were before. Driggs is vulnerable and that means that they have the upper hand now. Lark probably won't give him full credit for it and that's alright. It's not like one should get the credit for being lucky. Good fortune smiled on all of them by sending agent Oakley to dig them out of the clusterfuck that the past week has been. The Smiths are getting rescued, Miles is with Oakley in New York and he's back to minding his own business. There's hope in this world after all.

At first, Moonie didn't know what to make of Oakley.

Of course, he was suspicious. Everything was as fucked as it could possibly be, and about to get even worse, and out of nowhere, this guy shows up at their door like a fucking knight in shining armor and singlehandedly saves the day. A little too good to be true. But after they sat down, and Oakley gave them the details on Theo's and Maritza's situation, explained how he found him and Miles, and how he got Driggs to play ball, Moonie had to concede—he may be a spook, but he was their spook, the good kind.

When it was time for Miles and Oakley to leave, it was difficult to say good-bye. There was a moment where there might have been a tear or two shed. Even though he knew the opposite was true, Moonie couldn't help feeling like he failed Miles in some way by relinquishing his responsibility for him. Or, maybe it was because after bearing witness to Miles's cruel initiation to the world of adults, he felt culpable for its ugliness somehow. And of course, there was a nagging possibility that Oakley wasn't who he said he was and that his whole performance was a devious scheme hatched by Sheng Long. What if he chose to trust Oakley only because it was convenient for him to do so?

Moonie knew his balls were in a vise because Driggs was inevitably going to blame him for bringing trouble to his doorstep. Oakley offered to help him by squeezing Driggs on his behalf, but what good was that if the deal was going to fall through? He couldn't think of anything that would prevent freaked-out Driggs from killing it. The only way to possibly convince him that he had nothing to do with Oakley, was to appeal to Driggs's common sense, to tell him the truth, the whole story of what happened back in Concord, and how he ended up in this quagmire without asking for any of it.

When Moonie got to the mansion, Driggs was already packed up and ready to go. Driggs listened to what he had to say and then, to Moonie's great surprise, instead of menace and and anger, he offered an olive branch, sort of.

"The way I look at it," Driggs said, "we can both either destroy or help one another, so we might as well just move on as if nothing had happened. Business is business. I had this coming to me. Sooner or later somebody was going to show up here. Honestly, it's a good thing. I'm sick of it. Get your guys in here, do what you need to, but don't think for one second that I can't blow the whole place to rubble if you try to fuck me over. Do we understand each other, Belan?"

Driggs's one good eye was shining from behind his oversize sunglasses.

"Yes, sir," Moonie said readily.

"Good then."

Moonie extended his hand in a handshake, but Driggs snubbed him, heading straight to the waiting helicopter.

"I'll be in touch," he yelled out over the rising engine noise and soon afterward vanished in the sky.

Moonie had no idea what Driggs actually meant when he said that he could blow the place to rubble. Maybe he has the mines rigged with explosives. He was a weapons dealer after all, it wouldn't be much of a stretch for him to do that. Or, maybe he meant that he could bomb the place with guided missiles out of spite if he wanted to. Plenty of options to be anxious about.

*"Due to a temporary street closure we are unable to reach your desired destination,"* the taxi announces as it pulls up, three blocks from Russ's place. *"Sorry about that, Russell."*

The doors slide open, letting inside a blast of loud music from somewhere nearby.

*"Thank you for riding with Brooklyn Lizzie. See you around!"* the taxi bids farewell and takes off.

Mingled around a giant bouncy castle in the middle of the block, a group of workers is transforming the street into a playground, assembling red and blue plastic slides, lining up swing sets, and fitting soft foam grips over the metal handles of a merry-go-round.

"Block party," Russ extends his arm up like he's trying to snag the boomy rhythmic beats from the air and present them to Miles.

Dodging the crowd of vendors setting up craft booths and food stalls, they drift along the sidewalk, then squeeze through a row of A-frame barricades, skipping over a tangle of cables, rigging tools, and equipment cases to reach an open area in front of a small scaffold stage, where two men are conducting a soundcheck. Suddenly, the music stops and one of the men dives behind a pile of speakers and amplifiers.

"There'll be live music all day, local bands mostly," Russ takes advantage of the temporary silence. "Usually, the whole thing ends up being an all-around neighborhood jam."

A distorted, ear-cracking hiss rips through the air and the music commences, now even louder than before.

"Do you play an instrument?" Russ asks.

"What?" Miles can't hear him.

"Do you play an instrument?" Russ shouts out.

"Not really." Miles shouts back. "You?"

"No way. I have no ear for music. But, my girlfriend can bang out a beat. We should come down later. It'll be fun."

Rows of brownstones and turning trees spill over smoothly into the next block which, at first sight, looks the same as the previous one, except that some of the brownstones on this block are boarded-up, a few still bearing black marks left by the fire and others simply abandoned and left to the elements. Judging by the layers of faded graffiti, even vandals gave up on them a long time ago. In the jumble of washed-out blocky letters, spray paint drawings, crooked stencils, and squiggly tags, one message—written in red freehand—is still legible: "Respect the existence or expect the resistance!"

On Russ's block, a string of brownstone stoops is broken by the spacious front yard of an old mansion-like building. Inside the yard, behind a worn-out wooden fence, an old woman's raking leaves. She pauses when she sees them, leaning lightly on her rake.

"Hello, Russell."

"Good morning, Ms. Jablonsky," Russ speeds up a bit, hoping to avoid a lengthy neighborly chat.

"Can you believe this ruckus again? Didn't we just have a block party?"

"Yeah, I think that was back in June."

"Seems like it was just a couple weeks ago."

"What can you do? People like parties."

"They should find something useful to do with their time instead."

"I agree, Ms. Jablonsky. You have a good day, okay?"

Ms. Jablonsky waves after them and then goes back to

her raking. They continue to the end of the block then turn up the stairs to Russ's place, on the top floor of a four-story brownstone.

"Home sweet home," Russ kicks off his shoes with satisfaction. "Are you hungry? I can whip something up."

"I'm good, thanks," Miles replies.

Miles catches a glimpse of himself in the foyer mirror. A street person in the making, his eyes look weak with fatigue, his hair greasy and tangled, his cheeks streaked with grime and dried-up sweat.

"I wouldn't mind taking a shower, though," Miles says, his eyes darting away from the reflection in the mirror.

Six out of the fourteen microdrones they had trailing Fletcher since he crawled out of the bunker made it all the way inside his office with him, yielding plenty of visual data points along the way for Weiss to generate an access path for the dragonflies. It's up to the shooters now.

Both surveillance video feeds on Weiss's display are static. The first one shows Maritza and Theo at the opposite sides of their narrow room, both quietly staring at some point beyond their immediate surroundings; the other feed shows an unmoving image of Fletcher at his desk, absorbed in his display. Seizing the lull in action, Weiss takes a small plastic bottle out of his desk drawer, squeezes a few drops out of it into each eye, then leans back and shuts his eyes, letting the medicine do its work.

"What the fuck, Weiss?" a stentorian voice snaps him back to attention. "Are you sleeping?" Pratt's big head materializes inches from his face.

"Just resting my eyes," Weiss rolls back his chair, away from Pratt.

"Is that what you call it?"

"I have chronic asthenopia," Weiss replies hastily, not entirely sure if he did fall asleep for a moment.

"What's that?"

"Eye strain. My eye muscles tighten up, I get blurry vision. It's not a big deal, but I gotta unplug once in a while and close my eyes for a minute. It's fine now, I just put in the drops."

"Pilots are ready. Let's go. Time to end this ballsackary."

The pair make their way across the TOC floor to the circular lobby of the Drone Operations Sector, then head down one of the corridors to the designated flight deck.

In the cramped, windowless room of the flight deck, three twenty-something-year-olds seated in drone thrones with their immersion sets on are awaiting instructions. The display wall above their heads is showing an aerial view from the belly of the drone that's hovering over Epiphany's Elk Creek complex. Pratt and Weiss each grab a headset from the rack, put them on, and plug into the CoreCast.

"Put the target visual on," Pratt requests, and the surveillance feed from the skeeters in Fletcher's office pops up in the bottom left corner of the display, which shows Fletcher still seated behind his desk, gazing away, absorbed in thought.

"All ready?"

On Pratt's order, the drone's weapon bay doors spread open and, one by one, three miniature dragonfly drones zoom out, quivering and drifting precariously in high-altitude winds before the pilots manage to stabilize them. Once stable, the drones band together into a tiny squadron. As the drones swoop down toward the ground, the flight deck display switches to a triad feed from their onboard cameras. The malformed wrinkles of the oil sands pit below burst forth through the veil of clouds. Bitumen storage tank domes come into view, then smokestacks, crusher cones, coker towers, and building rooftops. In one synchronized dive, the drones swirl down into a controlled descent, touching down softly on top of the main administrative building. The pilots take a moment to reassess, overlaying real-time visuals on top of the projected access path Weiss generated earlier, then lower the drones and, one at a time, fly them inside.

The dragonflies zip up over the security station, out of the reach of the screening equipment and watchful eyes of the guards, then drop low to the ground and edge the walls while continuing to the lower level of the building, where the first real obstacle presents itself—the armored door at the end of the purple-tiled hallway. The bareness of the hallway offers no hiding spots, so drones stack up in the corner directly below the security camera to minimize their visibility, then switch to idle mode to conserve energy.

Pratt and Weiss stare wordlessly at the stagnant display wall for a few minutes, mulling their options.

"This'll take forever and a day," Pratt finally says. "If we even manage to stay unseen. We're totally exposed out there."

"True."

"What do you think?" He turns to Weiss.

"Still best to wait," Weiss responds. "We tickle Fletcher back out too sloppily and he'll get spooked, no doubt. No saying what happens after that. We might not even get our shot. Then we're back to square one, except now he knows something's up."

"Yup," Pratt replies briskly as Weiss confirms his own thoughts.

"I can't sit on this all day," Pratt takes off his headset.

"Let's just find you a face before you leave," says Weiss.

They step around and take seats at the curved console behind the pilots, Pratt in the middle, directly facing the display wall, Weiss right next to him. Weiss grabs a control tablet and taps on it a few times. A portion of the console top folds in unto itself and a communication panel slides up with three gooseneck cameras jutting out of it. Weiss throws the image of Pratt on the display wall, then adjusts the position of the camera lens to frame him properly. Once happy with the result, he scales down the camera feed and moves it to the bottom right part of the display wall.

"Give me the target's head," Weiss says into the headpiece.

A closeup of Fletcher looking straight into the camera pops up in the box next to the image of Pratt.

"Let's set up the I.D. trailback kill."

Pratt's face starts pulsing softly on the display, which then transforms into the face of an older Latino woman, then a bearded Middle Eastern man, a longhaired nymph, then a black teenage boy, an obese Indian man, followed by a corn-fed hunk, and then an Asian man in his seventies with piercing eyes and a stern jaw.

"This one'll do," Pratt stops the mug shuffle.

His face fades back in over the Asian man and red tracing dots sprinkle over the meshed image like a sped-up smallpox outbreak, detecting facial features and warping their contours. Finally, Pratt's face fully morphs into the Asian man's face, adopting a new set of facial expressions and gestures.

"Now voice," Weiss says.

In a deliberate tone, pronouncing each word like he's talking to a slow-witted child, Pratt recites a canned line out loud.

"And then he triumphantly wanders off into the sunset, never to be seen or heard from again."

"One more time." Weiss chimes in.

"And then he triumphantly wanders off..."

Slightly amused by the pitch of his modified voice, Pratt draws a smirk as he watches his new avatar replicate his words in real-time on the display wall.

*"... into the sunset, never to be seen or heard from again."*

"Negative trailback confirmed," Weiss declares, then points both of his index fingers up like he's about to shoot the ceiling. "We're anonymous and ominous, my luminous Dominus!"

"What?" Pratt looks at him like he's grown a second head.

"I like to throw a good rhyme out now and then," Weiss

chuckles, fully embracing the awkwardness.

"You need some social interaction, Weiss," Pratt sneers at him and gets up to leave. "Make some friends. Get a date. Although, I can see how it could be a challenge for anyone to spend time with you voluntarily."

"Ouch, that's mean."

"Yeah, yeah. Anything changes, let me know immediately. In plain, nonrhyming English, please," Pratt says, leaving the room.

"It's a deal, Mister big wheel," Weiss chuckles to himself after Pratt leaves.

Nothing happens on the surveillance feed for almost an hour until a slow-moving shadow starts creeping down the hallway, causing Weiss to spring up from his slouch. A robotic floor cleaner emerges from behind the corner, fitfully hissing short jets of steam from the bottom of its barrel-shaped body. It zigzags methodically from wall to wall, working over every inch of the already pristine floor, then finally reaching the door, where it draws in its brushes and mops, twists around with a jerky mechanical strut and aligns itself with the access reader, prompting the door to open.

Dragonflies follow the cleaner inside and then, floating behind it just a tick above the floor, continue down a long corridor that ends with two identical armored doors, the one on the right leading to the lab and the one on the left to Fletcher's office. The floor cleaner does its little dance again, cueing the lab door to swing open, and then disappears inside leaving the drones waiting in the corner outside the other door.

Miles's body longed for sleep, but his mind wouldn't rest, despite knowing that there's absolutely nothing he can do to affect the outcome of whatever is supposed to be happening in Alberta right now. Or maybe it's precisely because of that—the hard, bitter realization that his actions are just about irrelevant in this new absurd reality, leaving him feeling hapless and overwhelmed, struggling with the notion that you can do everything right in life, as his parents did—work hard, be kind and loving, try your best to be a worthy human being—and still, a complete stranger can one day crash into your life with deliberate intent and drastically alter the course of it in mere seconds. His dad lived through it once already after he lost his father in the fire. And he was even younger than Miles is now.

Theo never believed that what happened to Augustus was a random event. There were too many holes in the official story and too few of the people involved interested in the truth to pursue a robust, trustworthy investigation. And so, when the police came up with enough convenient conclusions to call it an accident they put a lid on it, brushing aside the myriad indications that pointed to a different, more sinister interpretation of events.

Frustrated with police indifference, Theo's mother Amelia hired a private investigation firm, but they backed out of the job after a few days without explanation, as did the other one she tried to hire after that. Reeling from the grief, with the help of friends and family she spent the next year trying to piece together incomplete clues on her own, hoping to come up with enough arguments to convince the authorities to reopen the investigation. But people move on, and as time went by, she found herself increasingly alone in her pursuit, spinning in concentric circles of anguish and futility, not an inch closer to resolution. Finally, when her request to reopen the investigation was denied by the District Attorney's office, she couldn't take it anymore. She picked up Theo and without a clear plan or direction left the city, hoping she had enough in her to pull off a fresh start someplace else and build a new life for her and her twelve-year-old son, a life not haunted by the tragic weight of the past.

They stayed at her sister's house in New Paltz for nine months, and waited for life to present them with a fighting chance. Then one day, Augustus's friend and colleague Matthew Sanders called to offer Amelia a position at UC Berkeley. She accepted it without hesitation and within a week they moved to California for good.

Miles slides out of bed and tiptoes into the living room. The block party outside had reached full swing, judging by the swarm of voices percolating through the soft booms of a soulful, hoppy track. He walks up to the window and looks outside. Below, empty brownstone backyards look drab and austere, rendered superfluous by cold weather.

A skinny white cat emerges from a pile of capsized patio furniture and with a nonchalant two-step leap, slings itself on top of a wooden fence. The cat sits there for a few moments, scanning her territory in search of food and enemies then, not catching sight of either, strolls along the narrow tip of the fence like a tightrope walker gracefully defying the laws of physics.

Theo never really wanted to talk about his Brooklyn days and Miles didn't press much, sensing he shouldn't stir up the old grief in him, but he managed to squeeze a few details out of his dad over the years. Miles tries to imagine Theo as a kid bopping around these narrow streets, the one-hundred-fifty-year-old house they lived in, and the amazing yard he heard so much about. It must have been ten times the size of these other cracks of sky between brownstones, connecting the main house with a single-story carriage house in the back that eventually became his grandad's lab.

The circular driveway in front of the lab was turned into a small flower garden with a three-tiered water fountain in the middle that Grandad's friend, the famous sculptor Franco Messa built for them from old millstone he found in some small town in Pennsylvania. There was an enormous oak tree in the yard, at least as old as the house itself.

One year, with ample help from his dad, Theo built a treehouse in it, if a simple plank platform with four upright beams topped with a flat piece of plywood could be called a house. Although it wasn't much, Theo was very proud of his accomplishment and started referring to it as his "castle." Emboldened by his early success, he quickly drew out improvement plans and presented them to Augustus, who had no choice, but to go along with it. By the end of the summer, they added side walls, two small windows, and a door, and replaced the plywood cover with a real roof. Next spring, they built access stairs that spiraled around the oak's trunk in an elegant twist and tacked a small watchtower on the roof, which ended up being a perfect nesting spot for neighborhood sparrows. Finally, when Augustus rigged up a power system using a couple of solar panels and a car battery, the transformation from a rickety raft in the sky to a glorious summer residence was complete.

The block party music eventually fades down and the muffled voice of the MC quiets down the crowd for a moment. Unable to understand what the MC is saying, Miles applies himself to crack the sticky seal of the window, but by the time he managed to open it the MC was done talking and all he could hear was the buzzing drone of the expectant crowd.

"Neighbors! Sisters and brothers!" A woman's voice calls out after a little while. "Focus here. Yeah, that's my name. Focus. Maybe you don't all know me, but you know me. And I know you all. We're all one, connected by the same blood we share. And that's what we need to do more of. Share. Help one another. Share what you got. Be it a piece of bread, knowledge, good fortune, responsibility, love, pain. Some have too much of one thing, some too little. That ain't right. We're all deserving. All I got is my music, and I'm here to share it with you."

The fragile, lonely sound of a trumpet brakes through the sparse applause and whoops of the crowd, spilling through the streets like a warm breeze. The soothing and forlorn melody unfurls at an insinuating rate, then grows bigger and more confident, tripping the listener's attention to the long tones at the upper end of the trumpet's register, delivered with breathtaking fluidity and precision.

"Nice, isn't it?"

Miles turns around to see Russ standing at the far end of the living room.

"Beautiful," Miles nods.

They stand unmoving until the song ends.

"Come," Russ waves Miles over, "Let's go up on the roof. The sound will be better up there."

Weiss stirs eagerly in his seat, shaking off the waiting stupor as Fletcher finally peels himself from the display and takes a few short steps around the office, proving that he's an animate being after all.

*"Drey, I need some food,"* Fletcher says out loud. *"The usual. And tell the new guy no melon in the fruit salad this time."*

Fletcher clasps his hands behind his head and does a few side crunches, wringing his back to the edge of pain and back, then takes his shoes off, sits on the floor in a cross-legged position, and shuts his eyes.

"We might be getting an opening here," Weiss says into his headset. "You should come back in."

Minutes later, Pratt huffs in through the flight deck door with an expectant air around his stolid face.

"What did I miss?"

"Absolutely nothing," Weiss replies. "The man hasn't moved from behind his desk since you left. He just asked for food delivery when I called you."

"What the fuck is he doing?" Pratt's nostrils widen at the sight of the motionless, cross-legged Fletcher on the display wall.

"Meditating?" Weiss guesses.

"Resting his eyes like you?"

"I'm telling you, it's a common affliction," Weiss shrugs jokingly.

"You guys ready to give this fucker his share of divine inspiration?" Pratt nudges his head into the headset.

"Ready, sir," the pilots answer in unison.

"Good." Pratt gives each pilot a quick pat on the back, then joins Weiss behind the console.

"Wetsmack," he hisses with contempt as he sits down.

"What's a wetsmack?" Weiss asks.

"He is," Pratt points at Fletcher.

Around thirty minutes later, a waiter appears at the far end of the hallway pushing a dining cart. As he gets closer, dragonflies stir up from their sleep, ready to move.

"Slow and steady now," Pratt whispers into his headset.

The waiter rolls up to the armored door, then steps around in front of the cart and leans in for a facial scan, giving the drones enough time to leap up onto the bottom shelf of the cart unnoticed. Once through the door, the waiter thrusts the cart into a narrow, windowless chamber and aims his face up at the security camera. One of the walls parts open, letting him inside Fletcher's office.

Back behind his desk, sponging off information from his display, Fletcher hardly acknowledges the waiter's entrance.

*"Sir,"* the waiter softens his movements to minimize his presence, and in a few practiced moves sets up a side table for dinner. Once done, he rolls out the cart and turns around to face Fletcher, arms by his side.

*"Have a pleasant evening, sir,"* he backs up with a short nod and leaves.

Without breaking his gaze, Fletcher reaches under the desk and pushes a small, flat button with his palm. The wall slides back in place, enclosing the room in its generic blandness.

"Go time boys," Pratt says into his headset, eyes locked on the display wall. "Aim for the skin."

A low purring buzz prompts Fletcher to take his eyes off his display. He sways his head around with incomprehension, looking for the sound source until one of the dragonflies hovers up into his line of sight. He freezes in shock, staring at the mechanical insect with stunned curiosity, dazed by the specks of light dancing through its translucent wings, inches from his face. He doesn't even flinch when the drone stutters upward and then recoils, firing a little arrow at him from its bowels. He feels the sting just below his cheekbone, a thorn scratch, a raw tingle. As the fear descends down from his neck and across his chest he reaches out with a shaky hand, runs his fingers over the tiny sharp stub lodged in his cheek, then pinches it with his nails and pulls it out like a pesky ingrown hair.

Pratt exchanges confirming nods with Weiss then gives an order to the pilots. "Blow up the drones."

With a puzzled frown on his face, Fletcher stares at the gleaming needle in the palm of his hand, then, still relatively collected, moves to get up, but three rapid bursts spark up the office, knocking him back into his seat. He ducks down and lifts his arms to protect his face from small pieces of flying debris. After a few moments, the explosive clouds thin out, leaving behind a faint sulfurous odor and tense silence. Fletcher slowly lifts his head, only to see the stern face of an older Asian man on his display.

"Sit up," the man says. "Look at me."

Fletcher rivets his eyes to the display.

*"What is this?"* he asks.

"No questions. It's time for you to shut up and listen. You've been injected with a fast- acting pathogen. You might not feel any different right now, but in about twenty minutes you'll start getting lightheaded and weak. After an hour, your joints will start aching and your lymph nodes will begin to swell. Then come muscle cramps, shortness of breath, and dizziness followed by vomiting and abdominal pain. After six hours, your endocrine system will be dramatically disrupted and seizures will begin. Unless treated, between twenty-four and thirty-six hours after activation of the pathogen, complete paralysis of all skeletal muscles will ensue, leading to death due to respiratory failure."

Pratt pauses shortly to measure Fletcher's reaction and then, resisting the impulse to revel in his fear, continues impassively through the avatar.

"The only treatment that can reverse this process is our proprietary pathogen inactivation system. Think of it as a serum. It contains pathogen-capture proteins that will remove infectants from your bloodstream. Once the pathogen is neutralized, your immune system can fight off the symptoms on its own and full health is achieved in less than two weeks. Do you understand the situation you're in?"

*"Yes,"* Fletcher's voice is reduced to a rough whisper.

"This is what's gonna happen. In exactly forty minutes from now, my men will drive up to the main gate of the complex. Without any conditions or delays, you will release Maritza and Theo Smith to them. In exchange, you will be given a metal safety box that contains one vial of the serum and the serum administration kit. Access to the box is protected by an encrypted electronic lock. Once the Smiths have been debriefed and assessed by my men, you'll receive an electronic key that will allow you to retrieve the contents of the box. This electronic key is the only way to safely access the box. Any attempt to forcibly open it will trigger a mechanism that will destroy the serum vial inside. Do you understand?"

*"Yes. Yes. I understand."*

The last few wails of Focus's trumpet flock together into a beautiful accord, daringly reaching for the sky, and for one ethereal moment it seems like its melody is going to shatter the constraints of the real world and envelop the entire city and all the people in it into a higher state of harmonious existence. But, the silence comes quickly, and the music falls back on the ground like a spent wave, leaving nothing but a fleeting recall behind.

"Thank you, all. Stay together. Share your lives with one another," Focus pleads over the applause.

Leaning over the rooftop wall, Miles gazes down into the cavernous void of the city blocks, hoping Focus will change her mind, pick her trumpet back up, and transform the murmur of the block party crowd into wild and sparking musical notes and send them chasing one another through the streets again.

"Come, I wanna show you something," Russ's voice brings him back.

Russ waves Miles through a maze of cedar planters to the back of a sprawling rooftop garden. Most of the planters are empty with only dried-out pepper and tomato vines scrunched on top of the gray soil like burnt fireworks snakes, but some are sporting hearty shrubs, and a few have small evergreen trees in them. Behind the trees, on a platform of stacked up bricks, there are three small, unwieldy towers, odd-looking file cabinets, each a motley assemblage of wooden crates of different colors and heights. Miles looks at Russ quizzically then notices a few bees buzzing in and out one of the towers through thin slits at the bottom.

"You have bees?"

"It's my pathetic contribution to the effort of slowing down the total collapse of the ecosystem," Russ smirks. "I know it's only three colonies, but it makes me feel better than doing nothing."

To the side of the beehives, resting against the red-brick chimney is a ramshackle cabinet made out of reclaimed wood, fashioned to look like a little hut. Russ reaches inside the cabinet and pulls out three mason jars containing a colorless liquid with whitish sediment at the bottom.

"Here, give these a shake." He hands two of the jars to Miles, then shakes the third one himself.

"What is this stuff?" asks Miles, watching the clear liquid inside the jar turn cloudy.

"Sugar water, mostly. They can't forage enough food on their own, so I gotta feed them pretty much all throughout the year. Extreme weather patterns are devastating for the bees. They shut down production when it gets too hot. The last few summers were particularly brutal around here. On top of that, crops get whacked by the late freeze almost every year now, late May, June even, so they don't have enough to eat to begin with. The ones still left in the wild are starving to death. It's cataclysmic, the rate they're dying off."

Russ cracks open one of the beehives. As he takes the cover off, Miles pulls back reflexively, expecting a swarm of bees to pour out, but nothing happens. He peeks inside over Russ's shoulder and sees that there's another layer on top, capping the beehive, a simple plywood panel with an empty mason jar turned upside down sticking out of it.

"It becomes a vicious circle," Russ continues, replacing the empty jar with a full one. "Declining crop yields means a smaller bee population, fewer bees means less efficient polination, inefficient pollination means declining crop yields and even less for the next generation of bees to survive on. And that's not even taking pesticide pollution into account. It's pretty grim all around."

Russ changes the jars in the other two beehives then slides out one of the brood boxes like a drawer, exposing a row of neatly stacked hive frames inside. Delicately, like he's handling a sleeping baby, he pulls one of the frames out and gives it a once-over.

"That's one plump and perky bunch," he smiles proudly, pleased with what he sees. "Almost ready for the winter."

Russ shoos off a crowd of teeming bees gently with his hand. They disperse in haste, revealing the lustrous mold of the honeycomb.

"Now comes the fun part!"

Russ breaks off a little chunk of the honeycomb and hands it to Miles. It feels both sturdy and fragile to the touch, shedding tears of glistening honey into his palm. Miles slurps up the runaway streams of honey off his fingers, taking a moment to let his taste buds relish the flavor, then nods approvingly.

"Single-origin, Brooklyn," Russ chuckles, breaking off a piece for himself. "It might not be the best you've ever tasted, but at least you know it's the real thing."

The front part of the garden is an open space with a cluster of graying Adirondack chairs huddled around a patio table, offering an unobstructed view of the Brooklyn shoreline, Lower Manhattan, and the New York Harbor. They sit down, sucking on their honeycombs like trophy popsicles, lapping up the sweet honey hidden inside while silently staring out at the serene glow of Indian summer that hangs in the air like an invisible veil, smoothing the visual chasm between stunted Brooklyn low-rises and gleaming skyscrapers across the water and making the two cities divided by the vast wealth disparity appear more cohesive, almost intimately reconnected. The way they used to be.

The sun slips into its daily routine of faking its own death, showing off its dramatic flair by drowning the skyline in napalm-like oranges and deep reds and igniting a sense of primal magnitude in any spectator's chest.

A dry bulk cargo barge appears on the horizon, skimming the water's surface like a wet-winged fly. Small waves buck and roll in its wake as it crosses the bay. After a few minutes, the barge slows down then halts in the water for no apparent reason. Miles finds it strange that it would just stop moving midway, thinking its motor probably gave away, until he notices an outline of a tiny island and realizes that the barge was actually headed there and now arrived at its destination.

The island is actually not an island at all, but some sort of floating platform, a working construction site. As the barge docks, the black arms of backhoe loaders stretch out in anticipation, flexing their scoops before bowing and feeding in unison.

"What are they building over there?" Miles asks.

"That," Russ replies with a prolonged stare "is going to be something called the Apocalypse Harbor."

"Apocalypse Harbor?" Miles asks, feeling utterly bewildered. The word *apocalypse* conjures up frightening images of death and horrible disasters associated with the end of the world.

"That's what some people call it. They call it 'The New York Harbor Terraform Peninsula Project.'"

"Who's they?"

"The ones building it," Russ points to Manhattan. "Rich folks across the river."

"But what is it?"

"They're adding a new landmass to the harbor, basically making a kind of a corridor from the bottom tip of Manhattan to the New Jersey side of the bay." Russ traces the path of the supposed structure with his finger. "From there, it connects back to Brooklyn and Governors Island, then loops through the East River back to Lower Manhattan. It's supposed to act as a protective barrier against a storm surge and, long term, a safeguard against rising sea levels."

"So, where is the excess water supposed to go?"

"Away," Russ scoffs. "The plan is to flood the New Jersey waterfront and a good part of Staten Island, both mostly no man's lands at this point, so that makes sense. They're accounting for a twelve to fifteen inch water rise, but climate models are not the most reliable science. What happens if we get more than that? Or what if this thing doesn't work the way we're told it will? People are afraid the water's is going to overflow into Brooklyn and Queens, that the whole project is just an elaborate scheme perpetrated by the Corporate to protect Manhattan at all costs."

"Do you think that's true?"

"Who knows?" Russ shrugs. "I try not to speculate too much without knowing the facts. The Corporate is paying for it, they're the ones calling the shots, so I can see how it could be perceived that way. When the masses are scared villains come in handy, but ignorance is a dangerous thing, especially when it comes from a place of fear."

Weary of looming unknown truths they abandon the conversation, losing themselves in the fiery sunset spectacle, hardly noticing the inky streaks of darkness seeping through the skies, slowly turning the molten slush of the sun-blazed sea into a murky mirror, and only when streetlights start trickling along the city grid do they realize that dusk has fallen upon them.

The fitful sound of percussions rises from the street, loose beats of cajon, tambourine, and congas looking for one another in the night. After a few incoherent minutes, the instruments agree on a cadence, settling together in a long-winded, forward pulling rhythm. Maracas and timpani join in from somewhere, a boisterous rattle, then a deep drum of some sort enters. The drum seems too loud, deliberately stepping over other instruments, and messing up the flow like it's begging for attention.

"Are you guys done slouching around here?"

They turn around to see Miriam behind them, thumping on a djembe strapped around her waist.

"Come on, we don't wanna miss the jam," she hits the rawhide with her palm one more time, then extends her arm out. "Hi Miles, I'm Miriam."

"Hi," Miles gets up and shakes her hand.

She holds Miles's hand in hers for a moment, looking him over with a warm smile, then makes brief, knowing eye contact with Russ, and with an imperceptible nod takes over the role of distractor-in-chief.

"Your hand's sticky, Miles," Miriam raises her eyebrow in mock suspicion. "If I didn't know any better, I'd say you guys raided the beehives."

Miles looks away as if not to incriminate himself and then turns to Russ, expecting him to admit the theft. It was his idea after all.

"It's okay, dear," Miriam chuckles, amused he took it seriously. "I'm just kidding. We steal their honey all the time. Now, what do you say we go down and make some music?"

She reaches inside her coat pocket and hands him a hollowed-out cylindrical piece of hardwood. Not exactly sure what he's looking at, or what to do with it, Miles twirls his fingers around it like he's testing its smoothness.

"It's a clave," Miriam clarifies. "Rumba clave, to be exact, because there's more than one kind."

"Yeah. Sorry, I..."

"This is what you do," Miriam takes the clave back and hits it with a wooden striker a few times, controlling the pitch of its clink with the squeeze of her palm. "Just follow the flow," she bobs her head with the rhythm.

Miles nods back in response, trying to catch the beat.

"It's easy," Miriam hands him back the instrument. "Anybody can do it."

"Except for me," Russ chimes in.

"It's because you don't even wanna try. I bought him these beautiful bongos a couple of years ago, I don't think he's touched them once. I bet you don't even know where they are."

"Yeah, I do."

"No way you do."

"I just mess everyone up. It's no fun when you're not good at it. I prefer to sit back and listen."

"See what I mean?" Miriam turns to Miles.

"Fine, let's go get the damn bongos," Russ gets up. "But I'm telling you, you're gonna regret it when you hear me play."

They head back down to the apartment.

"I'll be right back," says Russ and goes inside, leaving Miriam and Miles waiting on the stairwell, outside the door.

As soon as he gets in he calls Weiss, but gets bounced to the automated answering service.

"What the hell, Weiss?" He confronts the message box. "You dweeds gotta quit freezing me out. This is bullshit. I need to know what's going on."

He hangs up, mumbling a fruitless "Fuck!" to himself, then starts rummaging through the closets in search of the bongos.

"Miriam!" he yells out after a little while, realizing he has no clue where to look. "Where are the bongos?"

"What did I tell you?" Miriam turns to Miles, laughing.

"That's too funny," Miriam's infectious laugh makes Miles chuckle.

"Story of my life."

Outside, the jam session, now past its whimsy start, has unraveled into a self-sustaining sonic blanket, wrapping the neighborhood in a soul-soothing vibe, dampening all other city sounds. The street seems darker than it did from the rooftop and Miles realizes it's because none of the streetlights are working for some reason, except two, one at each end of the block.

They follow the drums down the block and as they turn the corner, Midtown Manhattan appears in the distance, suspended in a throbbing cloud of light. From their dim vantage point, the far-off skyscrapers look like jagged jaws bulging out of the dark, wet mouth of some mythical beast. Miles slows down, wowed by the view. Looking closer, he recognizes the glowing spire of the Chrysler Building then the trunk of the Empire State Building—once the tallest structure in the world, now humbled to just another tidy stack of concrete, metal, and glass that make up the labyrinth of the city, its art deco ambition out of place, almost naive, among the uninspired, utilitarian uniformity of the surrounding buildings.

Somewhere in the dark patch over the East River that separates Manhattan and Brooklyn, fragments of foggy light are swarming together, forming what looks like the figure of a person. A moment later, a humongous holographic image of a slender young woman wearing nothing but a long, translucent gown emerges from black water. Like a nymph out on a night stroll, she wades effortlessly through the waves then steps out on the shore, and with feathery steps, almost a dance, enters the city, the train of her gown trailing behind her like the flight path of a crane, curling up into an ornamental wreath bearing the logo of a luxury fashion brand.

A sudden clamor breaks out from somewhere nearby and a group of teens scamper out from a side street, pushing and shoving playfully, vying for each other's attention. Oblivious in their play, the kids sprint by them further into the night, without even taking notice. Looking after them, Miles catches himself feeling envious of their carefree goofiness, longing for his friends back home, but quickly shakes off the feeling, remembering how lucky he is to be here in the first place, free and in one piece, after everything that's happened.

He gazes back at the lights across the river. Blending into the city, the holograph of the girl has all but disappeared from view, only her locks still flowing between the buildings like silk ribbons in the wind, one last moment of relevance before her image gets consumed by the luminous flare of the midtown advertising jungle.

Gripped by anxious curiosity, Theo and Maritza stare out at the cloud of dust approaching along the road, still trying to wrap their heads around what or who could have orchestrated this total turnaround and why. Up until just a few minutes ago, they were helpless slaves condemned to a lifetime of misery in the hands of a cruel lunatic and now they're here, feeling alive again, trembling at the glimpse of freedom's proximity.

"I wouldn't get all perky just yet if I were you," Drey chimes in with fake concern as he unlocks the entrance gate. "Nothing's for nothing. You don't know who these people are, or what they want from you. You might just be jumping from one cage to another."

"As long as you stay in this one," Maritza snaps back at him.

Drey smirks, about to say something waspish, but instead stretches out his lips into a sapid, counterfeit smile.

"Maybe you'll end up missing me after all," Drey retorts.

"Somehow I doubt it," Maritza snaps back.

"You never know," Drey turns a short-lived smile into a contemptuous sneer. "Life's full of nasty surprises. You of all people should know that."

"Spare me the wisdom, you dumb ape!" Maritza wants to yell out but realizes she'd only be playing into his spiteful ploy to unnerve them. She scoots around him to get out, but

Drey reacts quickly, blocking the passage with his big frame.

"Hold your horses, lady," he pushes her back in, slam-locks the gate behind him, and then walks up the road, looking out at the distance.

A rolling dust cloud thins out as it draws closer, eventually revealing three unmarked utility vehicles with tinted windows swerving in unison like train cars. After a little while, the first and third vehicle flank out, pulling slightly in front of the middle one. The formation reels up towards the gate then stops some twenty yards from Drey, and four masked uniformed men step out of the side vehicles, brandishing submachine guns. At the sight of the weapons, Drey calmly lifts his hands midair then turns around full circle to show that he's not armed. A moment later, another masked man comes out of the middle vehicle carrying a metal briefcase in his hand. He walks up to Drey and lays the briefcase on the pavement between them. After they exchange a few words, Drey picks up the briefcase, comes back, and unlocks the gate.

"Good luck," he says, deliberately avoiding eye contact, hand outstretched to hold the gate open. "I mean it."

Not waiting to be told twice, Theo and Maritza scramble out, feeling the weight of desperation lifting off their shoulders like a lead blanket slipping off. But the bizarre sympathy in Drey's demeanor and voice still hang in the air. What did that man tell him? And what's in the briefcase? Are they just being traded to a higher bidder? What if, despite his hostile drift from before, Drey was right? What if these masked men are not their saviors, but their new jailers?

Theo and Maritza start walking toward the man in the middle, assuming he must be the one in charge. The man waits until they're far enough away from Drey's earshot then approaches them slowly and confidently.

"Mr. and Mrs. Smith, I'm special agent Arellano with Atlantic Commonwealth Intelligence. You can relax, you're free now."

# DAY_9

Three minutes before 7:00 am, the alarm clock squirts out a tiny vapor cloud from its flavor capsule, deploying the aroma of hot buttered croissants into the air. Russ stirs under the covers, widens his nostrils to better draw in the providential scent then, roused by it, opens his eyes to the sight of Miriam's masked face.

Miriam was always a good sleeper, but that changed after Russ's plane crash. The trauma of his death and eventual resurrection, and the uneasy recovery that followed had left her with residual anxiety that she couldn't set free. She began relying on aids to keep her asleep through the night—sleeping pills at first, then to shake the dependency she started using the Somni pillow, a teddy bear-like sleep bot that mimics affection and incites the release of oxytocin in the brain. But over time, the soothing noises the thing made became a distraction of its own, so they eventually had to kick it out of bed. Now this mask. Dreamcatcher six—two fleece-covered circuit-bands, the wide one strapped around her forehead and the other one pitched across the slope of her nose like some fuzzy facelift/nose job bandages. Scrunched in a ball with her head to the side, she looks like she passed out after a long day of skiing before she could even slip off her neck warmer fully.

Getting a second chance at life is a precious gift, one of those that would be a sin to let go to waste, a rare opportunity to let your mind wander off beyond the limits of comprehension and drift unhinged among the impregnable questions that populate the thin-air metaphysics of life and death. And if you're lucky, you'll understand that you won't find any answers up there because soon enough your mind will crash back down into the thick mud of quotidian ignorance and, like a lost dog eager to please with the one trick it knows well, it'll be back to waddling in the simple reality it's built for—and you'll find yourself entangled in the mundane comings and goings of everyday life again, reconciled with your insignificance, hoping that the brutal realization that the sun will rise in the morning with or without you won't be that painful anymore. Whatever time you get is luck. Now, tomorrow, or twenty years from today, your few cosmic nanoseconds of existence will come to an end and what was you once becomes something else, a speck of ash, a momentary flicker in the evening sky.

Nothing teaches humility like the proximity of death, but what really sets one's priorities in order is the threat of permanent physical disability. Nothing matters after you die, but while you're still alive, it's flat-out preferable to be in one piece and healthy. And so you start being truly grateful you're still on the right side of the dirt—walking, breathing, thinking, and feeling, and you struggle to make peace with the nothingness that's waiting with open arms to take you, once and for all, into a ghastly embrace when your time is up.

The alarm clock strikes the top of the hour with a peaceful progression of forest sounds: a gurgling brook, the distant song of a loon, the crackling of the forest floor under elk's hooves...

"I'm awake," Russ says out loud, silencing the alarm clock.

He kicks off the covers and slips out of bed.

"What the..." Miriam growls at the sudden morning chill nipping across her legs.

"Are you getting up?" Russ asks.

"In a minute," she yanks back the covers and curls up

under them, clearly without any intention of following through anytime soon.

"I'll make some breakfast. What do you want?"

"Go away!" Miriam moans, burying her head deeper into the pillow.

On the way to the kitchen, he pauses in front of the guest room and puts his ear to the door. Miles is still asleep. A smile curls Russ's lips. All's right with the world today. Or as close as it gets, at least for the moment.

Weiss finally called back around 8:00 pm last night. The op went without a glitch. They got the Smiths out, safe and sound. They brought them to the AC Trade Bureau in Saskatoon, where they are currently waiting for the next transport to New York, sometime this evening. Needless to say, Miles was ecstatic beyond words; he kept jumping up and down, and hugged Russ like he was a giant stuffed animal. His parents made a short video message for him that he ended up watching over and over again, perhaps to convince himself the whole thing wasn't just a dream.

A little while later, ACIS arranged a video conference for them. After the initial euphoria, with feelings gushing out of them quicker than they can find words to express them, the Smiths silently stared at their displays for a few moments, reading each other's faces, letting the anguish of the last nine days and the exaltation of the present moment meld into one. They talked for almost two hours before everyone went to bed. It was mostly Theo and Maritza asking Miles questions and Miles trying to remember everything that happened to him since he fled the house that morning—his and Moonie's escape from Concord, their adventures on the road, the time spent in Black Hills, his trip to New York with Russ. Theo and Maritza listened with a mixture of reverence and anguish, tearing up occasionally, all while delicately avoiding giving out too many details about their own experience so as not to upset Miles.

Being a witness to Smiths's sorrow and their joy filled

Russ's heart with affection and pride that he didn't always feel in his line of work. The abstract concept of "doing the right thing" becomes real when you can put faces on it.

"Kenji. On!" Russ activates CALO as he heads to the kitchen.

*"Good morning Russ. Coffee is ready."*

"Good."

*"Do you want the news?"*

"What do you got?"

*"HeatHub is reporting sporadic firefights in Munich between German federal forces and Sovereign Bavaria militias in response to the Federal Constitutional Courts decision to uphold the ruling of the trial court in the Klaus Klein case. Prediction platforms are now projecting that Klein will be assassinated within a week. It's currently the most popular bet on DeathWatch with more than three hundred thousand shares traded so far, which makes it the second most popular assassination bet of all time."*

"Follow the story."

Russ draws a sip of coffee and immediately spits it back into the mug.

"What's with this coffee?"

*"What seems to be the problem?"*

"It tastes like crap."

*"It's La Tortuga. You always liked La Tortuga beans."*

"Dishwater," Russ wrinkles his lips in disgust.

*"Too weak?"*

"Yeah."

*"Miriam changed coffeemaker settings two days ago. Do you want to revert to the previous setting?"*

"Yes," Russ empties the coffee pot into the sink. "Make a new pot."

*"On it. Should I continue with the news?"*

"Go on."

*"A research team from the University of Helsinki brings*

*the possibility of behavior modification through electrical stimulation closer to reality with a recently conducted study they claim shows that minimally invasive shocks to a person's brain makes them less likely to commit violent crime. Such shocks may also increase perceptions of violence and aggression as morally repugnant. A similar technique called transcranial direct-current stimulation has been used in the past to treat conditions such as Alzheimer's and opioid addiction or simply to boost memory. Perhaps the secret to holding less violence in your heart is to have a properly stimulated mind."*

"Perhaps," Russ mutters to himself.

*"The Florida Weather Force says it successfully tamed Hurricane Martha by spraying the ocean surface around Martha's eye with a biodegradable oil-based mix to slow down the evaporating that feeds hurricanes. Martha was originally predicted to become a category five hurricane before its expected landfall later today, somewhere between the western Panhandle and Louisiana, but now it's been downgraded to a category four hurricane.*

*Latest cholera outbreak in Manila is spreading at an unprecedented rate..."*

"Kenji, you know what? Skip the news. You're depressing me."

*"Okay. Maybe you should change your newsfeed preferences then."*

"Oh, is that's what you think?" Russ asks mockingly.

*"Mix in some humanities and art for good measure,"* Kenji continues undeterred. *"Sports maybe too. For example, I think you'll find this interesting: Earlier today, a twenty-two-year-old Ethiopian distance runner Negasi Seifu took a victory in the Berlin Marathon and broke the world record for completing the 26.2-mile race, finishing in 1 hour, 59 minutes, and 47 seconds."*

"Well, that's great."

*"See? Coffee's ready."*

"Go to sleep, Kenji."

*"Goodbye, Russ."*

Russ pours a new cup of coffee, takes a sip, then approvingly nods his head. He takes a look inside the fridge, not much to work with: Miriam's mutant food, milk, eggs, mushrooms, cheddar. Mushroom frittata it is then.

Maybe the damn bot is right, ignorance is bliss and all that. The world will keep spinning in circles of hell with or without him being a witness to it, so maybe he doesn't need to be aware of every little detail of the cataclysm. Better living through denial! It seems to work for some people.

The oven timer goes off. Russ pulls the frittata out and as he brings it out to the dining table sees Miles standing in the doorway.

"You're up!" Russ blurts out, surprised. "Perfect timing."

He cuts up the frittata, plunks one of the floppy squares on a plate and hands it to Miles, and then cuts another piece for himself and digs into it, nudging Miles with his fork to do the same. Miles gives the steaming egg pile a dubious look, deems it edible, then takes a small, reluctant nibble.

"Like it?"

"It's good," Miles nods his head, then realizing that he's actually hungry, takes another bite.

"It would have been better if I had bacon," Russ observes.

"I don't eat bacon."

"Well, that worked out perfectly then," says Russ, looking slightly offended.

They quietly finish off their plates then stand awkwardly for a moment, each wondering what to do or say next.

"Hey, today in Berlin a man broke the world record for running a marathon," Russ tries to strike up a conversation.

"Uh, okay," Miles mumbles back, not sure how to respond to that. "That's great."

"We got a few hours before we head back to the Directorate. We should do something fun," Russ tries again, unfazed by Miles's lack of enthusiasm about another great triumph of human tenacity and endurance. "Any ideas? Whatever you want."

"I don't know," Miles responds with a perplexed shrug.

"What are you guys up to?" Miriam's voice saves them both from further conversational deadlock.

"We're trying to think about something fun to do today," Russ turns to her, his eyes pleading for help.

"We should all do something fun every day," Miriam cranes her neck toward the table. "What do we have here? Yummy."

She grabs a plate then turns to Miles.

"How about a day trip to Manhattan? See firsthand what the whole hoopla is all about? Russ can get us day passes."

"Day passes?" Miles asks.

"Yeah. We need a permit to enter the Corporate zone, bellow Ninety-sixth Street. It takes about a week to get security clearance, but I bet Russ can expedite that through work."

"That shouldn't be a problem," Russ confirms, evidently happy with Miriam's suggestion.

"I kind of wanted to see where our old house is," Miles offers a gentle, apologetic smile. "Since we're in Brooklyn already."

"Sure!" Russ replies quickly, hiding his surprise.

"Grace Court. That's close, right?"

"Yeah, a ten-minute cab ride, tops. That's a great idea, Miles."

"And we won't need special passes," Miles's smile turns into a mild chuckle.

"True," Russ smiles back in kind. "Brooklyn still belongs to everyone."

Theo's eyes twitch open, revealing unfamiliar walls, and before he could make out where he is the terrifying thought of being back in that locked room grabs him by the throat. He springs up from the pillow, gasping for air in uneven breaths, then, realizing it's all over, he settles a bit, tuning in to Maritza's rhythmic, peaceful breathing. But the initial panic, bolstered by leftover fear, continues to well up in his chest as a slideshow of the harrowing experience of the past few days flashes in front of his eyes.

It's empowering to believe that we can fully determine our own fate through our actions, but for the most part, we're just puppets of happenstance bouncing around this tumultuous, discordant, unclassifiable mess that is life. One little thing tips the scale the wrong way and everything you've ever known, everything that makes you who you are, can be ripped apart into a thousand pieces. If you're lucky, you'll get another chance to put it all back together, but if you're not... Theo shudders, thinking about what could have been.

Careful not to wake Maritza up, he slides out of bed, gets dressed, and then parts the drapes just a fraction of an inch, letting a sliver of dim morning sunlight in. Outside, Saskatoon is shaking off the night's chill, indifferent and static, like a scale model of a generic city. Unremarkable in every way, the boxy pile of glass and metal housing the AC Trade Bureau blends in perfectly.

The insides of the building are equally as plain—a maze

of vinyl-coated drywall occasionally interrupted by patches of industrial paneling, low ceilings, and gray carpeting accentuating singularity of design, or lack thereof. Theo takes the elevator down to the common area on the second floor, where he finds Agent Arellano sprawled in one of the armchairs facing the elevators. Arellano springs to his feet when he sees him.

"Good morning," says Theo.

"Good morning, indeed. You slept well?"

"Better than the night before."

"I bet," Arellano winces. "Good news, we're on the six o'clock flight tonight. Arrangements have been made. We have a nice place for you in the ACIS Directorate housing complex on Governors Island, you'll stay there for the time being. Your son will be there when you arrive."

"How's he doing?"

"He's in good spirits. And in good hands. Agent Oakley is a seasoned guy, he'll keep him engaged. They're out now, visiting your old house in Brooklyn Heights, I believe."

The cab lets them out in front of Grace Church, then whirs off down the empty street. A gust of briny wind carrying distant seagull caws from the bay rustles through the tree branches, scaring the weakest of the dying leaves. The birds' high-pitched agitation tears through the echoey whispers spilling out from inside the church, then fades out in the open sky.

"That's Grace Court," Russ points across the street to a warped alley pockmarked with puddles.

The alley ends in a cul-de-sac of gray boards and a craggy chain-link fence ripped at the bottom corner, bent just enough so a person can pass through.

"And this should be seventy-seven," says Russ, while assessing the passage.

Miles nods in quiet comprehension then lifts the side of the fence, twisting his body to the opening, but before he could get his head through, he feels Russ's hand on his shoulder, gently pulling him back.

"Why don't you two wait here a minute? I'll go check what's out there first."

Miles and Miriam watch Russ disappear into the bushes behind the fence, then glance around the alley one more time with muted apprehension. Not a soul in sight, just two rows of decaying two-story buildings facing off across buckled cobblestone as if daring each other to see which one is going to surrender to time first.

"So, your folks are originally from Brooklyn, right?" Miriam asks.

"Yep, on my dad's side. He moved to the West Coast with his mom when he was twelve. But before that, yeah, I think as far back as anyone can remember, the Smiths lived in Brooklyn."

"Guess what? That makes you one of us."

Miles arches his eyebrows.

"Brooklynite," Miriam places her palm on her chest. "I'm from here too. Born and bred. Fort Green, just across Flatbush, that way."

"Is there something special about people from Brooklyn?" Miles smiles amusingly at her display of local pride.

"Damn right there is," Miriam exclaims without a flinch.

"What?" Miles asks when she fails to elaborate.

"If you have to ask, you'll never know."

"What?" He squawks incredulously, making her smile. "What does that even mean?"

"You'll figure it out, you're young," she says teasingly.

Russ pokes his head out from the bushes and waves them over. They squeeze through the chainlink fence and follow him down a shadowy path of fractured concrete and discolored grass.

Shrouded by wild tree branches and tall weeds, the house looks eerie yet strangely serene, weakened by the elements, but still composed, like a forgotten temple waiting for pilgrims. They walk up to the front porch silently, examining the invading armies of vine and ivy crawling over dingy brick walls. A portion of the front porch had collapsed, pulling askew wooden support columns with it. The smell of fungi feeding on the wet dust of rotting timber hangs in the air. The entrance to the house is sealed off with a solid steel door without a handle.

Miles sizes up the bulging square patch welded over the

spot where the lock should have been, then presses his palm on the smooth surface of the door, almost expecting to feel a heartbeat from the house behind it, but the steel is unresponsive and cold. One of the wood shutters on the first floor was bashed with a rock and now hangs uncertain on rusty screws, partially revealing a rolling steel curtain that protects the windows behind.

"Looks like somebody tried to get in, but gave up when they saw they need a flame cutter," says Russ.

"They probably just moved on to the next one," Miriam adds, then turns to Miles. "There are plenty of abandoned houses in Brooklyn nowadays, squatters are having their pick. A lot of people left for the countryside in the last five, ten years. Life is easier outside the city."

Miles drags his gaze across overgrown grounds. Heartened by unhindered growth, knee-high grass has collapsed at places under its own weight, stretching the length of the yard like an old, bedraggled shag carpet. The oak tree is still there, lording over the yard, big and proud, reaching for the skies. High up in its canopy, exhausted by the decades-long war between frost and heat, the remnants of Theo's treehouse are precariously balancing in the air like an ancient shipwreck, tethered to the ground by the narrow wooden staircase that wraps around the trunk in a crumbled spiral.

"We should call my dad," an excited smile breaks over Miles's face. "He's gotta see this."

"Let's try them," Russ whips out his Allcom. "They should be awake by now."

They wait for the Directorate to connect them to Saskatoon, glancing around the rest of the property with quiet curiosity. Toward the back of the yard, high grass yields its dominance to smaller, greener overgrowth that ebbs into the almost hidden, mossy relief of the cobblestone driveway. In the middle of the driveway, where the flower garden used to be, Franco Messa's fountain is still standing, besieged by a tangle of rough shrubs and stalky weeds.

"Miles!" Russ waves the kid over and hands him the Allcom.

"Dad!" Miles bursts out when he sees Theo's smiling face on the display.

*"Hey, buddy! How are you?"*

"Fine. I'm fine. Where's Mom?"

*"She's still asleep."*

*"No, I'm not,"* Miles hears Maritza's voice offscreen. *"Hi, baby!"* She bustles into the frame, nestling her head next to Theo's.

"Hi Mom," Miles's eyes soften with tenderness. "Hey, guess where I am?" he says with a sprightly giggle. "Do you recognize this?" Miles tilts the camera upward to the treehouse.

*"Oh, my,"* Theo sighs at the other end. *"What are you doing there?"*

"Can you believe it's still standing?"

*"It looks like it can use some fixing."*

"The rest of it too," Miles pans around the yard to the main house.

To give them privacy, Russ and Miriam walked to the back of the yard and are now shuffling their feet on the cobblestone between the jungle-like round of Amelia's flower garden and the flat open space overrun by nettle, where Augustus's carriage house lab once stood. Pecking through the velvety green blanket of nettle, the vibrant oranges, purples, and yellows of wild, late-blooming flowers glow like spilled stardust in a display of calm beauty that nature tends to create in the absence of humans. Creeping over the brick wall that separates two backyards, the naked branches of a neglected cherry tree hang snarled in a midair clump like a crown of thorns fit for a Goliath. The wall still bears the marks of the fire, red smudges of brick bleeding through a layer of petrified soot.

What a horrible way to go. Russ shivers at the thought that he almost ended up dying the same way when their plane caught fire in the sky above the desert. Hopefully, the carbon monoxide got him before the fire burned his body.

He turns his attention to Miriam who, for some reason, began clearing out the mess of broken tree branches, gray weed stalks, and bleached out rubbish that the wind deposited in the dry bed of the fountain. She rips out a few handfuls of dry grass clinging to the stone and brushes away dead leaves and twigs, then stands up with her hands on her hips and gazes at the carved image of the sun set at the center.

"Beautiful piece," she says after brief reflection, tracing the elegant cascading form with her finger.

A major portion of the top tier of the fountain toppled over some time ago, knocking the second tier off balance when it collapsed. Set free by the weakened mortar, some of the modular stone slabs have tilted apart, exposing a network of cracks, some of which reached the size of a child's hand. Most of the two-inch-wide stone planks that once fringed the outer walls have fallen off, leaving ghostly rectangular blemishes on the charred surface of the stone. Russ takes a closer look around and notices the word, "SHADOWS" inscribed on one of the remaining planks, and then the word, "FALL" on another.

"Shadows will fall behind you!" Jared Hiebert's feeble hiss comes out of nowhere, echoing in his ears.

Russ circles the fountain and sees three more planks bearing the words, "TURN," "FACE," and "TO" still attached, then crouches down looking for the rest in the grass.

"What do you think it says?"

"That's what I'm trying to figure out," Russ looks up to see Miles holding the Allcom in his outstretched hand.

Without getting up, Russ takes back his Allcom and puts it in his coat pocket.

"It's good to see their faces, huh?"

"Yeah, it's great."

"Found one!" Miriam yells out from the other side.

"What does it say?" Russ asks.

"YOU." And here's another! "BEHIND."

"That should be BEHIND YOU."

Miriam lays the planks on the ledge of the fountain then looks at the words with some scrutiny.

"How do you know? It could be YOU BEHIND. Like in leave YOU BEHIND. Maybe they don't even go together."

"They do. It's 'BEHIND YOU.'"

"You're just guessing."

"Trust me."

Miles squats next to Russ and starts inspecting scattered stone shards on the ground.

"My dad never wanted to talk about his childhood," he says. "Like it never happened."

"Everyone has their way of coping," Russ gives his two cents.

They search the grass for the rest of the words in silence, then Miriam digs out another plank.

"WILL," she announces her find. "WILL FALL BEHIND YOU?"

"Yes," Russ confirms. "It should say "SHADOWS WILL FALL BEHIND YOU."

"How do you know that?" Miriam challenges again.

Russ gives her a look that says "Please, stop talking."

"I think I found something," Miles lays down a few broken pieces on the ledge and starts shuffling them around. "YOUR... and this should be... SUN."

"I got AND and THE," Russ adds.

"Another THE here," Miriam shouts out.

"TURN YOUR FACE TO THE SUN..." Miles starts.

"... AND THE SHADOWS WILL FALL BEHIND YOU," Russ reads the rest.

"Turn your face to the sun and the shadows will fall behind you," Russ repeats out loud as they all gaze at the fractured words, grasping at their meaning.

Miles's mind wanders off into an unbidden memory of a photograph that he once saw on his father's desk. Wrapped tight in Augustus's hug, six-year-old Theo is looking straight at the camera, his eyes squinting with joy, his roguish smile revealing the gap from a missing front baby tooth. They're standing inside the dry bed of the unfinished fountain, both holding hammers in their raised right hands like trophies. Miles narrows his eyes, trying to determine the exact spot where Theo and Augustus were standing when the picture was taken, then steps inside the fountain, transcending time, becoming one with the image in his mind. He stands there for a few moments, unmoving, almost feeling their presence, then fixes his eyes on the carving of the sun in the middle. Intrigued by a faint beam of light fading into the crack between stone slabs right above it, he bends forward and peeks down into the crevice.

"Miles," Russ calls him, but he doesn't hear.

Miles lays down and presses his chest to the stone, cups his hands around his temples to block out the excess sunlight and, after a short survey of the dark hole below, reaches inside.

"There's something in there," he turns to Russ. "There's something in there, but I can't reach it."

"What is it?"

"I can't tell."

"Hold up," Russ says, before wandering off.

Russ starts scouring the ground for something, then comes back holding a medium-sized tree branch in his hands. He sticks the thicker end of the branch into the crack and starts levering. After a few pulls, the surrounding stone slabs begin moving apart, then the outer one slumps to the side, revealing a tiny chamber inside the structure. They flock to it, attracted by the sense of mystery, locking their eyes on the black cubical object laying inside the chamber. Unsure what to make of it, they look at each other with restrained trepidation.

"Well, we might as well see what we've found," Miles kneels down and takes a closer look at what appears to be a simple black box made of some sort of carbon alloy.

Sharp-edged and compact, with no markings or visible joints, the box resembles a scaled-down monolith. Gently, like he's touching a bird, Miles wipes mortar crumbs and pebbles off of it, then picks up the box and brings it out into the light.

# CODA

# DAY_207

It was still dark when Miles and Theo stepped out into the crisp April morning. Still asleep, its physical decay obscured by shadows, Grace Court Alley looked peaceful, almost serene, the way Theo remembered it before life in California faded its image in his memory.

Suspended in a faint halo of murky light seeping from side streets, the naked branches of poplar trees clattered above them in the wind as they negotiated the holes in the cobblestone pavement. Just as they were about to enter the intersection, a van emerged from Hicks Street and turned into the alley, heading straight at them. The flash of the van's lights blinded them temporarily, but they managed to scurry to the side. The van stopped abruptly, then after a few moments, slowly rolled up next to them.

"Mr. Smith. Miles," the driver's side window opened, revealing the burly head of Foreman Nick Hayes. "I almost didn't see you guys there in the dark."

"You're early today," Theo responded, hiding his relief.

"We got a fresh concrete delivery this morning. Those guys wait for no one."

A few of days after they settled in at ACIS housing, Miles started pestering Theo to go and visit the old house. Theo managed to rebuff him for almost two weeks, mainly because the big news they received in the middle of their second week at Governors Island diverted Miles's attention. Miles had won his final EternalQuest match against Chasm. It was the first truly happy, unfettered moment the Smith family had after everything that went down. Miles beamed with pride at his accomplishment and enjoyed the accolades that came his way from the EternalQuest community. But after the excitement wore off and the pressure of fandom eased, Miles started insisting they go to the old house again, leaving Theo no choice, but to finally agree to cross over to Brooklyn Heights and see his childhood home for the first time in more than four decades.

Theo knew he wasn't going to be ready for the whirlwind of emotions that hit him, the profound sadness that took over as old ghosts came alive in his heart, and if it weren't for Miles being there he would have broken down in tears for the better world that once was and the stunted promise of a different life that could have been. You can't go home again. But you can make something new from the memories of the past and maybe that's enough.

Theo felt grateful to his mother for keeping those memories alive for as long as she lived, telling him stories of their lives here that he was too young to remember. He finally understood her irrational decision to never sell the house. It was her way of keeping Dad with them forever, never letting go of the past and of the time they spent together on this Earth. They needed the money in the beginning when they moved out West, but she refused to sell.

"Never! I will never sell it," she was adamant, as if she knew that one day they'll return.

When Amelia died, Theo went with it out of respect for her wishes or maybe it was just inertia. There was no sense in selling anyway—the Brooklyn real estate market has been dead for ages, and he couldn't find a buyer even if he tried.

The final EternalQuest battle against Chasm was a doozie, but now, months later, it seemed to Miles like it blended into a blur of memories of those first few days on Governors Island. He was worried about his parents. Maritza has had bad headaches for a few days and has spent a lot of time in bed sleeping and Theo was unusually quiet most of the time. They didn't want to talk much about what hapened to them in Alberta. Despite their best efforts to appear okay, it was obvious that they weren't, and Miles didn't know what to do about it. The game came as a welcome distraction from everything, a chance to get out of his own head for a day.

Before he logged back onto QuestFrontier under his own name, Miles was told by Russ and Pratt not to say anything specific about the reasons for his disappearance or his actual whereabouts, even though everyone wanted to know what happened. Even the people who were nice and supportive started bugging him with constant messages demanding an explanation and then getting angry when they didn't get one. In retrospect, he should have made up some sort of story that would've satisfied the curious mob. The hive mind of the Frontier overwhelmed him in the end, so much so that he decided to go dark again. He didn't care if those conspiracy theories started swirling again. He realized that he couldn't please everyone. Besides, he felt that staying out of the chatter and rumor mill would do him good. The whole thing was starting to get on his nerves, which was the last thing he needed when he was trying to focus.

On the day of the match, Miles got up early and went to the building's gym to burn off some of his anxiety. After he got back from the gym, they had a big lunch on their apartment's terrace overlooking the bay and the Statue of Liberty. When it was time to go, Theo offered to accompany him to TOC, but Miles declined, saying that walking alone would help him get into the zone.

He's been getting a lot of looks walking around ACIS grounds, partly because people don't expect to see a fifteen-year-old bouncing around the campus of an intelligence agency, but it was probably more because the news of their fountain find had spread around, and people were just curious to see "the kid."

It took the ACIS data forensic team a full day to crack the encryption used to secure the electronic lock on the box. Nobody knew what to expect to find inside, so when they opened it, everyone was surprised to see a single metallic slab reposed in a bed of cutout foam—an ancient solid-state drive with no markings or labels. The hardware technician made a whole show of taking the drive out of its resting place; white cotton gloves, sprays of antistatic chemical agents, even administering something called corona discharge, a process that floods the air around the object with ions that neutralize any electrical charge. When they hooked up the drive, a prolonged moment of stunned silence took over the room as they all stared at the colossal display above the TOC main floor. No one knew what they were looking at.

"This is a third-generation blockchain database," one of the data forensics analysts finally divulged. "Smart contract setup of some sort. DAO. Decentralized autonomous organization," he added, bobbing his head in a slow, rhythmic manner as he scanned the display with his eyes.

The data forensics team took their time analyzing the contents of the blockchain database, but their findings were definitely worth the wait.

"Hands of Ali, heart of a lion, focus of samurai. Hands of Ali, heart of a lion, focus of samurai. Hands of Ali, heart of a lion, focus of samurai," Miles mouthed his pregame mantra, then eased up his grip on the fence railing and looked out at the restless surf gnawing away at the sea wall by the ACIS Tactical Operations Center.

A tang of ocean mist on his lips felt nourishing, sweet, and salty at the same time. He repeated his mantra one more time, then continued calmly to TOC. He was ready.

The guard nodded him in at the entrance with a smile, and Miles went inside feeling the excitement of a fighter entering an arena throbbing in his pulses, his body lifting with each breath, his feet barely touching the ground as he made his way through the corridors.

The TOC guys set up the room as an ascetic gamer's den—bare walls, a small table with a few bottles of Plenergy water, some high-energy snacks, and a souped up Portall that Weiss prepared for him, a bit more powerful, but a touch less responsive than his home setup, he thought. Miles strapped the immersion kit on and navigated to the EternalQuest gateway. Darkness took over his field of vision for a moment, then a single blue dot appeared in the center, gradually expanding through the void until the sphere of the Earth revealed itself in its full, fragile beauty. An uplifting soundscape of a soulful choir and distant tribal drumming sprinkled over the image, then a voiceover boomed in:

*"Empires rise and fall, but true greatness lives forever. Extraordinary feats touch the hearts of people, attract devotion, and invite the spirit of unity that extends beyond borders. What will your reign bring? Will you rise in the face of adversity or vanish into the ash heap of history? A great civilization expands horizons, strives for justice, and elevates all of humankind. How will the story of your people be written? What will your civilization be remembered for?"*

Moonie woke up with a smile on his face, feeling the warmth of Sofia's silken ass against his crotch. She didn't strike him as a spooner. He thought she was a model when he first saw her, maybe a daughter of some local el jefe. Wrapped in a short sequined green dress that fit like a snakeskin, with a copious mane of jet-black hair tamed in a horsetail and golden eyeshadow accentuating her burning green eyes, she moved like the world belonged to her. Which it did, at least for a moment, weeks ago, on the floor of a Santiago nightclub.

They hit it off immediately. Moonie was talkative beyond the pre-hookup routine, probably due to the multiple Terremoto cocktails he'd been imbibing since dinnertime. No wonder they call the thing earthquake. She seemed amused by his gringo naïveté and asked all of the right questions to keep him going—or maybe he kept blabbing because after the three-week grind of meet and greet with local politicos and businesspeople he was starved for a conversation that didn't involve terms like *overburden ratio, anomalous ore coefficient,* or *plata.*

After Driggs took off, Moonie stayed in the Black Hills, waiting for the feasibility team to come from Denver. When they came, twelve days later, he helped them settle and start with the mine testing. Driggs left one of his men in charge, an even-headed guy named Morris, who kept an eye on the day-to-day operations and reported back to him, wherever he might have gone. Morris and the Denver crew quickly established a good rapport and found a way to work together in a trusting way, rendering Moonie unnecessary, which meant that it was time for Lark to give his verdict on what was next for him.

Lark was royally pissed when Moonie told him the whole story about what happened with Miles, even though deep down, he probably understood that Moonie didn't have a choice, but to do what he did. It didn't matter. Moonie put Pardes Ventures in danger by messing with Sheng Long, and he almost fucked up the Driggs deal, aggravating Claymore in the process. Nobody needs more enemies. Especially among the PSCs. Despite his frustration, Lark, as always, kept a cool head and found a solution to benefit all sides.

After eighteen years of perpetual unrest that was by all standards closer to a slow-burning civil war, the people of Chile decided they had had enough, and they began working toward a compromise that would, if not reconcile, at least appease the warring parties enough to do their part to pull the country back from the precipice of complete disaster. It looked like peace was going to hold, and for Lark and Pardes Ventures that meant it was time to make their move.

Chile isn't a particularly rich country, but it's been blessed by the mineral gods: copper, gold, iodine, lithium, nitrates, rhenium, silver—they got a good bit of everything. But, like everyone else, they lacked a successful formula for how to solve the age-old problem of unequal distribution. So, after a violent eighteen year dispute between the left and the right about how to fairly divide resources, a bloody "debate" that took more than twenty-two thousand lives to settle and plunged the country into a severe economic depression, they came up with a wise conclusion that if they don't turn things around soon, there won't be anything left to divide and their quarrel will be all for naught.

The mining industry was generating three quarters of the country's revenue before the big international mining corporations were chased out with guns and laws at the beginning of the conflict. In a few short years, the locals ran it into the ground due to mismanagement, lack of expertise, and capital investment.

The current Chilean government, tasked with reviving the golden goose, was now forced to turn back to those same corporations to help them put their underperforming and idling mines back to work—except it's not easy to convince someone to fall for the same trick twice. Fearing the thuggery and bad treatment, most of them chose to steer clear from Chile, at least for the time being, which opened the playing field to allow smaller mining outfits with a higher risk tolerance to enter the fray.

Moonie was slated to leave for Santiago as soon as he was able to facilitate a smooth transition of responsibilities to a guy Lark picked to take over the Provo mine operations. He decided to keep his new identity, Max Madigan, for a little while longer, in case Sheng Long was keen on taking revenge against him personally—the way they took revenge on his house. Bobby discovered the house in disarray one day when he went back to check on it and called him right away. When he was finished in Provo, Moonie drove back to Concord to inspect the damage.

He left the truck on the side road, then walked up the narrow trail along a stream that carved its way between chunky boulders and tall oak trees. About a quarter-mile downstream he caught sight of solar panels on his rooftop. Once he was within eyesight of the house, he found cover behind some shrubs and thorny ferns and surveyed the area with field glasses.

The yard looked like it needed a trim. Flipped-over patio furniture laid scattered around like a pack of giant dead beetles on a bed of brown leaves. Detached from the top hinge, the warped screen door rattled in the breeze. One of the windows in the front was broken. He took a plastic case out of the inside pocket of his jacket and popped it open. Set snug in the cutout foam was a tiny drone and a seven-inch tablet. Moonie plucked the drone out and laid it on the ground, then picked up the tablet and tapped on its surface a few times. The drone lifted into the air and with an imperceptible hum flew off in the direction of the house. Moonie followed its progression on the tablet's display as it flew across the yard and through the broken window, then switched to drone's camera feed.

The place appeared like it was abandoned in a hurry ahead of an oncoming storm, then looted by marauding bandits before its occupants could come back home: a broken flower vase spilled on the foyer tile, rummaged-through cabinets, a toppled lamp in the corner, tea light candles and picture frames strewn across the floor, a linen scarf hanging by a thread off the side of one of the gaping drawers. In the kitchen, capsized chairs laid at the base of a cockeyed table, and the debris of shattered dishes cluttered the floor. The master bedroom was a ransacked mess, clothes everywhere, smeared boot-marks on pillowcases, knocked-over night tables, glass fragments sprayed throughout. Upturned on the bed like a gutted animal was the slashed-open mattress, fine wads of stuffing fibers spilled out of its insides and covered the floor in a mold-like white fuzz.

Moonie brought the drone back then walked over to the house and went inside. He stood up in the middle of the living room for a moment and gazed around, taking it all in. Up close, the violation felt even more unnerving.

The safe where he kept his walking around one-ounce gold bars was ripped out of its wet fridge hiding place, gone. He went to the basement and saw that they raked through it as well. Luckily they didn't know where to look. He cleared the rubble of broken armoire pieces and loose bric-a-brac in the far corner, ripped off the carpeting underneath, then got a hammer, chisel, and a couple of duffel bags from the garage. With a few precise whacks, he dislodged the floor planks, exposing the face of a safe with a dial combination lock built into the concrete below, then opened the safe and transferred all twenty-nine one-kilo gold bullion bars stored inside it into duffel bags.

Moonie lugged the bags up the stairs into the living room, then took a brief, solemn tour around the house. It's just stuff, nothing that can't be replaced. His anger softened after a while.

He found an unopened can of Quickstrike lying on the kitchen floor, partially covered by pieces of broken plates and cups, cracked it open, and took a long, thirsty swig out of it. Then he noticed his good luck ditty box wedged between the legs of the fallen kitchen chairs. He picked it up gently, checking its sturdiness. One of the tiny hinges had snapped broken and its top with the humpback whale engraving was dangling to the side. He walked back to the living room and put the ditty box in one of the duffle bags, looked around one more time, said good-bye to the fine house that was his home for the last four years, then lifted both of his arms in the air and, with a winning smile on his face, slowly swirled around and flipped off the hidden surveillance cameras Sheng Long left behind.

Moonie stashed the gold at his parents', then spent a day assuring them that it won't be long until he comes back, a few weeks, a couple of months at most. They wanted to believe him. He then drove down to Vallejo to hang out with the boys for a couple of days before boarding a flight in San Francisco. When he passed through Concord on his way to the airport, his mind was already zipping ahead to a new adventure waiting for him in Chile.

The first days in Santiago were a blur. New continent, new ways. The language barrier wasn't too bad because he mainly dealt with industry people and most of them spoke decent English. All of the mining materials were in English as well. For everything else there was UnBabel. Not that there was much of anything else for the first three weeks.

Then he met Sofia.

She moved to Santiago from Bogota, only six weeks before Moonie did, but she already had the lay of the land. The knowledge of the language and local culture certainly helped but it wasn't just that.

On the perennial seesaw of political and economic fortunes that is South America, Colombia was at the moment on top, and Chile close to the bottom, and, as anyone who's ever dabbled in financial speculation knows, the way to make money is to sell at the top and buy at the bottom. Similar to what Moonie was sent here to do for Lark and Pardes Ventures, Sofia was a spearhead of a Colombian real estate concern, tasked with finding good investment opportunities in Chile, which were plentiful if you were willing to run a little risk. After almost two decades of economic turmoil, the country was dirt cheap. With her brains and her looks, backed by powerful interests, she was a lethal facilitator of the once-in-a-generation wealth shift happening under everyone's noses.

Moonie and Sofia spent virtually all nonworking hours together, flying high above the streets of Santiago on the wings of a budding romance until the call of duty took Moonie up north to examine a few copper and lithium mines that looked like promising prospects. He spent a month in and around Antofagasta, a dusty gateway city to the vast plateau of the Atacama Desert, where most of Chile's mining business takes place. When he was done, they arranged to meet up about two-thirds of the way from Antofagasta to Santiago, in La Serena, where Sofia was looking at some seaside properties and tired hotels that needed a capital infusion.

Appropriately named, La Serena was a dainty beach town stretched across a coastal plain fringed by small hills, with Colonial Revival architecture and a laid-back vibe. They lazed away the day on the beach and around town and then, after a long boozy lunch at one of the thatch-roofed huts on Avenida del Mar, headed back to the hotel.

Regalo de Alma was one of the few places in town that maintained glimpses of the past resort luxury. Tucked behind a man-made lagoon, right on the beach, it towered over the town like a concrete obelisk, offering amazing views of the fertile valleys beyond nearby hills on one side, and the endless horizon above the ocean on the other. They stayed in the rest of the evening, making up for the lost time they spent apart, then after a couple of bottles of Carménère and a room service dinner called it a night.

Moonie laid in bed unmoving for a while, breathing in Sofia's intoxicating scent and then, feeling a morning thirst, he detached from her and stealthily slipped out of bed. He fetched a bottle of cold water from the minibar, stepped out on the balcony, and looked at the early autumn clouds floating over the dark blue water of the Pacific. The dampness of the ocean spray on his skin and the rhythmic shuffle of the waves reminded him of the lonely days he spent on the deck of *Vostok*. It seemed like a thousand years ago.

He remembered what Ms. Sherman, his sixth-grade teacher, once told him in class: "Vallejo is not the world." She talked about how the world is an oyster waiting to be cracked open, and that one should never lose a sense of wonder. He didn't remember everything Ms. Sherman said, but "Vallejo is not the world" was one thing that stuck in his mind. That simple statement probably changed the course of his life. Every one of his new beginnings, every fresh start originated there. It led him forward to explore what's beyond the invisible walls that kept most people content with just being fed, sheltered, and amused—until they forgot that they ever wanted anything else.

When he went back inside Sofia was still in bed with her hair rippled across the pillow in an obsidian halo, her lips plump from sleep. Her eyes fluttered open, sensing his presence in the room.

"Wanna get going?" she asked in a fine-grained voice.

"I like this place," Moonie said. "Maybe we should kick back here for a day or two. What do you think?"

"I think that sounds like a good plan."

Sofia lifted the covers and gently tapped the mattress with her palm, inviting him back to the warmth of the bed and her body.

"Come."

Sitting at a single table at the edge of the outdoor breakfast patio, hidden behind large sunglasses, Driggs watched horse riders in the distance. Sun-kissed and polished to a smooth finish, a group of polo players trotted by, flashing their toothy smiles at one another before disappearing behind the trees on their way to the polo grounds. Driggs took a couple of bites out of his açaí bowl feeling intense disdain for these useless creatures who never worked a day in their lives, then quickly packed away his acrimony before anyone could take notice.

Since he got here two months ago, he's made a lot of progress hiding his contempt for the citizens of Pardes, to the point that he thought nobody could call him unpleasant. The contempt was mutual, of course, but the unwritten rules of the place dictated that it should be veiled, so as not to interfere with the curated perfection of everyone's day. It's tough work being a Scrooge in paradise. Yes, paradise. That's what the word Pardes means. Well, more precisely, it means orchard in Hebrew, but a special kind of orchard, they told him. Paradise... Pardes... phonetically it's almost the same thing. According to an old Jewish legend, out of four rabbis who entered Pardes looking for divine presence one died immediately, another one went mad, and a third one destroyed all of the fruit trees in anger. Only one of them departed the orchard in peace. We'll see how it breaks down for all of them here, basking in this current iteration of Pardes, when the end times come.

After he abandoned his lair in the woods of Black Hills, Claymore helped Driggs disappear again. They took him to an old ranch outside of Cheyenne, one of their three tactical training centers, where he waited while the house in Vail was getting readied for his arrival. The place was nominally still a cattle ranch, but other than a dozen cows that decoratively adorned the sienna-colored hills surrounding it there was nothing else that suggested that Claymore was interested in raising beef there as much as raising an army of beefheads.

The old cattle pens were converted into training obstacle courses and shooting ranges, and the bunkhouse that once housed working cowboys now served as trainee barracks. The stench of cow shit, beaten into the mud for over a century by millions of cattle hooves that passed through there on their way to the slaughterhouse, hovered over the grounds like an invisible cloud. After two weeks of listening to the future PSCs grunt and bark outside his window and watching them sweat in the cow shit air while punching, stabbing, and shooting at imaginary enemies, Driggs finally boarded the helicopter and left for Vail.

Skiing season in Vail was supposed to begin in the second half of November, but the whims of the changing climate took the snow someplace else that year. They had a few flurries in January, but not enough to even cover the ground. Instead of the winter wonderland he was expecting, Driggs had to endure the dreary landscape of lifeless forests, barren mountain peaks, and hazy gray skies while he worked out the deal with Pardes Ventures.

Negotiations weren't particularly hard or lengthy. The feasibility team corroborated most of the initial diagnostic findings. Expectedly, Pardes Ventures lowballed him right out of the gate, knowing very well that he didn't have much choice, but to accept their paltry offer, which he did after a few upward adjustments. Driggs knew he was leaving a lot of money on the table but didn't really care. He already had enough to last him two lifetimes. He was tired of hiding, living the life of a troglodyte. He wanted to see the sun again.

The exfiltration went without a wrinkle, as promised. First, a helicopter from Vail to Denver, then a private jet to Havana, where they spent the night at an airport hotel. The next morning, they changed planes and continued south, landing at Porto Alegre in the late afternoon.

Porto Alegre used to be a rich city, one of the richest in Brazil, back in the day when the Brazilian federal state still existed. But over the last thirty or so years, the rising water levels in the Guaiba River delta, where the city was located, destroyed many of its neighborhoods and caused a population exodus. Porto Alegre became a shell of its former self.

First to leave were the rich. They bought up large swaths of cheap inland property southwest of the city and started building an exclusive gated community for themselves, away from the desperate masses. That first gated community, built upon the legacies of the founders' business acumen and their willingness to overlook morals in the interests of profit, became the foundation for what eventually grew into the transnational haven for high-value individuals known as Pardes Corporate.

The Pardes welcome crew was waiting for Driggs at the airport. After a short car ride, they ushered him onto a small yacht that took him across Lagoa dos Patos, a freshwater lagoon that separated Pardes and Porto Alegre. He arrived in Pardes at dusk, tired, but relieved that the trip was finally over.

"Your daily free radicals cleanse, Mr. Driggs," the servant said and softly placed a glass of pinkish foamy liquid on the table. "Ashwagandha root extract with goji berry foam," he expounded, clearing the table of the breakfast dishes.

Along with the customized nutritional program his personal wellness consultant created for him, she's been encouraging Driggs to acquire some other healthy habits—sleep more, drink less, exercise, and eat better. Driggs played along. It was working, he must admit. He felt much more energized, lighter, stronger. The problem was really what to do with all that newfound energy. There's plenty to do here in Pardes, it's just that he hasn't found anything that he actually wanted to do yet. Maybe he should pick up golfing. As silly as the game is, it might be useful as a distraction, and a way to make new acquaintances. After years of essential solitude in the Black Hills, he's fallen out of the habits of social relations. Strangely enough, he somehow felt freer there while alone. Despite its comforts, this place sort of felt to him like a big, beautiful jail—not that he should complain.

Driggs took a sip of the pinkish concoction, wincing at its sourness, then navigated his Allcom to HeatHub for a daily fix he actually enjoyed. He glanced at the HeatHub landing page, which featured competing coverage and analysis of the world's ongoing wars, then steered to his favorite—Texas versus California. The age-old divide finally escalated to heavy weapons and he couldn't wait to see who'd prevail. In his heart he was still a Texan, but his home country hasn't been very good to him for a long time and, quite honestly, it felt good to see Samuelson and his gang pull their horns in after they got their asses kicked in Yuma last month. But the war is still young, you can barely even call it a war at this point. They need to crank this thing up and fast, hit one of their big cities next, perhaps San Diego. Go big or drag their sorry asses back home. The meek shall not inherit the Earth—the brutes will.

The Smiths's decision to stay in Brooklyn, to renovate the old house, and try to restart their lives there started shaping up on the day the data forensic team invited them all to TOC to share what they found after they finished analyzing the blockchain database Augustus had left behind. Visibly energized, the head analyst explained that the database contains a master document of Augustus's invention—the scientific theory behind artificial photosynthesis, the source code, and detailed engineering instructions that define the physical aspects of the Chorus solar panel: product specifications, material requirements, design parameters, production guidelines, and procedures. A scientist by calling and a humanist by nature, Augustus found a way to ensure that his invention will be democratized—even if he wasn't around to witness it.

The whole thing was set up as a massive free token ICO, in which every country in the world gets an allotment of free shares relative to the sizes of their populations, which in effect gives an equal portion of ownership and governance of the enterprise to each person on the planet.

Shares cannot be bought or sold, making certain that no one entity can amass enough of them to take control of the organization by financial means, so people will have to be morally and politically mobilized. The smart contract built into the code transparently facilitates joint ownership of intellectual property and joint sharing in governance.

By taking for-profit monopolization out of the equation, participants can focus on public interest, motivated solely by the environmental and technological benefits the adoption of the new solar panel will bring to all humankind. Its decentralized autonomous organizational structure compels collaboration between countries to come up with a mechanism to select decision-makers, organize, incentivize production, and ensure a fair distribution.

Dr. Maya Savage, Sundance's chief engineer, was next to speak.

"As most everybody knows, history's littered with insufficiently examined proclamations of panacea, but looking at this data, I can't help but believe that we are witnesses to one of the most extraordinary moments in the field of applied science. I don't believe in God, but I'm inclined to think that this is as close to the divine solution as it gets, in every way imaginable. We're at the onset of something genuinely wonderful. The impact that Mr. Smith's invention will have on our lives will be immeasurable. Having an efficient, renewable, carbon-free source of virtually limitless energy will help resolve the most challenging existential problems of our time. A whole new future is waiting for us, one in which progress will not be constrained by energy scarcity, a future that will free up the great potential of humankind to explore new frontiers, untethered by today's limitations. And perhaps most importantly, we can start earning back our right to live on this planet by reversing the most damaging consequences of Anthropocene—and heal this fragile paradise of the sickness we inflicted on it with our irresponsible ways."

That same day, the Sundance team started setting up a lab in one of the newly built honeycomb-patterned buildings by the ferry landing, on the other side of the TOC. The building was unfinished inside, which made it easier to quickly purpose it for their needs. The ground floor was reserved for the workshop that will house materials development, prototype production, and testing; the upper floors are for the data center, product management, and common areas.

A few days later, they released the smart contract code to the public. The world rejoiced instantly, but facilitating the global collaboration needed to commence production had proven to be the hardest thing to do. After the initial euphoria petered out, the bickering started, followed by the dubious stalling tactics of certain parties designed to take advantage of the situation by holding the project hostage until their demands have been met. The political map of the world looked much different than it did in Augustus's time and that presented a problem. Who gets what? The heads of nations squabbled like a bunch of ungrateful offspring at a will reading. Legal issues arose, with different political entities claiming succession rights for their origin countries.

Finally, a consensus was reached that the smart contract should be reworked to reflect the new reality on the ground using the same principles of equality embedded in the original document. In a preemptive effort to escape the legal limbo that would inevitably take years to resolve, unnecessarily delaying the adoption of the new technology, the scientific community insisted that any agreement had to include an exemption that would allow a few countries with the means to carry out such a task to immediately begin producing a limited number of prototypes that could be tested and evaluated before mass production begins. The whole process would be monitored by an international body of experts and all of the information obtained would be publicly available in real time.

Things were moving at a breakneck pace at the lab, and Theo was too busy to do much of anything else. Every now and then he'd start feeling guilty that he wasn't doing enough to help Miles and Maritza transition to their new lives, only to realize that they've been managing just fine without his help. They were lucky enough to find a spot for Miles at Packer Collegiate, an old-time private school a few blocks from their home. Miles quickly took to the new school environment and has made a few friends there, good kids, mostly from the neighborhood, but you could tell he was missing his old Concord crew.

Every weekend, and very often during the week too, after he was done with school, Miles would take the ferry to Governors Island and hang out with Theo at the lab. They'd tinker on Simulacrum together for a while, then Miles would go down to the workshop and spend time with the engineers, learning firsthand how the Chorus prototypes were made. The production staff loved his curiosity and enthusiasm and always made him feel like he was a part of the team. Occasionally they would give him small jobs that he could do and he never let them down.

The house renovation all fell on Maritza. Granted, she was going to do most of the work anyway being the family architect, but Theo thought she could've used more of his help although she never asked for it. The house was structurally in pretty good shape considering that no one lived there for decades, but it needed to be gutted down to the studs. Russ and Miriam helped them find a local contractor with a great group of guys who Maritza declared was the best crew she ever worked with. Motivated by the good work they'd done on the house, she hired them to work with her on a project she was asked to do for a Manhattan-based architectural firm that specializes in parametric design. She fiddled with parametric modeling systems before, but never got to do a full project. It wasn't a big job, but with most of the work on their house already finished, she applied herself to it with complete commitment. It was a good stretch opportunity that will help her grow her skill set and client base.

Procreation sex isn't much fun. Not as fun as the passionate gotta-have-it-steamy kind or easy-living vacation sex, slow-road-to-sleep sex, or even just-for-the-sake-of-it sex. Procreation sex is scheduled copulation, a service appointment with the finicky client who comes out of hiding once a month demanding full and undivided attention. Those few days when the egg offers itself to the possibility of creation require serious focus, stamina, and no-frills dedication to the task of humping and sowing your seed. At least that's how it works when you hit Russ's and Miriam's ages. Yesterday was the last day of the cycle and last night they gave it their all. It's in the hands of fate right now.

Ever since they first knew they were going to end up together, Russ and Miriam both wanted to have kids. But somehow it was never the right time. At first, it was a knee-jerk fear of change, inert anxiety over the ultimate commitment. They were too young, they thought, they wanted to have some time just for themselves. After that, as Russ moved up the ladder at work, his increasingly longer absences took a toll. They learned to live apart, together. Then the crash and the years of rehab. All of a sudden, they were nearing the point where they were going to be too old to have kids. It was now or never; Miriam brought it up a couple of months back and Russ agreed.

Pier Six was busy at this early hour, the usual Friday morning scene when the weekly Manhattan Corporate service personnel turnover took place. Nurses, chefs, waitstaff, butlers, house help, maintenance workers, and security guards—the faces of invisible labor who make the city run—lined up on the security procedure conveyor belt, inches apart from each other. One by one, they scanned the built-in ID chips in their wrists, then climbed into the translucent biosecurity bubble to be checked over by hundreds of sensors measuring the levels of biological threat they could present to their employers across the river. The ones who cleared the bubble then climbed onto the ramp and disappeared inside the bowels of the ferry that'll take them to their jobs.

Russ's return to operations wasn't what he thought it was going to be. Two weeks after the Smith case was brought to conclusion, Pratt bumped him up to the position of Senior Watch Officer and put him in charge of a dozen junior agents. In addition to creating and overseeing their assignments, defining tactical approach standards to field cases, and appraising their analytical work, Russ was also responsible for grooming their skills and fostering their long-term development. Coaching a bunch of twenty-somethings right off the bench wasn't exactly what he wanted to do, but all things considered, it was the logical progression. As much as he wanted to be back to being his old self, Russ knew he wasn't physically able to hack it in the field. It was time to let go of that delusion—and it was surprisingly liberating once he finally did.

At moments, he even felt proud of his former champion and elder statesman status, knowing that someone could benefit from his experience and skills. That whole saying, "those who can't do, teach" is horseshit, he thought. Teaching is its own art. It isn't just about conveying information, it's about helping people be better versions of themselves, and that's a noble undertaking.

Good teachers are catalysts, galvanizers, and leaders. They help people bridge the distance between timid and bold, mediocre and great. Not that Russ felt he was a teacher per se, but he has seen his share of faceless taskmasters shouting orders from behind the scenes during his career, and he didn't want to be one of them. He strived to establish a personal relationship with his agents and to guide each one of them through the tangles of the job the best way he could. A little bit of compassion and the right kind of guidance can make a huge difference with young minds. Also, assuming a more active managerial role made him feel closer to the action. It was still a desk job, but infinitely more engaging than being mothballed at the DOA, and it had one significant benefit—it pretty much guaranteed that he wouldn't be killed on a mission someplace halfway across the world, leaving Miriam alone with a child if they were to have one.

Old habits die hard. It's been months since he's been reassigned to a daytime job, but Jiang still couldn't string together more than three uninterrupted hours of sleep per night. After more than eight years at the fusion center, his body worked on its own nocturnal clock that proved hard to reprogram.

Outside his window, Vancouver lights twinkled with the revelry of distant stars. Looking at the ornamental outline of the sky at night, one would never know that underneath it all the city was violently tearing itself apart. Despite being one of many operatives breeding its disunion, Jiang found something admirable in how Vancouver still managed to stay a unified city, and how the bums, wage slaves, and all the rich people who look like they're going to live forever still move freely in one another's worlds, without constraints. But it's just a matter of time. The money always gets what it wants in the end. West Vancouver has drifted away from the rest of the city and become an island unto itself, firmly on its way to seceding and becoming the newest addition to the Corporate city-state archipelago. No one can stop that now.

Knowing very well that Sheng Long didn't make a practice of giving people a second chance, Jiang felt suspicious that they decided to retain him, even in his current diminished capacity of an errand grunt. But he also felt cautiously optimistic. If that was his punishment for allowing the AC hack to happen on his watch, he could live with that. In a year or two he can hopefully prove himself worthy of their generosity and regain some of his credibility. But it might be that they didn't do it out of the goodness of their hearts. Maybe over the years he earned himself the coveted and dangerous label of "one who knows too much" and it was just safer to keep him close. Either that or... they decided that they can't knock people off every time they outlived their usefulness. They kept close tabs on him, that was a given.

Jiang made his case that the fusion center breach was not entirely his fault, but the blame game is never won by the small guy. Operations management never looped him into the whole AC's relay network hack. It was a ballsy thing to do, but in retrospect, incredibly stupid, or at least sloppily done. Whoever did it, they left their digital fingerprints all over the place, making it possible for AC to discover the source of the hack and strike back, inflicting maximum damage. Had he been told about it in advance, he probably could have done something about it. He could have at least taken measures to minimize the effects of the blowback.

Fortunately, Sheng Long's other two fusion centers were unaffected by the hack due to the prompt execution of contingency protocol that severed the correlation functions between the three systems at the first confirmation of the attack. Dynamic redundancy across the database allowed the other two fusion centers to take over the workload of the affected one, which meant that operations could continue uninterrupted, although at lower capacity. But the loss of confidential and proprietary information that AC swiped along the way will cost Sheng Long dearly in the years to come.

The first casualty was the long, successful relationship Sheng Long had with Macau Corporate, a consequence of the botched kidnapping of Theo Smith. After the whole thing blew up in everyone's faces, Macau Corporate disassociated themselves from Sheng Long and put a freeze on all ongoing jobs. The chatter on the street was that they're looking to switch to

Absolute Compliance for their North American operations. If that's true, Sheng Long stood to lose approximately twenty percent of its revenue. But the loss of reputation is not as easily calculated. Perception is everything. If Sheng Long doesn't quickly shed the stigma that they can't keep their data safe, its days are numbered.

About a month ago, Jiang was presented with a reminder of that disastrous job when he went to pick up a drop at Cáifù, a swanky health club in West Vancouver. He was there twice before, both times for the same reason—to collect the DNA samples that Sheng Long's source at the club covertly obtained from unsuspecting club members. Sheng Long was known to have the most extensive DNA databank of all of the PSCs operating on the West Coast of North America, rivaling only the government. With time running out, they recently doubled their efforts to compile as many DNA profiles of West Vancouver citizens as possible before its transition into a Corporate, which will make the whole process legally and operationally much more difficult.

When he got to Cáifù, Jiang ordered a double raw bean espresso at the bar, then found a secluded spot in the alcove of the café, by the windows and away from the media wall, where the news channels were competing for attention. Outside, below the main level and guarded from the eyes of strangers by knotty cedar trees and tall pines, was a small but immaculate Japanese garden with a little stream that galloped excitedly over moss-covered rocks into a koi fish pond, where bored gilded carp circled around waiting for the next feeding. Suspended over the garden was a glass cube filled with a bunch of scrawny septuagenarians in latex workout suits with built-in activity tracking sensors, jumping up and down.

Jiang couldn't believe his eyes, but there she was, leading the exercise class, the original weak link of the Smith operation, Rachel Fang. She swayed her small frame around like a slow-motion pole dancer, surprisingly flexible for a woman her age. On her command, the group stuck their necks out, stretched their arms forward, and ran in place. After some more jumping and running they laid down and started crawling on their bellies, wiggling like they were trying to escape a straitjacket.

Jiang spotted a waitress weaving between the tables offering complementary green tea to patrons. She made her way to him, then lowered her tray to his eye level.

"Green tea, sir?"

Jiang said the password phrase: "I prefer black tea."

"We can certainly accommodate that," the waitress replied. "Would you like a small snack with your black tea?"

"Yes, some biscuits would be nice."

The waitress finished her stroll among the tables, then a short while later came back with his black tea and a small paper box of biscuits. Jiang opened the box, checked its contents, nodded at the waitress, then took the two biscuits out of the box and put them on a plate in front of him, leaving the box open.

"Enjoy it," said the waitress, turning to leave.

"Hey, let me ask you something," Jiang stopped her. "What are they doing over there?" He pointed at the old people in the glass cube.

"That's a rejuvenation clinic class," the waitress explained.

"Rejuvenation? What are the trackers for?"

"Muscular charge sensors. It helps them monitor the learning progress."

"Learning of what?"

"Comparative biomechanics."

"What's that?"

"Basically, it's teaching humans the specifics of animal locomotion. We have a small institute here that does research on the structure and function of biological systems and their application in the overall wellbeing of the body. The class is a part of the program."

"So, if I had enough money and time to practice hard, one day I can learn to swim like a dolphin or fuck like a gorilla?"

"I don't think they took it that far yet, but thanks for the input," the waitress steered between discomfort and hospitality. "Is that all?"

"Interesting," Jiang mumbled to himself. "Very interesting, indeed."

He reached back into the tea biscuit box, grabbed the small plastic box of DNA samples from inside, and stuffed it in his jacket pocket. He took a sip of tea then looked up at the class cube one more time, feeling something like pity for Rachel Fang. Once a first-class agent, she was now reduced to a novelty act, a jumping clown in a glass cage. Life has a way of humbling all of us.

Where did we go so wrong that we ended up here?

Trapped in a haze of mental fatigue that rules the unclaimed hours between a late night and an early morning, Fletcher wasn't sure anymore who he was asking this question to, or to what purpose. Was he asking the whole of humanity to take a good, hard look at itself and admit, once and for all, that all of its efforts are, sooner or later, destined to fail? No matter what we tell ourselves, no matter how much we try, nothing we'll ever do can stand a chance against the great entropy of the cosmos. Or was he merely trying to drown his own flaws and hide them in the collective ineptness of humankind? No. As much as he wanted to believe otherwise, the monolithic "We" of mutual interest and vision did not exist. No. "We" is just a slapdash summary of each of us individually.

Where did he go wrong? After fourteen straight hours of staring at the holographic displays above his head, he wasn't any closer to an answer than he was yesterday, but he pressed on, hoping that the ghost of doubt that ate at his will to continue will fall asleep before he did.

Incertitude skulked up on him slowly, in the days and weeks after the whole Smith incident. It fed on his failure, corroded his mind, and grew more powerful with every unsuccessful attempt to create a sensible, comprehensive dataset that would support his abiotic oil generation theory out of the ocean of information populating the INDEX system.

A simple, superstitious mind might attribute his present lack of success to a curse, a spell that's been cast upon him for what he did to the Smiths, but Fletcher knew that this was just a temporary hitch, the darkness before the dawn. Despite the setbacks, he knew that resolution was close, patiently waiting for him to reach it.

The setbacks weren't trivial. It took him a long time to physically recover from the effect of the pathogen he was injected with. The first three days he was sure that the serum didn't work and that he was going to die. His whole body was on fire. The pain from swollen lymph nodes in his neck, armpits, and groin was unbearable. He felt like his bones had been pulverized and he had trouble breathing. The doctor they brought in from Edmonton started him on a treatment of antibiotics and anti-inflammatory drugs but the fever didn't budge. After a few days, they airlifted him to a hospital, where he spent a month recovering in intensive care. When he finally got released, he was so exhausted that he could barely stay awake for more than a few hours at a time. Even during those few waking hours he was dazed and unfocused, not able to work.

And if that wasn't enough, he had the fallout to deal with. The mandarins of the parent Corporate somehow managed to keep the Smith incident from blowing up, but there was a price to be paid. To clear themselves from responsibility, they made him the scapegoat and relieved him of his duty as COO of Epiphany. Perhaps he deserved it. He brought up the idea of kidnapping the Smiths to them in the first place, they just executed it. But, when they told him it was time to reevaluate the viability as well as the technical and financial soundness of his abiotic oil generation project, Fletcher was heartbroken. He feared that was only the first step of the process of killing it all together. It was one thing to betray him personally, but he couldn't let them betray his idea.

The process of reevaluation came and went as he expected. Claiming a lack of tangible results, the Corporate decided to scale down the project drastically, cease drilling of the borehole, and stop collection of new data from the surrounding strata. After he offered to sign away his current and all future patent rights relating to the project, they agreed to keep him around without pay, to continue analysis of existing data on the Simulacrum. He also had to give up his office and executive suite and move into workers' housing.

In an ironic twist of fate, they assigned him to Room 302, the same room where Theo Smith stayed during his brief time at the facility. Fletcher could have requested a different room, but he didn't. He knew that at some point he would have to face the morality of what he'd done to Theo and his family. Sleeping in the same room that Smith occupied before him was as direct of an impetus as he's ever going to get to do that. On a superficial level, he felt terrible about the monstrosity of his actions. The Smiths are likely scarred for life. They'll never feel truly safe again and that's a heavy burden to carry. But deep down he believed that the greater intentions should count for something. When you're trying to save the world, nothing should be off-limits. The Smiths's trauma, his own nagging conscience, none of it will matter when civilization collapses onto itself. And that's coming. Sooner than anyone thinks. Unless...

**The 6:00 am ferry materialized in the distance** like a ghost ship drifting through the dawn fog, prompting a small group of passengers waiting at the Fulton Ferry Landing in DUMBO to stir up in anticipation. Miles and Theo waited for everyone to get aboard, then climbed the shrieky gangway and found a couple of seats in the front of the cabin. After a few minutes of smooth gliding, the ferry slowed down with a slight lurch forward, then backed up its engines and pivoted in a tight curve to Pier Six. Miles's face lit up when he recognized Russ Oakley among the strangers coming onboard. Russ waved when he saw them and walked over and plopped into an adjacent seat.

"Excited for the big day?" Russ asked with a smile.

"Very," Miles replied.

"I think excited is a bit of an understatement," Theo chuckled slightly.

What Russ was referring to was, of course, the maiden launch of the twelve Chorus panels slated for this morning. The Atlantic Commonwealth was one of six entities granted permission to start developing the prototypes right away, and the first one to complete production of their allotted batch. Thanks to the existing Sundance infrastructure and all of the research and analysis the team had already done, they were able to significantly speed up the expected timeline and get to the testing phase long before the others. The tests went as smoothly as anyone could've hoped. The panels performed as expected, routinely achieving an efficacy benchmark of over ninety percent. The second phase of the project didn't present any new challenges since there was a well-established system that Sundance used for previous solar panel launches into the exosphere, and the microwave electricity transmission network was already in place.

They spent the rest of the trip engaged in small talk, the way they usually did when they happened to be on the same ferry. Miles asked Russ about Miriam and Russ wanted to know how the house renovation was going and if they needed help. Theo assured him that Maritza and Nick Hayes's crew had it under control. Miles grew very fond of Russ over the last few months, and so did Maritza. Theo, on the other hand, was kind of reluctant, even uncomfortable in the beginning, every time he was around Russ. He didn't know why. Was he jealous of the special bond Russ and Miles shared?

When he mentioned it to Maritza, she just smiled. "It's because you feel the need to repay him for what he's done for us, and you don't know how."

She was right. He'll never be able to settle that debt. Once he accepted that, he welcomed Russ in his heart without reserve. Another person he was indebted to, surely even more than to Russ, was Moonie. Theo wished he could do something for him, or just see him and thank him in person. Maybe the wind will bring him back their way one of these days.

By the time they got off the ferry at Governors Island, sun rays had splashed through the horizon and the majestic daylight began to rise from the surface of the sea. They parted ways at the lab entrance, saying that they should all get together soon, especially since the nice weather is coming—maybe a picnic in Prospect Park.

"Good luck," Russ shouted, watching Theo and Miles disappear behind glass reflections.

Russ then turned around and continued to TOC with the steady gait of a man of uncomplicated courage.

The ground floor of the lab was electric with expectation when Theo and Miles walked in. Gathered around workstations that for the occasion have been turned into makeshift hangout nooks, the members of the Sundance team had coffee and pastries while gazing up at the live mission control feed display hanging from the ceiling in the middle of the workshop. Voices trickled through the audio system, creating the texture of a subdued chant. The feed on the display was steadily switching between a composite visual of the carrier rocket's systems and a closer view of individual modules. Mounted at the tip of the rocket, the snow-white payload module shone like a high-priced gem.

When the countdown sequence began, everybody quieted down; all eyes were riveted on the display, everyone listened intently to the secret language of acronyms and shorthand phrases comprehensible only to a select few in mission control. After several minutes of intense anticipation, the launch clock started ticking down the seconds... nine, eight, seven, six... the engines lit up with a thunderous roar, engulfing the launch pad in a ball of fire. At the count of zero, the rocket bolted through the cloud of blasting fumes, rushing upward like heat from a candle flame. Applause and cheers cascaded across the lab as the rocket accelerated into the clear blue sky and neared escape velocity.

At orbital speed, the engines cut off and the thrusting blur of the feed smoothed out on the display. Without great force propelling it forward, the floating structure suddenly seemed insignificant against the vastness of space and time. And then, like a dandelion seed swept up by a light breeze, the payload module detached itself and began its silent, weightless dance toward the sun.

# ACKNOWLEDGMENTS

I would like to express my gratitude to my artistic brethren everywhere in the world for reaffirming my belief that we can change society through art.

Among them, I'd like to single out a Flying Elephant, Gregory Colbert, for always bringing his purest to this fight. I appreciate your friendship and support and your continuous pursuit of excellence.

I would like to thank Eric Titner, and also my Atmosphere Press team, for their hard work in forging the *ALT* manuscript into a book.

My biggest thanks goes to my wife, Sarah Coyne, for being an unwavering source of strength and inspiration throughout the years.

# ABOUT ATMOSPHERE PRESS

Atmosphere Press is an independent full-service publisher for excellent books in all genres and for all audiences. Learn more about what we do at atmospherepress.com.

We encourage you to check out some of Atmosphere's latest releases, which are available at Amazon.com and via order from your local bookstore:

*Twisted Silver Spoons,* a novel by Karen M. Wicks

*Queen of Crows,* a novel by S.L. Wilton

*The Past We Step Into,* stories by Richard Scharine

*Island of Dead Gods,* a novel by Verena Mahlow

*Cloakers,* a novel by Alexandra Lapointe

*Twins Daze,* a novel by Jerry Petersen

*Embargo on Hope,* a novel by Justin Doyle

*Abaddon Illusion,* a novel by Lindsey Bakken

*Blackland: A Utopian Novel,* by Richard A. Jones

*It Was Called a Home,* a novel by Brian Nisun

*Shifted,* a novel by KristaLyn A. Vetovich

# ABOUT THE AUTHOR

Aleksandar Nedeljkovic left his native Serbia in 1993 and moved to New York City, where he established his creative voice in the TV and film industries.

Although the seeds of ALT have been quietly germinating throughout the author's life, the sense of growing civilizational emergency ultimately compelled him to write his first novel and his impassioned plea to spread warning of the perils of climate change, economic inequality, and political discord.

Aleksandar lives in New York City with his wife Sarah and their son Luca.

CPSIA information can be obtained
at www.ICGtesting.com
Printed in the USA
LVHW010012120422
715960LV00001B/164